A KELLEHER

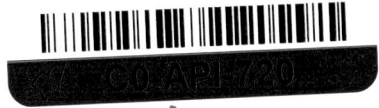

"Shea Stevens is just about the most interesting and sympathetic criminal you'll meet."

— PAULA BERINSTEIN, AUTHOR OF THE AMANDA
LESTER DETECTIVE SERIES

"A thrilling ride that will have you turning pages into the wee hours of the morning!"

— RENEE JAMES, AUTHOR OF SEVEN SUSPECTS

"Dharma Kelleher breaks new ground and breaths new life into a great genre. The best thing to happen to crime fiction since V. I. Warshawski."

— GREG BARTH, AUTHOR OF SELENA

# IRON GODDESS

# IRON GODDESS

A SHEA STEVENS THRILLER

DHARMA KELLEHER

Dark
Pariah
Press

IRON GODDESS: A SHEA STEVENS THRILLER

Ebook ISBN: 978-0-9791730-6-6

Print ISBN: 978-0-9791730-7-3

# ACKNOWLEDGMENTS

It's been thirty five years since I was a teenager typing out God-awful short stories on a manual Smith Corona typewriter. And now my dream of being a published novelist has come true. This would not have been possible without the help of countless friends and supporters. And so here is my chance to offer my humble thanks. If you weren't involved with the process, feel free to jump ahead to the story. Nothing in this acknowledgements section will be on the final exam.

First, let me thank Dr. Coleman Barks for showing up at key times in my writing career. I first met you when you came to my high school and recited poetry while tapping out notes on a toy xylophone. A few years later, I took two creative writing courses from you at the University of Georgia. And then about eight years ago, just moments after I reached the 50,000-word goal for my first National Novel Writing Month challenge, I heard your distinctive voice as I sat in my pickup truck in Phoenix, Arizona. Turns out you were being interviewed on NPR. It was a very serendipitous moment.

I also want to offer thanks to Denise Ganley, Nanor Tabrizi, Tina Wahl, David Waid, Rissa Watkins, and Carl Wilson, my fellow members of the Fantastic Seven critique group. You have kept me on task and provided me with amazing feedback. But more than that, you are the most treasured members of my literary family.

Thanks to John Daleiden, Bob Duckles, and all the wonderful writers at the West Valley Writers Critique Meetup and the West Valley Writers Workshop. You, too, have given me great feedback and inspiration.

Thanks to all of the sisters and misters of the Desert Sleuths Chapter of Sisters in Crime. You have been such a great source of information and inspiration. Where else can you watch a grisly slideshow about blood spatter while eating pizza? God, I hope that's tomato sauce.

This story would have never been written had I not become a biker chick. So I want to thank the Desert Dames and most especially the late Anne Suiter, the best leader that group ever had. You nurtured me as a fledgling biker and your safety lectures kept me safe. Ride with the angels, Anne.

Thanks to Omar and Geoff at MotoGhost for keeping Lady Midnight, my BMW R1200ST, running at peak performance. Their shop can't be beat when it comes to servicing German motorcycles. But don't ever bring your bike in with underinflated tires or Omar will put the fear of God (and physics) in you with one of his fatherly lectures. He scares because he cares.

Thanks of course to my agent, Sharon Pelletier of Dystel & Goderich, who put up with my constant pestering as she pitched *Iron Goddess* to publishing houses. Are we there yet? Are we there yet? Are we there yet?

And last, but certainly not least, thanks to my amazing team at Alibi—Julia Maguire, Kate Miciak, Ashleigh

Heaton, Erika Seyfried, Gina Wachtel, and Kelly Chian. I'll admit, I had some reservations about signing on with a digital-only imprint. But you have repeatedly demonstrated that you are all the cream of the crop. I couldn't have joined a better team. Thank you so much!

Okay, are we ready to ride?

*Thanks to my wife, Eileen*
*for picking me,*
*teaching me how to ride,*
*and believing in me.*

# 1

SPARKS EXPLODED from the left footpeg of Shea Stevens' motorcycle as it scraped against the pavement. She was going too fast through the curves that twisted up the south side of Sycamore Mountain. The road was dark—daybreak still an hour away. Getting up close and personal with an elk at sixty miles an hour would be disastrous. But Shea was in a hurry.

She tried to convince herself the call from the security company was another false alarm—a rat looking for a crumb, or maybe a glitch in the sensors. But she couldn't shake the fear that someone had broken into the shop. If the three custom motorcycles they'd finished the night before were stolen, it would be a quarter-million-dollar loss.

*Please, God, let it be another false alarm.*

The cold air blasting through the vents in her jacket caused her teeth to chatter. In her rush to alleviate her paranoia, she'd thrown on her jeans and T-shirt from the night before. Didn't bother with a bra. Her only precaution had been the .40-caliber Glock she'd slipped into a pancake holster at the small of her back.

Fifteen minutes later, her bike crested the hill and reached what the residents of Sycamore Springs, Arizona, call Olde Towne—a mile-long strip of locally owned shops including a café, a pharmacy, an antiques shop, and Iron Goddess Custom Cycles—her destination.

She screeched to a stop in front of the cycle shop, killed the engine, and ripped off her helmet. The pungent scent of creosote mixed with dead skunk made her nose crinkle. Moonlight reflected off the desert dust on the plate glass window, obscuring the Iron Goddess logo. Her gaze shifted left to the shop's front door. Shards of glass clung to the doorframe like broken teeth.

"Fuck." Her hands tightened into fists. She wanted to beat someone.

She climbed off the bike and scanned the street, hoping to spot the intruder skulking through Olde Towne. Fifty feet away at the Kokopelli Café, a Coca-Cola sign flickered on and off. Across the street, a security gate sliced the blue light of a fifties-era jukebox glowing from within the antiques shop. The rest of Olde Towne's shops slumbered in darkness.

She dug a flashlight out of her tank bag and drew the Glock, turning her attention back to Iron Goddess. She crept onto the cement porch, paused outside the door, and listened for anyone who might be inside. Somewhere in the darkness, a pack of coyotes performed a predawn symphony of yips and high-pitched howls over a recent kill. Two delivery trucks roared past three minutes apart. But no voices or sounds of crunching glass came from inside Iron Goddess. If anyone was in there, they may have hunkered down when they heard her motorcycle. She had to find out for sure.

Drops of a dark liquid on the concrete caught her attention. Was it oil or blood? She brushed it with a finger, creating a crimson smear. *Blood.* Her pulse quickened.

She pulled on the door handle. It was unlocked. Thief must've reached in and unlocked it after breaking the glass. She scolded herself for not getting a double-cylinder lock.

After slipping in through the door, she scanned the place with her flashlight. Tiny bits of glass sparkled like jewels across the floor. A bowling ball–sized rock lay near the front sales counter. The familiar industrial smell of the showroom mixed with the organic tang of blood. Her fist tightened on the grip of the gun.

More drops of blood led off to the right. She considered turning on the lights, but didn't want to blow what little stealth she had left. Broken glass crunched under her boots with each step. Moving slower didn't make it any quieter.

She followed the trail of blood around the counter to where three custom-ordered bikes and several production bikes had been parked hours earlier; they were now gone.

Clothing racks for motorcycle jackets and pants had been cleared. Empty hangers lay scattered on the floor. Shelves that once displayed helmets, boots, and other gear had been stripped bare.

Shea felt sucker-punched. Her mind kept telling her it was a dream.

Her heart leapt into her throat when someone coughed and moaned. She ducked down until she heard it again. Her finger slipped onto the trigger. She swung the flashlight around and found a man lying on the floor in the motor oil aisle. She approached cautiously, ignoring the pulse pounding in her ears.

With the light on the man's face, she recognized him as Derek Williams, one of her employees.

She slapped on the overhead lights. Derek was a

scrawny guy, just shy of his twentieth birthday. His stubbly face was pale and clammy. Blood covered his shirt, pooling on the floor around his chest.

"Aw shit, Derek!" She holstered her gun and knelt down next to him.

He opened his eyes for a moment. "They made me," he wheezed before coughing up blood.

"Who? Who did this to you?"

His eyes lost focus and closed.

She checked his pulse. Her own heart beat so fast she couldn't tell if he had a pulse or not. She pulled out her phone.

"Cortes County 911—what's your emergency?"

"I need an ambulance at Iron Goddess Custom Cycles, 8234 South Sycamore Highway. My friend is bleeding."

"How is he injured, ma'am?"

"I . . . I don't know. I just found him. He's got blood all over his chest. I think someone shot him."

"Is he breathing?"

"Uh . . . let me check." She put her ear to his mouth and could hear shallow, gurgling breaths. "He's breathing, but barely."

"We've dispatched an ambulance. It'll be there momentarily."

Shea hung up the phone and checked his pulse again. It was there, but weak. Then it stopped. She struggled to remember the lessons from a CPR course two years earlier. She clasped her hands and compressed in the center of his chest. Blood gushed from his wounds. That wasn't in the course.

She lifted up his shirt. His chest was smeared with blood. She wiped away as much as she could. Dark liquid oozed from two dime-sized wounds, one right above his heart, the other closer to his left shoulder.

"Shit!"

His shirt was soaked. Wouldn't work to stop the blood, even if she could get it off him. Shea looked for something else to use. The nearby shelves were stocked with bottles of motor oil, industrial cleaners, and cans of chain lube. No shop cloths or clothing.

She scrambled out of her jacket, pulled off her shirt, and twisted it into a tight wad. She pressed it over the wounds and compressed his chest again. The T-shirt kept the bleeding to a minimum. She continued pumping his chest. "Come on, Derek. Gimme a heartbeat."

After fifty compressions, she checked again. Still no pulse. She continued pounding on his chest, desperately trying to minimize the bleeding and hoping the EMTs would arrive before she ran out of energy.

Her back was beginning to cramp up when the silver bell on the front door jingled.

"Over here!" she yelled.

Two deputies rushed in, guns pointed at her.

"Sheriff's Office! Get on the floor. Hands behind your head."

## 2

Shea looked up at the deputy looming over her, his service pistol drawn. The aspiring commando's muscular frame blocked the aisle. His partner, who looked more frat boy than cop, penned her in from the other side.

She wanted to cover her exposed breasts, but was too busy with the chest compressions. "I'm the owner, Shea Stevens. I can't lay down. I'm trying to save my friend."

"Get on the floor," said Deputy Commando. "Hands behind your head. Now!"

"My friend has two chest wounds and his heart stopped. If you don't want me to continue CPR, come over and do it yourself."

"Winslow, get down there and take over for her."

"Roger that." Deputy Frat Boy holstered his weapon, knelt down, and replaced Shea's hands on the blood-soaked T-shirt covering Derek's wounds.

Deputy Commando turned back to her. "You! Get on the floor, now!"

"There's broken glass everywhere."

"Do it now!"

She brushed away the glass in front of her and lay down. Shards that she missed bit into her breasts and belly. She winced, but didn't want to give Deputy Commando the satisfaction of hearing her cry out in pain.

Boots crunched next to her ear. She felt him pull her Glock from its holster. "Are you carrying any other weapons?"

"No."

"Is there anything sharp or otherwise dangerous in your pants pockets?"

"No. My ID's in my back pocket."

"What are you doing here?" Deputy Commando's hand fumbled into her back pocket and pulled out her wallet.

"Holster your weapon, Deputy Aguilar. She owns the place."

That voice she knew. Shea turned her head. Sergeant Willie Foster stood beside her. They'd known each other since they were kids, and despite her previous run-ins with the law, the two of them had maintained a cordial relationship.

"Need a hand up?" He grabbed her elbow and helped her off the floor. "You all right?" He stood five nine, had put on weight since she'd seen him last, but still wore the same horseshoe mustache and horn-rimmed glasses.

Shea felt awkward with him seeing her topless and covered her breasts with one arm. "I'm all right, aside from some cuts. I ain't so sure about Derek." She wanted to pick the bits of glass out of her chest, but her hands were sticky with Derek's blood. He was an ex-junkie; using her blood-covered fingers to dig out slivers could be risky.

The EMTs arrived moments later and went to work on Derek. Willie waved over another EMT, a gal with dark hair tied up into a bun, caramel skin, and large, mahogany eyes.

"Jackie, can you help this woman?" Willie asked her. "She's got bits of glass in her chest."

"Sure," she said. "Is there a place where we can sit down?"

"Follow me."

Shea led Willie and Jackie the EMT to the customer waiting area—a half dozen stackable padded chairs upholstered in burnt orange tweed that had gone out of style about the time *Chico and the Man* went off the air. A small TV sat silent on its platform mounted near the ceiling. In the corner, a water dispenser stood next to a double-burner coffeemaker.

Shea gritted her teeth and tried not to wince while Jackie dug out the slivers of glass with a pair of tweezers and a penlight. Shea trembled, partly from adrenaline, partly from cold, partly from anger, thinking of the nastiest things she could do to whoever shot Derek. At the same time, a question haunted her. *Why'd Derek come back after everyone left?*

"How is he?" She craned her neck to see the EMTs working on Derek.

"I don't know." Willie pulled out a pad and pen and sat down. "The EMTs will do everything they can. Why don't you tell me what happened?"

Shea gasped as Jackie dug at an elusive shard of glass.

"Sorry." Jackie adjusted the angle of her penlight. "This one doesn't want to come out."

"Gotta call from the alarm company about four o'clock," said Shea as she glanced up at Willie. "Found the door smashed and a lot of our inventory gone, including three custom bikes for the Pink Trinkets."

"The Pink Trinkets? That all-girl punk band?"

"Yeah, they commissioned three bikes. Supposed to

unveil them down in Phoenix in a couple weeks to kick off their latest concert tour."

"What about Derek?"

"Found him on the floor bleeding. That's when I called 911." She looked at her hands covered in his blood. A wave of sadness mixed with anger overwhelmed her. The kid could be a smart-ass sometimes, but she liked him. Maybe because he reminded her of herself.

"He say anything when you found him?"

"Yeah, he said, 'They made me.'"

Willie's eyes narrowed. "'They made me'? What'd he mean by that?"

"No idea. Maybe someone set him up."

"Did he say who?"

"No."

"Any idea who woulda done this?" Willie asked.

She shook her head. "Naw."

"Maybe one of your other employees."

She raised an eyebrow. "Why would one of my employees do this?"

He shrugged. "You do tend to hire criminals."

She looked him square in the eye. "I hire ex-cons, just as Lenny Slater hired me when I got out. Keeps us from ending up back in the system."

"Yeah, you're doing society a great service." His voice dripped with condescension. She resisted the urge to tell him to kiss her ass. "That said, this place is the cycle shop of misfit toys. Anyone here have a beef with Derek? Any arguments? He owe anybody money?"

She glared at him. "None of my guys were involved, Willie."

"Whatever you say." He made a few more notes in his notebook. "Any suspicious people hanging around recently? Other than your employees, I mean."

She rolled her eyes. "No."

"Has Iron Goddess received any threats?"

"Nope."

"Was Derek working late last night?"

"We all were. Me, Derek, Terrance, Lakota, and Switch." Terrance was the co-owner of Iron Goddess and their business manager. Lakota was their engineer, Switch their electrician. "We were finishing up a bike till midnight."

"Was Derek the last to leave?"

"No, I was."

"Why would he come back?"

"Hell, I don't know." She shrugged. "Maybe he forgot his house keys. He had his own key to the shop. He wouldn't have broken the front door. I figure someone must've jumped him as he was leaving."

"He's a crystal meth addict, right?"

"Was. He's been clean two years."

"Maybe he's using again."

"If he is, I ain't seen no evidence of it."

"He been missing work or showing up late?"

"No." It wasn't the complete truth. He'd been coming in an hour or so late the past week. But considering he was at death's door, she wasn't going trash talk him to the law. If he'd relapsed, she'd deal with him later. If there was a later.

"Any problems with customers?"

"We had an old veteran rider complain about our imported helmets, but aside from that, no."

"Do you know what all they took?"

"Several bikes. They got a lot of our gear, too—helmets, jackets, boots. I can give you a complete inventory once we get this place cleaned up. "

When Jackie finished bandaging her wounds, there was more gauze than skin showing. Shea looked like a mummy. "You'll want to change the dressing and put antibiotic ointment on the wounds three times a day," Jackie said. "You might also consider getting a tetanus shot from your doctor."

"Thanks."

Jackie smiled and joined her comrades working on Derek.

"Willie, there's a box of Iron Goddess T-shirts in the office. Mind grabbing me one while I wash the blood off my hands?"

Shea walked into the women's restroom, still shaking. She wasn't normally emotional. Yet memories of her mother's death kept bleeding into the more recent images of Derek lying on the floor in the dark. She scrubbed the blood off her hands, arms, and a spot embedded in one of the deep scars on her cheek.

Willie met her outside the restroom and handed her a black T-shirt. "Wasn't sure what size."

The label said it was a men's XL, several sizes too big for her medium frame and small chest, but it slipped over the bandages.

Across the room, the EMTs lifted Derek onto a gurney with a metallic clang. "They taking him to Cortes General?"

"Yep." Willie looked up from his notes. "Now, Shea, promise me something."

"What?"

"You'll leave solving this case to me and the boys. We'll find out who shot Derek." He held out her Glock. She reached for it but he pulled it away. "Promise me."

She sighed. "Yeah. I'll leave it to you." He offered her gun again and she took it. "And if it ain't too much trouble, find my stolen bikes and other merchandise."

"Shea, those bikes are halfway to Mexico by now."

"Let's hope not." She holstered her gun as the crime

scene folks walked in. "I don't deliver those Pink Trinket bikes in two weeks, I'm up shit creek."

"You'll need to leave the premises while we process the scene." He pulled out a business card and handed it to her. "Call me if you think of something that might be relevant to the case."

"Fine." She ambled out the door and called her business partner, Terrance Douglas. It rang three times before he answered.

"Geez, Shea. You know what time it is? Somebody better be bleeding or on fire."

"Derek's been shot."

"What? Derek? Is he okay?"

"No, definitely not. Somebody broke into the shop and shot him twice in the chest. He lost a lotta blood."

"Geez! Where are you?"

"Still at Iron Goddess, but I'm gonna follow the ambulance over to Cortes General." She took a breath, stilling the emotion out of her voice. "Look, man, I know you scheduled the day off to spend with your family, but I need you here to help clean up the mess. No need to rush. The cops gotta do the whole crime scene thing."

"No, it's cool. My mom can take Elon to his soccer game."

"Oh, and T?"

"Yeah?"

"They stole the Pink Trinkets' bikes."

"Please tell me you're kidding."

"Don't worry. You know me—I'm good at finding things."

"Don't do anything stupid, Shea. Let the cops handle it."

"No worries, T. Got it all under control." She didn't. But no way in hell was she leaving this to the cops.

# 3

At four thousand feet above sea level, Cortes County was spared the brutal summer heat the poor suckers down in Phoenix endured six months out of the year. Since it was late August, temps were creeping into the low nineties during the day and down to sixty at night. Primo riding weather for those who didn't mind the seasonal monsoon thunderstorms and occasional flash flooding.

As Shea rode up Sycamore Highway to Cortes General Hospital, dawn broke over the grassy hilltops. The sun's warmth cut the morning chill, but didn't keep her from worrying about Derek. She couldn't shake the image of him bleeding out on the showroom floor. It filled her with rage, sadness, and the ache of having been violated.

*Why'd Derek come back to Iron Goddess,* she wondered. *Had he left something he needed at the shop? Or was he involved in the break-in?*

Derek could be a lazy shit when it suited him—always shooting off his mouth and goofing around when they were on a tight deadline. But he'd been with Iron Goddess long enough that Shea considered him family. She hated to think he might be involved in the break-in.

The tall, boxy shape of Cortes General Hospital rose on the horizon as she crested a hill. Shea followed the signs to the emergency room and parked near the entrance. In the parking lot islands, the normally dead-looking ocotillos bristled with tiny green leaves in response to the overnight rain. Their cheerful beauty mocked the bitterness she was struggling with.

As she locked up her bike, she remembered the Glock in her waistband. She knew from previous visits that guns weren't allowed in the hospital. But she didn't have any place to stash it. She sure as hell wasn't going leave it in her tank bag for some asshole to steal. She pulled the back of her leather jacket over it and hoped nobody would notice.

A half dozen people sat in the emergency waiting room. Most stared off into space or at the muted TV mounted on the wall. A petite woman with a lavender-tinted bouffant hairdo sat behind a flat-screen computer at the registration desk.

"I'm with Derek Williams. They brought him in by ambulance."

She typed the name into the computer and picked up the phone. "I have someone here for Derek Williams." She paused and looked up at Shea. "Your name?"

"Shea Stevens. Derek's a friend of mine."

The woman repeated Shea's name into the phone and nodded as she listened to the response. "Okay." She hung up. "Mr. Williams is still in surgery. The doctor will come out and talk to you as soon as she's done."

"How is he?"

She offered an apologetic smile. "I'm sorry, hon. I don't have that information." The crease between her eyebrows deepened. "Don't I know you from somewhere?"

With her scarred face, people tended to remember her, especially in a small town like Sycamore Springs. Ordinarily that might be a good thing, unless you had a history you'd prefer people to forget. She did.

"Naw, just got one of them faces." Shea smiled with feigned innocence.

She took a seat in one of the puke-green vinyl chairs that filled the waiting room. It wasn't as comfortable as it looked, and it didn't look that comfortable to start with. She shuffled through the magazines spread out on a side table —*Family Circle, Guns 'n Ammo, Sports Illustrated.* None of them caught her interest.

She pulled out her phone and dialed a number in the directory. It wasn't quite seven o'clock. She hoped it wasn't too early to call.

A familiar voice with a thick Mexican accent answered. "Good morning. AA Ajo Auto Repair."

"Goblin, it's me, Pantera." Goblin had given her the nickname during her previous career as a car thief.

"Panterita! Been a long time, *chica. ¿Cómo estás?*"

"Been better. Listen, you ain't been sending your guys up my way, have you?"

A stone's throw north of the Arizona-Mexico border, Goblin's garage in Ajo doubled as a chop shop. Back when she boosted cars for a living, he served as one of her more trustworthy fences. When she got locked up, she'd refused to rat him out. Goblin returned the favor by keeping his operation clear of Sycamore Springs after she started working at the bike shop.

That was ten years ago. Times had gotten tough. Goblin's need for cash flow might have outweighed any gratitude he had for her. *No honor among thieves,* Shea mused ruefully.

"Some of your bikes go missing?"

"Yeah, including three custom women's bikes. On top of that, whoever took them also shot one of my guys."

"*Lo siento, chica.* My boys ain't been north of Phoenix in years. Besides, we don't deal with custom bikes. Too easy to identify and the custom parts don't fit other bikes. Ain't worth the risk."

"Any idea who might've done it?"

"Lotta possibilities. You been keeping up with recent events in your old man's motorcycle club?"

The mention of her father stirred her anger more. "The Confederate Thunder? No. I ain't had contact with the MC since that bastard killed my mama."

"You know the Thunder used to deal heroin for Los Jaguares, right?"

"The Mexican street gang up in Ironwood? I remember."

"Well, a few years back, the Confederate Thunder told the Jaguars to take a hike. Decided to deal crystal meth from local cookers. Less risk, more money. The Jaguars, they not too happy about that."

"That I didn't know."

"It gets better. A month ago, DEA busted several Jaguars muling truckloads of H across the border for the Santa Cruz cartel. Word is *el jefe* at the cartel told the Jags they on the hook for the lost smack. Jags may be looking for new ways to earn."

"You think the Jags hit my shop to earn some quick cash?"

"Just a theory. Then again, maybe the Thunder did it. They're into motorcycles. Maybe they thought they could use a few more."

"Thanks, Goblin. You hear anything, you let me know."

"Will do, *mamacita.* What these bikes look like?"

"The custom bikes were pink and black cruisers with the Pink Trinkets logo on them."

"Shouldn't be too hard to spot. I'll ask around, see who's talking about pink bikes. There a reward if I find 'em?"

"Goblin, you get my bikes back in the next week, I'll make it worth your while."

She hung up. He could be lying, but she didn't feel like he was. He had connections she didn't. If anyone could find out who took the bikes, it would be him. Assuming they weren't already in Mexico.

Shea sorted through the magazines again and picked up an issue of *Arizona Highways*. She skimmed through the scenic photographs until she nodded off to sleep, haunted by dreams of blood, hot and slick, pouring through her fingers. The sound of someone calling her name woke her up.

"Shea Stevens for Derek Williams."

She took a deep breath and ambled over to where a woman stood in olive-green scrubs. Her short curls peaked from underneath a matching surgical cap. Her eyes were dark and hawklike, showing a hint of fatigue.

"I'm Shea Stevens," she said. Concern for Derek's condition drove away any remaining weariness she had.

"Hi, Shea. I'm Dr. Sossaman." She shook Shea's hand and motioned for her to sit in a nearby chair. The doctor took a seat beside her. "How are you related to Derek?"

"He works for me. I'm the one that found him and called 911." Her heart pounded in her chest as she sat down. "How is he?" *Please let him be okay. Please let him be okay.*

"Derek came in with two gunshot wounds. One hit the axillary artery, which feeds blood to his left shoulder. The other nicked the subclavian artery near the aorta. We removed the bullets and stopped the bleeding, but he lost a lot of blood." Her tone was matter-of-fact.

The details of his injuries left Shea queasy. "He'll pull through, right?"

"Hard to say. He's still in critical condition. We're trying to get his vital signs stable. If we can do that, his chances of surviving go way up."

Shea's face tightened with emotion. She kept seeing blood everywhere, making her want to throw up. "Can I see him?"

"We'll be taking him up to the ICU. I can have someone come get you."

"Thanks, Doc."

Thirty minutes later, a tech escorted Shea to Derek's room up in the ICU on the third floor. He looked pale, his face still flecked with blood. His hair was matted and greasy. Clear plastic tubes and multicolored wires were connected all over his body. He looked more cyborg than human. Her wobbly knees forced her to sit, afraid to breathe.

As a child growing up in the dysfunctional Confederate Thunder family, she'd seen the aftermath of beatings, stabbings, and shootings. She'd attended dozens of funerals. But only once before had she felt as shaken as she did now, staring at the ventilator pumping air in and out of Derek's lungs—the morning her mother was murdered.

For the past seventeen years, Shea had avoided the Confederate Thunder, hoping to live a normal life. She tried to tell herself this tragedy was a random shooting. Just one of those things that happens. Or had the club's violent world caught up with her at last?

After fifteen minutes of sitting vigil at Derek's bedside, Shea felt the walls starting to close in on her. Something deep inside dragged her into the nightmare of her past. She walked out of the room without a word to anyone.

When she reached the elevators, her phone rang to the

tune of Melissa Etheridge's "I Want You"—Jessica's special ringtone. "Hey, sweetie. Sorry, I didn't make it back. I'm at the hospital."

"Oh God, were you in an accident?" Jessica worried every time Shea rode, convinced some cager in an SUV was going to plow into her.

"No, I'm fine. Someone shot my employee Derek."

"Derek? Is he the black one or the skanky one?"

Shea sighed. "He ain't the black one. And in case you were wonderin', he's alive, but not doing too well."

"Sorry, that was rude of me. I'm glad he's alive, at least."

"Yeah, me, too."

"At the risk of sounding insensitive, are we still on for lunch? There's a new sushi restaurant I want to try in Iron-wood near the university."

Shea hadn't eaten anything since the night before. The morning's events had killed her appetite. The thought of sushi didn't help. In her opinion, sushi was a fancy word for fish bait. But since she and Jessica had started dating a few months earlier, she kept her mind open about her girl-friend's big-city culture.

"Sure," she said. "Stop by Iron Goddess around eleven. Maybe we can beat the lunch rush."

# 4

---

AT NINE THIRTY, Shea pulled her bike around to Iron Goddess' back lot and parked on the crumbling blacktop next to Terrance's beat-to-shit, industrial-green Ford pickup truck. A golden seal with the Sheriff Office's logo had been pasted on the back door of the building, warning folks not to come in or tamper with the sticker. She considered cutting it out of spite, but resisted the urge and walked around to the front of the shop.

A crime scene unit van occupied two motorcycle spaces closest to the sheet of plywood that now served as the front door. Yellow crime scene tape wound around the posts supporting the porch roof. She ducked under the tape and knocked on the makeshift door. Willie opened it. "Come on in. The boys are about done."

"Thanks." She didn't feel thankful. It was her shop, after all.

"How's Derek?"

She shook her head, pushing against a wave of sadness. "Doctor says he's in critical condition. Not sure if he'll make it."

"Sorry to hear that."

"Any idea who did this?" She stared into his eyes, looking for clues.

"Too early to tell."

"Think maybe the Jaguars did it?"

"The street gang? Why would they hit your shop?" Willie raised an eyebrow.

She didn't want to mention her conversation with Goblin. "Just a thought. The Confederate Thunder used to do business with them back in the day."

"Back when your old man ran the club."

Unpleasant memories pressed on the walls she'd put up against her childhood. "Yeah."

"You still hanging out with the MC?"

"Hell no! I put them in my rearview mirror years ago." Her jaw tensed with anger.

"I figured since your sister married the MC's current president—"

"I don't care if Wendy married the fucking pope, I ain't seen her in years. I don't have anything to do with the goddamn Thundermen. I'm busy building bikes. They're all ancient history, far as I'm concerned." She kicked a can of windshield cleaner across the debris-strewn floor. "Now I got all this shit to deal with."

Willie stood there looking at her without a word. She tried to get a handle on the bitter emotions twisting up inside her. "Sorry, this whole thing's got me upset."

He nodded. "I understand. You worry about cleaning up your shop. We'll get whoever did this. The Violent Crimes Division will be handling the investigation. I can have whoever's assigned to the case get in touch." He slapped her on the shoulder. "Real sorry about Derek. I'll let you know what we find out."

Willie led the last of the crime scene investigators out

the front door, leaving her staring at the empty shelves and an emptier showcase floor. She wanted a drink. A bottle of Bushmills sat in her desk drawer in the office, but she decided to wait. *People look at you funny when you start drinking before lunch.*

She stood over the place where she'd found Derek. Dried blood, broken glass, and medical trash littered the floor. Her blood-soaked shirt lay in the middle of it all. She picked it up and her stomach clenched. Old memories of growing up as the tomboy daughter of Ralph Stevens, the Confederate Thunder's former president, ripped through her mind.

For most of her childhood, Ralph had been her hero. A six-foot-five ex-Marine, he'd taught her how to ride a motorcycle, how to swap out the tranny in a car, and how to fire a pistol with deadly accuracy.

She'd participated in all but the most private of club business, much to her mama's chagrin—riding along on runs to move guns, drugs, and whatever stolen goods the club had acquired. She could pick locks, disable alarms, and hot-wire cars like a pro, all thanks to Ralph.

Living as Ralph Stevens' kid ruled until Mama died.

## 5

Shea stared at the bloodstained floor, pushing away the haunting memories of her mother's death. Her hand tightened on the shirt soaked with Derek's blood before tossing it into the garbage. She pulled out a mop and rolling bucket from the broom closet. With the bucket in the janitor sink, she poured in floor cleaner and turned on the water.

As the bucket filled, Shea caught a glimpse of her scar-riddled face in the aluminum cover of the paper towel dispenser. Something inside her twisted. She pounded the dispenser, denting her reflection.

*What's past is past,* she thought. She'd long since given up crying and feeling sorry about her disfigured face. Now she wanted to hurt whoever shot Derek. Whether it was the Jaguars, the Thunder, or a local junkie, she didn't care. One thing Ralph had taught her was when someone came at you, you had to push back hard. You had to send a message you weren't someone to be fucked with. Otherwise, they'd keep coming after you.

Shea dragged the mop bucket into the showroom. The

front door chimed. Terrance, Monica, Switch, and Lakota wandered through the showroom, surveying the damage.

Terrance stood a few inches taller than Shea, but with his bodybuilder's physique, he looked much bigger. His trim, full beard and tidy afro gave him a cuddly, teddy-bear look.

"We were next door at the café when we saw the CSU van leave." Terrance assessed the damage. "Robbers sure didn't miss much, did they?"

"Nope."

He followed her to the mess on the floor. "Man, that's a lot of blood. Sure hope homeboy pulls through."

"Me, too."

"How is he?"

"Still listed in critical condition. Doc's not sure if he'll make it or not."

"Damn. You think he was in on the robbery?"

She ran a hand through her hair. "Not sure. Don't want to think about that."

"He has been showing up late to work the past week. Maybe he's smoking crystal again."

She stared at the mess on the floor, refusing to acknowledge Terrance's point.

"I called the glass company," he said. "They're sending someone by later today."

The others approached. "Lakota, keep Switch away from this. Don't need her getting all triggered and freaky."

She had hired Lakota after the woman had transitioned out of a halfway house for alcoholism. Her deep-set eyes and strong nose, coupled with a gentle smile, gave her a motherly appearance. In addition to her skills as a mechanical engineer, Lakota's other gift was calming down Switch when she got triggered.

Switch, a lanky young woman with bushy hair that

always looked unkempt, had joined the crew after being released from a long-term mental facility. She'd been abused by her folks as a small child. Shea didn't know the details, but gathered it was the kind of horror story you read about in the papers. Whatever hell Switch had endured left her triggered by certain things like blood or people yelling. Once set off, she became a whole different person, and things tended to get broken.

"Come on, Switch," said Lakota, as if talking to a kid, "let's see what's going on in the workshop."

"Let me get some gloves and pick up that trash before you start mopping," said Terrance.

Monica walked over, covering her mouth and looking a little green.

"Mon, don't you go vomiting and giving me more shit to clean up," scolded Shea.

"I'm all right." She didn't sound convincing.

Monica, who served as Iron Goddess' salesperson, had worked there almost as long as Shea had. Her bleach blond hair and immaculate makeup reminded Shea of an aging biker magazine model. Still, she was the closest any of them came to normal. No criminal record or drug problems. Just a fondness for motorcycles. "You saved his life, huh?"

Shea shrugged. "Maybe. We'll see."

"They should write an article about you in the newspaper."

"Yeah, right: EX-CON SAVES FORMER JUNKIE AFTER BREAK-IN. Great headline."

"Okay, maybe not."

"Assuming they didn't steal our computers, I need you to print out our current inventory and figure out what got stolen."

"Yes, ma'am." She hurried away to the office.

"And stop calling me ma'am!" she called after her. "Makes me feel old."

Terrance gathered up the medical waste the EMTs had left behind. "Any thoughts on what to do about the Pink Trinkets' bikes?"

"I got a plan, but you ain't gonna like it."

"I was afraid you were going to say that."

∾

WITH THE MESS CLEANED UP, she and Terrance met in the office for an owners' meeting while Monica, Switch, and Lakota took inventory of what had been stolen.

Shea sat flicking the spark wheel on her Zippo. Lenny Slater, the former shop owner, had given it to her on her first anniversary at the shop. It no longer had any lighter fluid and hadn't since she'd quit smoking four years earlier. But she held on to it as a reminder of Lenny. Whenever she had trouble figuring something out, she flicked it until a spark of inspiration hit her.

"Shea, we need to call the Pink Trinkets and let them know what happened." Terrance swirled the coffee in his Styrofoam cup from the café next door.

"No fucking way!" She shook her head. "I don't wanna give the Trinks a reason to cancel the contract. We can't afford it. I'm gonna find them bikes and put a hurt on whoever shot Derek."

"The show's two weeks away. We don't even have time to rebuild them. So unless you know who has the bikes, we have to cancel."

"T, I ain't giving up on this project. I'll find the bikes and, with a little luck, get some justice for Derek." She could still feel the stickiness of Derek's blood on her hands, though they'd been washed.

"Okay, Miss Nancy Drew, what's your plan?"

"Goblin thinks the Jaguars might be behind the break-in."

"The Mexican street gang?" Terrance's eyes widened. "Sister, if they got your bikes, let them go. Don't go messing with those psychos and their drug cartel buddies unless you want to get yourself strung up from Memorial Bridge with your guts hanging out." He crushed his now-empty cup and tossed it into the trash can.

"They put Derek in the hospital, busted up our shop, and stole half our goddamn store. It's time for payback."

"Payback? Shea, do you hear yourself? You sound like your old man."

Terrance's words sent a shock of fury through her body like she'd been hit with a stun gun. Her fist tightened on the lighter. "Don't *ever* compare me to that fucking piece of shit."

"Shea, listen to yourself. Since when are you all revenge and stuff? This ain't you." He put his hand on her arm. She jerked it away.

"That was before they tried to kill one of our crew. You wanna survive in this world, you gotta set boundaries. When someone crosses 'em, you gotta let them know there's a price."

"We been building bikes together for what? Ten years? I care about you despite your pasty complexion and a face that resembles a shar-pei's ass."

Shea smirked at his attempt at humor. "Uh-huh."

"We are not a motorcycle club. We are not a street gang. We are business owners."

"Your point?"

"Point is, we care about our employees, but we don't go to war over them. Not with the Jaguars."

"These people aren't just my employees, T. They're my family."

"Fine. Family's good. I got my own son, Elon, to think about. You got Jessica. You want to put them at risk?"

"What's *your* plan? Put our tails between our legs, tell the Trinks, 'Sorry, ladies, your bikes got stolen. Here's your money back'? We can't afford it. We already spent the money on parts and materials."

"If we have to, yes. The Trinkets will understand. It ain't like we didn't finish the bikes. We got robbed."

"If we let this go unanswered, we look weak and are inviting more of the same. I grew up in the local criminal culture. Vulnerability is liability. We got a reputation to uphold. "

"Jesus H. Christ, Shea, what good's a reputation if you're dead? Maybe we can hire a few temps. Hellbent Cycles down in Phoenix has been wanting to collaborate for years. Maybe this is our opportunity."

"The Pink Trinkets didn't hire Hellbent to build their bikes. They hired us."

Terrance buried his head in his hands and groaned. "Fine. What do you suggest?"

"You used to buy Adderall from one of the Jaguars, didn't you? What was his name? Oscar?" She clicked away at her Zippo as a plan formed in her head.

"That was fifteen years ago. Dude's probably dead or in jail."

"Or maybe not. You mentioned once his family owns a taqueria, right?"

"Tres Olivos up in Ironwood." Terrance's voice sagged with defeat.

"Thought so." She smiled, clicking her Zippo all the faster.

"Shea, even in the unlikely chance you find him, you think he's going to rat on his own crew?"

Her smile faded. "I'll remind him I'm Ralph's daughter. Unless he wants a war with the Confederate Thunder, his crew needs to make things right."

"Oh, so suddenly you *are* Ralph's daughter. Have you lost your freaking mind? You don't have any pull with the MC."

"Yeah, but Oscar don't know that."

"This is going to go sideways, I just know it." He shook his head. "When do you plan to do this?"

"Today. After I call the insurance guy and we get this place cleaned up, you and I are having a late lunch at Tres Olivos."

Lakota opened the office door. "Geez, you guys! Can you keep it down? Switch is already freaky-deaky about Derek getting shot. You two yelling in here's getting her more wound up."

Shea sighed. "Sorry. Guess we're all a little worked up today. I'll go talk to her. Let her know Mommy and Daddy are done arguing. Where is she?"

Lakota pointed with her thumb. "In the garage, by the emergency eye wash station."

Shea followed her out to where Switch sat on a stool, facing the wall, twisting a strand of her long hair, muttering to herself. "I told her I never went in there. That's Daddy's drawers. I knew little girls aren't allowed in Daddy's drawers. But she didn't listen. No! She called me *mentirosa*. Liar!"

"Switch?" Shea pulled up another stool. She was tempted to put a calming hand on Switch's shoulder, but last time she'd done that, Switch broke Shea's nose with her elbow. "Hey Switch, it's me. Shea. You with us, kiddo?"

"She said, 'Don't you dare touch that razor.' Tried to tell

her wasn't me. It was Jamie that done it. Ouch! Ouch! No, Mommy. Please, Mommy!"

"Come on back, Switch. Nobody's gonna hurt you. Everybody loves Switch." She shuddered to think the hell the girl had endured at the hands of her sadistic parents.

Switch turned and looked at her, eyes wide with fear, arms tucked close to her frail body. "Everybody loves Switch?"

"Yeah. You're safe now, darlin'."

Like a puma, Switch pounced at her, wrapping her arms tight around her torso. The suddenness of the move startled Shea, but she held Switch for a few moments until the darkness faded enough for the young woman to reconnect to the present.

Switch leaned back, face blank. "I got work to do." She stood up and walked off to where she'd been working on a fuel injection module, as if the meltdown a moment earlier never happened.

Shea stood to go back to the office. Lakota stopped her. "Whatever's going on between you and Terrance, work it out quietly before she gets any worse."

"Yes, boss," Shea knew Lakota was right, but was too worked up herself to keep the sarcasm out of her voice.

No sooner had she sat down at her desk than Monica poked her head in the doorway. "Hey, your Scottsdale housewife girlfriend is here."

"Would you quit calling her that? She's not a housewife. She works at an insurance company." She looked through the office window and saw Jess, dressed to the nines as always. The perfect complement to Shea's baggy Iron Goddess T-shirt—sans bra—and grease-stained jeans. Shea waved, and Jessica blew her a kiss.

"Sorry, I figured Lady Jessica Taylor of the Snottsdale Taylors sounded a bit pompous."

"Gee, you think? Be nice." Shea walked out of the office and gave Jessica a hug. "Hey, babe."

"Hi, sweetie. Morning, Monica."

"Oh, *hi*, Jessica," Monica said with a saccharine grin. She went to assist a customer who'd walked in with Jessica.

Jessica looked her up and down. "You ready to go?"

"Go? Oh shit. That's right, sushi! Can you gimme a raincheck? We're still sorting through this mess. Besides, Terrance and I have a business lunch in a while."

"Oh, maybe I can join you."

"Would love you to, but you can't."

"Why not?"

"Well, it's sort of . . . there's gonna be some tense negotiating there. You'd be bored." *And in mortal danger,* Shea thought.

"When will I see you? I feel like you're more committed to this store than you are to our relationship."

Shea sighed. "Well, I *am* the co-owner and have been for several years. You and I've only been dating a few months."

"What're you saying?" Jessica pouted. Shea hated when she pouted.

"Look, sweetie, I'll be home after work and we can finally have some quality time. Maybe we can grab some fish—er, sushi for dinner."

"Okay. Kisses." Jessica gave her a peck on the lips and walked to the plywood-covered door. "Love what you've done with the place. Very minimalist."

## 6

---

WHEN THEY WALKED into Tres Olivos, Shea remembered eating there once as a kid. Ralph had brought her along to a meeting with the president of the Jaguars—a guy by the name of Victor Ganado, or Uncle Victor as he liked her to call him. He had a kind face, a ponytail, and a gentle voice like a grandfather—not the kind of man she'd expected to lead a Latino street gang. But then, people weren't always what they seemed.

The smell of carne asada and salsa filled her nose, causing her stomach to rumble. She hadn't eaten all day. Too many other things to worry about.

"May I help you?" asked the plump woman behind the counter. The crow's-feet around her eyes crinkled as she smiled. Her accent was heavy, but understandable.

Shea looked at the hand-printed menu on the wall. "Chicken burro."

"Rice and beans?"

"Yeah." She pulled out her wallet and turned to Terrance. "You're up."

"Gimme the *caldo de res* with rice and refried beans on the side."

"For here or to go?"

"Here."

The woman rang up the total. Shea paid and kicked Terrance's boot. He was stalling.

"Um, señora, does Oscar Reyes work here?"

The woman's smile drooped. "Why you ask about my Oscar? If you looking for drugs, you go. Oscar don't sell drugs no more."

Terrance shook his head. "No, no, señora, we aren't looking for drugs. This is something different."

"He owe you money?" Her eyes narrowed.

"Ma'am, we own an auto shop in Sycamore Springs." Shea handed her a business card. "We had a contest, and Oscar won a free car stereo. Unfortunately, we can't read the phone number on his ticket. If you'd have him call us, we'll give him his prize."

Señora Reyes' smile reappeared. "Oh, that's different. He'll be so happy. I have him call you."

Shea grinned. "Thanks. We'd appreciate it."

"You go sit down. I call Oscar. Then I bring your food."

The dining room was empty except for the two of them. Shea liked the idea of not having an audience, considering she'd promised Willie she'd leave the investigation to the Sheriff's Office. On the other hand, sometimes having witnesses could keep things from getting out of hand.

After a few minutes, Señora Reyes brought their food. "Oscar is on his way."

Shea smiled at her and turned to Terrance. "Told you it'd work out."

Terrance smirked.

She'd wolfed down her burrito and was eyeing Terrance's

beef stew when a lean man with a hard face and a shaved head joined them at the table. A tableau of ink featuring a growling jaguar extended below the sleeve of his plaid shirt.

"I didn't enter no contest, so who the fuck are you?" He looked her up and down. "Damn, *blanca*. What happened to your face? You look like my pit bull's chew toy."

She could picture this guy breaking into Iron Goddess and shooting Derek. Her creep-o-meter redlined, but she resisted the urge to pull the Glock in her waistband. She settled for glaring instead.

Oscar turned to Terrance and narrowed his gaze. "Don't I know you?"

"I used to buy Adderall from you." Terrance glanced away, looking uncomfortable.

Oscar tilted his head. "You got a sister? You remind me of this butch *marimacha* I used to sell to."

"That was me."

The burrito Shea had eaten sat like a rock in her stomach. It now hit her why Terrance didn't want to meet with Oscar.

She'd learned Terrance was transgender years earlier, after taking him to the hospital for an emergency appendectomy. She couldn't care less. He was as much a man as any other guy she knew. More so than some. But not everyone was so enlightened.

Oscar looked Terrance up and down. "No shit. Terry, right? You some superbutch dyke now?"

"The name's Terrance now. I'm a trans guy. Now if we can discuss the reason—"

"Trans guy? What's 'at mean? What you got tween your legs? A pussy or a dick?" He chuckled and tilted his head to look under the table.

Shea shoved the table toward him. "Eyes above the table, asshole!"

Oscar laughed all the harder. "And I guess this bitch is your girlfriend."

"Shea and I own a motorcycle shop," said Terrance.

"Oh yes, a motorcycle shop." Oscar pulled her card out of his shirt pocket. "Iron Goddess Custom Cycles. Shea Stevens. That you?"

"That's me," she said.

"Yeah, I hearda you. You make them girlie bikes, dontcha?"

"We build custom bikes for women, yes." Her patience wore thin. He was stalling. "Which is what we—"

Oscar turned back to Terrance. "I'm surprised at you, *ese*. Girlie bikes? I woulda figured you'd be making big ol' macho motorcycles. Harleys and shit. After all, you da man now, right?"

"Everyone makes big bikes. Women are an underserved market," he said.

She rolled her eyes. Typical Terrance and his business school bullshit.

"Ha! Underserved market," said Oscar. "I like that. You a real smart one, huh, *ese*?"

She was tired of letting Oscar run the show. She needed to find out who shot Derek. Her hand slipped around to rest on the grip of the Glock. "Listen, Oscar. It's our bikes we came to talk to you about."

Oscar waved her off like she was an annoying waitress. "Terrance, you musta liked girl prison. All the pussy you can eat."

That was it. She'd had enough of this bullshit. She pulled the Glock, chambered a round, and pointed it at Oscar's chest. "Forget about Terrance, Oscar! Let me tell you who *I* am."

"Look at you acting all gangsta, *blanca*." Oscar's smile turned sinister. "You think you the first *pinche puta* to point a gun at me? Get your ass out of my mama's restaurant 'fore I shove that piece up your *culo*."

Terrance put a hand over the Glock. "Shea, put that away before someone gets hurt."

She kept the gun trained on Oscar. "This morning someone robbed our shop and put one of our guys in the hospital. Word is the Jaguars did it."

"Why would Los Jaguares steal some *pinche* girlie bikes? And if we did, you think I'd admit it to you?"

"You know who I am? My father's Ralph Stevens, former prez of the Confederate Thunder Motorcycle Club. My sister's old man is the MC's current president. Unless you want a war between the Thunder and the Jaguars, you best start talking."

"Terrance, you best put a leash on your bitch, 'fore she finds herself hanging from a bridge."

Terrance shot Shea a look, then turned back to Oscar. "Man, we're just trying to get our bikes back."

"Shut the fuck up, girlie man. You *pinches maricónes* come into my restaurant threatening war and shit? Fuck you, bitches! Los Jaguares don't know nothing 'bout no pink bikes."

Shea raised an eyebrow. "How'd you know they were pink, asshole?"

"They *chica* bikes. What other fucking color'd they be? We ain't got your bikes, *blanca*. We don't ride fucking motorcycles." He pulled a Colt 1911 and pointed it at her. "And don't threaten me with your bullshit. If you were connected to the Thundermen, you'd know we already at war."

"Shea," said Terrance, a tremble in his voice. "I think it's time to leave."

The Colt still had the safety on. Her Glock had no safety. She had the advantage.

"Not so fast," she said. "If the Jaguars didn't hit our shop, then who?"

"Gee, let me think. Who I know rides motorcycles? How about your punk ass, white trash biker buddies the Thunder?"

Maybe he was telling the truth. Maybe not. Either way, she wasn't getting anything more out of him. Not like this. She holstered her gun, hoping Oscar would do the same. He didn't.

"Now, get the fuck out 'fore I have you carried out in a body bag."

She glared at him, refusing to move. Terrance stood up. "Come on, Shea. Let's let the cops deal with this."

She hated to admit it, but her plan sucked. She stood up, not taking her eyes off Oscar for a second. "We ain't done here."

"Count on it, *blanca*."

## 7

As Terrance drove them back to Iron Goddess, Shea replayed their confrontation with Oscar in her head. *Was he telling the truth? Maybe it* was *the Confederate Thunder who'd broken in and shot Derek.* But Oscar was hiding something; she could feel it.

"Do the Jaguars have a clubhouse somewhere?" she asked.

Terrance stared at the road ahead without glancing at her. "Give it a rest."

"Dude, we gotta figure out who shot Derek and teach 'em a lesson."

"No, *we* don't. I'm not throwing away everything I've worked for over this. Let the cops handle it."

"This guy Oscar shook you up, didn't he? I'm sorry he found out you're trans."

He pounded the steering wheel so hard she thought it would break. "I don't give a damn what Oscar thinks about me being trans."

"Then what're you so pissed about?"

"You, Shea! I didn't want to go there in the first place,

and then you pull a gun? In a restaurant?" He whacked the steering wheel again. "What were you thinking?"

"You're overreacting, seriously."

"Goddammit, you pulled a gun! They could throw us back in prison for that. You have any idea what a fucking nightmare that was for me?"

"It wasn't no picnic for me either, and I did twice the time you did."

"Not the same. Trans people *die* in prison. Everyone wants to fuck with you."

She hadn't thought about that. "Look, man, I'm sorry."

"Don't be fucking sorry, Shea. Sorry won't keep my black ass out of prison when you do something stupid. And this time it won't be women's prison. I'm legally male now, so they'll send me to men's lockup. How you think that'll play out?"

"All right, I'm sor—I mean, I get it. I'll let the cops handle it. Okay?"

Terrance grunted.

"Come on. At least look at me!"

"I'm driving."

She pulled out her Zippo and started flicking it. Terrance grabbed it from her hand and threw it out the window.

"Hey, Lenny gave me that."

He didn't say anything.

"Damn, T. You seriously need to get laid."

∾

TERRANCE PARKED the truck behind Iron Goddess. He hadn't said another word the rest of the way back. Shea followed him through the shop's back door, still marked with pieces of the crime scene sticker from that morning.

The workshop looked as it had before the robbery. Tool chests and other equipment were all where they should be. A few bikes were on lifts in various stages of assembly. Switch and Lakota were wiring up a large cruiser.

Terrance stomped through the workshop to the office, slamming the door behind him.

"How'd it go at your business meeting?" asked Lakota. A grease smudge marked her cheek.

Shea shook her head and scowled. Lakota shrugged and returned to her work.

Shea walked past the office to the showroom. Monica stood with a clipboard taking inventory of what remained on the shelves.

The showroom looked as empty as before, but Monica had cleared the floor of debris and put the remaining merchandise back where it belonged.

"Was that Terrance slamming the office door?" asked Monica.

"Yeah, he and I are havin' a disagreement."

"So he slams the office door? Guess I don't need to ask how your meeting went."

Shea smirked. "How's the inventory coming?"

"Just finishing up." Monica flipped to the front page of her list. "Looks like the thieves got nine production bikes, the three Pink Trinket customs, twenty-two helmets, four GoPro cameras, a couple intercom sets, seventeen pairs of boots, and twenty jackets. Not including the Trink bikes, wholesale cost for the stolen inventory comes to $160 grand."

"Fuck." Shea ran a hand through her hair.

"Any news on who mighta done this?"

"An old acquaintance of mine thinks the Jaguars did it."

"Oh shit. The Jags?" Monica dropped her pen as her

eyes widened with fear. "Is that what Terrance is pissed off about?"

"Terrance and me met with a Jaguar he used to know. Things got a little heated."

"Please tell me you're kidding."

"Don't worry about it, Mon. It's no big deal." Shea grabbed the inventory list from her and pretended to look through it.

"No big deal? Those psychos killed my cousins. You didn't do anything to piss that guy off did you?"

"I gotta call the insurance company." Shea walked away.

Monica trailed her. "Oh shit! You did, didn't you? That's why Terrance is all pissed off. I'm right, aren't I?"

"Isn't it time for your break?"

A loud crash from the office startled them both. "What the hell was that?" Monica asked.

"Sounded like Terrance's desk chair hitting the wall."

Terrance stood in the far corner of the office with his arms crossed, glaring at the floor.

"My purse is in there. How can I go on break with Terrance throwing shit around?"

Shea handed Monica a twenty. "Grab a bite to eat next door. He should be cooled off by the time you get back."

Monica strolled to the front door, the silver bell tinkling as she opened it. "Hey, Shea?"

"Yeah?"

"I hope Derek makes it."

"Yeah, me, too."

∾

AT THE SALES COUNTER, Shea thumbed through the inventory list. The thieves had gone after the more high-end gear, ignoring the cheap stuff. *Clearly someone who knows motorcycle gear.* A few Thundermen did, on occasion, buy oil or the odd motorcycle part from Iron Goddess. She'd never gotten the impression they were casing the place.

The MC made most of their illegal money selling crystal meth. *Have they added burglary to their list of ways to earn?* It was worth checking out. She just had to do it without ruffling any feathers. If her sister really had married the Confederate Thunder's current president, she might know whether they had hit Iron Goddess.

Her jaw clenched thinking of Wendy and the way she had betrayed Mama's memory. The idea of calling her made Shea sick. But Derek deserved justice and she needed to get the Pink Trinkets' bikes back. Seventeen years had passed since they'd seen each other. Who knew if Wendy would even talk to her?

With no other leads, Shea picked up the phone to call Willie.

"Cortes County Sheriff's Office, Sergeant William Foster speaking."

"Willie, it's Shea. You got Wendy's number?"

"I thought you didn't want nothing to do with her."

"Yeah, well, you got me thinking. Maybe it's time she and I patched things up. She's the only family I got left, after all."

"Well, her and your father."

Her body tensed. "Please don't mention that son of a bitch."

"Sorry," he said. "Listen, I'm not supposed to give information to civilians. This is the Sheriff's Office, not directory assistance. You try looking Wendy up on the Web?"

"Willie, be a pal and look it up on your computer. She's my sister, for chrissakes! I ain't stalking her or nothin'."

Computer keys clicked on Willie's end. "She might not have a number in our system, unless she's got a record."

"She's married to the president of the Confederate Thunder. She's bound to have been picked up for something. Speeding, shoplifting . . ."

"Grand theft auto," he added.

Shea rolled her eyes. "You're hilarious."

"Just kidding. She's in here, but nothing as exciting as your rap sheet."

"Dammit, does she have a phone number in there or not?"

"Yes, she does." He gave her the number.

"What's on her rap sheet?" *How had Wendy turned out after a lifetime with the club,* she wondered.

"Domestic disturbance. Guess her husband used her face for a punching bag a time or two. I shouldn't be telling you this."

"Domestic disturbance, huh? Imagine that—history does repeat itself." Shea almost felt sorry for her. Almost.

"You can't tell her I told you. I could lose my badge."

"Yeah, yeah. I won't. Thanks for your help, Willie."

"Hope the two of you can mend fences."

"We'll see."

Before she hung up, he interjected, "Oh, Shea! You wouldn't know anything about a disturbance at Tres Olivos, would you?"

*Shit.* "Tres Olivos?"

"Mexican restaurant up in Ironwood."

"Haven't heard a thing."

"Uh-huh. I got a report about a white female and a black male causing a ruckus there a little bit ago. Place is connected with the Jaguars street gang. The Sheriff's Office may not be the only ones looking for these two troublemakers, if you get my drift."

"I get your drift."

"I'll find out who shot Derek. I don't need you doing my job for me."

"Good to know you're on the case. Later, Willie." She hung up.

As Shea stared at the paper with Wendy's number on it, her heart pounded in her chest so hard her vision blurred. There was a whole lot of shit from her childhood she didn't want to remember. Reconnecting with Wendy could bring back a flood of painful memories. And she still couldn't forgive her sister for her last betrayal.

The office door opened. Terrance clomped through the showroom. He always seemed bigger when he was angry.

"Yo, T, I'm sorry for earlier."

He was her Jiminy Cricket, steering her away from her fondness for trouble. His anger intensified her loneliness.

He paused a moment, staring at her with a blank face until the front door jingled.

Monica walked in. "Hey, Terrance! Feeling better?"

He smiled at her. "A bit." He left without another glance at Shea. *Clearly I'm still on his shit list,* she thought.

"Good to see Terrance has cooled off," said Monica.

"Uh-huh." Time to see what Terrance had destroyed.

In the office, a dent the size of a fist now decorated the wall. One of the casters from Terrance's chair occupied a corner of the floor. The chair itself sat cockeyed behind his desk. No other obvious damage.

She sat in her chair, the Glock in her waistband pressing against her spine. *Don't need that sticking in my back while I'm dealing with this crap.* Shea pulled it out and locked it in her desk drawer.

Her fingers drummed on the wooden surface as her sister's phone number stared back at her. *This is ridiculous.* She could race her bike through twisties at breakneck speed, play bumper cars with semis on the highway, and go toe-to-toe with a Mexican gangbanger, but calling her own sister scared her shitless. *What the fuck is wrong with me?*

She forced her fingers to dial the number, the phone trembling next to her ear.

It rang four times before a voice that sounded like Mama said, "Hi, you've reached Wendy. Leave a message."

Her mouth felt like flypaper. After an awkward pause, she said, "Wendy, it's Shea. I . . . I need to talk to you." She left her number and hung up.

A wave of nausea pulled at her stomach. She forced herself to take slow, deep breaths, but it worsened until she dry-heaved over the plastic trash can by her desk.

After a few minutes, her stomach settled. At least she'd left a message. Now there was nothing left to do but wait for Wendy to call her back.

TWO HOURS LATER, Terrance remained holed up in the office ordering replacement merchandise, still refusing to talk to Shea. Monica was rearranging what inventory remained, so the showroom wouldn't look like Iron Goddess was in the final days of a going-out-of-business sale.

The glass guy hadn't shown up to repair the front door. No response from Wendy either. Shea was relieved, in part. She didn't want Wendy back in her life. Unfortunately, Wendy was Shea's only way to know whether the Confederate Thunder had shot Derek and robbed Iron Goddess.

In the workshop, Shea assisted Switch and Lakota, who were installing the fuel injection module Switch had repaired earlier. Switch seemed back to her usual, stable self. Shea hoped she stayed that way.

"Did I hear you leave a voicemail for your sister?" asked Lakota.

"Can't a girl have some privacy around here?" Shea unhooked the battery, while Switch secured the module.

Lakota laughed. "Office has thin walls, remember? How long since you saw her last?"

"Seventeen years."

"Screw." Switch held out her hand, oblivious to the conversation. Lakota fed her the screws, one by one, as requested.

"Seventeen years, huh? I can't imagine. I go more than a couple months without seeing my brothers and sisters, I get crazy homesick."

"After my mama got killed, I was afraid I'd end up like her. Or worse, like . . . like my father." The screwdriver trembled in her white-knuckled grip. "I needed space."

"Seventeen years is a lotta space."

"Yeah, well . . ." Shea reattached the battery once the module was in place.

Switch turned the key and pressed the starter. The bike rumbled to life. "It works." She looked at the others, beaming.

A vehicle squealed to a stop in the rear lot and honked its horn. A trim man in blue and white coveralls walked in the back door, pushing a dolly loaded with cardboard boxes. Shea flagged him down.

"How's it going?" The delivery guy handed her a tablet and a stylus.

"Been better." Shea recognized the shipment as helmets, jackets, and boots they had ordered the week before. "This helps." She signed the tablet with the stylus, then handed it back to him.

He unloaded the dolly and gave her a wave. "Hang in there."

She loaded the boxes onto one of the shop's dollies. "I'll be in the showroom if you need me. She backed through the door and down the hall. She knew Terrance would be pissed if she put the new stock on the shelves without first entering it into the system. She didn't care. The showroom was bare as Old Mother Hubbard's cupboard. They could enter the new merchandise later using the enclosed inventory list.

The bell on the front door jingled. Shea looked up hoping the glass guy had arrived, but it wasn't him. A thin woman with stringy red hair ducked behind the plywood, as if hiding from someone.

"Can I help you?" Last thing she needed was a crazy woman wreaking more havoc at Iron Goddess.

The woman turned around. Shea froze. The newcomer looked thirty with hard years under her belt. Her clothes hung off her frame like a painter's drop cloth. Shea stared at Mama back from the dead.

"Shealene, please help me!"

The voice was her mother's. How was this possible? *Am I going crazy?*

"It's me, Shea. Wendy!"

Shea's eyes widened. The last time she'd seen her baby sister was when the county sent her to live with Monster, her godfather and a member of the MC. Wendy had been a chubby seven-year-old back then. "Wendy? What are you doing here? I just wanted you to call me back."

Outside the roar of multiple bikes with unbaffled pipes shook the windows then stopped. Wendy glanced outside again. "Oh shit! Don't tell Hunter I'm here." She rushed past Shea toward the restrooms.

Three guys walked in wearing leather cuts with Confederate Thunder three-part patches. One of them, a bald-headed man with a scruffy, braided chestnut beard stood by the front counter and pointed toward the restrooms. "Mackey, check down there."

Mackey, a stout guy with the face of a weasel, nodded and sprinted toward the restrooms. A Confederate stars-

and-bars bandana circled his blond, greasy, shoulder-length hair.

"One-Shot, go 'round outside, make sure she don't sneak out the back."

"Roger that." One-Shot stood six-foot-something with a military-style crew cut. He ran back out the front door and around the building.

"I don't know what you boys want, but you're gonna have to leave." Shea approached the bald-headed man. The patches on his vest identified him as the president of the MC. No doubt this was Hunter, Wendy's old man.

"Mind your own business, bitch." Hunter tried to push her aside, but she caught his hand and twisted it around in an arm lock. He let loose a sharp squeal.

"This *is* my business, dirtbag!" She tightened the arm lock a pinch to drive home the point. "And in case you didn't see the sign on your way in, I don't allow club colors in my shop."

A scuffle erupted across the room. "Let me go, you asshole!" Wendy screeched as Mackey dragged her by the hair from the ladies' room.

Shea flipped Hunter around to face Mackey and her sister. A Beretta M9 protruded from Hunter's waistband. She considered reaching for it, but doing so meant releasing the arm lock. She opted to hold tight for the moment.

Mackey held Wendy with a tight grip on her hair, right at the scalp. Her face twisted in pain as she fell to her knees, her arms flailing.

"Let 'er go, or I rip your buddy's arm off," Shea yelled. *No one treats women like that in my shop,* she thought, *not even my good-for-nothing sister.*

"You stupid bitch," grunted Hunter. "You're good as dead."

Mackey pulled a snub-nosed revolver and squeezed off a couple of rounds in her direction. The deafening gunshots reverberated through the empty shop. Both bullets punched through the plywood on the door behind her.

Shea ducked down, using Hunter as a shield, and grabbed the Beretta. Hunter wheeled around to punch her until he saw the gun pointed at his head.

"Call off your dog." She stood up, keeping Hunter between her and Mackey.

Hunter glared until Shea flicked off the safety. "Mackey, hold your fire," he said.

Rather than dropping the revolver, Mackey pressed it against Wendy's temple, still holding her by her hair. *This guy is getting on my nerves,* she thought.

From the garage came a loud crash followed by shouting. It sounded like Lakota, Switch, and the other Thunderman.

"What the hell was that?" asked Hunter.

"If I had to guess, I'd say that was Switch." Shea pulled back the hammer on the Beretta. "Tell your buddy to put his gun on the floor and let Wendy go."

"Soon as she tells me where she took my little girl."

"Go fuck yourself, Hunter." Wendy's face flushed dark red. "I ain't telling you shit."

Mackey cracked her on the head with the revolver, dropping her to the floor, then pulled her back up again by her hair.

"You fuck!" Shea pointed the Beretta at Mackey but held her fire. Switch burst in shrieking like a bird of prey and knocked the revolver out of Mackey's hand with an exhaust pipe. Before he could recover, she swung again hitting him in the head. Mackey dropped like a fifty-pound sack of rice. Wendy recoiled against the wall and curled up into a ball.

Switch continued pounding him until Terrance ran up and took the exhaust pipe out of her hands. Lakota wrapped Switch in a bear hug, whispering in her ear until she settled down.

"Nice timing, guys," Shea said, enjoying the unsettled expression on Hunter's face.

"Got the other punk out back wrapped up with duct tape," said Terrance.

"This ain't over, you ugly bitch," said Hunter. "I got a right to see my little girl. Ain't nothing you or your overgrown monkey here can do to stop me."

Shea smacked Hunter in the face with the Beretta. A line of blood dripped onto his shirt.

"Listen, you redneck piece of shit." She put the gun to his forehead. "This ain't family court. We don't settle custody issues here. So unless you want me to pull the trigger, I'd suggest you leave and not come back. That goes for all the Thundermen. You got that?"

Hunter glanced at Terrance, then back at Shea, wiping blood from his nose. "I got it."

"One more thing—which of you rednecks broke in here last night?" She wasn't sure they had, but wanted to see how he reacted.

A sneer twisted onto Hunter's face. "What're ya talking about? Why would we wanna break into this dump?"

"Let's see. Scumbags broke into my shop. The Thundermen are scumbags who're always looking for a quick buck. You do the math."

"We were in Bradshaw City all night."

"Oh yeah? Doing what?"

"None of your goddamned business."

"You lying to me?"

In spite of the gun in his face, he smiled. "Guess you'll either have to take my word for it or shoot me."

She kneed him in the crotch. "Get out of my shop."

He doubled over in pain. "Bitch, you're gonna pay for that." He limped over to where Mackey lay on the floor and nudged him with his foot. "Get the fuck up. We're leaving."

Mackey groaned and struggled to his feet, massaging a lump on the back of his head.

Hunter turned back to Shea. "Where's One-Shot?"

"Terrance, drag that other guy up front. And don't be gentle about it."

"Will do." Terrance disappeared into the workshop.

She ushered Hunter and Mackey through the front door. One-Shot showed up a moment later, with Terrance on his heels.

One-Shot pulled at the duct tape on his mouth with a great deal of wincing.

"Let me get that for you, son." Terrance ripped the tape off One-Shot's face, leaving an angry welt.

One-Shot grabbed the side of his face. "Motherfucker!"

Terrance pulled him to his feet and pushed him toward Hunter and Mackey.

Shea pointed the Beretta at their bikes. "Now get the fuck outta here. Next person I see here wearing Thunderman colors gets two in the chest."

Hunter grinned. "Well, ain't you Daddy's little girl."

It took every ounce of restraint she possessed not to shoot him.

The three men started their Harleys in a deep rumble that echoed off the building. As they backed away from the curb, Hunter held up his hand in a gun shape pointed at Shea. She pointed his Beretta back at him.

Mrs. Brooks, the owner of the Kokopelli Café, came running out, looking alarmed. "Did I hear gunfire?"

Shea slipped the Beretta into her waistband, covering it with her shirt, "Naw, Mrs. Brooks," she said with her most innocent smile. "One of the bikes in the workshop back-fired a couple of times. Sorry to bother you."

Mrs. Brooks didn't look convinced, but went back into the café.

# 9

WHEN SHEA WAS sure Hunter and his boys were gone, she hurried over to her sister. Wendy sobbed so hard her body shook. Blood dripped from the top of her head where Mackey had coldcocked her with the revolver. The yellow-green of fading bruises colored Wendy's face and arms, reminding Shea of the countless times their mother had been black and blue from Ralph's beatings. The bitterness Shea felt toward her sister softened. History was repeating itself.

"It's okay; they're gone." Shea put an awkward hand on Wendy's arm.

"They'll be back," Wendy said between sobs.

"We can worry about that later." Shea helped her stand, guided her to a chair in the customer waiting area, and handed her a paper towel. "Put this on your head until the bleeding stops."

"Thanks." Wendy pressed the paper towel to her scalp and winced.

"Wanna tell me what that was about?"

"Hunter's my old man." Wendy offered an embarrassed smile.

"Yeah, I gathered that."

"He used to be real nice, but lately any little thing sets him off. I try to stay outta his way when he's like this, keep him happy best I can. But sometimes he gets pissed off no matter what." She took a deep breath and let it out slowly, like air squeezing out of a tire.

"The other day our daughter, Annie, asked why Daddy beats on me. I thought I'd been good about hiding it. But she's eight now and startin' to notice things." Wendy stared at the floor. "That was the last straw. I had to get us out of there."

*Wendy has a kid?* "Where's Annie now?" Shea asked.

"I left her at my friend Margaret's when I went to work this morning." She grabbed another paper towel and wiped her nose. "Then this afternoon, on my way back to her house, Hunter and the guys spotted my car and started chasin' me." She crumpled the paper towel and clenched it in her fist. "That's why I came here. I got your voicemail. Figured maybe you could help."

"How'd you know where I worked?"

"Oh please! I seen your booth at the bike shows in Phoenix. Word gets around."

Shea grimaced. "Was it true what he said?"

"'Bout what?"

"About the Thundermen being in Bradshaw City all night."

"I dunno. Me and him got into it last night. Then he got a call from One-Shot, some club business he had to deal with. Threatened to kick my ass when he got back. Once he drove off, I packed a couple bags and went to Margaret's with Annie."

She dabbed at the bloodstains on her blouse with the

paper towel, which smeared it more. "I should prolly head to Margaret's and check on Annie. Hunter ain't too smart, but he knows Margaret and I are friends. Sooner or later, he'll figure out we been staying there."

"Thought about filing a restraining order against him?" asked Terrance.

"Like a restraining order'd stop Hunter." Wendy managed a weak chuckle. She stood up and wobbled until Terrance grabbed her.

"You should go to the hospital first and make sure you don't have a concussion, " he said.

"I'm all right. Got a thick skull. Besides, I gotta check on Annie." Desperation tinged her voice. She looked at Shea with a pleading smile. "But I wouldn't mind if you tagged along. Margaret could drop you back here."

"Shea would be happy to," said Terrance.

Shea gave him the stink eye; it was the last thing she wanted to do.

"Wait here a moment," she said to Wendy.

Shea beckoned Terrance with her finger. "You and me gotta talk." She led him into the office and slammed the door shut. "What the hell you mean, I'd be happy to?" she asked in hushed tones. "I promised Jessica I'd take her to a new sushi restaurant in Ironwood for dinner. I ain't got time to be riding along with my sister to God-knows-where."

Terrance looked confused. "You hate sushi. You call it fish bait."

"So? Jessica likes it and I like her. Point is, I ain't getting in the middle of no custody dispute between my crazy-ass sister and her old man. I like not being dead."

"She's your sister, Shea. At least give her a ride to where she needs to go."

"She has a car. She's perfectly capable of driving to her

friend's house on her own." Shea crossed her arms and stared out the office window at the barren showroom.

"Have a heart, girl! She nearly got killed a moment ago."

"Yeah, and nearly got me killed in the process. I ever tell you she lied to protect that scumbag father of ours? So, fuck Wendy and her fucked-up life. If I wanna see trashy white people doing stupid shit, I'll watch reality TV where there's no chance of me getting my head blown off."

"What about your niece? Aren't you interested in meeting her? She's family, for God's sake."

Shea wanted to say no. Wendy chose to be a Thunderman's old lady. But a part of her wondered what would've happened if someone had been there for Mama. *What if Mama had gotten away from Ralph and taken me and Wendy with her?*

"Fine." Shea pulled out her phone to call Jessica. "Hey, hon. I'm gonna be a little late."

"No, you can't be a little late. We have reservations at six thirty. I already picked out an outfit for you to wear."

"Well, as much as I *love* you picking out my clothes," Shea said, rolling her eyes, "I have to give someone a ride up to Bradshaw City."

"Let me guess. It's a woman."

"No. Well, technically, yes, but it ain't like that."

"How did I know?"

"Jess, she's my sister."

"Oh baloney, you don't have a sister."

"Actually, I do."

"You never mentioned her before."

"That's 'cause we haven't spoken in seventeen years. We've been . . . what's the word?"

"Estranged?" suggested Jessica.

"Yeah, that's it."

"You haven't seen her in seventeen years, but suddenly

you have to give her a ride to the other side of the county?" Jessica's voice dripped with sarcasm.

"She and her old man are having problems. Listen, call the restaurant and see if you can push the reservation back to seven thirty. I should be back in plenty of time."

Jessica paused a moment before responding. "Fine, I'll call them. But you'd better be here."

"I swear. We'll be eating raw fish and that spicy green stuff in no time. Love you."

Shea hung up, walked out of the office, and stood in front of Wendy. *God, she looked pathetic,* thought Shea. *Mascara running, face swollen, blood everywhere.*

"Fine. I'll ride with you to your friend's house."

"Will you drive? I'm a bit wobbly." Wendy held up the bloody paper towel, as if to prove her point.

Shea frowned. "Got your key?"

Wendy held up a ring of keys with a Confederate battle flag charm attached. "It's the one with the Ford logo on it."

Shea took it from her. "Grab your purse," she said with all the warmth of a Popsicle.

# 10
———

WENDY POINTED Shea to an older model Mustang. The paint on the roof was peeling and faded, as if someone had taken a belt sander to it. The broken passenger side mirror hung limp like a dog's ear.

Shea opened the driver's door and sat down. Crumpled bits of paper, empty soda cans and the occasional french fry littered the floor. Wendy climbed into the passenger side.

"Where we headed?" asked Shea.

"Margaret lives on the east side of Bradshaw City. I'll show you."

Shea drove up Arizona 89 twelve miles to Bradshaw Highway. For the first five minutes, they rode in silence. Shea stared out at the road ahead, trying not to think about Derek or the Pink Trinkets bikes or how pissed Jessica was going be when she finally made it home.

"I missed you, you know," Wendy said, looking out the passenger window.

Shea tightened her grip on the steering wheel, her

anger igniting like gasoline fumes. "Maybe if you hadn't lied, I woulda stuck around."

"Lied? About what?"

Could she really not know? "Never mind."

"Well, whatever it was, I'm sorry, all right?"

"I don't want to talk about it."

"Fine." Wendy twisted a strand of hair. "It's cool you got your own bike shop. I remember you and Daddy working on bikes together all the time."

"Can we not talk about him?"

"Geez, is there any subject you ain't opposed to talking about?"

"Right now, I don't feel like talking about anything. I just want to get this over with."

"Whatever."

For the rest of the way, an oppressive silence filled the car, interrupted by occasional directions from Wendy. Shea turned off the main highway into a neighborhood of compact redbrick homes. She parked in front of a house with a rusted tricycle in the middle of the dirt yard and an older model minivan with a dented bumper in the gravel driveway.

As they walked to the front door, several of Margaret's neighbors stood staring at them from adjacent yards. Shea nodded at the onlookers and whispered to Wendy, "What's with the audience?"

"Something's wrong." Panic colored Wendy's voice. The door stood open, its frame busted in. "Annie!"

"Dammit, Hunter must have gotten here before us." Shea had hoped to avoid more of the MC's violent drama.

She moved Wendy away from the door and pulled Hunter's Beretta from her waistband. Her thumb pressed the button to eject the magazine. Eight rounds left. She hoped it would be enough. She slapped it back in.

"Wait here," she whispered. "They may still be inside."

"But my baby!"

"Sit tight." Shea left her sister sobbing on the front porch and slipped into the house. Her heart pounded in her ears.

The living room was small but uncluttered, decorated in a style Shea liked to call "early garage sale"—sort of shabby-chic, without much chic. Threadbare couch, milk crate bookshelves, and carpeting that reeked of mildew. On the upside, there wasn't any smashed furniture or other evidence of a struggle.

She tiptoed deeper into the house. A small hallway extended off to her left. To her right was the kitchen.

The familiar funk of blood filled her nose. *Maybe Margaret left a roast out on the counter too long,* she thought, calming herself against more sinister possibilities.

She stepped into the kitchen. The scent of blood grew weaker. No roast lay on the counter. Just a small pile of dishes in the sink. A voice in her head screamed at her to get out of the house, but she had to find her niece first.

Following the odor, she crept down the hall to the first bedroom on the right. A pile of plush toys sat on a bed with a faded patchwork gingham quilt. Posters of boy bands adorned the walls. She searched the room and wall closet, careful not to leave prints. There was no sign of the girl or the source of the smell.

She checked the bedroom on the left. A queen-sized bed with a tan and blue comforter dominated the room. A deep gouge marked the top of a bleached pine dresser that lined the opposite wall. She looked under the bed, in the attached bathroom, and the walk-in closet. The stink of blood grew stronger, but she found nothing to cause it.

"Shea?" Wendy called from the front door. "Can I come in? Is Annie in there?"

"Stay put. I'm still looking."

In the last bedroom, she found the source of the smell.

"Fuck."

Blood dappled the walls like a Jackson Pollock painting. The stench of blood, urine, and feces filled the room. A woman with shoulder-length black curls lay on the blood-soaked bed. *This must be Margaret.* She'd been shot twice in the face and several times in the chest. A smashed lamp and an overturned chair suggested a fight.

Shea's stomach grew queasy. The voice in her head grew more insistent, telling her to get out. *Where the hell's Annie?* She opened the closet door, hoping to find the girl curled up and frightened, but safe. Instead she found hand-me-down boy's clothes and an assortment of worn shoes.

"Shea?"

"Hold on."

"Shea, the cops are here."

"Aw, crap!" Shea ran to the front door only to be met by Deputies Aguilar and Winslow—aka Commando and Frat Boy—guns pointed at her head.

"Drop your weapon and get on the floor facedown." From the look on Aguilar's face, he wasn't cutting her any slack this time.

She dropped the Beretta on the floor and lay facedown on the carpet. At least this time there was no broken glass and she was clothed. She caught a strong whiff of mildew as Aguilar cuffed her. Sirens wailed outside.

"You got any other weapons on you?" His voice was cold and angry.

"No."

Winslow stalked down the hallway, clearing the rooms as he went.

Aguilar pulled her to her feet and patted her down.

"This makes twice in one day, Ms. Stevens. You going for a record?"

"It ain't what it looks like, Deputy. Honest."

"Oh Christ," called Winslow from the far bedroom. "Aguilar, we're gonna need a bus."

Aguilar pushed Shea down the hall and stopped in the bedroom doorway. Winslow had his arm wrapped around his face to ward off the smell.

Aguilar glared at her with fire in his eyes. "Shea Stevens, you have the right to remain silent."

# 11

SHEA SPENT the next hour and a half alone in an interrogation room with only a table and four wooden chairs for company. She'd lost all sensation in her right pinkie and ring finger because of the handcuffs. But her mind wasn't focused on the cuffs.

Since she'd woken up that morning, one person had been killed, another shot, and a third kidnapped. She herself had been shot at by an outlaw biker and had been in an armed standoff with a Mexican drug trafficker. She still had no idea where the stolen motorcycles were. And here she sat, stewing in a police station. Jessica was, no doubt, plotting ways to kill her for standing her up yet again. She was in the eye of a Category 5 shit storm.

Willie and Sheriff Buzz Keeler, whom she'd called Buzzkill since childhood, walked into the room. Buzzkill was in his late sixties, standing a few inches above six feet, and weighing north of three hundred pounds. His ruddy face had a permanent snarl on it, which darkened whenever he glared at someone he disliked. She'd been in the "dislike" category since as far back as she could remember.

Willie and Buzzkill sat down on either side of her. Two more people walked in behind them, both dressed in business clothes and carrying leather-bound notebooks. The first was a bespectacled white guy with a receding head of curly, black hair, wearing a dark suit, who looked more like an accountant than a detective. A petite Hispanic woman with bangs and a ponytail, dressed in a red blouse, a black jacket, and matching slacks, followed him in, dragging a fifth chair. Despite her size, she looked like someone who could handle herself.

Willie removed the handcuffs. "Shea, this here's Detective Micah Edelman and Detective Toni Rios. And you remember Sheriff Keeler."

She nodded at the detectives while rubbing her wrists to get the blood flowing back into her fingers.

Buzzkill leaned back in his chair and slammed the door shut. He'd aged a bit since she'd seen him last. He reeked of Old Spice and sweat. But that beer belly of his was coming along nicely.

"Been awhile, Miss Stevens." He slapped a folder down on the table.

"Yeah." She wasn't feeling talkative.

"Seems we have ourselves a situation here." Buzzkill pulled a photo of Margaret's body from the folder. "This poor, young lady, name o' Margaret Ortega, got herself kilt this afternoon, round 'bout five o'clock. You know anything 'bout that, missy?"

"Margaret was dead when I got there."

"Why were you at Ms. Ortega's house?" asked Detective Rios.

"My sister dropped by my motorcycle shop this afternoon. She wasn't feeling well afterward, so I agreed to drop her by her friend's house."

"Why her friend's house?" she asked. "Why not her place?"

Shea shrugged. "Have to ask her."

Willie pulled out the notebook he'd used that morning to take notes about the break-in at the shop. "After seventeen years of not seeing Wendy, you two must've had quite the reunion. How come she looks all beat up? You two get in a fight?"

"No." Shea's hip ached from the hard chair she sat on. She shifted her weight from one side to the other, growing restless from the endless questions.

"Uh-huh." Buzzkill glared at her. "Two people get shot on the same day, and you happened to be at both crime scenes. How you explain that?"

"A coincidence."

"Is that so? Ya know, I ain't a big believer in coincidences."

"Coincidences happen all the time, Buzzkill. Look it up."

Buzzkill's face turned purple. "You gettin' smart with me, girl? 'Cause you're lookin' at charges of murder and kidnappin'."

"Come on, Shea," said Willie. "I also have a report of gunfire coming from your shop this afternoon. What the hell's going on?"

"Nothing, I swear!"

Detective Edelman, who'd been taking notes the whole time, looked up at Shea. "I'll be honest, Ms. Stevens; right now, all the evidence points to you for the murder of Ms. Ortega." He spoke like an Ivy League blue blood from Boston or New York—Shea could never tell the difference. "If you're innocent, it'd behoove you to tell us what you know. Otherwise we *will* have no choice but to charge you."

*Time for me to shut up now,* she thought. "I ain't saying nothing else without my lawyer."

~

JUSTIN BRYCE WAS A SOFT-SPOKEN, pear-shaped guy in his late fifties. Back when she was arrested for grand theft, he'd served as her public defender. Didn't keep her out of prison, but he got her sentences to run concurrently. After getting out, she'd hired him to get her rights restored and to handle legal matters for the shop. He'd become kind of a family friend—albeit an expensive one.

"You're lucky," said Justin after Buzzkill and the others stepped outside the interrogation room. "I finished a case up in Prescott an hour before you called."

"Not guilty?" she asked, hoping for a positive sign.

"He did better than he would have without me. Let's leave it at that." He frowned. "Tell me what's going on here. Why're they looking at you for this woman's murder?"

"Early this morning, someone broke into Iron Goddess and shot Derek. Stole a bunch of merchandise, too. I called 911. They took Derek to the hospital."

"Sorry to hear about that." He scribbled down some notes. "How does that relate to this woman's murder?"

"I thought the Confederate Thunder mighta been the ones who broke in, so I called my sister, Wendy. She's married to the club's president—a guy by the name of Hunter Wittmann. Thought maybe she'd heard something one way or the other."

"The Sheriff's Office isn't investigating the break-in?"

Shea smirked. "Between illegally profiling Latinos, pulling people over for 'driving while black,' and staking out the county's doughnut shops, Buzzkill's boys are probably too busy to do any real police work," she said. "Figured it'd be faster if I did the investigating myself."

Justin chuckled. "And?"

"Apparently Hunter's been using her as a punching bag. Wendy and her daughter, Annie, spent the last night with her friend Margaret. Then this afternoon, she showed up at Iron Goddess, followed by Hunter and his boys. They started knocking her around, asking where Annie was. When I told 'em to clear out, one of his guys shot at me. He missed, fortunately, and we kicked them out without any further incident."

"How'd y'all manage that?"

"Oh, you know us ex-cons." She smiled for the first time in hours. "We're resourceful."

"Uh-huh. So you kick the Bowery Boys out and then what?"

"Wendy was all shaken up and asked me to drive her to Margaret's—promised Margaret would gimme a ride back. When we got there, we found the front door busted in. I went in looking for the girl and found Margaret dead in the back bedroom. No sign of Annie. That's when the cops showed up."

"Anything else I should know?"

"Like what?" Shea recalled her run-in with Oscar, but figured, why bring it up? It didn't have anything to do with Margaret or Annie.

"Like anything else the sheriff might surprise me with. I'm not a fan of surprises."

She shook her head. "No, that's it."

"Okay, let's bring them back in here and see if we can't get all this cleared up and go home."

Justin brought Buzzkill, Edelman, and Rios back into the room.

"Where's Willie?" she asked.

"Sergeant Foster had other business to attend to," said Edelman.

"Your client ready to confess, Counselor?" asked Buzzkill.

"Sheriff, the only thing my client is guilty of is giving a ride to her sister, Wendy, who is separated from her husband, Hunter Wittmann. She has been staying at Ms. Ortega's residence. If you're looking for a suspect in the child's abduction and Ms. Ortega's murder, I suggest you look at the girl's father."

Rios looked confused. "Why would Mr. Wittmann kill Ms. Ortega?"

"He's a Thunderman. Feels he can shoot whoever gets in his way," Shea said. "I've heard he's been picked up a few times for assaulting Wendy."

"Now folks," said Justin, "who do you think's more likely to have done this—a hardworking businesswoman or an outlaw biker with a history of violence?"

"Your client has a criminal record herself and was caught holding a gun at two different shootings," said Buzzkill. "I'd say that makes her a suspect."

"My client never met the deceased before she found the body. Her employees can confirm that she gave her sister a ride to pick up the girl."

Edelman shuffled some papers and pulled one out. "The ones at Iron Goddess Cycles?"

She nodded. "That's right."

"Would that include Olivia White River, who served two years for DUI?" he asked.

She rolled her eyes. "You mean Lakota? Yes."

"And Amy Marana, nickname Switch, who spent several years committed to the Cortes County Behavioral Health Center after putting three students and a teacher in the hospital?"

"She had schizoaffective disorder after her family abused her. She's better now."

"And your business partner, Terrance Childers, previously known as Theresa Childers," said Edelman. "He served four years for illegal possession of prescription narcotics, did he not?"

Buzzkill leaned over the table, sneering at her. "Seems like your alibi hangs on the word of criminals, junkies, and lunatics, all of whom work for you. Hardly enough to convince a jury. Why don't you quit lying and tell us the truth?"

Her blood boiled. "I *am* telling the truth, you fat piece of—"

Justin put a hand on her shoulder. "My client had no motive to kill the deceased, much less abduct her own niece. These charges are absurd."

"The motive could be any number of things. Drugs, money, who knows?" said Rios. "There's been a sharp rise in drug trafficking and related violence throughout Cortes County. A lot of it ties back to Mexican drug gangs."

"What's that got to do with me?" Shea asked. "I ain't Mexican."

Edelman referenced his sheet of paper again. "You know a man named Oscar Reyes?"

Shea shook her head, wondering how much worse this would get. "Name doesn't ring a bell."

"We received a report that a white female—medium build, short hair, and a scarred face—threatened him with a firearm earlier today at his family's restaurant. What can you tell us about this?" asked Edelman.

Justin leaned over to her and whispered. "What's he talking about? You know this Reyes character?"

She shook her head.

Justin turned to Edelman. "My client has no knowledge

of this. What does this have to do with Ms. Ortega or the missing girl?"

"Mr. Reyes is a member of Los Jaguares, a street gang that smuggles heroin and guns for the Santa Cruz drug cartel," said Edelman. "Margaret Ortega is Mr. Reyes' cousin."

That was news to Shea. In her mind, she could hear Terrance telling her he told her so—that the meeting with Oscar would come back and bite her. Guess he got that one right.

Edelman continued. "My guess is you've been using your business as a front to sell heroin for the Jaguars. Maybe a deal went sour, so when someone robbed your shop and shot your guy, you suspected the Jaguars. You retaliated by killing Ms. Ortega."

"Really?" asked Justin, arms crossed, looking rather unimpressed with Edelman's theory. "And the missing girl?"

Edelman shrugged. "We're still investigating that. Maybe the child's father does have her."

She stood up. "That's nuts. I got no idea who killed that woman. And I couldn't've kidnapped my niece. I was in the house when y'all arrested me."

Buzzkill pointed at her. "You sit down, missy, or I will cuff you again."

Rios smiled with a look of concern in her eyes. "Shea, we get it. You were in a tight spot. Economy's bad, making it harder to make ends meet. So you made deals with the Jags to keep the doors open. Anybody in your situation would have done the same thing. We just need you to tell us what happened."

"That's horseshit. I already told you what happened."

"Everybody, relax." Justin pulled her back down in her

chair. "Sheriff, have you checked my client for gunshot residue?"

Buzzkill squirmed. "We did, but the results were inconclusive."

"You mean the results came back negative."

"Don't mean nothing." Buzzkill sat back and crossed his arms. "She coulda been wearing gloves or washed her hands."

"Had the gun you found on my client been fired recently?"

"Again, inconclusive."

"I see. So the only thing you do know is my client was in the house with no motive and no evidence of having fired the weapon she was holding. Is that the case?"

The sheriff frowned. "We're still investigating."

"You sound like a broken record, Sheriff." Justin stood up. "Let me suggest an alternative theory, if I may. Hunter gets wind that Wendy is leaving him and staying with someone with family ties to the Jaguars. Believing his wife has betrayed him and the club to the enemy, he and his fellow outlaw bikers grab the girl and kill the Mexican woman. Doesn't that seem much more likely given the evidence?"

"Maybe."

"Well then, unless you plan to arrest my client, this interview is over."

Buzzkill sat there fuming. It pleased Shea to watch Justin put him in his place.

He closed the folder and stood up. "Detective, please release this woman. For now."

## 12

HALF AN HOUR LATER, Shea and Justin walked out of the police station.

"I guess your meeting with that Reyes fella must've slipped your mind," he said with a sour expression on his face as they approached his car.

"Look, I didn't think it was relevant. Thought he might know who broke into Iron Goddess. Things got a little heated."

He opened the passenger door for her. "Do yourself a favor, kiddo. Stay away from the Jaguars."

"Trust me, I intend to. Where's my sister?"

He climbed into the car. "I didn't see her in there. They probably questioned her and let her go. Want me to make some phone calls and find out?"

"Naw, I'm more worried about her daughter, Annie. Hunter's a violent son of a bitch."

"The Sheriff's Office put out an AMBER Alert. I'm sure they'll do everything they can to get her back to your sister safe and sound."

"You think they'll try to pin this murder on me?"

"They don't have much of a case. Hunter is the more likely suspect, anyway. All they have on you is wrong place/wrong time."

"I wouldn't put it past Buzzkill to frame me. He's still bitter about the time I boosted three of his patrol cars."

Justin laughed while he drove them back to the shop. "That was eighteen years ago. Not even Sheriff Keeler holds a grudge that long. He just wants to see justice served. As long as you don't do anything further to incriminate yourself, you should be fine."

She wasn't convinced, but let it go and stared out the window. A billboard advertising the new sushi restaurant caught her eye. "Oh shit, Jessica!"

On her phone, Jess had left sixteen voicemail messages. Shea dialed. It rang four times and went to voicemail. Maybe she's in another room and didn't hear it. She redialed. On the third ring, Jessica picked up.

"I don't want to talk to you," said Jessica before the line went dead.

"Crap."

"What's wrong?" asked Justin.

"My girlfriend's pissed."

Justin chuckled. "Guess it don't matter whether you're straight or gay. Relationships are hard work."

"Ain't that the truth."

When they reached Iron Goddess, Justin pulled around back next to her bike. Terrance's truck was still there. *What was he doing here so late?*

"Thanks for your help." She got out, closed the door, and poked her head back through the open window.

"Stay out of trouble, ya hear?" He waved and drove off.

Fatigue hung on her like a bag of wet sand. Her body ached from the day's excitement. More than anything, Shea wanted to crawl into bed. But first she wanted to make sure

Terrance was all right and not lying dead on the showroom floor. Maybe she could also clear the air between them.

Terrance sat staring at his computer when she poked her head in the door.

"Still here?" she asked.

"Just about to lock up." He looked up from his work. "Where've you been? Jessica's freaking out. Been calling every thirty minutes wondering where you are. I thought you'd be back in an hour."

Shea sighed. "That was the plan, till I got picked up by Willie and the boys."

"You got arrested?" He shook his head. "Dammit, I told you that stunt with Oscar would come back and bite us."

"This wasn't about Oscar. Wendy's friend Margaret—the one watching her daughter—someone murdered her."

"Oh no. That's horrible."

"Happened right before we got there. Door was all busted up, so I told Wendy to stay outside while I went in. That's when the cops showed up."

"Tell me you weren't armed."

"I had the Beretta I'd taken off Hunter earlier." Shea grimaced. "After all the shit that went down today, I wasn't taking any chances."

"Dammit, Shea! I can't believe you."

"You're the one who wanted me to drive her. This is the kinda drama I was hoping to avoid."

"They're not charging you, are they?"

"They wanted to, but Justin got me clear of it for now."

"At least there's that. Where's Wendy's little girl?"

"Dunno. Most likely with Wendy's old man. My guess is he figured out where Wendy was staying, grabbed his daughter, and shot her friend."

"Poor kid." Terrance shook his head. "And Wendy?"

"Don't know, don't care. I'd hoped she could tell me if

the Thunder shot Derek, but . . ." Shea shook her head. "Last thing I want now is to get pulled into any more of her drama. I feel sorry for the kid being caught in the middle of her parents' shit."

She sat down at her desk, took the Glock out, and tucked it into her waistband, mulling over the situation. "What're you doing here so late?"

"Figuring out how to pay for the new inventory until the insurance money comes in."

"Days like this, I miss boosting cars. Cash money, no overhead."

"Prison."

"No job's perfect."

The shop phone rang. The caller ID showed it was Wicked, lead singer for the Pink Trinkets. Shea picked it up. "Wicked, what's going on?"

"Not too late to call is it? We're in London. I can never figure out the time zones back in the States." Music blared in the background.

"No, it's cool." *Shoulda let it go to voicemail,* she thought.

"I wanted to see how the bikes are coming."

Her stomach knotted. "Finished 'em last night. They look great. Ride like a dream."

Terrance glared at her and mouthed, "Tell them."

"Awesome! Send pics. I can't wait to see them. Vicious and Nasty are excited, too."

"Pics? Sure, I'll email some tomorrow."

"Excellent! Our publicity gal is mentioning the bikes in all the radio and Web promos. Maybe after the concert, we can take them for a test ride. You can show us the sights." She sounded excited as only a twenty-something rock star can be.

"Sounds like a blast," Shea said, ignoring Terrance's glare.

"See you in a couple weeks." Wicked hung up.

"Dammit, Shea."

"What?" she asked, feigning innocence.

Terrance looked ready to spit nails. "You need to tell them the bikes are gone."

"T, we can't. The Trinks are already promoting the bikes. I'll find the bikes."

"How?"

"You know me. I got a gift for finding lost objects. Just last week I found Switch's socket wrench that Derek had borrowed and not put back. And before that I located that receipt you couldn't find. I'll find the bikes, too."

"It's not as if you misplaced the bikes in the workshop. They were stolen. If you don't want to tell Wicked they're gone, then I'm calling in help to build replacements."

"We ain't got enough time, nor can we afford to pay someone else to build 'em. I don't wanna give credit to another shop for bikes we already built once. That's just wrong.

"Well, we need to do something."

She resisted the urge to say something snarky. "I don't want to discuss this right now."

"Smartest thing you said all night. Go home and rest. We'll figure this out in the morning."

She slapped him on the back as she walked out. "See ya."

~

SHE FOUND Jessica asleep on the couch, dressed in her knee-length, midnight-blue silk robe. Shea sat beside her and kissed her on the cheek. "Hey, I'm home."

Jessica opened her eyes, which were bloodshot and puffy. "Where were you? I called your cell, the shop, even

the hospital. I was afraid you'd killed yourself on that
motorcycle." Her voice cracked as a tear ran down her
cheek.

Shea hugged her. "Sheriff's deputies picked me up for
questioning."

Jessica sat up. "You got arrested? For what?"

"Not arrested. Questioned. My sister's old man grabbed
their daughter and killed the friend she was staying with. I
found the body."

"Oh God." She covered her mouth with her hand.

"Right now I just want to sleep," Shea said, touching her
forehead to Jessica's.

"Oh honey." Jessica kissed her. "I'm glad you're okay."

They groped and kissed their way to the bedroom. Shea
kicked off her boots and jeans as Jessica's robe fell away.
Jessica said something, but the cool sheets of the bed
pulled Shea into the oblivion of sleep like a drug.

## 13

SHEA'S PHONE rang a few hours later. She tried to ignore it until Jessica started shaking her. "Shea, your phone is ringing. Please, make it stop."

Shea picked it up. "If this is the alarm company, call the fucking cops."

"Shea? It's me." It wasn't the alarm company. But the voice was familiar.

Her half-asleep mind tried to put a name to the voice. "Mama?"

"What? No, it's Wendy."

She sat up and looked at the clock. It was four in the morning. "Wendy." It took a moment to recall the previous day's events. "You find Annie?"

"No." Wendy sounded like a wounded puppy. "Can you come over? I need your help."

Shea groaned in frustration. *How do I tell her no without being a self-centered bitch?*

"This is between you and your old man. After what happened yesterday, I think it's best if I stay out of it. I got my own shit to deal with." She sighed, knowing she sounded cold and selfish. "Isn't the Sheriff's Office looking for Annie?"

"Buzzkill and his doughnut-eating storm troopers couldn't find shit in a horse trailer. They don't give a damn about anyone affiliated with the MC. I need *you,* Shea."

"Call the FBI. They handle missing kids, don't they?" Guilt tugged at her. She steeled her resolve. There were the problems at the shop to worry about.

"Trust some suit to rescue my little girl? Are you nuts? You're the one who was always good at finding things."

"I ain't no bounty hunter. I'm a bike builder. Besides, I'm already in enough trouble over this. The damn cops think I shot your friend."

"If you help me get Annie back from Hunter, she can tell Buzzkill you didn't kill Margaret."

"I can't. Sorry." Shea hung up.

"Was that your sister?" Jessica's voice was raspy with sleep.

"Yeah." Shea cuddled up with Jessica, ashamed of her refusal to help. "I guess her old man still has their kid somewhere."

"Maybe you should go help her."

"And risk getting my head blown off again by that maniac? I got a better idea." Shea nuzzled Jessica's neck. "How 'bout I stay here in bed with you and make amends for missing our date last night."

Jessica pulled away. "If some asshole had *our* kid, would you want your sister to blow you off?"

"Don't say that. It's Wendy's mess. She married that fucker. I'm sure she can figure out how to get her kid back from him."

"If he's crazy enough to kill a baby-sitter, what'll he do with his own daughter?"

Shea lay there stewing in her guilt. She could hear their

mother in Wendy's voice, pleading with her, reaching out. The memory of blood filled her nostrils. "Fuck."

She called Wendy back. "Fine. I'll help. Where the hell are you?"

"At the Getaway Motel in Bradshaw City. Room 213. It's on the second floor." Her voice was so choked with tears Shea could barely understand her.

"I'll be there as soon as I can." She rubbed her face, trying to wake up.

Wendy whimpered a thank-you and hung up.

Shea pulled off the covers and stood, admiring the curves of her girlfriend's cocoa-colored skin. "If I get killed doing this, you're gonna feel bad. Just sayin'."

Jessica smiled. "You're a good person."

"No, just too tired to argue with the women in my life."

Shea peeled the bandages off her chest and took a cold shower to wake herself up. Jessica handed her a cup of coffee when she got out. After putting on some clean clothes, she geared up, slipped her Glock into her waistband, and drove north on her bike to Bradshaw City.

～

THE GETAWAY MOTEL was a popular spot for hookups and illicit affairs. Desk clerks never checked IDs. Rooms were often paid in cash. A yellow sign illuminated the motel's parking lot, advertising their extensive selection of porn channels. Shea wondered why Wendy'd gotten a room at a dump like the Getaway.

Shea parked her bike, climbed the outdoor stairs, and knocked on the door to room 213. Wendy opened it a moment later, her eyes swollen and lifeless. She let Shea into the dim room without a word and sat down on a queen-sized bed covered with a stained polyester bedspread. The room stank of mildew and sex. The only light came from a small lamp on the nightstand. Shea opted to remain standing for fear of catching something.

"I don't know what I can do to help. The cops are already looking for Annie."

"Cops don't know shit. They think you took her. How stupid's that?" Her voice sounded distant and detached, eyes half lidded. Shea wondered if she was high or only sleep deprived.

"So what now?"

"It's all my fault." Wendy began to sob.

Shea felt sympathy tugging at her and tried to ignore it. "Don't be stupid. It ain't your fault. You figure Hunter's got her?"

"I thought so. But why would he kill Margaret?"

"Gee, lemme think—because he's a psycho?"

"He's not a psycho. He just has anger-management issues sometimes."

Shea decided not to argue the point. "Where would he take her? The Church?" she asked, referring to the Confederate Thunder's clubhouse.

"Most likely."

"How do we get her back?"

Wendy's phone dinged. She picked it up, touched the screen, then dropped it as if burned. "Noooooo . . ."

Shea picked up the phone. A video of a blindfolded girl played on the screen. She whimpered despite the duct tape covering her mouth. Her wrists and ankles were bound with duct tape.

A man's deep voice with a thick Latino accent said, "I have your daughter. You give me four million dollars in nonsequential, twenty-dollar bills delivered to me in two duffel bags within forty-eight hours. No marked bills. No tracking devices. No cops. You don't pay or you break my rules, I gut the girl and hang her from a bridge. I contact you again soon."

Acid burned the back of Shea's throat. Her hand shook with anger and disgust as she held the phone. "Where'd this video come from?"

Wendy lay curled in a fetal position on the bed, sobbing, hands covering her head.

Shea waited a moment for Wendy to respond, but the crying intensified. Shea shook her sister's shoulder. "Wendy, listen to me. Where'd this video come from?"

"From a link in an email."

Shea found the email. The subject read, "I Have Your Daughter." The sender's email address looked like a random jumble of letters. There was nothing in the body of the email but the hyperlink with a Mexican Web address.

"It wasn't supposed to happen like this," Wendy wailed. "What do I do? What do I do?"

Shea tried to focus. "It's gotta be the Jaguars. It's the only thing that makes sense."

"No, please. Why would they take Annie? What did I ever do to them?"

"Think about it. How better to hurt the club than to go after the president's kid? And then there's the video— Mexican accent, threatening to hang her from a bridge. It's the Jaguars all right."

Wendy shook her head back and forth. Her hands cupped her ears. "Oh God, this is all my fault. I never should've tried to leave."

"This ain't about you, Wen. The Jags are using Annie to get at the MC."

"No. Please, not my baby. Can't we convince them to let her go? She's only a little girl." Her eyes pleaded with Shea.

Shea's resentment toward Wendy softened, loosening

the tightness in her chest. She wiped the damp hair from Wendy's face. "We're in over our heads."

Shea thought about calling Terrance, but didn't want to put him at any further risk. "Much as I hate to say it, I think we should tell the Sheriff's Office about the ransom demand."

"No! You heard what the kidnapper said. They'll kill her."

"Kidnappers always say that. But we're out of our league here. The Sheriff's Office has experience with these things."

"I am *not* trusting those assholes with my daughter's life."

"Fine, but that doesn't leave us with many options." Shea sighed, considering alternatives. "Maybe we need to call Hunter."

A mix of emotions played across Wendy's face. "Why?"

"Because the only way we're getting her back is with four million dollars."

"Who you think Hunter is? Donald Trump?"

"Cut the bullshit. We both know the Thundermen are the biggest crystal meth dealers in the state. The Jags know it, too, which is probably why they took Annie. We either come up with the money, or . . ." Shea held out the phone. "Call Hunter."

Wendy pushed it away, closing her eyes. "You call him. I can't talk to him." Wendy turned away from her and sobbed.

An amber pill bottle on the nightstand caught Shea's eye. "What's this?" She picked it up. The label identified it as an OxyContin prescription for someone named Bertha Daniels. "Jesus, Wendy. Just when I thought you couldn't be more pathetic. Where the hell'd you get this?"

"Hunter got it for me to help with stress. Took some a little while ago, trying to sleep."

"Goddammit, your daughter gets kidnapped, and you go poppin' Oxy? Shit." Shea looked up Hunter's number in the directory on Wendy's phone and dialed it.

"Where's my daughter, bitch?" he bellowed.

"We ain't got her."

"Who the fuck is this?"

"Shea, Wendy's sister. Annie's been kidnapped."

"Bullshit, kidnapped! Put Wendy on the phone."

"Wendy's fucked up on that hillbilly heroin you gave her. You're dealing with me now."

"Goddamn cunt."

Shea wasn't sure if he was talking about her or Wendy.

"Where the fuck's my daughter? And don't give me that kidnapped crap. I know she's got her."

"Listen, asshole, Wendy left your daughter with her friend Margaret. When we got to the house, someone'd killed Margaret and took Annie."

"You better not be lying to me. I already owe you for what went down at the bike shop."

"I ain't lying. Wendy got an email a few minutes ago with a video of Annie all tied up. Kidnapper wants four million dollars within forty-eight hours or he'll gut her and hang her body from a bridge. Didn't see his face but he had a Mexican accent."

"Muthafuckin' Jaguars!"

"My thoughts exactly. You got the four million?"

"Hell no, I ain't got four million dollars! Do you?"

"No, but then I don't deal crystal like you do."

"You don't know shit."

"Look, I don't care if you earn selling stolen tricycles. You need to come up with the four mill or find a way to rescue her. Otherwise, those Mexican gangbangers are gonna kill your daughter."

"Fuck!" He went quiet for a few moments.

"You there, Hunter?"

"Yeah, I'm here." He sounded choked up. "Goddamn beaners! I'm gonna fuck them up."

"That's the spirit. Why don't we meet up and figure out how to handle this."

"Fuck you, bitch. This ain't your business. This is between me, Wendy, and the club."

"You ain't the only one with a score to settle with these guys. The Jaguars shot one of my employees and stole a dozen of our bikes. You wanna get Annie back safe. I want my motorcycles. Maybe if we work together, we can both get what we want."

He didn't say anything for about a minute. "Fine. Meet me at Bradshaw City Diner in half an hour."

# 14

SHEA SHOOK WENDY, who was snoring on the bed. "Get up! We gotta go."

Wendy pushed away her sister's hand. "Let me sleep a few more minutes."

Shea pulled her up by her arm. "Wake the fuck up, Wendy, or the Jaguars are gonna kill Annie."

"What? Oh fuck, Annie!" She buried her face in her hands and wept.

"Get your shit together. We're meeting Hunter at the Bradshaw City Diner to figure out what to do."

Wendy reached for the bottle of Oxy, but Shea snatched it. "Nuh-uh. You had enough of this shit." She dashed to the bathroom.

"Hey! Give those back. They're mine." Wendy stumbled after her.

"Oh really? Your name Bertha Daniels? 'Cause that's whose name's on the bottle." She lifted the toilet lid and dumped the pills as Wendy made a desperate grab for the bottle.

"No, I need those!"

The pills swirled down the drain as Shea flushed it. "What you need is to get your shoes, so we can get outta here."

Wendy pounded on Shea's back with her fists. "I hate you!"

Shea spun her around and pushed her out of the bathroom. "Yeah, you and everyone else."

A knock on the front door startled Shea. She looked at Wendy. "You expecting anyone?"

Wendy shook her head.

"Hide in the bathroom." Shea pulled out her Glock and crept to the door. "Who is it?" There was no peephole, naturally.

A male voice said, "Detectives Edelman and Rios with the Sheriff's Office. I'm looking for Wendy Wittmann. Is she here?"

Shea secured the chain on the door, and opened it a few inches. The detectives from the interrogation room stood on the concrete walkway that ran along the second floor, backlit by the sulfur glow of a nearby streetlamp. "All right, give me a sec."

She holstered the Glock, closed the door to unlatch the chain, and opened it again. Edelman stood in the doorway, with Rios a few feet behind him.

Edelman leaned in and took a quick scan of the room. "Mind if we come in?"

"You got a warrant?"

"Miss Stevens, we're not here to arrest anyone. We're trying to get Wendy's daughter back from whoever took her. Is Wendy here?"

*If the kidnapper finds out we talked to the cops, he might hurt her,* Shea thought. On the other hand, if she turned the detectives away, they might suspect something was up. "Yeah, she's here."

She stepped back to let them in and shut the door. Wendy stumbled out of the bathroom, hair disheveled, eyes unfocused. "Who is it?"

"The detectives are here to help get Annie back," she said.

Edelman helped Wendy sit on the bed. "Ms. Wittmann, have you heard back from your husband on where your daughter is?"

Wendy looked at her, wide-eyed, as if expecting her to tell her what to say. "Um, maybe."

"Wendy, we're here to help." He pulled out a notepad and pen. "Anything you can tell us that can help us find her?"

Rios put a hand on Shea's arm. "Why don't you and I step outside, and let them talk."

Shea knew this move. Divide and conquer. It made her all the more suspicious. Cops were always there to help until they're weren't. She could refuse to leave the room, but again it might make them suspect the kidnapper had contacted them.

Shea followed Rios outside onto the concrete walkway. She leaned back against the railing, arms crossed, and stared casually at the detective. "How'd you know we were here?"

"We had one of our guys keep an eye on your sister after she left the Sheriff's Office."

"Why? She didn't do nothing wrong."

"We were concerned for her safety." Rios smiled. "Now that I've answered your questions, how about you answer mine. When was the last time you saw Annie?"

"Never met 'er."

The detective raised an eyebrow. "You've never met your eight-year-old niece?"

"Nope."

"Why's that?"

"Until yesterday, Wendy and me hadn't seen each other for a while. After our fa—" She couldn't bring herself to say father. "After our mother was killed, Wendy went to live with a member of the Confederate Thunder. I didn't want to have anything to do with the MC, so I split."

"Your father was president of the Thunder before he went to prison, right?" Rios had been doing her homework.

Shea stared down the walkway at the other rooms. "Yeah."

"Wendy looks all beat up. Care to explain that?"

She didn't. With most of her employees being ex-cons, she didn't want them looking into the confrontation with the Thunder at Iron Goddess. "Ask her."

"I'm asking you. Did her husband Hunter do that?"

"Yeah, I reckon." Close enough to the truth.

"They having marital problems?"

"Like I said, I reconnected with her yesterday. Now her kid's gone. It ain't like we're gossiping about boys and braiding each other's hair."

"Shea, when children go missing, it's often a relative who has them. You think Annie's father has her?"

"No. We called him a little bit ago. He's looking for her, too."

"Have either of you heard from whoever took Annie? Maybe a ransom demand?"

Shea thought about telling the truth, but the truth might get Annie killed. "Nothing so far."

Rios tilted her head. "You'd tell me if you had, right?"

"Why wouldn't I?"

"A lot of families get scared, especially if the kidnapper says not to contact police. But Annie has a much better chance of getting home safely if we're here to help coordinate. Kidnappers know how to play on your fears and use that power to get what they want. We shift the power in your favor because we know what works and what doesn't."

The detective made sense, but it wasn't enough to overcome Shea's distrust of cops. "I hear what you're saying."

"Good. So I'll ask you again: have you or your sister heard from whoever took Annie?"

"No."

"If that changes, get in touch with me right away." She handed Shea a card with her name, Detective Antonia Rios, on it. "Any time of day or night, give me a call."

"I'll do that."

"One other thing, I heard about what happened at your shop yesterday."

Shea's pulse quickened. "What'd you hear?"

"About the break-in. How's your employee doing?"

Shea shrugged. "Critical condition. You involved in the investigation?"

"No, Sergeant Foster assigned that case to someone else. You think it's related to Annie's abduction?"

"Why would it be?"

The motel room door opened. Edelman appeared shaking his head. "You ready?" he asked Rios.

"Yeah, we're done." Rios pointed to the business card in Shea's hand. "Call me if you hear something."

"Right." Shea tucked the card into her wallet and watched them drive off in a navy blue sedan into the hazy, predawn light. Once they were out of sight, she dashed into the motel room. Wendy sat on the bed, staring at the floor.

"What d'you tell him?" Shea asked.

"Nothing." Wendy's eyes darted around the room, avoiding Shea's gaze. "He asked if we'd heard from the kidnapper, and I told him no. But I ain't sure he believed me."

"Let's hope he did. Don't need Buzzkill's goons getting in the middle of this mess. C'mon, let's go meet Hunter."

## 15

FOR TEN MINUTES, Shea nagged Wendy to get her out of the motel room and into the passenger seat of the Mustang. The egg yolk of a sun had crested the horizon, painting everything in a golden glow. Aside from Wendy's Mustang and Shea's bike, only a black Nissan SUV and a red Toyota pickup with an NRA sticker remained in the hotel parking lot. Not a lot of the Getaway's guests spent the whole night there, Shea noted.

Shea didn't like leaving her bike in the empty lot, but Wendy didn't seem fit to drive. Her skin was clammy, and her pupils dilated. Her voice rattled with congestion. Shea hoped whatever Wendy was coming down with wasn't contagious.

Shea turned the key in the ignition. "Buckle up, Bug."

"Bug? You ain't called me that since we were kids."

The nickname had slipped out without Shea realizing it, and it pissed her off. She didn't want any more trips down memory lane. "Just put your damn seatbelt on."

"You ain't the boss of me." She crossed her arms and stared at Shea with a smug expression.

Shea wanted to slap her stupid. "Suit yourself." She threw the car in reverse and stomped on the gas. The Mustang jolted backward out of the parking space. Wendy's head bounced off the glove box, leaving a red lump, but no blood.

"What the fuck?"

"Oops." Shea pulled out of the parking lot and cruised toward the diner, ten miles away. The black SUV pulled out behind them. Shea wondered if it was the deputy who'd followed Wendy to the motel, though all the other Sheriff's Office vehicles were painted either gold or white.

Shea's phone rang. She pulled it out. "Yello."

"Hey babe," said Jessica, "I got an AMBER Alert on my phone. Any luck finding Annie?"

"She's been kidnapped. We got a ransom demand a little while ago."

"Oh, the poor kid! Have you told the cops?"

"Kidnapper said no cops. We're handling it ourselves. Me and Wendy are meeting her old man for breakfast."

"Mind if I join you? I'd like to meet your sister and her *old man*."

"I don't think that'd be a good idea."

"Why not? You're not ashamed of me, are you?"

"Ashamed? Why would I be ashamed of you?"

"Because I'm black."

"No, that ain't it at all. It's . . ." She glanced at her sister. Wendy stared out the window, head resting against the glass. "Wendy's old man is a redneck biker and not a big fan of people of color. I'm afraid he'd say something disrespectful to you, and I'd have to kick his ass."

"Uh-huh." She didn't sound convinced. "You couldn't make it to lunch or dinner yesterday, but you got time to hang out with your racist brother-in-law?"

"It ain't by choice, believe you me. I'm trying to get

Annie back. I know I owe you for standing you up for dinner last night."

"And lunch."

"Yes, and lunch. How about dinner tonight?"

"Okay, but no more rainchecks."

"I promise." She hung up.

Wendy coughed and sniffled.

"You coming down with something? You look like shit."

"I'd be better if you hadn't flushed my stuff down the john." She gave Shea a resentful look. "Who's that on the phone?"

"Jessica."

"Who's Jessica? Your roommate?"

"Sorta."

"What's sort of a roommate?"

"She's my girlfriend." Normally coming out to someone was no big deal for Shea. But discussing her love life with her sister made her uncomfortable.

"You mean a friend that's a girl, like a bestie, or—"

"She's my lover."

"Oh." Wendy perked up and looked at her. "Holy fuck! You're a dyke?"

"What? The short, spiky hair and clothes stained with engine grease didn't give it away?"

"I don't know. I thought you were . . ."

"Butch?"

"A tomboy. You and Daddy were always doing stuff together." Wendy grew quiet for a moment, eyes cocked as if remembering something. "Is that what made you gay? Doing all that boy stuff with Daddy?"

"No, dingbat, that ain't why I'm gay. I did stuff with Ralph 'cause Mama was all into shopping and manicures and shit." Shea made a gagging gesture. "Boring."

"Then why do you like girls?"

"I don't know. Just do. Why do you like boys?"

She giggled. "'Cause, you know, they're hot."

Shea shrugged. "I think girls are hot."

"Maybe you haven't met the right guy."

"Maybe you haven't met the right girl."

"Huh. Never thought of it that way." Wendy twisted her face in thought, then snorted. "My sister's got an old lady."

~

FOUR MILES LATER, the black SUV remained behind them. To see if it was tailing them, Shea made a last-second left turn onto a side street. The SUV squealed its tires and tipped onto two wheels through the turn.

"Geez, Shea. Drive much?" whined Wendy.

"I told you earlier to put your seatbelt on."

"Why?"

"We're being tailed. Now put your goddamn seatbelt on."

Wendy twisted around to look behind them before snapping on her seatbelt. "The black one?"

"Uh-huh." Shea pressed the accelerator and weaved past a few cars. "Please tell me you got the eight-cylinder Mustang and not the six."

"Why?"

"If we're gonna outrun these guys—"

"I got the six. It was cheaper."

"Fuck." Shea considered her options. "This is gonna get a little bumpy."

The SUV honked and flashed its lights at the cars separating them. The drivers gave way and soon the SUV was back on their tail.

"Who is it?" Wendy asked, the fear obvious in her voice.

"I thought it might be the deputy who followed you to

the motel. But now I wonder. Seems a little aggressive, even for one of Buzzkill's goons."

"Why would they be following me? We just talked to them."

"I ain't real keen on finding out." Shea swerved into a shopping center parking lot, dashing across lanes, dodging grocery carts, and sending pedestrians scrambling. The SUV didn't let up. It smashed grocery carts out of its way and scraped paint with a parked Audi. *Definitely not a deputy,* Shea thought. That worried her more.

Running out of parking lot, she pulled back onto the road, making sure the SUV followed. It did. At the next intersection, she pulled hard on the parking brake and turned the wheel to swing a bootlegger's turn, a trick she'd learned when boosting cars. The car spun around, heading the way they'd come, and whizzed past the SUV.

"Holy shit, that was some move! D'we lose 'em?" asked Wendy.

Shea glanced in the rearview mirror. "No sign of them."

Before she could congratulate herself, a sheriff's cruiser pulled onto the street behind them and turned on its flashing lights. "Damn, just can't win today."

She considered running from the cop, but they wouldn't have stood a chance. It was one thing to outrun a single patrol car, quite another to outrun a police radio. She pulled over to the curb as the black SUV whizzed by too quickly for her to read the license plate.

The cruiser parked behind her, blue lights flashing. "Wendy, where's your registration?"

"My what?" Her sister seemed jittery. Her face was flush and sweaty. She let loose with a fit of coughing.

"Your vehicle registration. You know, the little paper they give you when you pay for your tags every year or two."

Wendy searched through the glove box, tearing through the papers like a Tasmanian devil. Shea glanced in the mirror to see Willie walking up to the car. She rolled down the window, not sure whether to be worried or relieved.

"Willie, how is it everywhere I go, you show up? You fire all your other deputies?"

"You tell me how every time there's trouble, you're in the middle of it. Where you two going?"

"To meet Wendy's husband for breakfast."

"Breakfast with Hunter Wittmann? The man you accused of killing the Ortega woman and kidnapping his own daughter? Am I missing something?"

She felt like she was back in the interrogation room. "Turns out it wasn't him."

"You sound convinced. Why the change of heart?"

"'Cause we talked to him on the phone. He thought we had Annie."

"You tell this to Detectives Edelman and Rios?"

"Yeah, we told them. Geez, what's with the third degree? I thought we were friends."

"I hate to break it to you, but right now you're our main suspect."

"How could I kidnap my own niece if I was still there when you guys arrived? Don't they teach you guys anything at deputy school?"

"Listen, I'm not in charge of this investigation. Edelman and Rios are. I'm sure they're following up on every lead. You heard from the kidnappers?"

"No."

He kept her gaze a minute longer than she was comfortable with. "You hear anything, you let us know."

"Yeah, yeah. We free to go?"

"Not so fast. You mind explaining that little stunt you pulled back there?"

"Did you not see the black SUV chasing us?"

"Now why would someone be chasing you?"

"How the hell should I know? Why'd someone break into Iron Goddess and shoot one of my guys? Why'd someone kidnap Wendy's kid? This world's gone fuckin' crazy. For all I know, Buzzkill's framing me."

"Don't be ridiculous. Why would the sheriff want to frame you?"

"Maybe he resents me making something of myself."

"That's absurd. Now show me your license, insurance, and registration."

"Fine." She handed him her license and the insurance card for her motorcycle. "This is Wendy's car. She's looking for the registration."

Willie leaned down to look through the window at Wendy, who had papers strewn all over her half of the car. She sniffled and coughed, as she gazed absently at a wrinkled receipt. Between the bruises on her face and her feverish complexion, she looked messed up. "You all right there, Wendy?"

"Her daughter's been kidnapped, Willie. Of course, she's not all right."

He examined Shea's license and insurance card, then handed them back to her. "You found that registration yet?"

Wendy dug under her seat, pulling out empty paper cups and candy wrappers. "I'm sure it's here somewhere."

"No registration." He walked around to the back of the car, bent down, then returned to the window. "Plate's current. I'll let it slide. As for the reckless driving, I didn't see any SUV. But I'll let you go with a warning."

"Well, don't do me any favors. I'd hate to impose on you any further." Letting her smart mouth run wild was apt to get her in deeper trouble, but she was hungry and in desperate need of coffee.

Willie leaned in, his face inches from Shea's. "I don't know what's going on, but I get the impression you're messed up in something you shouldn't be. Unless you want to spend the rest of your life in jail, I'd suggest getting your shit together. Childhood friendship only goes so far. Now get on outta here before I change my mind. And do drive more carefully."

"Gee, thanks, Sarge," she said, her voice dripping with sarcasm.

She pulled out slowly and cruised on to the diner. A mile down the road, Wendy held up a piece of paper. "Found it. No, wait, this is from two years ago."

"Give it a rest, Wen."

## 16

SHEA PULLED into the diner's crowded parking lot. The aluminum skin of the building gleamed like an oversized Airstream. Near the entrance, a Harley Fat Boy and a Road King sat parked next to a Ford Bronco. All three sported the skull and Confederate battle flag—nicknamed the Johnny Reb—that served as the club's logo. Shea resisted the urge to spit on the Road King's seat as they walked past to the front door.

Inside, plates and glasses clinked over a hum of conversation. Most of the tables were filled for the breakfast rush. Waitresses in yellow and orange outfits, armed with pots of coffee and trays of food, glided through the aisles like ballerinas.

Hunter sat in a large round booth in the corner.

"Over there." Shea nudged Wendy in his direction and followed behind her.

Hunter looked up from his steak and eggs. "Well if it ain't my prodigal wife and her sister, Scarface."

"Nice to see you, too, asshole." Shea approached the table.

A heavy hand gripped her shoulder. She turned around to see One-Shot looming over her. According to the patches on the front of his cut, he was the club's VP. Mackey, the club's sergeant-at-arms, stood next to him. The place felt way too crowded. Shea wondered if Hunter might be looking for payback.

"After you." She tried to step away to let Mackey and One-Shot go first, hoping not to get boxed into the booth between them and Hunter.

"Ladies first," said Mackey with a crooked smile. He pushed Shea and Wendy onto the seat and slid in after them. The side of his face was purple and swollen from where Switch had walloped him with the tailpipe.

One-Shot took a seat on the other side of Hunter.

Shea hooked a thumb at Mackey. "What're Tweedledum and Tweedledee doing here, Hunter? I thought it'd be just the three of us."

Hunter smirked at her. "You thought wrong. Where the fuck's my gun?" He stuffed a piece of steak into his mouth, chewing so everyone could see the show. He cut up a piece and offered it to Wendy. She took a sniff and scrunched up her nose at it.

"Talk to Sheriff Buzzkill. One of his deputies took it when Annie's baby-sitter got killed. I reckon they're running ballistic tests to see if it matches the murder weapon."

Hunter growled. "Stupid bitch, you don't know the shitstorm you stirred up."

"Forget the gun. Let's talk about how we're getting Annie back."

"Fine, but you ain't off the hook."

Wendy cuddled up to him, then erupted into a fit of raspy coughing over Hunter's food.

Hunter pulled his plate away from her. "What the hell's

wrong with you?" He turned to Shea. "What's wrong with her? She looks like shit."

"Beats me."

"Shea threw away my medicine," Wendy said with an exaggerated pout on her feverish face.

He glared at Shea. "What the hell'd you do that for?"

"We don't need her all fucked up while we're rescuing Annie."

"Stupid bitch! Can't you see she's in withdrawal?" He cupped Wendy's chin in his hand. "Don't worry, baby. I'll hook you up. Mackey, call Goatsy, tell 'em to bring me some Oxy."

Mackey pulled out his phone and made the call while Hunter and Wendy got all lovey-dovey, whispering, giggling, and making out like a couple of lovesick teenagers.

Despite her hunger, Shea's stomach soured at her sister's public display of affection. "Holy mother of fuck, are we gonna rescue Annie or are you two playing tonsil hockey all morning?"

Hunter's face flushed as he sat up and straightened his leather cut. "Any more calls from the kidnapper?" he asked.

"Not yet."

"Where's the phone?"

She patted the inside pocket of her biker jacket. "I got it."

He held out his hand. "Give it to me."

Shea frowned. "I'm holding on to it for now."

Hunter's eyes blazed. "I said, gimme the goddamn phone, lesbo."

Shea's upper lip curled in frustration. "You told him I was gay?" She normally didn't care who knew, but she wasn't in the mood to deal with these idiots' bigotry.

"What? I didn't think it was a big deal."

One-Shot whispered something in Hunter's ear. Hunter nodded. "Fine. You can keep the phone. For now."

*Score a point for me,* she thought. "So what's the plan?"

Mackey played absently with the pepper shaker. "Jaguars got a warehouse in the Cortes National Forest, fifteen miles east of Ironwood. Use it to store guns, drugs, whatever shit they don't want the cops to find. Probably holding her there."

She wondered if the Jags were also storing the stolen Pink Trinkets' bikes there. "How do y'all know about it?"

"Been there a time or two, back when we sold weed for the beaners."

"Is it guarded?" Shea didn't want to get caught in the middle of a gunfight between the Thunder and the Jags.

"Not usually. They keep it locked up." said Hunter. "If they got Annie there, they may have someone watching her."

"When we going?"

"Ain't no we, rug munch," said Mackey. "This is club business. Don't need no cunts getting in the way."

Her hands balled into fists. "We had a deal. We're in this together."

"I changed my mind." Hunter raised his chin as a smug grin creased his face.

"Oh yeah? Lemme ask you something. If this warehouse is locked, how y'all getting inside? Any you boys pick locks?" She looked at Hunter, then at One-Shot and Mackey. None of them spoke. "That's what I figured. What're ya gonna do? Knock and see who's home?"

"We'll fucking shoot the locks." Mackey sneered.

"And whoever's guarding Annie can blow her head off."

Wendy shook her head, tears streaming down her face. "Don't say that!"

"Point is, Hunter, you need me. I can pick anything that takes a key and a bunch of stuff that don't."

One-Shot again leaned over and had a whispered conversation with his president. Hunter smiled with a smug look that sent a shiver down Shea's spine. "You can come. Just keep outta our way."

Mackey grunted. "Hunter, man, why we gotta bring this dyke along?"

"'Cause I said so," snapped Hunter.

"What about me?" asked Wendy.

"I'll drop you back at the motel and pick up my bike." Shea glanced back at the guys. "I'll meet y'all back here in an hour."

Hunter turned to Wendy. "When she drops you off, I want you to head to the Church."

"Oh baby, can't I just stay at the motel for a while? I don't feel good. Probably shouldn't be driving."

"Fine. I'll have someone pick you up."

"No, you don't have to do that. I'll be okay at the hotel."

"Why would you want to stay in that shithole? You'd be more comfortable at the Church. You can take a nap upstairs in our suite."

Wendy glanced at Shea, then back at Hunter. "I wanna spend some time alone with my sister. We ain't seen each other in forever. Please? Just a little while. Then I'll meet up with you at the Church. I promise."

Hunter narrowed his gaze at her. "I ain't so keen on you being by yourself with all this shit going on."

"Nobody knows I'll be there."

"The cops know."

"I ain't telling them shit, you know that." She showered his face with kisses.

Hunter threw up his hands. "Fine. Do what you want. Just don't stay too long."

"Thanks, baby!"

Hunter followed them out into the parking lot. A guy with a goat patch beard wearing a Confederate Thunder cut over an NRA T-shirt sat on Hunter's Harley Road King.

*Must be Goatsy,* Shea thought, watching him out of the corner of her eye. He slipped something into Hunter's hand as they walked past on the way to Wendy's car.

Shea climbed in and started the Mustang. Wendy sat down in the passenger seat, as Hunter handed her a small plastic bag. "This should hold you till I get back with Annie," he said.

"Thanks, baby." She kissed him on the lips.

When Hunter left, Wendy opened the bag, took out two pills, and chased them down with a swig from a half-empty water bottle in the center console. She shut the door. "Okay, let's go."

Shea's lip curled in disgust. "Real mother of the year, you are." She pulled out of the parking lot and raced down the road. Wendy didn't say anything.

~

SHEA DROVE BACK to the hotel, keeping an eye out for the black SUV or anyone else who might be following. Either no one was tailing them or their pursuers were getting harder to spot.

To her relief, her bike remained in the motel parking lot. *At least something's going right,* she thought.

They climbed the stairs to the room. As Wendy opened the door, the phone in Shea's jacket rang. Wendy gasped and dropped the key on the floor.

Shea pulled the phone out of her jacket pocket. "Hello."

"You the little girl's mother?" The voice was deep and gravelly with a Latino accent, the same one on the video.

Shea directed Wendy into the room and closed the door behind them.

"She's not feeling well. I'm her sister. You can talk to me," she said, taking a seat on the bed. Wendy sat beside her, eyes frantic.

"*Órale.* What's your name?"

"Shea. Where's Annie?"

"You got my four million dollars, Che?" he asked, mispronouncing her name.

"Put Annie on the phone, so I know she's okay."

"You don't make the rules, *puta.* I'm in charge. *¿Comprende?* You got the money, or do I kill her?"

"Put her on the phone or you don't get shit, asshole."

A shrill scream filled Shea's ear, followed by the choking sobs of a child. Shea inhaled sharply, wondering if she'd overplayed her hand.

"You hear that? She's alive, but not much longer, you keep playing games. You got my money?"

"Four mill? No, I don't."

"That's too bad. She such a pretty girl. But when I cut her open and hang her from a bridge, she won't look so pretty."

Shea struggled to keep the image of Annie's broken body out of her mind. *Keep it together or you're no good to her,* she told herself. "Look, I can get some money. Just not four million."

"You think this a game? Maybe I cut off the girl's ear, show you I don't play games."

"Don't you fucking touch her, you miserable dirtbag. I'll try to get the money. It's gonna take time."

"Time's something you don't got. Get the money now or the girl swings from a bridge."

"What the hell you expect me to do? Rob a fucking bank?"

---

"Maybe you should, if you love your niece."

"I ain't robbing no bank. I'm willing to pay, but you gotta come down on the ransom. Otherwise, nobody gets what they want."

"Why should I believe you, when you already talked to the cops?"

The phone trembled in her hand. *How'd he know?* "We didn't contact them. They just showed up. We didn't tell them nothing."

"Better not. If you want Annie back alive, you get my money."

"I can come up with maybe a couple grand."

"Two fucking grand?" He scoffed. "For two grand, I give you a piece. What part you like? Her eyes or her heart? Maybe a finger or two."

"You sick fuck. We ain't got that kinda cash."

"Girl's *papi* got *mucho dinero* from selling crystal. Only question is what he loves more—his money or his daughter."

"You said we got forty-eight hours. I'll talk to the girl's father about getting the ransom."

"Get the money. Then take out ad on craigslist. Subject say, 'Come Home Annie.' In the ad, you say 'We have room ready.' You do that, I know you got the money and ready to make the drop. I don't see the ad by nine tomorrow night, I kill the girl. You talk to the cops again, I carve your name in her chest so everybody know it's Che's fault the girl's dead. *¿Comprende?*"

"Yeah. I *comprende*." The call ended.

"What'd he say?" Wendy looked worried but less feverish. *Maybe she really was in withdrawal,* Shea thought.

"He ain't budging. Says we gotta come up with four million dollars or he'll kill Annie."

"Four million? That's not— That's way too much! Where we supposed to get four million dollars?"

"We aren't. Hunter and I are gonna rescue her."

"What if you can't find her? What then?"

"We'll find her, all right? Sit tight in the room." Shea handed her the phone.

"What if he calls back? What do I say?"

"He ain't gonna call before I get back. And if he does, tell him we're putting the money together."

Shea walked to the door, adjusting the pistol in her waistband.

Wendy followed her and handed her a key to the room. "Shea, please bring my baby back."

"That's the plan."

# 17

WITH THE BREAKFAST RUSH OVER, the diner's parking lot was a lot emptier when Shea returned. Hunter and One-Shot sat waiting on their bikes, with Mackey in the Bronco, looking antsy. Shea pulled up in between Hunter's bike and the Bronco.

Mackey looked at his watch and threw up his hands. "What the fuck? You're late."

"Got a call from the kidnapper."

"You learn anything?" asked Hunter

"Sounds like he's got Annie with him. Wouldn't put her on the phone, but I heard her scream."

His face twisted in anger. "Motherfucker!"

"Point is, if she is at the warehouse, she ain't alone." Shea narrowed her gaze at Hunter. "And FYI, he took her 'cause the club deals crystal. Figures you got the four mill for the ransom."

Mackey held up a full-sized Ruger SR9. "Guess he'll have to settle for a nine mill, instead. Right between the eyes."

"Enough of this chitchat," said Hunter. "Let's get this

done."

The Confederate Thunder engines roared to life. Shea followed the guys out of town and down South Chaparral Road into the mountains of the Cortes National Forest. The sweet scent of ponderosa pine, mesquite, and juniper trees filled her nose, taking a bit of the edge off the tension. Campgrounds sprawled on either side of the road, catering to tourists escaping the heat of Phoenix.

Ten miles later, the pavement gave way to hard-packed dirt and gravel, forcing those on motorcycles to slow down or risk catastrophe on the less stable surface.

Near a vine-wrapped stone chimney, the last remains of a pioneer homestead, Hunter turned down an unmarked side road. Here and there, large rocks protruded through the earth, forcing Shea and the bikers to navigate around them. Muddy ruts and washboard ripples rattled the bikes so much that Shea wondered if she would lose a filling.

After a dozen turns through a labyrinth of dirt roads, they stopped and shut off the bikes. The sudden quiet of the forest felt like a shock after an hour of listening to the rumble of the engines and the roar of the wind through her helmet. The crunch of pine needles underneath her boots and the soprano chorus of birds were a welcome sound.

Shea had lost track of where they had turned and wasn't sure she could find her way back if she needed to.

"Where's the warehouse?" She wondered if they had led her here to get revenge for their tussle at the bike shop.

"We walk from here." Hunter chambered a round on what looked like a .44 Magnum Desert Eagle.

"Walk?" She considered drawing her Glock. "How far?"

"The warehouse is over the next ridge."

"Why the hell'd we park here then?" Her pulse quickened as she resisted the urge to make a run for it.

"Don't want them wetbacks to hear us coming, do ya? Come on."

Hunter and Mackey led the way. She stepped aside to let One-Shot follow. He gestured with an open hand toward the others. "After you," he said in a baritone voice.

She studied his face, looking for hints of conspiracy. After a moment, she fell in behind Mackey, keeping an eye out for possible cover and escape routes should things go south.

They retraced their route on the gravel road to the most recent turn, veered right around the crest of the hill, then up a ways to the summit. The road dead-ended in front of a fifty-foot-wide, sage-green corrugated metal building. She breathed a sigh of relief. *Maybe this wasn't a setup.*

Keeping to the trees, they stopped ten feet from the building. A garage door dominated the front with a side door painted black to the right of it—both closed. No vehicles outside.

The only sounds came from a pair of ground squirrels chasing each other through the underbrush.

"Don't look like nobody's home," said Mackey in a hushed tone. "Maybe they ain't got her here after all."

"Coulda parked inside." Hunter turned to Shea. "Well? Get us in there."

"The garage door's probably padlocked from the inside. Best bet is through the side door."

"What are you waiting for? Do your thing, master thief, and hurry the hell up."

She pulled a leather case from her jacket and unzipped it to reveal a collection of slender steel instruments. She kneeled down in front of the door and studied the lock in the door handle and the dead bolt above it. With her riding gloves on to avoid leaving any prints, she tried the doorknob. It was locked. She inserted the short end of an Lshaped tension wrench into the doorknob's keyhole, resting her ring finger on the long end with the gentlest of pressure, then inserted her half-diamond pick above it. As she slowly pulled it out, she counted the clicks. Only five pins. No problem. One by one, she set each pin until the cylinder turned. She turned the doorknob and pulled. Sure enough, the dead bolt was locked.

"C'mon, ya dumb bitch, we're wasting time," Mackey hissed. "We're sitting ducks out here."

She glared at him, keeping the knob turned. "You wanna do help, smart guy? Keep this knob turned so I don't have to pick it again."

"Quit yapping and get it done," said Hunter.

Mackey grabbed the doorknob, muttering under his breath.

She started in on the dead bolt and counted six pins. She knew from experience a few would be hourglass-shaped security pins. Picking them would be that much trickier. She started from the back, testing each pin with a gentle push upward. Two set right away. The next couple were not so easy and required her to adjust the tensioner and start over.

"Goddammit, can you do it or not?" A corkscrew vein on Hunter's temple throbbed as he loomed over her.

"Shut up and give me a minute." Her racing pulse made it hard to concentrate on what was going on unseen inside the lock. She slowed down her breathing and let her pick once again give her the lay of the land. One pin, three pins, five, then at last the tensioner turned the cylinder. *I still got it,* she mused with a smile.

"Okay, it should open now. Let's hope there's no alarm."

Mackey pulled on the knob and the door opened. Shea stepped back and let Hunter take the lead, his gun at the ready. If someone was going to get shot, she wanted it to be him. One-Shot followed carrying a large revolver, possibly a Smith & Wesson .500.

Mackey gestured with his Ruger that she should go before him. When she didn't move, he bared his teeth. "Get in there, bitch."

She drew her Glock, chambered a round, and stepped into the shadows of the building's interior.

A narrow hallway led forty feet to the back of the building with two doors on the right, followed by a single door on the left. One-Shot ducked inside, then out again, shaking his head. Shea glanced in—just an empty restroom. The door to the second room was open. A small lamp and a computer monitor, both off, sat on a metal desk. On the floor next to the desk, a computer hummed quietly. They continued to the door on the left at the end of the hall. A window in the door revealed it opened to the warehouse's storage area. One by one, they filed in.

The room was forty feet by forty feet with a concrete slab floor and a door along the back wall. Daylight filtered through skylights in the ceiling, giving the place a surreal atmosphere. Floor-to-ceiling shelving units took up most of the space. In the middle of the room a small forklift sat idle near a table surrounded by three metal folding chairs. A musty, chemical smell hung heavy in the air. They spread out to search the place.

Red plastic bins the size of beer coolers were stacked on the shelves alongside fifty-pound sacks of cornstarch, which Shea assumed was used to cut the heroin. Wooden crates filled the shelving unit on the far wall.

On the table, bricks of black tar heroin wrapped in clear plastic were piled next to digital scales, three large mortars and pestles, a large bag of what Shea guessed to be ecstasy, and several industrial-size rolls of plastic wrap.

She recalled a recent conversation she'd had with

Derek. A new drug called hex had hit the streets in the past year—heroin cut with ecstasy. Hex was potent, cheap, and popular with the nightclub scene.

With no sign of Annie or her bikes, Shea's hopes of finding either dimmed.

Mackey lowered his gun. "Don't look like nobody's home."

"Annie!" Hunter called so loud Shea's heart skipped a beat.

They waited, but there was no response.

"Think maybe she's in one of these boxes?" Mackey asked.

A cloud of worry darkened Hunter's face. "Open 'em all up—the wooden crates and the red bins."

One-Shot located a pry bar near the forklift and pulled the lid off of a wooden crate with a loud crack. He reached in and pulled out an AK-47. "Guns," he said.

Shea turned her attention to the red plastic bins, as did Mackey. She holstered her gun, popped the side locks on the first bin, and opened it. It held gallon-sized plastic bags filled with brown powder. "Jesus Christ, that's a lot of hex."

"Hot damn!" Mackey stuck a knife in the bin he'd opened and snorted a small amount of hex. His eyes rolled back. "Damn, that's some good shit, man."

"You're an idiot, Mackey," she said. "I hope you OD."

He flipped her off and grinned like a madman. "Look at all this shit, Hunter! We hit the mother lode."

Shea grabbed his collar. "Hey, asswipe! This dope ain't ours. Now keep looking for my niece!"

Hunter stepped between them and shoved her away. "Don't tell my guys what to do. You got me, lesbo? Annie ain't here. Don't mean we leave here empty-handed. Everybody grab a bin."

"What about the rifles?" asked One-Shot.

"Leave 'em. Got plenty of guns back at the Church. We can sell the hex for a lot more than the guns."

As Hunter walked toward another bin, she stepped into his path. "Listen, moron, you steal the Jaguars' shit, they'll figure out who did it."

"So what? This gives us leverage to get Annie back."

She couldn't blame him for wanting a bargaining chip, but stealing drugs from the Mexicans was a sure way to find yourself on the wrong end of a rope. She walked away toward the hallway door. "This is insane. I'm outta here."

Hunter's fist latched on to her arm. "I said, grab a bin."

She shook his hand loose. "I ain't grabbing nothing. You do what you want."

He pointed the Desert Eagle at her. "Grab a bin, bitch, or I'll put you in one."

Her vision narrowed to the gaping gun barrel in her face. He was close enough, she might be able to disarm him, but she'd still have One-Shot and Mackey to contend with. Fuming, she picked up a bin and walked toward the hallway door.

"See? Things go much better when bitches obey orders," said Hunter.

Energy erupted in her body. She spun and heaved the bin at him. He staggered back. His gun clattered to the floor. He rushed her, driving his fist into her jaw. She fell hard on her back. Ignoring the crushing pain in her head, she drew her Glock, but he kicked it spinning across the room.

"This is why bitches don't wear patches," he said, standing over her. "You don't understand who's in charge. You on a job with me? You do what I say." He kicked her in the gut a few times. Her armored leather jacket took most of the impact, but it still knocked the wind out of her. "That's for stealing my gun and disrespecting me."

He kicked again, but she grabbed his leg and twisted, throwing him to the floor. She pulled herself up, clinging to one of the shelving supports. As she got to her feet, someone lifted her up from behind. For a moment, gravity lost its grip on her. She flew through the air until she collided with one of the gun crates. Everything went black.

## 18

When Shea came to, her body was slumped against a wooden crate. Her head and chest throbbed. Hunter and the guys were nowhere to be seen.

Thoughts drifted through her mind—some urgent, telling her to get the hell out of there, others suggesting she stay put until the room stopped spinning. She coughed and spit up blood. Her bottom lip felt fat and tender.

She scanned the room. Half a dozen bins full of hex were missing. *Street value must be a few mill, easy,* she thought. *The Jaguars'll be pissed when they find out it's gone.* She'd already pushed her luck with Oscar. If they found out she was here, God knows what they'd do to her and those she cared about.

A blinking red light near the ceiling caught her eye. A security camera on the wall had recorded the whole damn thing. "Oh fuck."

The urgent need to destroy the recording energized her. When she pulled herself into a wobbly stance, the room spun and a wave of nausea caused her knees to buckle. Shea grabbed a nearby shelf to steady herself.

*Where would they keep the security recordings?* Dizziness kept sliding thoughts out of her grasp. *On the computer in the office, most likely.* Using the shelves for support, she shuffled across the room.

She spotted her Glock underneath the rear tire of the forklift. She eased herself into a crouch, grabbed the gun, and put it in her waistband. The shakiness faded as she continued to the hallway.

When she reached the office door, the distant roar of an engine disturbed the silence. *Not a motorcycle. A truck.* Whether it was Hunter returning for more hex or the Jaguars themselves, the growing rumble lit a fire underneath her. She tried to pick up the computer, but it was bolted to the floor. She was out of options. Time to get out of there.

Shea raced out the back door and took cover in the woods. Her pulse pounded in her ears, merging with the thrum of the approaching truck. She scrambled through the underbrush around the side of the building as a black Nissan Pathfinder backed up to the garage door. Was it the same one that chased them earlier? She wasn't sure.

Two men got out. The driver was Oscar Reyes. No surprise. The other man had a hippie-turned-bank-executive look. His silver-gray ponytail and goatee contrasted with the precise cut of his tailored black suit.

"Well, well, Uncle Victor," she whispered to herself. Absently, she traced a scar on her cheek as she remembered the last time she had seen him. Victor Ganado, the president of the Jaguars, was one of Ralph's former business associates.

Shea remembered him as a sweet grandfather of a man who spoke with a funny accent and smelled of cigars. But the kindly *abuelito* persona was a façade to hide the ruthless Latino gang leader who'd left countless mutilated bodies hanging from bridges. He'd wiped out entire families as a warning to anyone who might consider crossing him.

The two men approached the warehouse's side door. Oscar turned the doorknob, opened the door, and shouted excitedly in Spanish, while pointing at the lock. Victor turned, scanning the woods in Shea's direction.

Panic swept through her as she ducked down. *Did they see me?*

When they entered the building, Shea barreled through the woods, like a deer running from wildfire, down the hill to where she had parked her bike. The Thundermen's vehicles were gone. Her motorcycle lay on its right side—a final fuck-you from Hunter.

With her heart racing, she set the side stand down, then crouched down, with her butt against the seat. She extended her legs out as far as she could without losing balance. Her left hand grabbed the handle bars and her right the chassis below the seat. She took a deep breath and pushed up with her legs. But instead of rising, the bike slid sideways.

"Fuck!" Her head pounded, making it hard to focus. *Gotta get outta here now.*

She heaved again, angling her shoulders to get traction underneath the tires. The bike slid further across the loose surface.

Her jaw clenched while she struggled to maintain control against the rising panic. She scrutinized her surroundings and spotted a flat, two-foot-long rock on the side of the road. Shea lobbed the rock toward the bike and pushed it flush against her back tire.

Once again, she crouched down against the bike and lifted, her body screaming in pain. The front tire shifted a few inches, then got enough purchase to lift the bike.

She laid it over on the side stand, gasping for air. The

Jaguar's Pathfinder would be charging down the road any minute. Drawing on the last of her energy, she adjusted the side mirror that'd been knocked loose and pulled on her helmet. She pressed the starter, put it in gear, and raced down the hill.

Her mind swam as she attempted to retrace the route back to civilization. *Left turn, then another left, followed by a right, or was it a right followed by a left?* She thought she had figured it out until she hit a section of road filled with deep ruts and large rocks. *Crap! Wrong turn somewhere.* She flipped a u-ey and charged back to the last intersection.

While she made the turn, the Pathfinder roared from a side road, bearing down on her. Her heart stopped.

She twisted the throttle, skidding around the SUV, before racing down the road. She glanced in her left mirror, adrenaline pumping through her system. The tires rumbled over the gravel, vibrating the mirror and blurring the reflection of the Pathfinder, only a few feet from her rear tire. She focused back on the road in front of her and swerved, narrowly missing a large, half-buried rock.

Ahead the road curved sharply to the right. Shea eased up on the throttle to avoid taking the curve too fast. The Pathfinder kissed her rear fender. The bike wobbled, but stayed upright. She leaned hard into the corner, hanging way off the bike, and accelerated through the turn. The bike skidded across the road, sending up a rooster tail of rocks before straightening up again.

She glanced back. Several cracks spider-webbed across the SUV's windshield. It now hung back about fifteen feet. *That'll teach 'em to ride my ass.*

Shea approached another turn—a hairpin to the left with a sheer wall of rock on one side and a fifty-foot drop on the other. A loud bang behind her made her duck. Her right mirror shattered. *Those fuckers are shooting at me!*

She turned on the speed, pulled to the left, then pressed hard on the rear brake an instant before coming into the hairpin. Her back tire fishtailed. She whipped left into the turn, then pinned the throttle in the corner. Behind her, the Pathfinder skidded and slammed into the cliff face with a loud crunch. Before she could breathe a sigh of relief, it roared back to life and resumed the chase.

Over the next mile, the truck caught back up with her. Large rocks and potholes forced her to weave left and right, while someone in the truck fired another three rounds at her. Her back tingled in anticipation of the bullet that would kill her.

Shea rounded another corner and glimpsed paved road in the distance. If she could make it to the blacktop, she'd have the advantage over the top-heavy Pathfinder. She pushed the tachometer into the red, pouring on speed, closing the distance between her and the paved road.

Without warning, an elk bolted out from the side of the road. Shea jerked the handlebars to avoid it. The back tire slid out, causing the bike to lowside on top of her right leg. She screamed in pain while gravel tore away at the fabric of her jeans and bit into the flesh of her leg.

At the last second, the elk retreated, clearing her path. She turned the handlebars and accelerated. The front wheel caught the lip of the pavement. The bike jerked upright. She flew down the road once again.

She glanced at her left side mirror. The Pathfinder spun out at the spot where she had dropped the bike, but soon corrected and resumed chasing her. However, on the pavement, the advantage was hers. The high-performance engine roared as she leaned hard into the curves like a MotoGP racer. The Pathfinder couldn't do the same without flipping over.

By the time she reached the main highway, the SUV

had disappeared behind her.

As the adrenaline wore off, the throbbing on her right leg intensified. The pain became distracting. Shea forced herself to take slow, even breaths until a stoplight on the outskirts of Bradshaw City brought her to a stop. She looked down at her leg. Her Kevlar jeans were black and wet with blood. She didn't have time for this. She pressed on into town, groaning in agony every time she had to use her right foot on the rear brake.

She was growling Pink Trinkets' tunes to keep her mind off the pain until she pulled into the Getaway Motel's parking lot. Potholes filled with pea gravel reminded her of the grit imbedded in her leg, making her wince.

The bike rumbled to a stop near the stairway to Wendy's room. Shea would have preferred parking someplace a little less out in the open, but that would mean a longer agonizing walk to the room.

A jolt of pain took her breath away when she lifted her right leg over the back of the bike. She gripped the handlebars, standing on one foot until the worst of the pain subsided. She looked down at her injury. The side of her leg from her ankle to her knee looked like raw hamburger mixed with dirt and rocks. Blood dripped onto the pavement.

Gingerly, she limped up the staircase to the room where she'd left Wendy a couple of hours earlier. She pounded and waited. No answer. She fumbled in her pocket for the key Wendy'd given her and opened the door to the room.

"Wendy?" There was no response. "Wendy?" She hobbled into the bathroom, half expecting to see her sister passed out on the floor. But Wendy wasn't in the room. "Goddammit, where'd you go?"

The words summoned a childhood memory she'd suppressed until now. Mama and Ralph had left her to baby-sit Wendy. Instead of keeping an eye on her, Shea had disappeared into her room and cranked up the latest Ramones album. When her folks got home around midnight, Wendy wasn't in the house. After three hours of calling neighbors and hospitals, Ralph found her wandering in the desert. She'd heard a pack of coyotes yipping and wanted to "sing along with them." Ralph had beaten Shea bloody until Mama threatened to call the cops. Thirty years later, Wendy was still wandering off, while Shea was taking a beating.

"Fuck her." Her focus shifted from finding Wendy to treating her injuries.

She set the Glock on the back of the toilet. When she pulled off her boots and dropped her tattered, blood-soaked jeans, the pain took her breath away. Shea draped her bleeding leg into the tub, gritted her teeth, and turned on spigot, which only had one flow setting—firehose. She bellowed when the water hit the chewed-up flesh. The room swayed.

After a moment, the cold water numbed her leg. The pain became almost bearable. She looked for soap; there wasn't any. No surprise in this sleazy motel. She was probably increasing her risk of infection by coming in contact with the tub. *Who knows the last time it was cleaned?*

After a few minutes of white-knuckling the spigot, she turned off the water and looked again at the wound. It looked cleaner, but raw, angry, and still seeping blood. She grabbed the cleanest towel from the shelf above the toilet and pressed it to her leg.

The front door of the room creaked open. Was it Wendy or had the Jaguars tracked her down?

Her fingers wrapped around the Glock's grip. With her hand trembling from the pain, she pointed the gun at the bathroom door.

# 19

WENDY POPPED her head in the bathroom and jumped when she saw the gun. "Jesus Christ, Shea! What the hell?" She seemed less jittery, eyes more focused. The clammy flush of fever was gone. Her hair was brushed, makeup not quite concealing the shiner Mackey had given her.

"Sorry. Didn't know it was you." Shea tossed the Glock onto her jeans, piled on the floor next to her. "Where the hell you been?"

"I got hungry. Where's Annie?"

Shea shook her head. "She wasn't there."

Tears filled Wendy's eyes. She collapsed onto the toilet seat, burying her face in her hands. "What are we gonna do? I want my baby back."

Gritting her teeth against the pain, Shea pivoted toward her and put a hand on her sister's knee. "We'll get her back. Just gotta figure out a way to get the ransom."

Wendy looked up at her. "Where's Hunter?"

"I don't know. We, uh, parted ways at the warehouse."

"What's that mean?"

"Ask that asshole you call a husband."

Wendy tilted her head with a confused look on her face. Her gaze dropped to where blood seeped through the towel Shea held on her leg. "You're bleeding."

"You noticed." She peeled the towel away and bit her lip to keep from screaming. Looking at the wound made it hurt worse.

"Shit, how'd that happen?"

"Learning how not to drive on gravel."

"Maybe we should go to the Church. One of the guys is a doctor."

"Can you drive?" The sudden departure of Wendy's withdrawal symptoms made Shea wonder.

"Whaddya mean? Of course I can drive. I have a car."

"I mean, are you high?"

"No!"

Shea couldn't tell if she was lying or not. "Uh-huh."

"I took some medicine to feel better, but I'm fine."

Shea thought about asking her for some of whatever she'd taken to help with the pain. "Then drive me to the hospital."

"The Church is closer. Our doctor, Dopey, knows his stuff."

"Club's got a doctor named Dopey? No, thanks. Drive me to the fucking hospital, okay?"

"Okay! Jump down my throat, why dontcha?"

"Sorry. My leg feels like it went through a wood chipper." With the black pocket knife she kept clipped inside her waistband, she cut off the lower half of her right pant leg.

"What're you doing?"

"Don't want my jeans pressing against the road rash. You got anything clean I can use to cover the wound? Something you don't mind getting blood on?"

Wendy retrieved a purple nightshirt from her suitcase

and handed it to her. "You can use this. It's kinda ratty, anyways. Had it since I was pregnant with Annie."

Shea looked it over. The words MAMA IN TRAINING were printed in faded letters on the front. The hems were ragged in spots, but it looked clean. "Thanks."

She wrapped it around the wound and cut strips on the end to tie it off. She gingerly pulled on her tattered jeans, followed by her boots, then holstered the Glock.

Wendy helped her to her feet. "Can you make it to the car?"

Again, she thought about asking Wendy what she'd taken, now wondering if she had some to share. Her pain tolerance had neared its limit. "I can make it. Is there an elevator?"

"Yeah, but it's at the other side of the building. The staircase is a lot closer. Just lean on me."

It felt weird relying on Wendy to help her walk. Shea was always the one looking after her sister. She kept reminding herself not to trust Wendy, not to like her. But right now she needed her help.

Wendy held open the passenger door as Shea lowered herself into the Mustang's bucket seats with help from the oh-shit handle above the doorframe. Getting her right leg inside required some gymnastics.

"You in?" asked Wendy.

Shea nodded and put on her seatbelt. Wendy shut the passenger door, climbed into the driver's seat, and drove south toward Cortes General Hospital.

"You hear from the kidnapper?" Shea asked through gritted teeth.

"Ummm . . . no, not really."

"What do you mean not really?"

"I got a call from Margaret's brother, Eduardo."

"Why'd he call you?"

Wendy shrugged, keeping her eyes on the road ahead of them. "Well, we kinda know each other. I mean, he's her brother. Or was."

"You *kinda* know him? There's something you ain't telling me. I can hear it in your voice. Were you dating him?"

"Ew, no! He's just a teenager. We're just friends. Not even friends, really. He's just the kid brother of a friend. I barely know him."

"So what does he have to do with the kidnapper?" Shea thought for a moment when Wendy didn't respond right away. "Shit, he's a member of the Jags, isn't he?"

"You know, I really don't want to talk about this right now. I gotta concentrate on driving."

"Is he the one who took Annie?"

"No, he ain't like that." Wendy's voice became choked with emotion as her eyes filled with tears. "He was upset about his sister getting killed. He was calling me asking if I knew anything."

"He should be talking to his fellow gangbangers."

"That's what I told him. But he swears the Jaguars ain't got her."

"Yeah, that's a load of crap." Shea's leg began to throb more as she became angrier. She took a deep breath and let it out slowly. She pulled out her phone. Jessica had left a voicemail message. Rather than listen to it, she called Jess directly.

"Tell me the truth, Shea. Are you seeing someone else? I'm tired of these crazy stories."

She took a deep breath as the throbbing in her leg intensified. "No, sweetie. I ain't seeing no one else. I had a minor accident on the motorcycle."

"Oh my God, are you all right? Where are you?"

"Wendy's driving me to Cortes General now. Got a little

road rash on my leg. I'll live." A pothole on the road sent a jolt of pain through both her leg and head. "Fuck!"

"I'll meet you there." Jessica hung up before she could tell her not to bother.

"She coming?" asked Wendy.

"Guess so." She lay back in the seat, relaxing into the pain.

"Interesting. I get to meet my sister's old lady."

"Don't call her an old lady to her face. She might not get the context."

"Why not?"

"She's an insurance adjuster who moved up here from Scottsdale. The whole biker scene's new to her." Shea opened one eye and looked at her sister.

Wendy grinned. "This oughta be fun."

"Oh yeah. Tons."

"What happened at the warehouse?"

Shea didn't feel like talking about it, but as Annie's mother, Wendy deserved to know. "All we found was shit-load of hex. Hunter decided to commandeer it. When I objected, the three of them jumped me."

"Hunter did this to your leg?"

"Not directly. He just left me for the Jags to find. Barely got out of there when Uncle Victor and one of his goons showed up. They were the ones in the black SUV that chased us." The car hit another pothole, sending Shea's pain level through the roof. "Gah! Tore up my leg getting away. Fucking gravel roads."

"Damn Hunter! You see why I ran away from him?"

"Seemed awful cozy at the diner."

"I wasn't feeling well. I was hoping he could hook me up with something."

"Sounds fucked up, if ya ask me."

"Well, I didn't."

Shea's phone rang. "Hello?"

"Panterita?"

"Goblin! You hear anything about my bikes?"

"An associate of mine got a visit from a couple guys looking to unload some pink bikes."

"Fucking A! Best news I heard all day. He got 'em?"

"Not yet. He supposed to check 'em out in the next day or so."

"What'd the two guys look like?"

"My associate said one was a cholo with Jag ink. The other guy was bald and talked like a cop. My guy's not sure about doing the deal. Might be a sting."

"A sting with my stolen bikes? Doubt it." She wondered if the cop was Deputy Commando. "Tell your guy to set up a meet. Give me the details and I'll be there."

"I'll pass the word, amiga."

"Thanks, Goblin." She hung up.

"Who's that?" Wendy asked.

"A friend from back in the day. Might have a lead on who's got my stolen motorcycles."

"You think it's the same people who took Annie?"

"Could be. One of the guys sported Jaguar tattoos. My friend'll call me when they set a meet."

## 20

WHEN THEY PARKED near the ER entrance, Shea stashed her Glock in the glove box. Wendy helped her limp into the emergency waiting room. The heady smell of antiseptic hung in the air.

The same woman with the pale lavender bouffant hair sat behind the check-in desk. Her brow crinkled when she looked up at Shea. "Weren't you here yesterday?"

"Yeah. Tore up my leg in a motorcycle accident a little bit ago." Shea gave the woman her personal information.

"Have a seat. Someone will be with you shortly."

Jessica arrived twenty minutes later, right as a nurse named Bruce, sporting Harry Potter glasses, showed up with a wheelchair. Shea gave Jess a quick hug, taking a moment to enjoy the scent of her perfume. "Glad you came."

Shea sat in the wheelchair and Bruce wheeled her into one of the ER rooms, with her sister and girlfriend trailing behind.

"You need help getting on the bed?" asked Bruce.

With his help, Shea climbed onto the bed and lay back.

Jessica and Wendy stared at each other in awkward silence, while Bruce took Shea's vitals and asked the usual medical intake questions.

"The doctor should be in soon." Bruce shut the sliding glass door behind him as he vanished down the hall.

"Jessica, meet my sister, Wendy. Wendy, this is my girlfriend, Jessica."

"So, you're my sister's old lady?" said Wendy with a smirk.

Jessica looked at her, horrified. "Old lady?"

Shea shook her head. "Biker lingo, darling. It means we're in a relationship."

"Oh yeah, right. I knew that." Jessica blushed. "How'd this happen?"

"The leg? An elk jumped out in front of me. I laid down the bike to avoid hitting it."

Wendy raised an eyebrow. "You said it happened when you were running away from the Jaguars."

"Jaguars? I think you mean mountain lions. There aren't any jaguars this far north," said Jessica.

"Not that kind of jaguar, honey," said Wendy. "We're talking about Mexican gangsters who traffic heroin for the Santa Cruz drug cartel." Angry tears filled her eyes. "And kidnap little girls."

"We'll get her back, Wen." Shea put her hand on her sister's arm.

"A Mexican drug gang has your niece?" asked Jessica. "I thought you said the girl's father had her."

"We got a ransom demand from the kidnappers," Shea said. "Me and a few of the Thundermen thought we could rescue Annie."

"From Mexican gangsters? Are you insane? Have you told the cops what you know?"

"No!" Wendy shook her head. "We tell the cops, they'll kill her."

"I don't like this, Shea. You'll get yourself killed." Jessica looked angry. "Look at your leg, for crying out loud."

"Don't worry, sweetie. We'll find a way to pay the ransom and get her back. No more heroics. I promise."

～

A LITTLE WHILE LATER, Dr. Sossaman, the same doctor who'd treated Derek, walked in. "Ms. Stevens, I didn't expect to see you again so soon."

"That makes two of us," she said.

"What brings you back?"

She pointed to her leg wrapped in the bloodstained remnants of Wendy's nightshirt. "Laid my bike down in gravel."

"Ouch! Let's get that off and take a look." She untied the strips used to secure the shirt and held one end of the makeshift bandage. "This will hurt a bit."

Shea's leg trembled as the doctor unwrapped the improvised bandage. When she got to the point where the T-shirt was pulling off her chewed-up flesh, the pain forced a string of obscenities from Shea's lips. She gripped the edge of the hospital bed, struggling for breath.

Jessica took her hand. Shea struggled to compose herself while the doc examined the wound.

"Not too much dirt or debris, but I want to rinse it with saline to make sure we got it all out."

Dr. Sossaman injected a local anesthetic at several spots along the length of the wound. "This should help." She picked up a bottle with a long tapered tube on top and let a stream of saline flow onto the wound.

Despite the anesthetic, the saltwater trickling over the

exposed nerves burned like fire. Shea clinched her teeth. "Fuckity fuck fuck fuck."

"It'll leave an ugly scar, but you should live." The doctor squeezed ointment onto a large bandage and covered the wound.

Shea smirked. "Just adding to my collection."

Dr. Sossaman wrote out a prescription for oxycodone and handed it to her. "Take one of these every four to six hours as needed for the pain."

"Thanks. Any word on how my friend Derek is doing?"

"He's still up in ICU, last I heard. I think Dr. Rinku Patel is taking care of him."

"How do I get there from the ER?" Her recent trauma muddled her memory of her previous visit.

She pointed. "Around the corner, take your first right, then down the hall to the elevators. ICU's on the third floor. Follow the signs."

"Thanks."

After settling up with the hospital cashier, Shea hobbled down the corridor, with Wendy and Jessica in tow.

"Where're we going?" asked Jessica.

"To see a friend." Her leg hurt less than it had. Maybe the local was kicking in.

At the ICU nurses' station, she checked in with an RN named Marcy, according to her name badge.

"How's Derek Williams doing?"

Marcy looked up his information on the computer in front of her. "Are you family?"

"He ain't got no family. I'm the one who brought him to the ER. He's a friend of mine. Why?"

"I'm sorry to tell you this, but Mr. Williams is in a coma."

Sorrow consumed Shea. "What happened?"

"He had a seizure due to extreme blood loss."

"He gonna live?"

"We're doing everything we can for him." Marcy gave her an apologetic smile. Shea didn't want sympathy. She needed reassurances he would come out of this alive.

A husky man with dark skin, a wreath of graying hair, and dressed in a white lab coat sat on the other side of the nurses' station typing at a computer. Shea hobbled over there. "Dr. Patel?"

Marcy chased after her. "Ma'am, the doctor is occupied at the moment."

Shea ignored her and planted herself in front of the doctor. "Are you Patel?"

"Yes," he said with a slight Indian accent. "Can I help you?"

"You're taking care of my friend Derek Williams. He was shot."

He scratched the top of his balding head. "Yes, I remember."

"Is he gonna make it?"

"He's in a coma right now."

"When will he come out of it?"

"It's hard to say. He's had a terrible trauma. He lost so much blood, his whole system has been impacted—his heart, his brain."

"Did he say anything? Did he say how he got shot?"

"Not that I'm aware of. The police visited with him shortly before he went into the coma. I don't know if he told them anything or not."

Anger and sorrow pressed on her chest, making it hard to breathe. *What had he said to me? "They made me?" Who? Who made him?*

"Is there anything else I can do for you? I am very busy."

"No. Thanks."

Pressing against the crush of emotions, she walked to Derek's room and sat next to his bed. A large ventilator tube was taped over his mouth. A tangle of IVs and vital monitor leads were attached all over his body. On the plus side, his face had more color than when she'd seen him last. Seeing him, her leg hurt less. "Hey, kiddo, you gotta wake up and tell me who did this to you, so I can go kick their ass."

Jessica kneeled down. "You okay, babe?"

Shea forced a grim smile. "I'll be all right."

"Someone shot your friend?" Wendy's eyes darted around the room.

"Yeah. You know something about it?"

"No, why would I know anything?" She shifted from one foot to another, as if there was someplace else she wanted to be. "You don't think Hunter shot him, do you?"

"Whoever shot Derek robbed my shop and took the good stuff. They know motorcycle gear." Shea ran her fingers through her hair. "And Hunter? I don't trust him as far as I can spit. So yeah, he's high on my list of suspects."

Wendy's phone rang. "Speak of the devil."

Shea pointed to the door. "Take it out in the hall. The nurses don't allow phone calls in the ICU."

Wendy rushed out of the room and down the hall to answer the call.

Shea took a final look at Derek. "Get better, kid." A lump formed in her throat. Her eyes met Jessica's. "Let's go see what Hunter is saying to Wendy."

# 21

Shea and Jessica caught up to Wendy, who was by the elevators yelling at Hunter on the phone.

"What the fuck were you thinking, Hunter?"

Shea grabbed the phone from her. "Hey, asshole! Remember me?"

"Well, look who's still alive. I thought for sure the wetbacks got you."

Her grip tightened. "Almost did, thanks to you."

"Payback's a bitch, ain't it?"

"I guess you'll find out. You notice the security camera at the warehouse? They're gonna know you took their hex."

"That's why I want Wendy here. Club's on lockdown."

Shea looked at Wendy. "He wants you at the Church."

Wendy leaned over and yelled at the phone. "Tell him to go fuck himself."

"Hear that, asshole? You screwed things up. I only hope Annie's still alive."

"Long as I got their dope, they ain't doing nothing to Annie."

"You'd bet your child's life on that?"

He didn't say anything. Maybe he realized he wasn't so smart after all.

"What's your plan to get Annie back now?" she demanded.

"We'll pay the ransom." Defeat dampened the tone of his voice. "But there ain't no way we can get four million dollars. A few hundred thousand, maybe."

"I tried negotiating with the kidnapper. He ain't budging."

"Try harder."

"You try harder to get the four million. We only have one shot at this, so don't fuck it up."

"You giving me orders, bitch?" he asked, getting back a little of his fire.

She hung up and tossed Wendy the phone.

"The kidnappers want four million dollars?" asked Jessica. "That's insane! Who has that kind of money?"

"The Confederate Thunder. At least the kidnappers think they do."

"Why would they have four million dollars?"

"Because they are the biggest crank dealers in the state."

"He gonna get the ransom?" Wendy asked when the elevator doors opened.

"So he says," said Shea, keeping a wary eye on her sister.

"What about the Jaguars' heroin? They'll want that back, too, right?" Agitation and fear colored Wendy's face.

"I reckon. I'm surprised we haven't heard from the kidnapper about it. Maybe he don't know yet." A new possibility occurred to Shea. "Or maybe the Jaguars ain't the ones who got Annie."

"Not the Jaguars? If it ain't them, then who's got her?"

Shea shook her head. "I don't know. For now, Hunter needs to put the ransom together."

"You said something about a church," said Jessica. "What church?"

"It's what the Thunder calls their clubhouse," Shea said. "Hunter wants everyone affiliated with the club there. The MC's on lockdown. Guess he's expecting blowback from the Jaguars."

"All the more reason for you to let the cops handle it." Jessica looked worried.

"We can't." Shea stared at a smudge on the stainless steel doors. "They'll kill her."

"And if you don't, they'll kill you."

"It's a risk we gotta take. I grew up around punks like this. I can handle myself." The doors opened. Wendy strolled out of the elevator toward the building's exit. Shea limped along as fast as she could, every step increasing the pain. Jessica put her arm around her and helped her to the parking lot. They found Wendy standing by her Mustang.

"Where are we going now?" asked Wendy.

"I wanna pick up my bike from the motel and go home." Sympathy eroded Shea's resentment toward Wendy. "You're welcome to crash at our place if you want. Beats staying in that shitty motel or at the Church with your old man."

Wendy offered a grim smile. "Thanks, I'd like that. I can give you a ride to the motel. I'll grab my stuff and you can pick up your bike."

Jessica looked down at Shea's leg. "Can you ride?"

The anesthetic the doctor had injected into her leg was wearing off. But she didn't want to leave her bike at the motel any longer than necessary. "I'll manage."

Jessica shrugged. "I'll head home and throw something together for dinner." She kissed Shea. "Be careful. Keep the sunny side up."

Despite the throbbing in her leg, Shea chuckled. "I

think you mean, 'Keep the shiny side up.' Biker talk for 'Don't have an accident.'"

She followed Wendy to her car and climbed into the passenger seat.

≈

THEY ARRIVED BACK at the motel at five in the afternoon. Shea retrieved her pistol from the glove box, wrestled herself out of the car, and hobbled toward her bike.

While Wendy grabbed her suitcase, Shea pulled on her helmet, zipped up her jacket, and threw her leg over the bike with a grunt. The engine roared to life and she hit the highway heading south to Sycamore Springs, with Wendy following behind in the Mustang.

The constant braking at intersections aggravated the stiffness and discomfort, making Shea want to grind her teeth. Once they got clear of the stoplights in Bradshaw City, the open road gave her leg a break.

The summer air, scented with the gin-like aroma of juniper, cooled while the late-afternoon sun dipped below the mountains. The sensation of flying low over the landscape calmed her. Wind therapy, as bikers called it. Her mind drifted, sorting out the chaos.

The kidnapper's Hispanic accent and threats of hanging Annie from a bridge had led Shea to believe he was a Jaguar. But then why hadn't he called about the stolen hex? And who had her bikes? Goblin had said one of the guys talked like a cop. Why would a member of the Jags team up with a cop for a heist? None of the pieces fit together.

She thought about Jessica's suggestion of calling the detectives. *God knows, I'm out of my depth.* Oscar Reyes had her business card and had probably seen her face on the security feed. How long before they tracked her down? Had she put Terrance and their employees at risk?

On the other hand, the kidnapper knew the detectives had met with them. If she told them what she knew, the kidnapper might find out. Then what would happen to Annie? She didn't want to think about it. Her best bet was to wait for Hunter to call to confirm he had the ransom.

Once she reached Sycamore Springs' Olde Towne, she stopped at the Rexall Drugs across the street from Iron Goddess. The lights were on in the motorcycle shop's showroom. She thought about checking in with Terrance, but her leg was getting worse by the minute. She wanted to pick up her pain meds, go home, and zone out.

Wendy poked her head out of the window of her car. "Why are we stopping?"

"Gotta pick up the pain meds for my leg."

"Can't we get 'em tomorrow?" She looked impatient.

"Not if I wanna sleep tonight. Just chill. I'll be out in a minute."

Shea limped past the unmanned front register and the displays for sunscreen and bath products.

"We're closed." Her friend Aracelli was sweeping the floor near the pharmacy counter, her back to Shea. She turned around. "Oh, Shea! I was just locking up."

"Do a favor for a friend?" Shea limped over to her.

"What'd you do to your leg?"

"Road rash."

"Ouch!" Aracelli winced.

"You mind filling a prescription for pain meds before you close?"

"Sure."

Shea reached into her outside jacket pocket. The prescription wasn't there. She checked the outside pocket on the other side. Empty. She checked the pockets inside her jacket and in her shredded jeans. It wasn't there either. "Crap!"

"What's wrong?"

"Can't find the damn scrip." *Was it with the rest of the paperwork the hospital gave me?* "Never mind. I'll get it tomorrow."

"Sorry. You want something over the counter?"

"No, I'll be all right." She walked out wanting to kick something. If her leg hadn't hurt so much, she would have.

"Follow me," she told Wendy as she hopped back onto her bike.

## 22

As SHEA ZIGZAGGED down the switchbacks of Sycamore Mountain, the wind grew warmer until it became a blast furnace across her chest. The air in her helmet grew stuffy, but opening the face shield even a crack would only let in more heat. The increasing temperature intensified the throbbing in her leg into a steady drumbeat of pain.

When the hill leveled out, she turned right onto a side street. Homes nestled in the shade of twisted mesquites, sweet-smelling sycamores, and cottonwood trees that filled the air with fairy fluff. This wasn't like the pretty suburban neighborhoods down in Phoenix populated with carbon-copy houses, manicured shrubs, and yards covered with monochromatic crushed rock.

The rugged, untamed lots here each spanned a few acres, some dominated by horse corrals and the fragrance of manure. After a half mile, the road took a dogleg left, then paralleled a low ridge crested with boulders the size of automobiles.

Shea's house sat at the end of the lane. She pulled into one of the few paved driveways in the neighborhood and opened the garage with the remote in her jacket. The late-afternoon sunlight revealed her stable of a dozen custom motorcycles and cabinets full of tools. She parked in the one empty spot.

Her right knee refused to bend when she tried to dismount. Her arms strained to pull her body closer to the handlebars to get enough room to slide her foot around. The effort left her winded. While she caught her breath, Wendy parked her Mustang next to Jessica's car on the side of the house.

"Geez, got enough bikes?" Wendy locked up her car.

"What can I say? I like motorcycles."

"Your garage is as big as the rest of the house."

"I didn't need the third bedroom, so I knocked out the wall to make room for more bikes."

Wendy's face darkened. "Hunter called."

"What'd he say?"

"He's not sure he can come up with four million. He wants you to get the kidnapper to lower the ransom."

"How much has he got?"

"Couple hundred grand."

"Shit." Her brain was a train wreck of ache, hunger, and exhaustion. Concentrating took more effort than she could spare. "Every time I tried to negotiate, he threatened to hurt Annie. Hunter's gotta come up with the money somehow."

"What if he doesn't?" Wendy stared out at the horizon, arms wrapped around her like she was keeping something from escaping.

"We'll figure something out." Shea hugged her for the first time in seventeen years. It felt strange, but comfortable. "We'll think better once we've had something to eat. Come on, let's see what Jess is cooking."

Her home was a bit snug on the inside—two small bedrooms, a compact kitchen, and a living room with seating for five, if you didn't mind getting cozy. Shea'd ripped out the carpeting in the living room years earlier and replaced it with rugs on the bare slab. It helped keep the place cool and she could pull a bike inside if she needed to work on one of her bikes away from the summer heat.

As they walked in the door, the aroma of curry, meat, and onions filled the air. Jessica stood in the kitchen to their right. Meat sizzled in the wok on the stove.

"I hope no one's allergic to peanuts. I'm making Thai beef," said Jessica over her shoulder.

"Sounds delicious, hon." Shea led Wendy to the living room. Mismatched rugs covered the concrete slab. An oversized recliner sat at one end, next to a leather loveseat, with a glass and brass coffee table in the middle. A projection TV occupied the far corner.

Wendy took the recliner, Shea's usual spot. Shea resisted the urge to say anything and instead plopped down on the loveseat, resting her hurt leg on the coffee table.

"What's Thai beef?" whispered Wendy.

Shea shrugged. "Dunno, but Jess is a damn good cook."

Moments later, Jessica handed Wendy and Shea warm plates covered with strips of beef swimming in a spicy brown sauce over rice. *"Bon appétit,"* she said.

Shea took a bite. Her mouth exploded with a combination of fiery chile paste, garlic, lime juice, and peanut. The beef melted on her tongue. She groaned with pleasure and for a moment forgot about the pain in her leg.

"Good?" Jess carried over a plate for herself, nestling next to Shea on the loveseat.

Shea nodded, too focused on eating to speak. Not a grain of rice remained when she set the plate on the coffee table.

While her stomach was now full, the ache in her leg

had grown worse. She could have used the pain pills the doctor had prescribed. She wondered if Wendy still had any of the Oxy Hunter had given her at the restaurant. She also wondered if maybe her sister had palmed the prescription when Shea wasn't looking.

She took a deep breath, grimacing as she pulled herself to her feet. If she couldn't have pain pills, there was always vodka.

Jessica looked up from her dinner. "You need something?"

"No, I got it. Butt's getting sore from sitting, anyways." She limped to the kitchen and pulled a frost-covered bottle of vodka out of the freezer. The icy glass surface was so cold it made her hand ache holding it. "Anyone else want some?"

Wendy's hand shot up like the teacher's pet. Shea frowned, not surprised in the least.

"Jessica?" She held up the bottle.

"No thanks."

She poured three fingers' worth into a glass for herself, and two fingers for Wendy. With the bottle tucked under one arm and a glass in each hand, she returned to the loveseat, careful not to spill any of the precious liquid.

"How long you two been together?" Wendy asked as Shea's cat, Ninja, crept out of the bedroom to investigate the strange human who'd invaded her house. Wendy reached out to pet her, but the cat scampered away. "Fraidy cat!"

Shea looked at Jessica. "What, about three months now?"

"Closer to four, I think."

"And already living together?" Wendy asked with an air of mock judgment. "How scandalous."

"I recently moved up from the Valley," said Jessica, referring to Phoenix. "I'm hoping to find a place of my own soon. They opened some cute condos up in Ironwood near the university."

Shea rolled her eyes. "I keep telling ya you're welcome to move the rest of your stuff in here. I'll make room."

Jess made a face. "I'd prefer something a little less industrial. It's like living in an oversized storage unit."

"I thought you yuppie types were into that whole reclaimed, urban-industrial style," said Wendy.

Shea threw a cat toy at Wendy. "Don't be starting nothing."

"Geez, I'm teasing." She looked at Jessica. "I'm teasing. Really."

Jessica took a sip of Shea's vodka, made a face, and walked to the kitchen. "I don't know how y'all drink that stuff."

Shea emptied her glass and poured herself another three fingers. Wendy stuck out her glass. Shea gave her a shot's worth. Her sister made a face and Shea added a little more.

Jessica fixed herself a glass of wine from the fridge and sat back down. "How did you meet your husband, Wendy?"

"He was a prospect for the club when we met. I thought he was cute. He made me smile."

"What's a prospect?" Jessica asked.

"Prospective member," Shea said.

"Oh, like a pledge to a fraternity."

Wendy laughed and choked on her vodka. "Only not as dorky."

"Hey, my brother's in a fraternity." Jessica crossed her arms, frowning.

"Then I guess you know. Pretty little frat boys with their dorky polo shirts and penny loafers and Daddy's gold card. Bunch a pansy-ass dicks, if ya ask me. Bikers ain't like that, not even the prospects."

Jessica's eyes narrowed. "No, of course not. Bikers wear stupid little leather vests, nasty-ass beards, and chains on their wallets." Venom poisoned her tone.

"Like you would know, bitch."

"More than you, you backwoods redneck." Jessica stood up, as if poised for a fight.

Shea made a T with her hands. "Yo! Time out, ladies. No fighting while I'm injured."

"Whatever." Jessica slammed her glass onto the coffee table and stormed to their bedroom, closing the door behind her.

# 23

PART OF SHEA wanted to chase after Jessica and apologize for her sister's rude remarks. She settled for glaring at Wendy.

"What's her problem?" Wendy asked, as if nothing had happened.

"Listen, I don't mind you staying here, but don't piss off my girlfriend."

"Sor-ry!" She held up her hands to emphasize her fake apology. "Didn't know y'all were so touchy."

The vodka was settling into Shea's brain, taking the edge off the pain. Her mind drifted to other subjects. "If Annie's eight years old . . ."

"I got pregnant when I was fifteen." Wendy blushed and stared at the dark screen on the TV.

"How old was Hunter?"

"Nineteen."

"Nineteen? That's statutory rape."

"I know. Monster wanted to kill him when he found out, but I told him we were in love. So the Thunder threw us a big-ass, leather-and-lace biker wedding." She poured herself another glass of vodka. "God, that was beautiful."

"How'd Mr. Wonderful turn into such a psycho?"

"When Hunter became the club's sergeant-at-arms, he got more secretive. I mean, I know he can't always share about club stuff, but it got to the point we didn't have shit to talk about. Sometimes I didn't see him for days."

"Sounds like Ralph."

"You know what they say, girls marry their fathers," said Wendy.

Shea shook her head. "Not this girl."

Wendy turned to her, all humor gone. "No, you just stole cars for a living. Big-time felon, just like Daddy."

"Fuck you, Wendy. I am nothing like that murderous son of a bitch. All I did was boost a few cars to survive." Shea felt like punching her, or at least kicking her out of her house. But she needed to see this through. For Annie and for Derek.

"You coulda lived with us, had a normal life instead of living on the streets."

"If growing up with those bigoted motherfuckers is your idea of normal, I'm glad I missed out."

"Monster and Julia were good godparents."

"I seen what the club does to people. What it did to Mama."

"You coulda at least stayed in touch."

"After what you said at Ralph's trial, I didn't want nothin' to do with you or the club."

Wendy's brow crinkled. "What the hell you talking about?"

"Don't deny it, Wendy. I was in the courtroom. I heard you."

"I never testified at Daddy's trial."

"I remember seeing you."

"It wasn't me you remember."

A wave of nausea swept over Shea. *Must be the vodka,* she thought. A dark memory threatened to bubble to the surface. "What're you talking about?" Her voice cracked with nervousness.

Wendy took Shea's hand as if she were a child. "It's okay. I mighta done the same thing on the stand. We'd already lost Mama. We were scared of losing Daddy, too. And you two were so close before."

"You saying *I* testified that Ralph acted in self-defense? You're off your rocker. I'd sooner die than protect that piece of shit." Shea turned away from her, downed what remained in her glass, and poured herself another.

"Shea, it don't matter. Daddy went to prison. And we both turned out okay, more or less."

Shea stood up. Her head swam and she fell back onto the loveseat. Fire rippled up her leg. "Fuck!"

It took a moment for her to catch her breath and get control of the pain. Her pulse pounded in her ears like a bass drum. "You're fulla shit, you know that? Why would I care about losing the club? They're a bunch of violent, racist assholes who treat women like shit. They weren't my family. I got a family of my own."

"Who? Your cat?"

"Jessica, for one. And the people I work with. These people respect me and I respect them."

"The club takes care of its own."

Shea grabbed her sister's chin and turned her face from one side to the other. "I can see from the bruises on your face how well they take care of you. Same way they took care of Mama. How many times did Ralph beat the shit out of her? And no one did a damn thing. Real family don't do that shit to each other."

Wendy twisted her face out of Shea's hand. "I tried to get out and look what happened."

Shea stumbled to the kitchen and put her glass in the sink. The vodka was kicking in strong, but it couldn't stop the dread creeping in from the past.

Maybe Wendy was right. Maybe if her sister could get away from the Thunder, she could turn her shit around, too. Be a decent mother to Annie.

"Whatever's past is past," said Shea. "I'm willing to let it go. If we get Annie back—*when* we get Annie back—if you still want to get away from Hunter and them, I'll help. Might even find a job for you at Iron Goddess."

Wendy sighed. "Yeah, I'll think about it. Thanks."

"Until then, you can crash in the spare bedroom."

"You sure?"

"Yeah." Shea sighed. "I gotta hit the hay." She limped toward the main bedroom.

"Hey, Shea, member that time we all went tubing down the Salt River?"

"Shit, hadn't thought about that in years." She'd forgotten almost everything about life before Mama died. "We got caught in that dust storm."

"Everything turned all orangey brown," said Wendy. "We couldn't see where the river was taking us. It felt like drifting through a fog."

The memories wriggled to the surface like earthworms in a rainstorm. "Mama insisted we get out when it started thundering. So we piled into a rusted-out horse trailer till the storm passed."

Wendy giggled the way she did as a child. "God, did that stink!"

"When we got in the car to go home, Daddy told Mama to drive because he'd left his license at home."

"And Mom told him no 'cause she'd had too much to drink."

"But he made her do it anyway, said if she ran off the road and killed us all it'd serve her right for drinking so much."

Wendy's smile evaporated. "He was a real bastard, wasn't he?"

"Yeah, I hope someone made him their prison bitch. Serve him right."

Wendy's phone rang. She looked at it, then held it out to Shea, her forehead creased with worry. "I think it's him. The kidnapper."

Shea took it from her. "Hello?"

"You got my four million dollars, Che?"

"I talked to Annie's father. He don't have four million dollars. The club don't neither. Best we can do is a couple hundred thousand."

His laugh sent chills down her spine. "*Puta,* I show you what two hundred grand get you." A child screamed an instant before the line went dead. Shea's knees weakened.

"What'd he say?"

"We gotta find a way to come up with four million dollars. Anything less than that and he's gonna hurt her." *If he hadn't already.*

"What are we gonna do, Shea? I can't let them kill my baby." Wendy buried her face in her arms, sobbing.

Shea shook her head. "We'll call Hunter tomorrow and figure something out. In the meantime we need to get some sleep."

"How'm I supposed to sleep when that monster has my child?"

Shea wrapped her arms around her sister, feeling her body quake with fear, anger, and anguish. "Just do the best you can. That's all any of us can do."

## 24

PAIN AND WORRY refused Shea the oblivion of sleep, despite the abundant amount of vodka coursing through her bloodstream,. The road rash made finding a comfortable position impossible under the clingy warmth of the bedsheets. Jess lay like the dead beside her, leaving Shea all the more frustrated. Even the tap dance of monsoon rain on the windows couldn't drown out the memory of Annie's screams.

A little after four in the morning Ninja's relentless mewing and pawing pulled her from an endless series of troubled dreams. Half asleep, Shea stumbled into the kitchen, trailing behind the cat. The worst of the pain in her leg had settled into a dull ache, while worries about Annie and Derek clawed at her lethargic mind.

Worry amplified to frustration as she flipped on the kitchen light. Cornflakes and freeze-dried strawberries surrounded an overturned cereal box on the breakfast bar that separated the kitchen from the living room. *Another fucking mess to clean up.* Ninja must've been foraging in the night. She'd clean it up later, hoping the cat would let her sleep once she'd been fed.

She gave Ninja's empty food bowl a quick rinse in the sink. The can of wet cat food opened with a scrape-pop, filling her nose with the rank fragrance of processed fish. Ninja devoured the mush with the fervor of a crack addict getting a much-needed bump.

On her way back to bed, the open door of the spare bedroom caught Shea's eye. She poked her head in, wondering if her sister was getting any sleep. But Wendy wasn't there. Not in the hallway bathroom either.

Panic tugged her mind awake. She returned to the kitchen. Drops of blood glistened among the dried strawberries and cereal flakes on the counter. One of Jessica's Japanese knives lay beside the box, a stripe of scarlet marking the razor-sharp blade.

"Wendy?" she called.

Her sister didn't answer.

Maybe she stepped outside the front door for a smoke. Blood on the doorknob sent a chill down her spine. Had someone grabbed Wendy in the night? If so, why hadn't she heard them? Why hadn't they come after her, too?

Footsteps creaked on the front porch. Shea picked up the baseball bat in the corner and prepared to bash the intruder. The door opened. She tightened her grip.

She was in mid-swing when Wendy's head appeared. Shea diverted her swing, smacking the door instead. Wendy jumped back, shielding herself with her arm. "Jesus Christ, Shea! What the fuck?"

"Where the hell were you?" Shea lowered the bat.

Wendy held up a bloodstained paper sack from the Kokopelli Café. "I was hungry."

"Why is there blood on the doorknob?"

"I cut my hand opening the damn bag in the cereal

box." She held up her hand. A red-black line marked her palm surrounded by smears of dried blood.

Jessica walked out of their bedroom, dressed in her robe. "What's with all the yelling?"

"Your girlfriend tried to kill me." Wendy glared at Shea. "Again."

Jessica gave Shea a funny look.

"I thought she was an intruder, Jess," said Shea. "Maybe if Wendy hadn't left blood all over the damn place, I wouldn't have picked up the goddamn bat."

"Maybe if I knew where the goddamn Band-Aids were."

"In our bathroom," said Jessica. "I'll get you one."

Jessica seemed civil considering the previous night's drama. Between the three of them, she was probably the only one who got a decent night's sleep, Shea thought.

"Don't bother with a Band-Aid. The bleeding stopped." She pulled a breakfast burrito out of the bag, then offered the bag to Shea. "Got y'all some, too. You're welcome."

Shea hesitated to grab the bag for fear her sister's blood might've contaminated its contents. Last thing she needed was to catch some disease from her junkie sister. Wendy frowned as the moment grew awkward.

Jessica took the bag from her. "Thanks for buying breakfast. That was considerate of you." She handed a burrito to Shea. "How's the leg?"

"Hurts." Shea put the bat away while Jessica made coffee.

Morning light filtered through the drapes as they sat down in the living room.

"Any word from Hunter?" Shea asked between bites.

"He's freaking out. A black SUV tried to run a couple of Thundermen off the road last night. He wants me up there."

"They getting the ransom together?"

"He said he's taking care of it. All patronizing, you know? Like I shouldn't worry my pretty little head about all the manly details. He can be such a prick sometimes." The calmness of her demeanor unsettled Shea. Wendy's pupils were pinpoints, though maybe it was from the sun shining through the window.

"Maybe we should go to the Church," suggested Shea. "I don't want to risk Hunter fucking things up again."

Jessica looked at her. "You don't want me to go, too, do you?"

"Safer for you here, sweetie." Shea gave her a quick kiss. "The club ain't big into diversity."

"Suits me fine. I was planning on checking out those condos up in Ironwood, anyway."

Wendy tied her hair back into a ponytail. "You ready to go?"

"I wanna take a shower first." Shea took a final bite of burrito and crumpled the wrapper.

∼

A HALF-HOUR LATER, Shea was dressed and ready to go. She'd clipped the spring-assisted jackknife next to the Glock's holster in her waistband, out of sight but easy to reach.

"Be careful," said Jessica.

"Always." Shea smiled and followed Wendy out to her car. "I guess I got shotgun."

Wendy donned a pair of orange shades. "Got that right, sister."

The morning air was warm, humid, and heavy with the promise of an afternoon monsoon. They drove back to the main highway and wound up the hill. As they cruised

through Olde Towne Sycamore Springs, Shea spotted a
dark SUV parked in front of Iron Goddess.

A jolt of fear hit Shea. *Were the Jaguars at Iron Goddess
looking for her and their stolen hex?*

"Stop!"

"What's wrong?" Wendy tapped the brakes.

"Pull into Iron Goddess. Swing around to the back lot."

Wendy followed Shea's instructions. Several vehicles
she didn't recognize occupied the employee spaces. *Was she
too late?*

"Wait here." She drew the Glock, tiptoeing to the back
door of the shop and pressing her ear against it to listen.
From inside came the sizzle of a welder and the chatter of
casual conversation. She reholstered the pistol and covered
it with her shirt before opening the door.

To her right, Lakota tack-welded a bike frame together.
A heavyset guy with wild hair and a face full of stubble was
bending tube steel on the pipe bender. Closer to the office,
Switch and a man with a walrus mustache rounded out a
fender on the roller.

Except for the two strangers, everything looked business as usual. Shea's concern eased a bit, tempered with the
realization outsiders were working in her shop without her
permission.

Mr. Wild Hair looked up at her from the pipe bender.
"Can I help you, ma'am?"

"Yeah, who the hell are you, and what're you doing in
my shop?"

"'Scuse me?" He tilted his head, took a few steps toward
her, puffing out his chest.

"You heard me."

Lakota threw herself between them. "Easy, Shea.
Terrance brought these guys up from Hellbent Cycles in
Phoenix."

"You're shitting me." Shea balled her fists.

"We needed help rebuilding the Trinkets' bikes."

"Where's Terrance?"

"In the office."

"Go talk to your boss, lady," said Wild Hair.

Between the lack of sleep and the gnawing pain in her body, something in Shea snapped. She swung at him. Lakota caught her arm.

"Hey, work it out with Terrance. Not here." Lakota nodded in Switch's direction.

No fighting around Switch. Shea grimaced. "Whatever."

Shea hustled to the office, throwing open the office door. "I thought we weren't hiring the guys from Hellbent Cycles."

Terrance looked up from his computer, a cup of coffee in his hand. "Good morning to you, too."

"T, I'm this close to getting the bikes back. Two guys are looking to sell them to one of Goblin's contacts." She leaned back against the door frame, taking the weight off her injured leg.

"I'm trying to salvage the project." His calmness made Shea madder.

"By outsourcing it to another shop?"

"It's not costing us anything in labor. Scotty Parsons lent us a couple of his guys in exchange for equal billing."

"I don't want equal billing. I want all the billing. The Pink Trinkets hired us, not Hellbent."

"The Trinkets are on board with this."

Shea's jaw dropped. "You told them?"

"What was I supposed to do? Communication with a client is important in maintaining a good relationship." *More of his business school bullshit.*

She took a deep breath and let it out slowly. *There are*

*more pressing issues,* she reminded herself. "Fine. Do what you think's best. That's not what I stopped by to tell you."

"What's going on?"

"Yesterday I rode with a few of the Thundermen to a place we thought my niece was being held, to rescue her. It's a warehouse the Jaguars use to store their heroin."

Concern creased Terrance's brow.

"Annie wasn't there," Shea continued, "but Hunter stole a shitload of the Jaguars' hex."

"Oh fuck! You stole dope from the Jaguars?"

"I wanted nothing to do with it. Hunter pulled a gun on me and forced me to carry a bin full of hex."

He shook his head. "Please tell me the Jags don't know you were there."

"There was a security camera. I tried to get rid of the recording, but Oscar Reyes and Victor Ganado showed up before I got a chance. I got away from them, but not before I dropped my bike on gravel and tore up my leg. It really hurts." She pouted a little, hoping her injury might mitigate his anger. It didn't.

Dread and rage darkened his face. "Oscar has your business card. He knows where we work."

"Yeah, T. I know. I didn't expect Hunter to steal the hex." She stared at the floor, feeling stupid. "Hopefully, when the Jags look at the video, they'll see Hunter forced me to carry the dope."

"You think the Jaguars will give you a pass?"

"What do you suggest we do?"

"Call the cops."

"And tell them what? That I got caught stealing dope from the Jaguars?"

"Tell them you were looking for your niece."

She shook her head. "I can't. Kidnapper said not to get the cops involved or they'd kill her."

"Then I need to close down Iron Goddess until all this blows over. I can't put everyone's lives at risk over this." He picked up the phone and pressed the intercom button. "I need all personnel in the office immediately."

"I'm sorry, T. I didn't mean for it to get this out of hand."

"Any update on Derek?"

"In a coma. Doesn't look good."

He shook his head. "How are you and your sister getting along?"

"She's a junkie. Caught her with a bottle of Oxy written out in someone else's name."

"Can't choose your family," Terrance said with a bitter laugh.

The door behind her opened. She turned, expecting Lakota, Switch, and the guys from Hellbent.

Instead Wendy stood with arms crossed. "And here I thought we moved beyond that."

## 25

WENDY'S EYES blazed as she glared at Shea. "Sorry I didn't turn out to be the standup citizen you did. How many years d'you spend in prison? I forget. Was it six or seven?"

"Better an ex-con than a junkie who defends murderous assholes."

"Believe what you want." She pivoted and marched down the hall.

As much as she enjoyed telling her sister off, Shea knew it wasn't helping the situation. "Wendy, wait." Shea sighed. "I'm sorry."

Wendy turned on her, anger radiating from her face. "I only came to tell you Hunter called. The club should have the money ready by this afternoon. He wants us there now."

Lakota and the others squeezed past Wendy in the narrow hallway on their way to the office. Wild Hair bumped Wendy, knocking her purse to the floor with a thud. The contents rolled across the floor.

"Dammit!" She bent down to pick up her belongings.

"Sorry, lady." Wild Hair walked on without offering to help.

An amber pill bottle rolled to Shea. She picked it up. Her own name was printed on the label. It was her prescription for OxyContin from Dr. Sossaman. "What the fuck, Wendy?"

Wendy's face turned red. "I was gonna give 'em to you. Geez!"

Terrance poked his head out of the office. "What's wrong?"

Shea held up the bottle. "This is what's wrong. She stole the prescription the ER doc wrote for my pain meds."

"I didn't steal shit. I picked them up for you."

"That's a load of bullshit. You picked 'em up for your damn self." Shea slammed her against the wall. "I want you outta my shop, you lying junkie. You and Hunter deserve each other."

Terrance pushed them apart. "All right, all right. Let's everybody calm down."

Rage boiled inside of Shea. Flashes of childhood memories bubbled under the surface of her mind, but she couldn't make sense of them. Her mother's blood. Ralph's trial. A guy in a suit saying what a good girl she was.

Wendy stood up with her purse, its contents recovered. "Look, I'm sorry I didn't give you your meds right away. I meant to. I forgot, okay?" She looked sincere, but Shea didn't want to believe her. Once a liar, always a liar.

"Shea, you have something to say to Wendy?" asked Terrance, sounding like their father.

"I'm sorry you turned out to be a junkie."

Terrance rolled his eyes. "Not helpful, Shea."

"I just want my baby back." Tears of desperation filled Wendy's eyes. "Please come with me to the Church, Shea. I

don't want to go there by myself. Not with all the shit
Hunter's been doing."

"Hunter's your problem. Not mine."

Wendy held up her interlaced fists in supplication.
"This ain't about me, Shea. It's about my little girl. I can't
imagine what she must be going through. If you can't do it
for me, do it for her. Please."

Guilt tugged at Shea's heartstrings. "Fine. I'll go." Shea
pocketed the Oxy. "Then once Annie's safe, I don't want to
see your scrawny junkie ass in my shop ever again."

"I promise."

"One big happy family," Terrance said with a half smile.

Monica's scream rang out from the showroom. Terrance
sprinted from the office with Shea on his heels. Monica
stood behind the sales counter, eyes wide with horror. Her
hand covered her mouth as if suppressing another scream.
A cardboard box sat open on the counter.

"What's wrong?" Shea asked.

Monica pointed at the box and twisted away from the
counter.

Terrance stared into the box. "Oh shit."

Shea limped up to the counter. Inside the box, a small
bloody ear had been sealed inside a plastic bag. It took
everything inside her to control her gag reflex. Her attempts
to negotiate had cost poor Annie her ear, perhaps her life.
"Where did this come from?"

Monica shrugged. "Delivery guy dropped it off a little
bit ago. I just now opened it."

"What'd he look like?" asked Shea.

"I don't know. White. Maybe Latino. Bald. About thirty."

Aguilar, thought Shea.

"What is it?" asked Wendy from across the room.

Shea rallied to control her writhing emotions. "Get
some ice from the freezer in the office," she said to

Terrance. "We may be able to preserve it long enough for it to be reattached." He nodded and ran to the office.

"Tell me." Wendy's voice cracked with fear.

Shea was torn between telling her the horrible truth or letting her suffer in ignorance. "It's an ear," she confessed, unable to meet her sister's gaze.

"But not Annie's ear, right?"

"I think it may be."

Wendy crumpled to her knees. "No."

Monica spewed into a trash can. Shea wanted to do the same. Lakota cradled Wendy on the floor.

Terrance returned with a large resealable bag full of ice and held it open. Shea lifted the bag with the ear by the corner and lowered it into the bag of ice.

"I hope we don't remove any fingerprints," said Terrance.

"Better that than Annie losing her ear for good."

"Yeah." A stern look darkened Terrance's his face. "I'm closing up shop until we can get this situation with the Jaguars figured out."

"I'm with you." Shea walked over to Lakota and Wendy. "How's she doing?"

Lakota looked up at her, grim faced. "Not well. I think she's in shock. She keeps saying this wasn't supposed to happen."

"Wendy," Shea squatted down in front of Wendy. "I know you're upset, but we gotta go rescue Annie."

Wendy looked up and their eyes met. Her face was flush with anguish. As Shea held her gaze, Wendy's expression hardened. "I'm gonna kill those fuckers who hurt my baby."

Shea gave her a hand up. "I'll help you." She turned to Terrance. "Do what you need to do to keep everyone safe."

"Will do. Be careful out there." Terrance ushered everyone back to the office.

Shea followed Wendy out the back door to the parking lot.

"You want me to drive?" Shea asked.

"I'm all right." Her voice was monotone.

Shea climbed into the passenger seat. Wendy started the car with a roar and pulled onto the street, heading north. As they left Olde Towne, Shea caught sight of a dark SUV a few cars behind them, maybe a half mile back. She couldn't tell if it was black, dark blue, or maroon. It wasn't driving aggressively, but she suspected they were once again being tailed.

"What's wrong?" asked Wendy.

"Remember that SUV chasing us the other day?"

"Yeah."

"I think it's back."

Wendy glanced in her rearview mirror. "You sure it's the same one?"

"No, but there's a way to find out. Turn right up here onto Highway 134."

"I wasn't planning on going that way. I was gonna take the Ironwood Bypass."

"Just do it. If I'm wrong, they'll stay on 89. But if I'm right, they'll follow us onto 134."

Wendy slowed down and turned at the junction. The two cars immediately behind them continued straight on Highway 89. The SUV turned, following them. "Shea . . ."

"Yeah, I know. Speed up a little bit, see what they do."

Wendy accelerated from sixty-five miles per hour to seventy-five. The SUV drifted behind.

*We're in the clear,* Shea thought. The Mustang crested a hill and the SUV disappeared from view.

Wendy glanced back again. "They gone?"

"Yeah . . . wait, no, there they are. Shit." The SUV reappeared, closing the gap between them. "Dammit. They're after us."

"What should I do?"

"We'll have to lose them."

"Who you think I am? Dale Earnhardt?"

"Just go fast as you can to I-17."

"Whatever you say." Wendy floored it. "Hope we don't pass any cops."

"Better the cops than the Jaguars."

"You got your gun, right?"

"Yeah, why?"

"Maybe you can get them to tell us where they got Annie." Wendy wove past a cluster of cars in their way.

Shea gritted her teeth on each bump and swerve, trying to avoid hitting her leg or wrenching her neck whenever she glanced back. "You think these guys don't have guns? Keep going."

The SUV continued to close the distance.

"There's a red light coming up," said Wendy.

Shea looked ahead. There weren't any cars approaching the intersection. "Run it, then turn north onto the interstate."

"Maybe you should take the wheel." Wendy squinted while she flew through the intersection, then slowed down when they approached the interstate on-ramp.

"Don't slow down! They catch us, we're dead. Now punch it!"

Wendy complied, but without as much punch as Shea would have liked.

They merged onto I-17 North. A few miles in the distance, the road climbed up through a twisting mountain pass. "If we can make it to the mountains, maybe we can lose them. Those SUVs can't corner for shit."

The landscape of prairie grass dotted with thirty-foot

junipers whizzed past in a blur, but the SUV stayed on their tail.

"Oh shit. Hang on!" Shea hunkered down and grabbed the oh-shit handle above her.

The SUV slammed their rear bumper. Shea's head bounced off the headrest.

"What now?"

"Go faster!" Shea yelled. The SUV hit them again, harder this time.

"I've got the pedal to the floor. Maybe I should do one of your fancy U-turns."

"Not at this speed. You'd flip us. Get to the mountains. We can make it." The twisties were still half a mile away.

The SUV pulled into the lane to their left and rammed them from the side. Wendy screamed, struggling to stay on the road. The right shoulder of the road fell away as the highway rose up toward the mountains.

"Hit the brakes!"

"What?"

"The brakes! Do it!"

She slammed on the brakes. The Mustang shuddered while the antilock brakes struggled to keep the wheels from skidding. The SUV blew past, then locked up its brakes with a high-pitched scream and a cloud of dust.

Wendy turned to her. "Now what?"

Shea glanced in the rearview mirror. There were cars approaching from the south, so going in reverse wasn't an option. Ahead of them, the SUV was now backing up.

"Hold tight. When I tell you to, floor it."

The truck stopped forty feet away. The driver's door opened and Oscar Reyes climbed out, a yellow bandana on his head representing his membership in the Jaguars.

"Okay, go!" Shea yelled.

Wendy hit the gas and ducked down, peeking over the

dash. Oscar jumped back in as they flew by. Shea looked back. The SUV roared to life and came charging after them again.

Ahead, the road climbed steeply. Soon they'd hit the first tight turn up the side of the mountain. Shea hoped Wendy could control the car enough to not go flying off the cliff.

"Shea..."

Shea turned back in time to see the SUV pulling up beside them once again, this time on their right. Oscar was gesturing wildly and shouting something but Shea couldn't make it out over the road noise.

He turned the wheel and hit them, pushing them across the median. Wendy swerved onto the southbound lane. An oncoming semi blew past—horn blaring—a split second before they skidded across the southbound lane toward the far shoulder. The SUV kept coming. Shea grabbed the wheel to help Wendy to keep them on the road. The car shook violently. The wheels screamed as they were swept sideways by the SUV's superior weight and engine.

The left wheel slipped off the side of the road. The car spun, then careened down the steep hill, flipping sideways over boulders and mowing down yucca. Shea clung to her seatbelt through a roller coaster of crunching metal and shattering glass. The airbags blew in front of her and on her side as the car came to a heart-pounding stop. Everything went black.

## 26

SHEA FOUND her nine-year-old self wandering aimlessly outside Victor Ganado's home. Ralph had chased her off while he and the Jaguars' president talked business inside. It was a cool day, the sky royal blue, the air filled with the sweet fragrances of citrus blossoms. She preferred playing outside anyway, when the weather was pleasant.

The fenced-in lot next to the house caught her attention. Discarded machines of all types—cars, motorcycles, mowers, bicycles, even a snow machine—were jam-packed into rows like a rusty wonderland of hidden treasures. She spied a 250 cc minibike about three rows in. Ralph had been looking for one for her to learn on. This might be the ride they'd been hunting for.

She paid no heed to the KEEP OUT and NO TRESPASSING signs. Ralph had taught her those signs were for other people. That sort of thing didn't apply to them. The Stevenses were biker royalty. They could do what they wanted, go where they wanted, whenever they wanted.

The fence was twice as tall as she was, crowned with three strands of barbed wire. No problem. She grabbed the welcome mat from Victor's front door and tossed it over the barbed wire. It took a few attempts, but she nailed it on the third try. With her heart racing, she climbed up the chain links, up and over the mat covering the barbed wire, then down the other side where she stepped onto the hood of a rusted out VW Rabbit with all but one window busted out.

She hopped down. The broken windows tempted her mischievous side. She picked up a rock and threw it at the VW's remaining window. It cracked but didn't shatter. She picked up the rock again, threw harder, and was rewarded with a loud crash. "Yes!"

Satisfied, she walked down the row, tapping on various surfaces with a green palo verde stick, noting the different tinks and thunks each object made.

She was halfway to the minibike when a low rumble disturbed the quiet. She looked around the sea of abandoned junk, but didn't see anything. Then she heard it again—a throaty growl. She turned down a different aisle and came face-to-face with a black dog as tall as her chest. All the dogs she knew were friendly. Their only threat was covering her in slobber. This dog was different. It held its head down, teeth bared, eyes aflame.

Instinct did for her what experience couldn't. She swung the stick in front of herself to fend off the dog. It barked several times and snatched the stick out of her hand.

Adrenaline flooded her system as she ran. The beast was almost on her when she rolled under a nearby car. The dog growled, then hunched down and crawled toward her on its belly. She scrambled to the other side, leaping over a riding lawn mower. When it emerged from under the car, she threw a broken tricycle at it. It dodged the trike and kept coming. She ran toward a golf cart, clambering onto the roof.

As she caught her breath, the dog grabbed her pant leg. She clung to the roof of the golf cart with all her strength, but her sweaty palms couldn't get enough purchase. She landed face first on the ground with the wind knocked out of her. She flipped around onto her back, but before she could get to her feet, the dog leapt onto her chest. She punched wildly at the monstrous mouth full of teeth snapping at her. She grabbed hold of its throat, but it overpowered her easily.

Powerful jaws sliced into her face. Pain exploded in her head. She continued punching, but it had no effect. Blood obscured her vision.

All at once, the growling faded and her screaming stopped. The rapid heartbeat hammering in her ears remained the only sound. Every beat screamed for her to wake up. *Wake up. Wake up. Wake up.*

∾

SHEA OPENED HER EYES, the memory of teeth tearing at her flesh replaced by the Mustang's seatbelt pulling against her chest. The roof had caved in, the windshield cracked but still in place. The world outside had taken a ninety-degree turn clockwise. Steam hissed from the cracked radiator.

She remembered tumbling down the hill. "Wendy?"

Blood speckled Wendy's face and the deflated driver-side air bag. Sand filled the view outside the driver's window. The car had landed on its side. Shea shook Wendy's shoulder. She groaned. "What happened?"

"We crashed. Can you undo your seatbelt?"

"What?" Wendy's eyes were unfocused, jaw slack like a large-mouth bass.

"Your seatbelt. Can you get it open?"

Wendy stabbed at the button. "It won't let go."

"Crap." Shea reached down but couldn't get it to release. "Hold on a sec." She pulled out the knife clipped inside her waistband. The spring-assisted blade opened with a sharp clack.

Wendy looked worried. "What're you doing with that?"

"Cutting your seatbelt."

Using the serrated edge at the base of the blade, Shea sawed through the seatbelt. Wendy dropped a few inches to the ground as the seatbelt gave way.

"You okay?" Shea asked.

"My head hurts."

Shea tucked the knife back into her waistband. With one hand on the oh-shit handle and her feet braced against the side of the footwell, she pressed the seatbelt release. It opened.

"We gotta get out of here." Shea assessed their options. The windshield was cracked but not shattered. There wasn't enough room to kick it out. Their best route was up through the passenger-side door.

She stepped onto the center console and tried the door. It wouldn't open. No surprise, considering how much damage it had sustained from rolling down the hill. But the window was gone. She reached through, her arms, back, and legs protesting as she wriggled up through the window.

Standing on the door, Shea inspected their surroundings. They had rolled two hundred feet down a steep hill. At the top, the SUV sat parked on the side of the road. Oscar was already a third the way down the hill, struggling to maintain his balance on the steep, uneven slope.

"Wendy, we need to leave."

Wendy shook her head. "Let me lay here awhile."

"What the hell's wrong with you?" Shea feared she might have a concussion. "The guy who ran us off the road is halfway down the hill already. If we stay here, he'll kill us. Gimme your hand." She leaned down into the car, reaching for Wendy.

Wendy took Shea's hand. "I'm scared."

"Yeah, me, too. Step on the console. Careful with the broken window. The glass can still cut you."

Wendy's skinny frame made her ascent easier as Shea pulled her out of the smashed Mustang.

"My beautiful car." She tucked a string of hair behind her ear with a blood-smeared hand as she sat on the crumpled fender.

"Worry about the car later."

A bullet thunked the car's exposed undercarriage, followed by the report of a gunshot.

"You *putas* need to come with me!" shouted Oscar.

Shea thought about shooting back, but Oscar was more than a hundred yards away, well outside the range of her Glock. Wendy crouched down looking like she would dive back into the car.

"Don't go back in there. Follow me." Shea slid off the side of the car onto the ground, then turned back to her sister. "Jump down. It's not as far as it looks."

Wendy closed her eyes and leapt, landing in a heap on the ground.

Shea pulled her to her feet. "Let's go." She led Wendy further down the hill through waist-high prairie grass that made running difficult and offered little cover. Another shot echoed. Shea resisted the urge to look back. It would slow them down more.

At the bottom of the hill, a dry wash meandered through a grove of palo verde trees. "There. Head for the wash." Shea pointed.

"We ain't gonna make it."

"Yes, we are." Shea pushed her sister ahead of her. Her heart thundered in her chest. Her lungs ached for air.

When they reached the edge of the grove, Wendy ducked down to hide behind a paloverde.

Shea pulled her up and pushed her ahead of her again. "Can't stop. He knows we're here."

Another shot sounded, this time shattering one of the tree branches. "He's gonna kill us!" cried Wendy.

Shea pulled her Glock and fired a couple of shots at Oscar. He fell. "Got him."

Her hope evaporated a moment later when he struggled to his feet and resumed the chase. "Fuck. He's wearing body armor."

In the distance, the high-pitched drone of an engine approached. Possibly a motorcycle or an ATV. Further down the wash, a dirt road intersected the dry riverbed. "Make for that road."

When they reached the dirt road, two ATVs—one blue, one red—appeared on the far bank of the wash, thundering their way. Shea put away the Glock and waved her arms. "Stop! Please!"

The guy on a blue ATV pulled up beside them, his buddy on a red one stopped a few feet behind. "What's going on?"

"A man," Shea said between breaths. "With a gun. Trying. To kill us."

The guy on the blue ATV look up the wash. "Get on. We'll get you out of here."

"Thank you." Shea pointed for Wendy to climb onto the red ATV while she got on the blue one.

"You set?" asked her driver.

Before she could say yes, his head exploded in a spray of blood. Shea turned to see Oscar approaching. He fired again. Shea ducked behind the blue ATV. Wendy screamed. The other ATV driver lay on the ground, bleeding from a chest wound. "Wendy, get on." Shea pushed the driver's body off and reached out for Wendy to join her. Wendy rolled onto the ground, curling into a fetal position behind her ATV.

Shea crouched beside her and drew her Glock. She peeked above the ATV and fired a shot at Oscar. It missed. He fired back as she ducked down.

"Call Hunter," she said. "Let him know what's happening."

"I left my purse back in the car."

"Dammit!" Shea pulled her phone out, tossing it to Wendy. "Use this."

She took it. "It's cracked."

"Try it anyway." Shea looked above the ATV.

One of Oscar's shots ricocheted off the handlebars inches from Shea's head. "Put down your gun, *blanca,* and give yourselves up, or I will blow your fucking heads off."

"Kiss my ass, Oscar!"

"Shea, your phone ain't working."

"Shit." Shea rose up to take another shot. Pain exploded on the left side of her head. She fell to the ground dazed. She forced her eyes open despite the horrendous agony. Wendy loomed over her, saying something she couldn't make out. Everything was spinning. She had trouble getting her mind to focus.

"You're okay. Just a graze."

The world felt out of sorts. Wendy turned and screamed with her hands in the air. "Please don't kill me."

Shea turned, causing her head to swim, her vision darkening. When her mind cleared, Oscar stood over her with the Colt pointed at her chest. "I should kill you for making me hike down this fucking hill. But *el jefe* wants you alive. Guess this is your lucky day, *blanca.*"

He stuck her Glock in his waistband and pulled Shea to her feet.

Wendy put an arm around her. "C'mon, sis," she said with defeat in her voice.

Oscar pointed his gun up the hill. *"Andale, putas."*

While they trudged along the wash and back up the hill, Shea's mind began to clear. Blood stained her shirt. Halfway up the hill, Wendy collapsed onto the ground. Shea wobbled but stayed on her feet.

"I can't," said Wendy.

Shea felt the same way, but lacked the energy to say it.

Oscar pointed the gun at Wendy, who ducked away, fending him off with her arms. "Get moving or I blow your *pinche* head off."

Shea forced air into her lungs. "Leave her alone, you piece of shit."

He turned the gun on Shea. "Listen here, *blanca*. I got the gun now. You do as I say, or I kill you anyway."

There was nowhere to run. He wasn't bluffing.

"C'mon, Bug. Let's keep moving," Shea said.

She helped Wendy up. The two of them, leaning on each other, continued up the hill. Shea turned to Oscar. "Why?"

"Oh, I think you know."

He pressed the gun into Shea's back. Anger forced her to dig deep, giving her a burst of energy. She twisted to the side, coiling her arms around her chest, then nailed him in the face with her elbow. He staggered back a step. Before she could punch him again, he caught her on the jaw with butt of the pistol. She fell onto the grass with the taste of blood in her mouth, seeing stars and feeling dizzy.

"I gotta give you credit. You don't give up without a fight. But you gotta face facts—you gonna lose. Now get your ass up."

He held the gun to Wendy's head. Shea forced herself

up. Wendy put a hand under Shea's arm and helped her up the hill.

When they reached the road, Victor stood there waiting beside the black Nissan Pathfinder, dressed in a dark gray pinstripe suit.

"Hello, Uncle Victor."

"*¡Hola, mija!* You cause me much trouble." Victor's eyes flickered with anger. No pretense of the kind grandfather now.

## 27

Oscar patted them down and pulled the bottle of OxyContin from Shea's pocket. He shook it and examined the label. "Well, well, Oxy. Nice!"

Victor took the bottle from him. "I'll just hold on to this for you." He pocketed the bottle while Oscar zip-tied their hands behind their backs.

"Get in." He shoved them into the back of the Pathfinder, with Shea on the driver's side. Sirens wailed in the distance while they crossed back over the median and drove away, going north into the mountains toward Ironwood.

"What're you gonna do with us?" asked Wendy in a trembling voice.

Oscar laughed. Victor remained silent.

"Just keep quiet," Shea said. She wanted to comfort her sister, to tell her it would be all right. But she wasn't sure it would be.

"Are they gonna kill us?"

"Shhh."

Wendy sobbed quietly.

The ride gave Shea's head time to clear. It ached to the point of distraction, but the dizziness was fading. She slowed her breathing, focusing on how to escape. If she slipped her bound wrists under and past her legs, she could use the zip tie as a garrote to strangle Oscar. But considering he was driving, that could lead to another accident. A crash in the mountains could prove fatal, since she and Wendy weren't buckled in. She sat back hoping a new opportunity would present itself before it was too late.

Oscar turned onto a now-familiar side road. They were headed back to the warehouse—a great place to make bodies disappear. The crunching of tires on gravel set her further on edge. The chances of them surviving were growing thinner by the minute. But still, Shea paid closer attention to the turns, clinging to hope.

When the SUV stopped in front of the warehouse, the two men got out. Oscar opened Shea's door, grabbed her collar, and pulled her from the vehicle, causing her to stumble. When she regained her feet, something hard pressed against the back of her head. *A gun barrel, no doubt.* Victor held Wendy with a firm grip on her arm.

"Walk." Oscar's voice purred with delight and malice. He grabbed Shea's arm and led her over the gravel drive-way. Victor unlocked the side door, releasing the bolt with a clack. The door squeaked open.

Using his gun as a prod, Oscar pushed Shea and Wendy down the hallway and into the main room of the ware-house, then pushed Shea backward into a folding chair. The familiar pungent sweetness of black tar heroin hung heavy in the air.

Wendy slumped in a chair to Shea's right, her eyes red and swollen from crying. Her sweaty hair was plastered against her head. *I'm sure I'm no beauty to behold either,* she thought. *Not that I ever was.* Behind them sat the table Victor's guys used to cut heroin into hex.

Oscar stood a few paces back, with his Colt 1911 in his hand and Shea's Glock sticking out of the front of his waistband. Victor towered over her. His face had the rumpled, worn texture of a discarded snake skin. His eyes sizzled with indignation.

"I liked you kids. So full of life and curiosity." Victor cupped Wendy's chin in his gnarled hand. "I remember you were a little *gordita*. What happened? You smoking your old man's product? Or maybe selling crystal not so profitable, eh?" A venomous smile twisted his face further.

"Why are you doing this?" Shea asked.

Victor slithered over to her. "*Pobrecita,* you were so pretty until my Cesar attacked you. Now you look . . . well." He shook his head. "I loved Cesar, *mija*. Hated to put him down. It was a knife in my gut. But to keep peace with the Thunder, I did it. Sometimes one does unpleasant things in this business."

*A knife in the gut,* Shea repeated to herself. A knife. Of course, her knife! Was it still there?

Careful not to give herself away, she reached around the back of the chair and found her knife clipped to the inside of her waistband underneath the gun holster. Oscar must have missed it. She inched it out with her fingertips.

Victor's gaze grew icy. "We had a good thing, your *papi* and me. The Jaguars supply him with *mota* and heroin. He sold it for us. Good business. But when he go to prison, the Thundermen no longer respect me."

He bent down beside Shea. She covered the knife with her hand.

"They got greedy, *mija*," he hissed in her ear.

He turned to Wendy. "Your old man, Hunter—he the most greedy. He stopped buying from me to sell crystal cooked by his toothless junkie buddies. Became a competitor. Very disrespectful."

The knife pulled free of Shea's jeans. She held it solidly in her hands. The familiar weight of it gave her confidence. Her thumb found the peg on the blade and eased it out of the grip. The blade locked in place with a loud click.

*Did they hear it?* Her heart stopped. Oscar glanced at her and narrowed his eyes, but didn't say anything.

"But it was not enough to steal my business. I arrive yesterday to see someone stealing my heroin." Victor pointed up to the surveillance camera. His voice thundered with anger. "Notice that camera up there? I see everything!"

He leaned into Shea's face. "This, *mija,* was the most disrespectful. I kill my dog for you, and you steal from me?"

"Hunter took your dope. I had nothing to do with it."

"I see you on my video. In *my* warehouse carrying *my* hex. That makes you guilty."

"Hunter forced me to." She maneuvered the knife blade to the spot on the zip tie between her hands. She applied pressure and began sawing at the tie, hoping she didn't slit her own wrists in the process.

"If you not here to steal my dope, why you here? Huh?"

"The Jags kidnapped my niece. You also shot one of my employees and stole a dozen of my bikes. I was looking to get back what was mine."

Victor looked confused. "What are you talking about? We did not kidnap your niece or steal any motorcycles."

"Don't lie to me, Victor."

Oscar kicked Shea's chair right between her legs, almost causing Shea to drop the knife. He pointed his gun at her, while sweat beaded on his forehead. "You full o' shit, *blanca.*"

"Why would we do these things?" Victor looked indignant.

"You said it yourself. The Thunder's cutting into your business. You needed money and wanted to punish Hunter, so you kidnapped his daughter for ransom. You stole my bikes to sell to a chop shop."

"Enough of this shit." Victor looked her square in the eye. "Where's my hex, *mija*?"

"Where's my niece, asshole?"

"*Órale.*" Victor looked at Oscar, who met his gaze. For a moment, she thought he might start asking questions of Oscar. "*Mijo.*"

"*Sí, jefe.*" Oscar looked nervous.

"Encourage our guests to talk. Start with that one." He pointed at Wendy.

A smile broke out across Oscar's face. "*Sí, jefe.*" Oscar handed his Colt to Victor, pulled out a stainless steel lighter, and walked up to Wendy. Shea furiously cut at her bonds, hoping to break free before he hurt Wendy. But without seeing what she was doing, progress was slow.

Wendy's face blanched with fear. "No, please!"

Oscar clicked the trigger. A blue flame hissed from the lighter like a tiny jet engine. He grabbed Wendy's arm and pressed the flame to her skin. She screamed, the acrid stench of crisped flesh permeating the air.

"Stop it, you bastards!" Shea said. "She doesn't know anything."

Victor held a hand up to Oscar. The old man leaned into Wendy's face. "Where. Is. My. Hex?"

Wendy choked and gasped, her face distorted in pain. "Don't know."

"We don't have it, Victor," Shea said. "Hunter does."

"Where would he take it?" said Victor, turning to Shea.

"The MC's clubhouse most likely." Shea had no idea if it was there or not, but a wrong answer was better than no answer. She pulled on the zip tie, hoping she'd cut through enough to break it. It held, cutting deeper into her wrist. She resumed sawing at the notch she had made.

Victor smiled in a way that reminded Shea of the Grinch. "Now we get somewhere. Perhaps you get Hunter to return what he stole, perhaps we let you go. Where is your phone, Wendy?"

Wendy tried to speak, but could only choke out a series of gasps and guttural moans.

"We lost our phones when you ran us off the road," Shea said.

Oscar pulled out his own cellphone and looked at Wendy. "What's your old man's number, *puta*?"

Wendy struggled for breath. "Can't remember. Never memorized."

Oscar set down his phone and tore open Wendy's shirt, sending buttons flying, then pulled up her bra, exposing her breasts.

"No!" she shrieked.

"*Estúpida.*" Oscar shook his head. He pressed the trigger on the lighter, letting it hiss near her left nipple. "What's the fucking number?"

Wendy whimpered. "If I knew . . . I'd tell you. Please . . . believe me."

Shea's knife slipped and nicked her wrist. She bit her lip to keep from crying out. She located the notch again and resumed cutting it.

"You don't know your old man's phone number? I find that hard to believe." Victor nodded at Oscar, who pressed the blue flame against her breast. Wendy's raw screams tore at Shea's soul.

Shea gritted her teeth, pulling on the zip tie with all her strength. With a quiet snap, it broke. She adjusted her grip on the knife and leapt at Oscar.

## 28

Oscar turned as Shea flew at him. She stabbed him in the chest, but the blade hit a rib, barely penetrating his skin. The lighter fell to the floor as he dropped to one knee.

She reached for her Glock in his waistband. He punched her in the face before she could grab it. The pistol clattered to the concrete as she reeled backward onto her chair from the blow. When he went for the gun, she drove her boot into his temple. He collapsed onto the floor.

Out of the corner of her eye, Shea saw Victor raise the Colt. She rolled, grabbed the Glock in her left hand. A bullet whizzed overhead. She returned fire putting two in Victor's chest. He slumped against one of the shelving units.

Oscar seized her left wrist, weakening her grip on the gun. His eyes blazed with hatred. "I'm gonna rip you apart, *blanca.*"

She stabbed his forearm. He let go with a yelp, blood gushing from the wound. She plunged the knife into this neck. He bellowed as arterial spray showered them both.

She scrambled to her feet, wiped her face with her arm,

and looked down at Oscar. Blood pooled around his now-still body. His eyes were half closed, mouth agape.

With her ears ringing from the gunshots, a darkness crept over her, as if she'd crossed a threshold with no hope of return. She'd never killed anyone before. God knows, they deserved it. But she couldn't shake the fear that she'd become like them. Like her father.

The grief-stricken face of Oscar's mother appeared in Shea's mind. *Why you kill my Oscar?*

"Help." Wendy's ragged plea pulled Shea out of her head.

Shea rushed over to her sister and cut her restraints. With her hands free, Wendy wrapped her arms around her chest and sobbed.

Shea knelt down and put a hand on her shoulder. "I know you're hurtin', but we gotta go."

Wendy nodded. With a whimper, she pulled off her bra and tied a knot with the corners of her now-buttonless shirt to cover herself. Shea dug through Oscar's pockets and found his keys and his phone. To her surprise, the phone didn't require a pass code to use it. Oscar was either too confident or too stupid to worry about anyone stealing it. There was a single bar's worth of cell signal. She slipped it into her pocket.

"Shouldn't we do something with the bodies?" Wendy grimaced against the pain as she stood over Oscar's body.

"Why?" Shea trembled from adrenaline.

"Hide the evidence."

"Two dead gangbangers in a warehouse full of dope? What all you planning on hiding? I just want to go."

Wendy kicked the lid off one of the plastic bins. "Jesus." She picked up one of the bags of hex.

"Leave it." Shea opened the garage door and walked toward the Pathfinder.

"Please? I'm in pain. I could seriously use a hit right now." Her eyes pleaded with Shea. "Besides, this shit is worth a buttload on the street."

"I said, leave it!"

"And if I don't, what? You gonna kill me, too?"

Shea put away her knife and holstered the gun. "Just get in the truck."

Wendy dropped the bag and sauntered to the Pathfinder, sulking the whole way. Shea started the engine. As Wendy climbed in, Victor began to stir and moan.

"Hurry up," Shea said. "Victor's alive."

Victor raised the Colt and fired, putting a hole in the upper right corner of the windshield. Ducking down, Shea threw the truck in reverse and floored it. Victor fired three more shots.

"How's he alive?" Wendy asked while they hurtled backward down the hill. "You shot him."

"Must've been wearing a vest." Shea stared out the back window, struggling to keep the Pathfinder on the narrow gravel road.

They reached an intersection a quarter mile from the warehouse. Shea spun the Pathfinder around and raced back through the labyrinth of unmarked roads.

Shea's leg began to throb. She pounded the steering wheel. "Fuck!"

"What's wrong?"

"Forgot to get my pain meds back from Victor."

Wendy put a comforting hand on Shea's shoulder. "Once we get to the Church, I can have Dopey give you something."

Shea scoffed at the idea. "Great."

Moments later, a red triangle appeared on the dash. The engine temp had redlined.

"Dammit!" Shea ran her hand through her hair as steam poured from under the hood. "This is not good."

"Now what's wrong?"

"Victor must've hit the radiator. Engine's overheating."

"What do we do now?"

Shea pulled out the phone and handed it to Wendy. "Think you can remember Hunter's number now?"

"Don't matter whether I can or not. There's no bars on the phone. We're outta range."

The truck lurched and whined. "Looks like we'll have to hoof it soon."

"Hoof it? We're in the middle of fucking nowhere."

For the next mile the engine started rattling, growing louder until the whole thing seized up and quit. The truck coasted to a stop.

"Well, that's it. No choice now." Shea searched the back of the truck for a first-aid kit, a bottle of water, or anything that might make a long trek through the wilderness easier. All she found was a worn spare and a dusty navy-blue windbreaker. She tossed Wendy the jacket. "In case it starts to rain."

"Thanks," she whispered.

Shea opened up the maps app on Oscar's phone. Despite the lack of a cell signal, the GPS pinpointed their location. "The closest highway is five miles southeast." She pointed in the direction they had come.

"Back toward the warehouse?"

"We'll get off the road and stay in the woods. I think we can avoid Victor. How's your chest?"

"It hurts. A lot. I wish I had your pain meds right now."

Shea grimaced. "Wish I did, too."

The GPS led them off the road and into the dense woods. Poison ivy and prickly pear cactus permeated the underbrush. With no trails to follow, it would be a tough five miles across steep, rugged mountains.

"If I tell you something, you promise you won't be mad?" Wendy sounded like a kid again, terrified of getting in trouble.

"What?" Shea struggled to keep her balance as a rock hidden by leaves twisted her ankle.

"You gotta promise."

"Tell me already."

"Okay, I wasn't going to give you your prescription."

Shea didn't say anything. She wasn't in the mood to have deep emotional conversations with her junkie sister.

"Ain't you gonna say something?"

"Like what?"

"I dunno, like, 'I forgive you,' or, 'Hey, that's okay, we all make mistakes.'"

"No. I don't forgive you."

"As if your shit don't stink, Miss Grand Theft Auto."

"I don't want to talk about it."

"News flash, Shea! We all got issues."

"Whatever. Keep walking or Victor *will* find us."

The terrain fell away steeply, forcing Shea to grab on to trees to keep her balance. She looked for signs of the road, but the horizon was too hazy to make anything out. After thirty minutes of tripping through underbrush, Wendy collapsed onto a fallen log.

"Ugh, I need a break."

"We gotta keep moving. Victor is looking for us."

"You're just saying that. No one could find us in this jungle."

"It ain't no jungle. Just a forest."

"I'm in pain and I'm thirsty."

"I am, too. But the only way outta here is to keep moving." Shea pointed down the hill.

Wendy looked in the direction Shea pointed. "What's all that?"

"All what?"

"Red. Looks like a field of flowers down there."

Shea stared down through the trees and caught a glimpse of color. "Wildflowers, I reckon." Wendy was stalling, making Shea all the more frustrated.

Wendy shook her head. "Wildflowers bloom in the spring. It's August. It looks like the fields of roses they grow outside of Phoenix."

"Whatever they are, that's the direction we're headed, so I guess we'll find it out."

Above them, a wall of slate-gray clouds swallowed the sun, deepening the gloom of the woods. "We best get going. Even if Victor doesn't catch us, that monsoon might."

Wendy gazed at the approaching storm. "Geez, can't catch a fucking break."

"Whatever. Come on."

With a grunt, Wendy stood up and trudged along behind Shea down to where the terrain leveled out and the trees ended in a field of scarlet. They weren't wildflowers. Dense lines of chest-high plants topped with blood-red petals grew in precise rows, complete with drip irrigation lines. A chill ran down Shea's spine. "We shouldn't be here."

"Why?"

"They're poppies."

"Opium poppies? I didn't think they could grow here in Arizona."

"Victor musta figured a way to do it. We better get outta here before someone sees us." Shea crept back up the hill into the trees, looking for a route around the poppy field. When she didn't hear Wendy behind her, she turned around.

"What are you doing?" Shea rushed back down to the field to find Wendy pulling up poppy plants and collecting them in her arms.

"I'm taking a few samples. No harm in that."

"What the hell's wrong with you? Hunter stole heroin from Victor and you see where it got us. Seriously, how stupid are you?"

Wendy glared at her. "It ain't like I'm taking several keys' worth of smack. Geez, you're such a square."

Something whizzed past like a supersonic bee, followed by the boom of a gunshot echoing across the valley. "Shit! Get down."

## 29

SHEA AND WENDY dropped to the ground.

"Shit, that hurts," Wendy said under her breath.

"You hit?" Shea looked her over but didn't see any fresh blood.

Wendy shook her head, eyes closed. "No, but I landed on my chest."

"This is why I didn't want you picking flowers. Fields like this aren't left unguarded. Now follow me and keep low. And try not to bump any of the plants."

Someone shouted in Spanish from the other side of the field, maybe fifty yards away. Shea couldn't make out the words, but from the tone of his voice, he was pissed. She crept along the row of flowers to the southern end of the field, hoping the poppies would give them enough cover to reach the trees. Another shot whizzed overhead.

"Fuck," Shea muttered. "He's getting closer."

"You've got a gun. Shoot him."

"Yeah, easy for you to say. I don't know where he is. Last time I stuck my head up in a firefight, almost got it blown off. Remember?"

"So what's your plan?"

"Right now my plan is not to get shot."

"Great plan, sis."

Shea looked at her, frustration mixing with fear. "I'm open to suggestions."

Wendy held out her hand. "Give me the gun."

"You know how to shoot?"

"Of course. Hunter taught me. Now give it here, if you don't want to use it."

"Fine." Shea handed her the Glock.

Wendy sat on her haunches and peeked above the tops of the flowers. The guard fired again, blasting a seed pod next to her head. Wendy squealed and fell back. Another shot whizzed by, not far from the last. Wendy scrambled on all fours toward Shea. "Go, go, go!"

Shea ducked through a gap in the plants to move across a couple of rows, then lay flat. Wendy hit the deck beside her. They had reached the end of the row. Nothing but fifteen feet of open terrain between the poppies and the trees. Chances of reaching cover without getting shot were slim.

"Okay, bad idea," Wendy said.

"Where's the gun?"

"I dropped it."

"You what?" Shea's body shook with frustration. "You said you knew how to handle a gun."

"Not when someone's shooting at me, turns out."

"Any other bright ideas, Annie Oakley?"

Another shot. This time the bullet ripped through a poppy plant next to Shea, shearing off the flower from the stem. The ring of petals spun in the air like helicopter blades and landed delicately in front of her.

"Maybe if you talk to him," said Wendy. "Tell him we're just looking for the road."

"You wanna get chatty with Mr. Trigger Happy, be my guest. I'm getting my gun back." Shea slid past her, retracing their steps.

"Hey! Señor Guardo!"

Shea listened for the guy's response to her sister's call. No shots. No words in Spanish or English.

*"No el shoot-o, por favor."*

Wendy's butchered Spanish alone should have earned her getting shot, thought Shea. But the guard held his fire.

*"¡Manos andale!"*

Shea hurried back to where they were when Wendy dropped the gun, but didn't see it anywhere. She looked in neighboring rows, up and down the way.

"Don't shoot." Wendy stood with her hands up in surrender. She'd discarded the jacket and was looking all Daisy Duke with her shirttails tied around her chest, showing off a lot of skin.

"You done lost your mind?" Shea whispered.

*"Ay, ay, ay, mamacita!"* The guard swished against poppy plants as he approached.

Fighting against the rising panic, Shea resumed her search for the pistol before the guy could do more than ogle her half-naked sister. She spotted it one row over and dove for it.

"He's coming closer, Shea," Wendy muttered.

The guard's approach grew louder. Shea rolled onto her elbows and looked through the plants, gun in hand. Thunder rumbled in the distance. She guessed he was twenty feet away. Through the stems of poppy flowers she caught a glimpse of denim.

She raised the pistol and fired. The man fell to the ground, screaming in pain.

"You got him!" Wendy sounded gleeful, like Shea had caught her first fish.

Shea wasn't so filled with joy. The darkness in her was growing, numbing her emotions.

She pushed through the field to where the man lay on a bed of crushed poppy plants, moaning and crying out in Spanish. He smelled as if he hadn't bathed in weeks. His skin was dark, his clothes dirty and sweat stained. Blood poured from a wound above his left knee. He looked more day laborer than gangster, despite the AK-47 just out of his reach.

"*¿Por que? ¿Por que?*" he cried over and over. He looked up at Shea, eyes begging for mercy. "*Lo siento. Lo siento. Por favor, ayudame.*"

"He says he's sorry." Shea pushed back against the darkness, fearing what would happen if she gave into it. Memories of her father's trial and a lawyer with slicked-back hair played in her head.

"Yeah, well, fuck him. He's only sorry we shot him first." Wendy spit at him, while pulling the windbreaker back on.

"What do we do with him?" The darkness in Shea wanted to finish him off. Tit for tat. "Eye for an eye," said the darkness in Ralph's twangy rumble of a voice.

"You gotta finish him."

"Why?" Something in his face made Shea wonder who he was, if he had a family somewhere.

"You didn't finish off Victor and now we're hiking all over creation to get to the road. Then this fucker tries to blow my head off."

Shea pointed the Glock at his head, willing herself to pull the trigger. Her hand trembled, as he sobbed with pleading eyes.

"Do it! For God's sake, if he was a wounded buck, you'd shoot him and put him out of his misery."

"He ain't no animal. He's a human being."

"He's a fucking spic working for the Jaguars."

"¡*Ayudame! Por favor, ayudame!*"

Rain started falling in large, cold splats on Shea's arm. The longer she stared at him, the more her hand shook.

Shea holstered the gun. "I'm gonna save him if I can. There's a blue tarp across the field. Probably his camp," she said. "Put pressure on the wound while I go look for something to stop the bleeding."

"Like hell I will. You wanna save him after he tried to kill us?"

"Do it, Wendy!"

"Fine! You're fucking crazy, ya know that?" Wendy knelt down.

"Yeah, I know."

While Shea trudged through the field, the rain came down harder until it was a deluge. The wind howled, whipping the rain in sheets across the rows of poppy plants. The ground turned to muck that pulled at her boots.

The man had strung a blue tarp into a makeshift lean-to with a pile of belongings stashed in one corner. Among the empty freeze-dried food wrappers and assorted camping gear, she found a faded photograph of the man with a woman and five kids.

A loud boom shattered the patter of the rain. Shea ducked down, gun raised, not sure if it was nearby lightning strike or another guard shooting at them. Wendy stood with the guard's AK-47 tucked under her arm, pointed at the ground.

"What the fuck'd you do?" Shea ran back as fast as she could. "What'd you do?"

Wendy stood over the man with a satisfied grin on her face. Blood oozed from a bullet hole in his forehead, mixing with the mud around his body.

"Had to be done."

"He had kids, goddammit!" Shea held up the photo.

"So do I, and these fucking wetbacks took her." Wendy glared at her.

Compassion softened Shea's anger.

"Let's go." Wendy slung the rifle across her back and marched across the field.

"I'm sorry," Shea whispered to the guard's body. She tucked the photograph of his family into his dead hand, then ran to catch up to her sister.

～

As they marched onward, Shea's mind drifted back to when she was fifteen and skinny with Ralph's chestnut hair, long and wild. She was sitting at the kitchen table with her seven-year-old sister, Wendy, both of them eating bowls of Fruity Pebbles, watching the milk turn that funky purple-brown color. Wendy's strawberry-blond curls bounced as she hummed tunes in her head. Ralph sat between them dressed in a wifebeater, smoking a cigarette and drinking coffee.

Mama walked in, wearing a yellow dress with white polka dots. She was dragging an old blue suitcase with a broken wheel and a smaller one Shea and her sister used for sleepovers. Her long red hair was put up in a bun. With her face made up, which was a rarity, she reminded Shea of a World War II pinup girl—except for the new shiner peaking out from beneath a layer of concealer. Ralph took one look at Mama and said, "Where the fuck you going?"

"I had enough of your shit."

"What the hell you yammering about?"

"Your drinking, your abuse, and your insatiable need to tap every piece of ass that comes your way." Her voice trembled with anger. "I will not have my daughters grow up in this environment."

Ralph's face darkened. He bumped the table as he stood up, spilling milk from the kids' cereal bowls. He'd been grousing all morning 'cause Mama hadn't fixed him breakfast. "Where you gonna go, bitch? Everything you got belongs to me." He grabbed the suitcases away from her and threw them clattering across the kitchen. "You got no money. No car. Nothing."

Wendy looked up from her bowl and ran to Mama, wrapping her little arms around Mama's legs. She was always Mama's girl.

"I got my daughters."

Mama reached for Shea's arm, who pulled away. "What are you doing, Mama? I ain't going anywhere. This is crazy!"

"Shealene, please! You deserve better than this. You stay here, you'll end up like me or worse. Remember Auntie Gina? And Beverly? You wanna end up dead or in prison the way they did?"

"I'm gonna be a Thunderman, like my daddy."

Mama stretched out her hand. "Shea, you're a girl. They'll never let you be a Thunderman."

"You can't tell me what to do!"

Ralph put an arm around Shea. When she nestled into his embrace, he grinned. "Shea stays with me. You wanna take that redheaded brat, you go right ahead. Never thought she was mine anyways. So go on. Everybody'll see you walking down the street like the drunken whore you are."

A car horn beeped three times on the street.

"Who the fuck is that?" Ralph's tone turned icy, sending a shiver down Shea's spine. Trouble was coming. She slipped out of his embrace and stepped away from him.

"None of your damn business." Mama picked up the suitcases and strode to the front door, but Ralph caught her.

Wendy panicked. She let go of Mama's legs and ran out the door.

"It's that douchebag boss of yours, ain't it?"

"Larry's giving me a ride."

"Ha! I'll bet he is. You been fuckin' him?"

Shea backed away into the corner of the cabinets farthest from the door. "Daddy, let her go."

Mama escaped his grasp, pulled open the door, and looked at Shea. "Baby, please come with me."

Ralph dragged his wife back in and slammed the door shut. "You ain't going nowhere, cunt, till I get some answers." He threw her against the stainless steel fridge next to Shea, leaving a dent.

She looked dazed but managed to stand. "I've taken your shit for fifteen years, Ralph Stevens. You don't frighten me."

"No?" He pulled a butcher knife from the knife block and stepped toward her. "Scared now?"

Mama stood taller, her chin high, and glared at him.

Shea crouched on the floor beside her, wide-eyed. "Daddy, stop! Please!"

"I ain't gonna ask again, woman. You been sleeping with that pencil-pushing dick?"

"I ain't telling you shit, you no-good excuse for a man. It make you feel tough, beating up on women?" She looked down at Shea on the floor. "See what you got to look forward to, Shealene? Nothing but—"

Ralph swung the knife, slicing open Mama's throat, sending a spray of cranberry blood across Shea's face. Mama crumpled and fell on top of her. Shea struggled to cover the wounds with her hands, but the cut was too deep and wide. Slick blood flowed through her slender fingers. Mama lay gurgling and gasping, eyes wide with shock until ... until there was nothing left of her.

Shea's final memory of that day was looking up at Ralph's blood-spattered grin. She didn't want to believe he'd done it. He'd been her hero. But there he stood with the knife, gloating over Mama's lifeless body. It was the last time she'd called him Daddy.

～

ON THE OTHER side of the poppy field, the hillside grew rockier. According to the GPS, they were two miles from the road. Shea plodded in silence, lagging behind Wendy, who groaned and grunted with every other step.

Shea remembered her fury watching Oscar hurt her sister, and her satisfaction hearing his cries as the knife pierced his neck. The darkness spread deep into her chest, a black hole swallowing up all light. Maybe they were more alike than she wanted to admit.

After another mile, Wendy stopped on the crest of a hill and stared down at something. The rain had eased to a steady drizzle. The roar of rushing water drowned out the patter of the rain. Shea caught up to Wendy and saw what she was looking at.

A ten-foot-wide stream raced down the mountainside, cutting across their intended path. During most of the year it would've been a dry wash. But now it churned with muddy water and debris. Even if it was only a foot deep, the current could knock them off their feet, carrying them downstream.

"What now?" Wendy asked.

## 30

SHEA'S LINGERING anger at her sister left her reluctant to answer. She stared at the seething flash flood blocking their way. It was too wide to jump and too treacherous to wade.

"Look for something we can use for a bridge," Shea said.

Paloverdes, covered in a nest of spiny green branches, hung over the gravy-colored water. Higher up on the bank, mesquites with twisted, gnarled trunks competed with column-like sycamores for space among muddy chunks of granite the size of a motorcycle engine. A sycamore would've worked great if they had a way to cut it down—which they didn't. None of the other trees were suitable for a bridge.

Shea used a stick to loosen the dirt around a rock the size of a tire. Her fingers slipped under the edge, lifted up one end, then dropped it with a whomp. It must have weighed a couple of hundred pounds. "Gimme a hand with this."

Wendy had wandered downstream and was inspecting a pile of debris. "Just a minute."

Shea sighed. "Fine, I'll do it my damn self." Gripping the side of the rock, she dragged it to the flooded stream. With a deep breath, she heaved it into the water, three feet from the water's edge. After a cannonball splash, it vanished beneath the murky water.

"Fuck."

"How about this?" Wendy was dragging the trunk of a young sycamore, six inches in diameter at its widest end. The bark had been worn off, leaving the bare ash-gray wood cracked and hollow in places.

"Will it hold our weight?" Shea asked.

Wendy put a hand on her hip. "You got any better suggestions?"

The water was getting deeper the longer they scratched their heads.

Shea shrugged. "Let's try it."

They pivoted the sycamore trunk, extending the narrow end across to the opposite bank, and planted it in the mud.

Wendy looked at Shea with a nervous gaze. "Who goes first?"

"You're the lightest by a good measure. I nominate you."

"Fine."

With knees bent, Wendy straddled the tree trunk and shuffled across. When she got to the middle, the log sagged and creaked. Water rushed over her shoes.

"Damn, that's cold." Wendy continued on and reached the other side unscathed. "Your turn."

Shea tossed her the cellphone and put a tentative foot on the trunk. It drooped. She looked around again for anything else that might make crossing a little less risky, but there was nothing. As she straddled the trunk, it creaked and sagged under her weight. Chilly water soaked her boots, then crested her jeans, leaving her gasping. "Fuck, it's like ice water."

"Quit staring at the water and c'mon!"

"I'm coming." Shea inched toward the middle. The tree sagged so much the water came up to her waist, numbing the muscles in her legs and bringing temporary relief to her road rash.

Wendy reached out to her but Shea shooed away her hand. When she did, the log gave way with a loud crack. Her body plunged into the freezing water. The current pulled her under, tumbling and smashing her against rocks and other debris. Her arms flailed, struggling toward the surface. She pulled her head up for a second to gasp for air before the water dragged her down once again.

Her shin smashed into something solid. A submerged tree trunk. She grabbed at it, but the wood was slippery. Before she could get a firm grasp, the current pulled her on, spinning her like a boat without a keel. Her hip slammed into a large rock. She cried out and got a lungful of water.

Blindly, she reached for anything to grab on to and found a paloverde branch. She clung to it, even as spines dug into her hand.

She planted her feet in a hole, pushing against the flow. Using the paloverde for balance, she pulled herself out of the river and collapsed on the stony bank. She lay shivering and coughing up water. Hypothermia threatened to pull her into unconsciousness.

"You okay?" Wendy stood over her.

"Am I?" Her mind numbed.

"Anything broken?" Wendy's eyes were red, like she'd been crying, but it was hard to tell with the rain trickling down her face.

"Don't think so." Everything hurt. Shea's hands were bloody from the paloverde branch. A scrape ran down the side of one of her arms.

Wendy helped her sit down on a rock. "I's afraid I'd lost you."

"Me, too." Shea's body quaked, teeth chattering like a Teletype machine.

Wendy brushed something from Shea's face and looked at her the way their mother used to. "We need to get this off you." She grabbed the bottom of Shea's shirt and pulled.

Shea resisted. "What're you doing?"

"Your lips are turning blue. We gotta warm you up."

"By taking off my clothes?"

"Trust me for once, will ya?"

Shea gasped while Wendy pulled her shirt off. "Doesn't feel warmer."

Wendy slipped out of the windbreaker, draped it over Shea, and helped fish her arms through the sleeves. After a few moments, the worst of the shivering passed, though Shea's teeth still chattered in spurts.

"Better?"

Shea nodded and looked at her shirt laying in the mud, stained with Oscar's blood. After what he'd done to Wendy, why couldn't she shake this brooding emptiness? She threw the shirt into the rushing water and watched it drift away in the current.

"Can you walk?" Wendy's words startled her.

"I think so."

Wendy helped her up from the rock. Gravity slid sideways for a moment and Shea took a step to steady herself. When the vertigo passed, she said, "Let's go."

They climbed the rocky bank up the next hillside. The physical activity helped warm her and clear the cobwebs from her head.

At the top of the hill, Wendy stopped and pointed. "There it is."

A hundred feet down a steep incline, a ribbon of pavement snaked through the forest. The rain had dissolved into a swirling mist.

As they descended the hill, Shea's knees wobbled like jelly. At the road's edge, Wendy led them under a rocky overhang and pulled out Oscar's phone. "Looks like we're on White Juniper Road, about ten miles east of Ironwood."

"Don't suppose you remember Hunter's number at this point?"

Wendy gave her a sly smile. "Never forgot it."

"You what? Why'd you let Oscar torture you if you knew the number?"

"Because *fuck Oscar,* that's why. He was gonna kill us anyway."

Shea shook her head in amazement. "Damn, the balls on you."

"A little something I learned from my big sister."

Wendy called Hunter. "Hey, it's me. I need you to come pick us up. We're sitting on the side of the road on White Juniper, ten miles east of Ironwood." She paused for a moment. Shea caught distorted bits of Hunter's response. "The Jaguars ran us off the road and took us hostage, but we got away. How long before you can be here? Okay, see ya then."

Wendy hung up. "He'll be here in half an hour."

After their adventure with Victor and Oscar, Hunter was the last person Shea wanted to see. This was all his fault. But he was their only hope for the ransom money. "How's your chest?" Shea asked.

"Hurts, but I've survived worse."

"Worse? From who?"

She stared at the pavement. "Guess."

"Hunter?"

Wendy nodded without looking up.

"Hand me the phone, I need to make some calls while we're waiting."

Shea first called Jessica.

"Shea? I've been worried about you. You weren't answering your phone." Her voice made Shea feel warmer.

"Sorry, we had an accident. My phone got smashed."

"You okay? Sounds like your teeth are chattering."

"Fell in a river, but I'm all right."

"Shea, I have to tell you something. I called the cops. Told them you'd heard from the kidnappers."

"Dammit, Jess. Why?"

"This whole situation has gotten way too violent. I'm worried about you."

Shea shook her head, not sure if she should be angry or relieved. "Well, what's done is done. Did they come by and ask you questions?"

"Worse. A couple of detectives from the Sheriff's Office were here looking for you. They had an arrest warrant. What did you do?"

"Arrest warrant? I didn't do nothing. What are they trying to arrest me for?" Shea sighed. Was this about Oscar? Would Victor have dumped his body somewhere for the cops to find?

"They wouldn't tell me."

"Gotta be a mix-up." Maybe Aguilar was trying to frame her. "Jess, is there someone you can stay with temporarily? A coworker maybe? Just until we get this all cleared up."

"Not really. I have a few friends at work, but I don't have their numbers. Am I in danger?"

"Probably not, but I don't want to take any chances. I'll call Terrance and see if he can put you up until this gets resolved."

"When will I see you?"

"I don't know. We're making the ransom drop tonight. If

all goes well, we'll have Annie back, and I can clear my name with Buzzkill and his goons."

"Please be careful, sweetie. I miss you."

"Miss you, too."

Shea punched in Terrance's number.

"T? It's Shea."

"Where are you? I've been trying to get ahold of you."

"Long story. Listen, I talked to Jess. The cops dropped by my house with a warrant for my arrest."

"Why would they want to arrest you?"

"No idea." Shea cupped her hand over the phone so Wendy couldn't hear. "What happened with the ear?"

"I have it. Not sure how long it'll stay viable."

"Fuck," Shea said. Annie's scream rang in her ears.

"What about you? Where are you?"

"Middle of nowhere at the moment."

"You need me to pick you up?"

"No. Hunter's on his way. But there is something you can do for me."

"Name it."

"I'm worried about Jessica. I'm not sure it's safe at my place. I told her she could crash at your place until we get all this business straightened out with the cops."

"No problem. Stay safe, Shea."

"Thanks, T." She hung up and pulled out a damp business card from her wallet and dialed the number, hoping to get ahead of this nonsense with the Sheriff's Department.

A familiar voice answered. "Homicide and Missing Persons, Detective Toni Rios speaking. How may I help you?"

"Detective, it's Shea Stevens. Why's there a warrant out for my arrest?"

"Shea, where are you?"

"Never mind where I am. What's with the arrest warrant?"

"The Beretta you were carrying when we picked you up matched several unsolved homicides. Where'd you get that gun?"

Shea facepalmed. She'd forgotten about that. "Borrowed it from a friend."

"Well, if you want to clear your name, you'll need to come down to the station and answer some questions."

"Fine. I'll do that. Just can't right at the moment."

"Shea, we're trying to help your sister get her daughter back. I can't help you get Annie back safely if you don't provide me with the information I need."

"The kidnapper threatened to kill Annie if we got you involved."

"Annie has a much better chance of getting out of this alive if we're working together."

"I'm sorry. I don't believe you." Shea hung up.

"You talking to the cops?" asked Wendy.

"Just that female detective. Buzzkill's got a warrant out for my arrest. Just trying to find out why."

"What'd she say?"

"That gun I got off Hunter was apparently used to kill some folks."

"This surprises you?"

"No, what surprises me is you married him."

"And I tried to leave him."

Shea scoffed. "And yet here we are waiting for him to pick us up."

"You got any better ideas?"

"Nope."

"Hey, the other day you said I lied about something, that it was the reason you quit talking to me. What were you talking about?"

"Ralph."

"Daddy? What about him?"

"You testified at the trial he killed Mama in self-defense. You lied to protect that murderous son of a bitch!" Shea's voice came out as a growl.

"Are you nuts? I never testified."

"Like hell you didn't. I remember all too well."

"You're delusional. Why would I defend him? I loved Mama." Wendy got misty-eyed.

*Was Wendy lying or choosing not to remember?* Shea herself had blocked out a lot about that time, but Wendy's testifying to protect Ralph had burned itself into Shea's memory. "Yeah, you loved Mama so much you went and lived with her murderer's best friend."

"Monster and Julia were our godparents. They took me in and treated me like family. Woulda taken you in, too. But, no, you had to run away and steal cars for a living. Some upright citizen you turned out to be."

"Whatever." Shea pulled the Windbreaker tighter. "Keep protecting the club. That's what you do."

"I'm telling you, I didn't testify. Besides, even if I had, he still woulda gone to prison. End of story."

"Yes, he did, no thanks to you."

"You know, Shea, you think you got it all figured out. But you don't. And it hurts me to think that I would have betrayed Mama like that."

"Never mind. Just drop it." Shea closed her eyes and tried to think warm thoughts.

## 31

Forty minutes later, Hunter arrived in his Bronco. Behind him rode One-Shot and Mackey on their Harleys, their hair soaked from the rain. Wendy handed Shea the rifle and climbed into the Bronco next to Hunter. Shea slipped into the back, holding the AK-47 next to her.

Hunter turned toward Shea, eyeing the rifle. "Where'd ya get the hardware?"

"From someone who don't need it no more." Shea glanced at Wendy.

Hunter looked at her as well. "What the hell's going on with your shirt? You look like a goddamn hooker."

Wendy shrank away from him, staring out at the rain, shoulders slumped. "Don't wanna talk about it."

"Hey, I asked you a question." He grabbed her arm.

Shea knocked his hand away. "Leave her alone."

He turned and threatened Shea with a fist. "You want some of this?"

"Cut the shit, asshole. Wendy's hurt 'cause of you." said Shea.

"What're you talking about, hurt?" He turned to Wendy. "What's she talking about?"

Wendy rubbed the ruddy mark his grip had left, but wouldn't look at him.

"The Jags tortured her to get back the hex you stole."

"What'd you tell 'em?"

"Nothing, I swear." Wendy's voice was almost a whisper.

"She didn't tell 'em shit. Wouldn't even give up your phone number. Just let them burn her with a lighter to protect your thieving ass."

"Ha! Guess I trained my bitch right, then."

A high-pitched horn sounded behind them.

*The boys must be tired of sitting in the rain,* thought Shea, managing a weak smile.

Hunter put the truck in gear and roared down the road. Shea stared out the window as they drove north toward Bradshaw City. A double rainbow arced across the eastern sky. Her dark mood muted its jeweled colors. Air from the truck's vents warmed her skin, but the heat didn't penetrate the cold emptiness in her core.

It pissed Shea off to see Wendy cower from Hunter. *Where's the badass chick who defied Oscar's abuse and shot the guard in the poppy field?*

She wanted to punch Hunter for treating Wendy like a disobedient child. Wendy was under his thrall, same way Mama had been under Ralph's. Nothing Shea could do to change that. Wendy had tried to leave him once; maybe she'd do it again, once Annie was safe.

By the time they approached their destination, the setting sun had painted the blanket of clouds with hues of lavender and peach. They were a few miles outside of Bradshaw City when Hunter pulled off onto Pinellas Parkway, an isolated road meandering between grass-covered hills west of town. A few minutes later, he turned onto a driveway, stopping at the gate of a ten-foot-tall chain-link fence. Two men wearing prospect cuts and armed with AR-15 assault rifles opened the gate, letting them through.

A hundred yards past the gate, Hunter drove up to a worn brick building that had been like a second home to Shea when she was growing up. What once had been a church in the days before Arizona's statehood now served as the Confederate Thunder clubhouse, which they continued to call the Church. Up in the bell tower, a sniper's rifle barrel extended from the balcony railing.

Hunter pulled the truck into the nearby lot among a small assortment of cars and three dozen bikes, some concealed with covers. When the truck stopped, Shea grabbed the AK-47 and hopped out next to her sister. They'd taken two steps when Hunter appeared with his hand extended. "Gimme the AK."

Shea didn't have much interest in the assault rifle, but held it away from him in defiance. "This ain't yours."

"You're in my house now. I say what's mine and what ain't."

Wendy looked at Shea with dull eyes. "Give it to him." Her voice was flat and lifeless. Shea wondered if her sister was again jonesing for a hit of oxy.

She held up the rifle. Hunter snatched it away and inspected it. "Can't never have too many of these."

One-Shot and Mackey walked past them, both pale and wet, lips lavender with cold. Hunter, Wendy, and Shea followed them around to the front of the building.

A rain-soaked Confederate battle flag fluttered on a flagpole attached to one of the four-by-four columns on the porch. Shea put her hand on the wooden façade that covered the front of the building. The paint, cracked and faded to the color of butter, felt like lichens growing on boulders.

"'Member when we used to play tag and hide-and-seek here with the other bikers' kids?" asked Wendy.

Shea recalled her sister's childish laughter, tinkling like the tiny silver bells some of the Thundermen put on their bikes to ward off road gremlins. "Long time ago," she said.

Shea followed the others inside. The air vibrated with the sound of Lynyrd Skynyrd and reeked of stale smoke, beer, urine, and sweat.

The walls of the entryway were covered with photos of past members, many of them mug shots. In one club family photo, a young Shea and her sister sported goofy grins. Interspersed with these were framed letters of appreciation from local charities for contributions. Images of the Confederate stars and bars, along with the club's Johnny Reb logo, were everywhere.

Part of her longed for the innocence of her childhood, but she knew the sweet memories were only part of the story. The trauma of the dog attack and the recurring terror of her father's abuse poisoned the recollections. Despite its promised commitment to its members and their families, the club was a cesspool of racism, misogyny, and violence.

Shea stepped into what had been the sanctuary of the old church. A bar stood where the altar must have once been. A dozen members of the MC, along with a few of their old ladies, were drinking and laughing around wooden tables that had replaced the church's pews.

Hunter, One-Shot, and Mackey marched down a hallway on the right side of the barroom-sanctuary.

"There she is!" A heavyset man with thinning gray hair and a well-worn cut stood up from one of the tables and approached Shea and her sister. He looked familiar, but Shea couldn't place him.

"We was worried about you, sunshine." He gave Wendy

a bear hug. She yelped when he squeezed her. "What's wrong?"

"Is Dopey around, Papa?"

Wendy calling him Papa eliminated any doubt. This was Monster. Or had been at one time. Not nearly as scary looking as he'd been seventeen years earlier.

"He's around here somewhere. Why? You hurt, sugar?"

"Uh-huh."

He grabbed the arm of one of the other Thundermen, the same guy with goat patch on his chin who had brought Hunter the pills for Wendy. "Goatsy, fetch Dopey for me, will ya?"

Goatsy ran off. Monster turned to Shea. "Jesus fucking Christ! Can't be. Little Shea-Shea?"

"Hey, Monster." Nostalgia once again tugged at her. She could smell his Old Spice aftershave.

He shook her hand with a strong grip. "Good to see you, kiddo." He looked her over. "You look like a drowned rat. You fall in a river?"

She shrugged. "More or less."

A lanky man with John Lennon glasses and a port-wine stain on his right cheek walked up to Monster. "You looking for me?"

"I am," said Wendy. "Can we talk someplace private?"

"Sure." Dopey waved her on and she followed him down a hallway. "Come on down to the infirmary."

Shea watched them leave. "He a real doctor?"

"Sure enough, board certified and everything. One of them Doctors without Boundaries."

"I think you mean Doctors without Borders."

Monster crinkled his brow. "Naw, pretty sure he said Doctors without Boundaries. Either way he sewed me up one time after a serious scrap with them Mexican bangers. Hey, ya want anything? Whiskey, coffee, both?"

"Coffee'd be nice."

"Hey, Jimbo! Bring us a cup of coffee," he called to the man behind the bar. "Shea, let's you and me have a seat and talk. I'm getting too old to stand for long." He ushered her over to where he'd been sitting and drinking a bottle of Miller.

A moment later, Jimbo, who reminded Shea of a scary version of John Belushi, dropped off a cup of coffee. "Thanks," she said.

"What in the world happened to y'all?" asked Monster. "We were 'specting you hours ago."

"We got ambushed by the Jaguars," Shea said. "We tried to get away, but they caught us, took us to their warehouse out in the forest." Her voice rippled with anger. She tried to calm herself.

"Why would them damn beaners be going after the two of you?"

"Hunter," she said.

"Hunter?" Monster looked surprised. "What's he got to do with this?"

"Yesterday, I rode with Hunter, Mackey, and One-Shot up to the Jags' warehouse looking for Annie."

"Heard about that. They said she wasn't there though."

"No, but a whole lot of the Jaguar's hex was. Hunter and the boys helped themselves to a few hundred kilos. When I protested, they jumped me and left me there."

Monster gave a low, throaty grumble. "That boy. He got more dollars than sense sometimes."

"How come *you* ain't at the head of the table?" she asked.

He chuckled. "There was a time I wanted it. Believe me, I did. But I had enough on my plate raising your sister, especially after what she been through. What y'all been through, I should say." His face darkened. "Wish you'd come to live with us, too. Wendy missed having her big sister around."

"After Ralph killed Mama, I didn't want nothing to do with the club. I had to find my own way."

"Can't say I blame ya. This life can be brutal sometimes."

"So why you still part of the club? Why not leave this shit behind?"

"These folks is family. Besides, somebody's gotta be here to put some sense into these little punks."

She shook her head. "Don't sound like they're listening, old man."

"Not enough, that's for sure."

"What happened? Ralph and Victor used to have a good partnership."

"They did. When your old man got locked up, Roadster took the gavel. Wasn't too keen on doing business with brown. Tried a few other things to earn. Dogfighting, guns, crystal. Jags didn't take too kindly to it."

"Imagine that."

"What about you? What's keeping you off the streets these days?"

"Building custom bikes for women."

He smiled. "Yeah, think I heard something about that. Never knew there's such a thing as women's bikes. Figured a motorcycle's a motorcycle."

"For the most part. Lotta women are shorter. Most bikes are too tall in the seat, even with lowering kits. So we make smaller bikes."

"No shit. That's something else."

"For our best customers, we design the bikes like a tailor custom makes a suit. I measure arms, legs, torso, then build the bike to spec."

"I'll be damned. Purty clever there, girl." He took a sip of his beer. "How's business?"

She shrugged. "Okay till we got robbed a few days ago."

"Know who did it?"

"Friend of mine owns a chop shop, says someone wearing Jag ink was trying to fence a few of our custom bikes. Him and someone who looked like a cop."

"Huh! Fucking beaners and pigs. Now them Jags got my grandbaby." He slammed his bottle on the table. "Serves 'em right, Hunter stealing their dope."

"I'm worried about Wendy, Monster."

"Wendy?" He raised an eyebrow. "How come?"

"For starters, she's hooked on Oxy."

He frowned. "Yeah, been noticing that, too."

"Then there's Hunter abusing her. I'm afraid what happened to Mama will happen to her. Annie, too."

"Hunter gets a little rough sometimes, but Wendy holds her own."

"A little rough? He and his boys came charging into my shop and nearly killed her for leaving him."

"Yeah, well. That's the life, ain't it?"

"Being someone's punching bag? That ain't no life, Monster. She deserves better and you know it."

He frowned. "I ain't arguing with ya. I want her to be happy."

With the coffee, Shea felt warmer. She started to unzip the windbreaker and stopped when she remembered she had nothing underneath. "Y'all got a spare shirt I can borrow?"

## 32

MONSTER FLAGGED DOWN GOATSY AGAIN. "We got a change of clothes for my goddaughter? She needs something to wear while her clothes dry."

Goatsy looked at Shea. "Let me see what I can come up with." He hustled down the hallway.

"Goddaughter?" She raised an eyebrow.

"I know you blame the club for your mama's death. But in my mind, you're still my goddaughter. You and Wendy both."

Shea let it sink in.

Moments later Goatsy brought Shea a faded Sturgis T-shirt and pair of drawstring sweatpants. "The pants are a bit short on me but they should fit you."

"Thanks. I should have the pants back to you in a bit. I may need to hang on to the shirt a little longer."

"Keep 'em long as you need." He hustled off.

"The dryer still where it used to be?" Shea asked Monster.

"Same place, newer model."

She carried the clothes down the hall to the bathroom.

A handwritten note taped to the wall advised people to use the sliding bolt lock rather than the lock in the doorknob. She wriggled out of the windbreaker and slipped off the wet jeans, socks, and underwear. The bandage on her leg was similarly soaked. She peeled it off. The scabs that had formed were now soft and oozy. The skin glowed bright red.

The medicine cabinet contained no first-aid supplies. She squeezed a glop of hand sanitizer into her palm and smeared it across the tattered flesh of her road rash. The alcohol burned like fire on her exposed nerves, causing her to wince.

She looked at the shirt and sweatpants Goatsy loaned her. Her skin crawled at the idea of putting on a strange man's clothes, especially without any underwear. *God, I hope he don't have crabs or anything else contagious.* How would she explain that to Jessica? She gritted her teeth and pulled them on. The pants were a little long, the shirt baggy. She pulled the windbreaker over it.

At the end of the hall, she popped the wet clothes into the dryer and returned to the clubhouse's main room.

Wendy sat at a table with several other bikers' old ladies on the other side of the room. They were all skinny with long hair and way too much makeup. Aside from her sister, Shea didn't recognize any of them. All of the women's eyes were on Wendy, as if she were holding court as the young queen of the club. Their expressions were somber and consoling. An older woman in a tube top held Wendy's hand.

*Is that Monster's old lady?* wondered Shea. *What was her name? Julia?*

Hunter walked up to Shea, brooding. "We got the money. One-Shot and Mackey are putting it in duffel bags now."

"How'd you come up with four million so quickly?"

His eyes narrowed. "None of your business."

"Fair enough. You got a computer I can use? The kidnapper told me to post an ad on craigslist once we have the ransom."

"Yeah, in the office. I'll show you."

She followed him back down the hallway to a door on the left. He pulled out a set of keys and opened up a small office decorated with framed photos, biker memorabilia, and an assortment of Confederate flags. A rolltop desk sat in one corner with a computer and monitor. She sat down, logged into her craigslist account, and created the personal ad with a subject "Come Home Annie." In the body of the ad, she wrote, "Your room is ready, but no allowance until you're safe." She added Oscar's phone number.

"What's that mean?" He pointed to the text.

"It means he doesn't get the ransom without first giving us Annie."

"Now what?"

"We wait for the kidnapper to tell us where and when to make the drop."

They returned to the main room. She joined Monster, though the two sat without saying anything. The music had been turned off, replaced by an occasional creak of the building or the scrape of a chair across the floor. During her childhood, this room would shake with raucous laughter or the odd heated argument. The silence made Shea's ears ring.

An hour later, Oscar's phone dinged. The kidnapper had sent a text message with a video. "Better get Hunter," she said to Monster.

He brought Hunter and Wendy both, who stood behind Shea's chair.

Shea looked up at Wendy. "Maybe you shouldn't see this."

Wendy's chin trembled. "Play it."

Shea did so. On the screen, Annie held up a tablet displaying the current time and date with large, readable numbers. A strip of gauze wrapped around her head held a bulky, blood-soaked bandage where her right ear had been, reminiscent of Van Gogh's self portrait. "Mommy," she sobbed.

"What've they done to my baby?" Wendy's knees buckled. Hunter grabbed her and put her in a chair.

Monster held out his hand. "The time on that tablet she's holding could be faked. Lemme check the time stamp on the video."

"How you know about time stamps?" Shea handed it to him.

"From my granddaughter there." He adjusted his bifocals. "Video was shot about an hour ago."

He was handing it back to Shea when it rang. No caller ID appeared on the screen. *Was it the kidnapper or someone trying to reach Oscar?*

She answered it. Her insides shook. "Hello."

"Is this Che?" The same Mexican voice mispronounced her name.

"Yes."

"Why you using Oscar's phone?"

"Borrowed it from him." *What else could she say?* The connection went silent for a moment. "You still there?"

"You like the present I send to you?"

Her body trembled as she resisted the urge to throw the phone across the room. "I just want Annie back."

"You got my money, Che?"

She looked up at Hunter, not sure if he'd told her the truth. "We got it."

"All of it?"

"All four million dollars."

"*Bueno.* Bring the money to 1437 North San Juan Boulevard in Ironwood. Be there at midnight. Just you. If I see anyone else, I kill them, you, and the girl. *Comprende?*"

"I understand." Her voice shook with anger.

"If you call the cops, I kill you and the girl. *Comprende?*"

"Yes, I *comprende.*"

"If all the money isn't there, if there are any sequential bills, if there are any tracking devices . . ."

"Yeah, yeah, you'll kill me and you'll kill the girl. I got it. Now here are my demands, asshole. I don't let go of the money until Annie's safe. Otherwise, I will light the whole bag of money on fire and you get nothing. *Comprende?*"

"What are you doing?" Hunter whispered between gritted teeth.

"Oh, so you making the rules now, *gringa*? Let me remind you I'm in charge. Not you." Annie screamed in the background.

Shea's jaw clenched. "What did you do, asshole?"

"I see you at midnight, *gringa*." The call ended.

Hunter grabbed her shirt collar. "What the hell you doing? Getting my little girl killed?"

She grabbed a fistful of his braided beard, gave it a yank. He released her collar.

"I'm making sure he doesn't take the money without giving us Annie," she said.

He rubbed his chin, glaring at her. "Where's the drop?"

She gave him the address, then looked it up on the map app on the phone. "It's in the Ironwood Barrio. Probably an abandoned building."

He pointed a finger at her. "You better not have messed this up, you fucking dyke. Anything happens to my Annie, you die, ya hear me?"

She stood up and got in his face. "Maybe if you weren't dealing crystal, nobody woulda took Annie in the first place."

His left eye twitched, but he said nothing.

Shea marched outside and stood on the front steps staring out at the night, bristling with rage. She kicked one of the wooden columns and left a dent with the toe of her boot.

The door opened and she wheeled around, fists raised.

Monster held up his hands in surrender. "Easy, kiddo. It's me."

Shea grunted as she paced along the porch.

"Don't pay him no mind, Shea. He's worried bout his little girl is all."

"I think I may have got her killed."

Monster sighed. "You done what you thought was right."

A chill ran down her spine, coupled with a sense of déjà vu. "You said that to me before."

"Did I?" Monster crinkled his forehead, then nodded. "When was that?"

"After Ralph's trial. Why'd you say that to me?" A growing sense of dread gripped her.

"Yeah, I remember now. Why you wanna stir up old hurts?"

"Please, Monster. Tell me the truth."

"It was after you testified your old man acted in self-defense."

Shea shook her head. "No, that was Wendy. I would never."

"Kiddo, you're a little confused. Wendy never testified. She wasn't in the room when your Daddy . . ."

Shea's stomach twisted into a tight, painful knot. "Why would I do that? It makes no sense."

"Sweetie, you were scared. That shyster lawyer your old man hired bamboozled you, got your head all twisted round. Said you and your sister'd end up in the system, away from the club with no one to take care of you."

"No! It can't be true. Please, tell me it isn't true." As she said it, the memory of the lawyer's words cut like a knife in her gut. "How could I have forgotten that?"

"Hell, I ain't no shrink. But you sure was tore up when you realized what you done." He put his arm around her. "That's when you ran away."

Shame wrapped around her throat. Her lungs spasmed, and she struggled for air.

"Relax, darlin'. It's all okay. The jury saw you for what you were."

She took a deep breath. "A liar?"

"Naw, a scared little girl who witnessed something ain't nobody oughta see. Ralph still got what was coming to him."

She remembered her mother's bloody face lying on the kitchen floor. "I'm a horrible person."

"Don't you be thinking that. You're a good kid living in a not-so-good world."

When she regained her composure, she asked, "Whatever happened to that lawyer?"

"Ended up getting shot by one of his clients. Must not have been satisfied with the service."

"Guess not."

"Everything'll be all right, kid." Monster pulled a card from his wallet. "Here's my number. Call me if you ever need anything. Or even if you don't. I'd like to stay in touch."

"Vernon Mueller, handyman? Huh, all this time, I never knew your real name."

"Yeah, well, putting 'Monster' on a business card kinda scares off customers."

"I reckon it would." She tucked the card into her wallet.

Mackey appeared in the doorway. "Yo, Monster, we got a meeting."

## 33

SHEA FOLLOWED Monster and Mackey inside to a room down the hallway. A long Formica table was surrounded by an assortment of mismatched chairs. Mackey stepped in front of her, barring her entry. "Sorry, only patched members."

"Is this about the drop?"

Hunter rose from his seat at the head of the table and strutted over to her. "This is a club meeting. You ain't welcome."

"We'll be out in a bit, kiddo." Monster put a hand on her shoulder. "Let us men talk for a bit."

Shea glared at Hunter. "You best not put Annie at more risk."

He tilted his head. "What kind of father you think I am?"

"You want me to answer that?"

He shoved her into the hallway and slammed the door in her face.

Shea slunk back to the laundry room, pulled her clothes out of the dryer, and slipped out of Goatsy's sweatpants, which she folded and set on the washing machine. Her now-dry clothes provided much-needed warmth.

Back in the main room, she took a seat at the unmanned bar. She considered helping herself to some whiskey, but opted for a cup of coffee instead.

The club's old ladies were still comforting Wendy, though the tone of the conversation had lightened. Wendy had them all enthralled with the tale of their capture and escape from the Jaguars, leaving out the part where she executed the man in the poppy field. The discussion then turned to shopping, manicures, guys with cute asses, and daycare nightmares.

None of it interested Shea in the least. Her left leg bounced on the barstool as she grew restless. She wasn't an old lady to be sequestered while the menfolk formulated their master plans. So far, all of Hunter's schemes had made things worse. At Iron Goddess, she was the decision maker. *Time to take charge,* she told herself.

She crept back to the room where the Thundermen were meeting and pressed her ear to the door. At first she couldn't make out what they were saying, but the conversation grew more lively and heated.

"I don't like this," said Monster, his voice muffled. "What if someone realizes you substituted one of our guys for Shea? Or they find you padded the bundles of cash with newspaper before they give up Annie?"

"We'll all be there and will have the place surrounded," replied Hunter. "If he tries something, we take him out. If he shows up without Annie, we'll force him to tell us where she is. And if she's . . . if she's not okay, he dies."

Shea opened the door. A room full of eyes zeroed in on her. She felt like a juicy steak falling into a pack of wolves. But someone had to look out for Annie. "You're gonna get her killed."

"Get the fuck out." Hunter stood and kicked away his chair, sending it tumbling into the wall.

"Leave it to you boys to turn something simple into a complicated mess. Here's the rules. I go into the house, alone, with the ransom. None of you boys are to be anywhere near the place. If the kidnapper shows up without Annie, he gets no money. He already knows it."

"Ain't no way I'm giving you four million of our money."

"From what I heard, you boys don't have the full four mill."

"Ain't none of your concern. She ain't your daughter."

"What's wrong, Hunter? Ain't Annie worth four million dollars? You getting cheap on rescuing your daughter?"

Hunter charged at Shea with alarming speed, slamming her against the wall, his fist holding her up by her shirt collar. She tried to twist away, but his grip was too strong.

"Listen here, you fucking bitch. You are not in charge. *I* am. So as long as you're in my house, you do as I say." He threw her to the side. She staggered back. Someone's leg swept her feet out from under her. They laughed when she collapsed onto the floor.

Shea scrambled up and flew at him, but strong hands held her back. She wriggled to break free, but it was no use.

"Easy, kid. Let it go." Monster frowned at her. "Come on, I'll walk you out." With a firm grip on her arm, he led her out of the room.

"He's putting her in danger, Monster."

They walked down the hall to the laundry room. Monster shut the door behind them. "She's already in danger. Hunter's doing what needs to be done to control the situation."

"So why not let me make the drop?"

"Darlin', he don't know you. Not sure he can trust you.

Four million dollars, or however much he's got of it, is a lotta damn money."

"What happens when the kidnapper discovers he ain't got the whole ransom?"

"We put in everything we got. It'll have to do."

She looked at him. "You think he can get her back safe?"

"He don't always do things how I think he oughta, but then I ain't sittin' at the head of the table. He's brought us through some mighty tight situations on numerous occasions. I trust him. You busting in don't help things none."

"Look, I'm not saying do everything the kidnapper says, but we gotta be smart about this. Soon as he sees it's not me making the drop, he's gonna know something's up."

"I hear ya, but it ain't your call and it ain't mine. Hunter's in charge here."

"Fine." Her jaw clenched. *Like talking to a brick wall,* she thought.

"All right then. You hang out with the old ladies at the bar. The guys'll have a quick vote and then we'll all get this thing done."

≈

FIFTEEN MINUTES LATER, Hunter marched past her carrying the bags of money. A dozen Thundermen followed, armed with shotguns, rifles, pistols, and boxes of ammunition. Monster didn't glance at her when he walked past.

"Where y'all going?" Shea asked Monster. He didn't acknowledge her.

Shea trailed them out the front door to the parking lot, with Wendy right behind her. Despite the late hour the air had warmed again, now with the added humidity from the monsoon.

As Monster threw a leg over his bike, Shea grabbed his arm. "What about me?"

He cupped her chin. "Just wait here, kiddo. We'll be back with Annie soon enough."

Wendy appeared beside her. "Take me with you, Papa. Please, I gotta see my daughter."

"This ain't no situation for a couple o' girls. It's likely to get dangerous. Don't want you two getting into trouble."

"Don't treat me like a child, Monster," said Shea. "I'm the one the kidnapper's expecting, not any of y'all. I can take care of myself."

"Papa, you can't leave me behind. She's my daughter." Wendy stepped on the rear footpeg and pulled herself onto the passenger seat.

Monster twisted toward her, wrapped a meaty arm around her middle, and swung her back onto the blacktop. "Stay here. I mean it." He started his bike and drove off. One by one the Thundermen roared off into the night, leaving a handful of Harleys and cars in the lot. Shea kicked the dirt, hating that she was once again stranded.

"C'mon." Wendy pulled her back inside and they sat at an empty table. "Might as well wait in here. It's muggy out."

"I'm not waiting around." Shea pulled out the phone. "Yo, T, I could use a ride."

"You're not still stranded in the middle of nowhere, are you? It's damn near ten o'clock." He sounded concerned.

"I'm at the Confederate Thunder clubhouse. Hunter picked us up a few hours ago. But now they drove off to make the ransom drop without me. They're gonna screw this thing up and get Annie killed. I can't let them do that."

"You want me to pick you up from the KKK Honeycomb Hideout? Did you forget I'm black?"

"There ain't no one here but a couple of prospects. I can stand outside the gate and wait for you."

"And take you where? To the ransom drop?"

"Yeah."

"Where all them cracker bikers are."

"Well . . ."

"Tell me one thing: are they armed?"

"Yeah." She understood his reluctance.

"Shea, I love you like a sister from another mister, but ain't no way in hell I'm driving my black ass to someplace surrounded by racist outlaw bikers armed to the teeth, looking for someone to kill."

"T, if I don't make the drop, the kidnapper will kill Annie. I need you, man."

"If you need me to pick you up, I will. But only to bring you back to my place. Jessica's already here."

"No, that's all right. Tell her I love her. I gotta focus on saving Annie right now."

"Stay safe, Shea."

"I'll do my best."

Wendy plopped a bottle of Jack and two glass tumblers on the table. "On the house."

"No, thanks." Shea pushed away her glass.

Wendy reached into her pocket and pulled out an amber pill bottle. "Here's something to help with your leg."

Shea picked it up. "Vicodin? This from your guy Dopey?"

"Yeah. He's all out of Oxy at the moment."

Her tumble down the wash had left her aching all over. A couple of these would really help. She grimaced and tossed it back at her sister. "No, thanks. I need to be able to concentrate."

Wendy tucked the bottle back into her pocket. "Suit yourself. More for me." She popped two into her mouth and chased them down with a long draft of whiskey.

Shea stared at Oscar's phone, flipping through his

contacts and recently called numbers. All were unfamiliar names and numbers except one with the caller ID of Foster. Over the past few days, Oscar had made and received numerous calls from that number. Was Oscar working with Willie?

Shea showed the phone to Wendy. "Oscar's been talking with Willie at the Sheriff's Department."

"Oscar's a rat?"

"That, or maybe the two of them got something else going on. I got a lead that one of the guys fencing my stolen motorcycles is a Jaguar. The other guy looked like a cop."

"You think Willie broke into your shop?"

"I don't know. I've known the guy since forever. As cops go, he's all right. But how else do you explain the warrant for my arrest?"

"You think he kidnapped Annie, too?"

Shea shook her head. "I ain't sure what to think. I do know I can't just sit here."

"What can you do? My car's wrecked, and your bike's at your place."

Shea glanced at the prospect sat at the bar, reading an issue of *Guns & Ammo* magazine. "I got an idea." Shea walked outside, Wendy tailing her.

"What're you gonna do?"

In the gravel lot, under the dim light of a streetlight, a Dodge Challenger sat parked next to a few remaining bikes. Shea crossed her fingers hoping for a break. She pulled on the Challenger's door handle, hoping to find it unlocked. It wasn't. Without a slim jim or something to pop the lock, her only other option was to break the window, which would attract attention.

She checked out each bike until she found what she was looking for. "Hallelujah. Someone left his key in the

Iron Goddess 233

ignition. Must've figured it was safe enough sitting here at the Church."

Wendy shook her head, a worried expression on her face. "You steal a bike, they'll crucify you."

Shea looked her sister in the eye. "You trust your old man to bring Annie back alive?"

Wendy stared at the ground. "No."

"Well?"

"Before we do this there's something you oughta know."

"You already admitted you stole my prescription. I forgive you, all right?"

"No, not that. Something else."

"What?"

Wendy looked her sister in the eye. "This is not how I planned for this to go."

"What are you talking about?"

"Honestly?"

"No, I want you to lie to me. Of course honestly." Shea glared at Wendy, feeling her blood pressure rise.

"I needed help getting away from Hunter."

"What kind of help?"

"Money, mostly. I don't make shit at my job. Hunter controls the bank accounts. So Eduardo came up with a plan."

"Eduardo? Margaret's brother?"

"Uh-huh."

"You made a plan with a member of the Jaguars? Are you insane?"

"He was supposed to pick me and Annie up from Margaret's after I got off work. He was gonna call Hunter and say he kidnapped us and was demanding a ransom. Not a lot. Just a few grand. Enough to get me started somewhere else."

"I don't believe this. So what the hell happened?"

"I don't know. Eduardo don't know neither. I'm thinking he might have mentioned our plan to his cousin Oscar."

"Oscar Reyes, the man that tortured you? The man that I killed? Geez, Wendy, when you fuck up, you really do it big time. Couldn't ya have just gone to a women's shelter?"

"Look, I'm sorry, all right? I never meant for any of this to happen."

"Yeah, well, it happened. And now I gotta risk my ass again to keep your old man from fucking things up more."

Shea threw a leg over the bike, trying to ignore the mixture of anger and frustration building in her mind. She needed to focus on the task at hand.

She familiarized herself with the controls of the bike. She was never a fan of Harleys, despite their popularity. They were overpriced, underpowered, and always in the shop. But being stranded as she was, she couldn't afford to be picky. She pulled on the half helmet the prospect had left dangling from the handlebars and started the engine. She had to admit the trademarked Harley rumble was a sexy sound.

Wendy climbed on behind her.

"What the hell you doing?" yelled Shea over the roar of the engine.

"If you're going, I'm going."

"How am I supposed to bring back Annie if you're riding bitch?"

"We'll figure it out. Just drive."

Shea wanted to argue, but it would have been pointless. What could she say to Wendy that the Thundermen hadn't said to her? She took off the helmet and handed it to Wendy. "Put this on."

## 34

As SHEA CRUISED through the parking lot, one of the prospects charged out of the building and tried to block her way. "Where the hell you going with my bike?"

She swerved around him and pinned the throttle down the hill toward the perimeter fence. The Harley felt sluggish compared to her Iron Goddess bikes.

A Thunderman armed with an AR-15 stood next to the closed gate, talking on his cellphone. He stepped into the middle of the driveway and raised the rifle. "Stop the bike!"

She considered running the gate, but it was too risky on a bike. Frustrated, Shea screeched to a halt inches from the guard, her mind racing.

The guard walked alongside the bike, lowered his rifle, and shined a flashlight in Shea's face. "What the hell you doing?"

"Wendy OD'd. I gotta get her to the hospital."

The guard shined the light at Wendy. She raised her head. "Please, Hooch," she said in her most pitiful voice. "I don't feel so good."

"You can't take her to the hospital on the back of a bike.

She could fall off," said Hooch. "Let me have Razor bring a car around."

"We ain't got time. She's having trouble breathing. Open the damned gate," said Shea through gritted teeth.

Hooch glanced up the hill at the Church, then back at Shea. "Oh all right, but I better not get in no trouble for this." He unlatched the gate and rolled it open.

Shea roared through the gears driving south and caught the highway to Ironwood. Wendy held on tightly to Shea's battered chest, making it hard to breathe. Not that Shea blamed her. The bike didn't have a sissy bar to act as a backrest. One hard bump and Wendy could go flying off the back.

When they reached the outskirts of Ironwood, traffic grew heavy. Central Arizona University students, having arrived from all over the country for the upcoming semester, were enjoying a late Saturday night on the town. Cars with out-of-state license plates clogged Ironwood's Downtown Square. Music poured out of bars, restaurants, and open car windows on Prospector Avenue, the square's main drag. Shea crept along, anxious to get past the rolling roadblock. The aromas of burgers, fried foods, and ethnic cuisine hung thick in the air, tantalizing her stomach.

"We gonna make it in time?" asked Wendy.

The digital clock on the motorcycle's dash read 11:47 P.M. "Not at this rate. Hold on."

Shea swerved, splitting the narrow southbound lanes. Horns blared while she whizzed between the cars, accelerating through an intersection as the light turned red.

Past the square, traffic thinned out. They pressed on, following the directions to Ironwood's south-side barrio, the less affluent side of the city. The recession had left a lot of businesses and homes in the barrio empty, either reclaimed by banks or simply abandoned. Streets were dark and littered with trash from the day's monsoon.

Shea's pulse quickened. The barrio was the heart of Jaguar territory. Riding a loud, throaty Harley with the Johnny Reb painted on the tank made Shea feel like a sitting duck every time she stopped at a light.

The directions led them to a dilapidated house on Washington Street. Shea pulled up to the house and killed the engine. There wasn't a vehicle anywhere on the block. Most of the streetlights were out.

"Where is everybody?" Wendy asked.

"Something's wrong." Shea drew her Glock and stepped off the bike. "Let's go inside."

"What if the kidnapper shows up? We ain't got the ransom."

"We'll have to wing it. I don't like hanging out here exposed."

As they walked up the house's broken driveway, something white on the concrete walkway by the door caught her attention. Shea used Oscar's phone for a flashlight and picked up an envelope with the word *Che* written on the outside. It was empty.

"The kidnapper must have changed the drop location." Shea balled up the envelope and tossed it on the ground. "We got no clue where we're supposed to be. Fucking Hunter!" She pounded the front door a few times.

"I got an idea." Wendy reached out her hand. "Give me the phone."

"Why? There ain't no message or anything."

"Gimme the damn phone, Shea."

Shea complied. Wendy tapped away at the screen.

"What are you doing?" Shea looked over her shoulder.

"A few months ago, I put an app on Hunter's phone. It links to his GPS and tells me where he is. If I can load the tracking app onto this phone, I can log in and get his location."

"You're spying on your old man?" Shea smirked. *Girl had gumption after all.*

"I got tired of not knowing where he was."

"Didn't he wonder about the strange app on his phone?"

"Naw, the app doesn't show up on his screen." Wendy continued typing on the phone. "There! Found him."

A map revealed Hunter was four blocks east and one block south.

"Way to go." Shea rubbed the top of Wendy's helmet. "Let's go join the party."

They cruised along past dark houses and parked a couple of streets from where the app said Hunter was. Shea drew her Glock. Wendy set the helmet on the bike's seat and turned on the phone's flashlight app.

"Turn it off," snapped Shea. "They'll see it."

"You had yours on earlier."

"Just do what I tell ya for once."

"How we supposed to see where we're going?"

"Follow me."

The moonlight provided enough light for Shea to navigate between two houses. When they came to a chain-link fence, Wendy started to climb.

Shea grabbed the back of Wendy's shirt. "Hold up. How you know there ain't a dog in there?" The thought gave Shea a prickling sensation in her scarred facial muscles.

"Does it look like anyone lives on this street?"

Shadows in the fenced-off yard shifted back and forth, swallowing up the moonlight. Tall weeds surrounded an in-ground pool.

*Was something moving in there among the weeds or was it*

*the wind?* Her hand trembled while it gripped the wire fence. "All right. Let's go."

Shea followed Wendy over the fence and into the yard's chest-high weeds. If anything lurked in there, it'd be on them before they knew to run.

Movement near the pool caught Shea's eye. She drew the Glock and zeroed in on a doglike shape. It raised its head, its eyes reflecting like glowing coals. Shea fired a shot. The creature retreated into the brush and scaled the fence in a single bound.

"Geez, Shea, it's just a fucking coyote."

Shea pushed back against the wave of panic that gripped her chest. "Sorry."

"And you think *I'm* a screwup."

On the other side, a six-foot-high cement block wall ran the length of the yard.

Wendy slapped the wall. "Now what?"

"Up and over." Channeling her fear into motion, Shea leapt up and got an elbow over the top. She threw a leg up, which sent lightning bolts of pain as the road rash rubbed the inside of her pants. She gritted her teeth and forced herself into sitting position atop the wall. From her vantage point, she had a good view of the next street, where the Thundermen's bikes were parked.

"How'd you do that?"

Shea chuckled. "Ten years of wrestling motorcycle engines—that and a strong desire not to be in that yard anymore. Gimme your hand. I'll pull you up."

On the other side of the wall, they crept past the parked motorcycles. The engines *tink-tinked* as they cooled. Shea walked along a row of bushes beside a house on the other side of the street. The ratcheting action of several guns being cocked brought them to a halt. Shea raised her hands.

"Who the hell are you?" asked a voice she recognized as Hunter's.

"It's me," said Wendy. "And Shea."

"Aw fuck, what the hell are y'all doing here? I told ya to stay at the Church."

"I know how much fun you boys have playing with each other," Shea said. "But the situation needed a little girl power."

"Goddammit, you really know how to piss me off, don't ya? I'm guessing that gunshot was you."

"Deal with it, asshole. Where's the new drop point and where's the money?"

He pointed to a house on the next street over. "The house over there with the lights on. I got a guy inside with the money."

Shea started to stroll toward the house. Hunter grabbed her and pulled her back. "Where the hell you think you're going, bitch?"

"The kidnapper told me to make the drop."

"Forget it. My guy's already in place. We wait."

"Hey, Hunter . . ." A voice squawked on a walkie-talkie Hunter had on him.

"Yeah, Goatsy?"

"You should see this. Someone put metal plating along all the walls. Even the front door's reinforced. This place is like a fucking bunker."

"Shit, it's a setup. Get outta there."

"What about the money?" asked Goatsy.

"Bring the goddamn money."

A car turned the corner onto the street and stopped in front of the drop house. The Cortes County Sheriff's logo glimmered in the moonlight.

"Hold up, Goatsy. A cop just pulled up in front of the house."

"Roger that."

The interior light in the police cruiser lit up. Shea couldn't make out the driver's face. The door opened and a man in a suit climbed out of the driver's seat. The profile revealed the cop was Willie. Shea and the others ducked down further into the shadows, while Willie scanned the area. He pulled a large duffel bag from the backseat, drew his sidearm, and walked into the drop house.

"Holy shit," said Shea. "What the hell's Willie doing here?"

"Did you call the fucking cops?" Hunter glared at Shea in the dim light.

"Not me. Maybe he's working with the kidnapper." *And maybe he's also the one fencing the Pink Trinket bikes,* she thought.

"You think Annie's in the bag he's carrying?" Wendy's voice trembled.

"Too small," said Hunter. "If she's here, she's probably in the car."

"Looked like someone in the front passenger seat before the inside light went out, but Willie blocked my view." Shea's body tensed, as if she were watching the timer of a bomb count down the last few seconds. "What do we do now?"

"Shut your trap, that's what. Whatever happens don't nobody shoot the damn car, in case Annie's in there," said Hunter.

The lights inside the house went dark. A gun fired.

"What the hell?" Shea chambered a round on the Glock.

"Goatsy, what's happening?" asked Hunter into the walkie-talkie.

"I should have known you bikers would screw things up."

"It's Sergeant Willie Foster," muttered Shea.

"Where the hell's my daughter, you fucking pig?" asked Hunter.

"She's nearby and in much better shape than your boy in here. I'm afraid he isn't going to make it."

Jimbo, the bartender from the Church, stood up.

"Get back down," Hunter whisper-shouted.

"Like hell. That's my brother in there." Jimbo hustled toward the house and reached the edge of the driveway when another gunshot sounded. Jimbo fell, screaming.

The air exploded with sound as the Thundermen returned fire. Muzzle flashes flickered like a strobe light inside the house.

Shea pushed Wendy to the ground. For a solid minute, the earth shook with the thunder of open warfare. Shea's ears were ringing when it stopped. The odor of spent gunpowder made her nose twitch.

"Gordo, go check it out." Hunter's voice sounded dull and distant.

A Thunderman with a big head of thick, curly hair sprinted behind the cruiser. No response from inside the house. When he stepped away from the car, a shot from the house dropped him. Another volley of bullets rang out from both sides. The car's two front windows shattered.

Shea caught a glimpse of movement inside the front seat of the police cruiser.

*Annie,* she thought. It had to be.

## 35

SHOTS CONTINUED to ring out while Thundermen converged on the house, ducking behind planters, telephone poles, and anything else that would serve as cover. Wendy and Shea remained on the ground behind a bush.

"I think I see Annie in the car." Shea said. "You stay here. I'll go get her."

"She's my daughter. I'm coming with you."

A gunshot ricocheted off a rock a foot from Wendy's head. She shrank back, covering her head with her arms.

"Just stay here. Don't need you getting your head blown off by this fucking cop."

With her Glock in hand, Shea sprinted to the cruiser and crouched down with her back against the rear door. "Annie? You in there? It's your Aunt Shea."

Shea heard a muffled moan, followed by a thump.

Shea took a breath, leaned over the windowsill, and peeked inside. A shot rang out from the house. She ducked down too quickly to make out any detail in the dark, but someone was hunkered down in the front seat. She hoped it was Annie and that she was alive.

Shea pulled on the handle of the front door and found it unlocked. She threw the door open wide and the interior dome light went on. When she looked inside, a beefy Latino rose up from the passenger seat and pounced on her chest like a cougar, knocking the Glock from her hand.

"¡*Puta!* You shoulda followed my rules," he growled in a familiar accented voice as he pinned her to the pavement. A large knife in his hand flashed in the moonlight.

Shea grabbed his arms, desperate to keep the knife from plunging into her chest. Inch by inch, the tip of the blade pushed closer. The inked jaguar on his arm looked hungry for her blood. She pushed with the last of her strength, but couldn't stop the blade from creeping toward her. "Nooooo . . ."

The kidnapper's body shuddered when two gunshots thundered a few feet away. The knife clattered to the ground. He gripped his chest, face tight with anguish, and fell onto his side. Shea raised herself up on her elbows. Wendy knelt in front of her holding the Glock.

"Oh thank God," said Shea.

"You okay?"

Shea sat up and took the gun from her. "I thought I told you to wait across the street."

"You think I should've let him kill you?"

"No. Thanks for that."

"Was it him? Was he the one who took Annie?"

"Yeah, it was him."

Shea pulled on the back door handle. It was locked. She stuck her head up to look into the backseat. The back windows exploded in a shower of tempered glass and she ducked back down, gasping for breath. She fired a couple of shots at the house, then rose up again and glanced into the backseat. It was empty. "Fuck."

"What's wrong?" asked Wendy.

"She's not in there."

"I thought you told him to bring Annie."

"Guess he doesn't follow directions either."

"Where can she be? Oh God, you don't think they . . ."

"Don't say it. I'm sure she's alive. Just gotta figure this out." The ringing in her ears and the hammering of her heart made it hard to concentrate. "Wait."

Shea pressed her hand flat against the car's rear fender and felt a pounding. "Someone's in the trunk."

"Annie?" Wendy's eyes grew wide and hopeful.

Shea crouched behind the rear of the vehicle. Occasionally a bullet thunked into the car. She wondered how bulletproof the cruiser was until a round ripped through the back door inches from her face, leaving a hole the size of a grapefruit in the fender. "Fuck!"

She fought the urge to run for better cover. "Annie? Is that you? Are you in the trunk?" Shea yelled.

A muffled cry, followed by a couple of thuds—definitely in the trunk. It had to be her. Staying low, Shea slunk into the cruiser, looking for a trunk release.

A gunshot shattered the windshield. She lay pressed against the seat, jaw clenched, waiting for the shot that would kill her. After a moment of silence, she turned and spotted the release. She pulled it, but nothing happened. "Shit."

"What's going on?" Wendy whispered.

"Trunk won't open."

"Are the keys in there?"

Shea looked up at the steering column. "Yeah. They're in the ignition."

"Car might need to be on for the trunk release to work."

Shea rolled her eyes, kicking herself for not realizing the obvious. "We'll have to move fast. You ready?"

"Just do it already."

Police sirens wailed in the distance. Either Willie had called for backup or someone had called 911 to report gunfire.

Shea turned the key. Three shots from the house were followed by a volley of gunfire from the Thundermen. She pulled the release lever and was rewarded with a satisfying thunk of the trunk lid popping up. She scrambled out of the cruiser, past Wendy and toward the outside of the trunk. *It's now or never.*

Shea took a deep breath, stood up, and fired four rounds into the house. Several Thundermen joined her in the volley. While they continued to fire, she ducked under the trunk lid. Inside lay a young girl with short, curly dark hair, wrapped with a large bandage on one side of her head. Duct tape covered her mouth and bound her hands and feet. Shea lifted her out of the trunk and pulled her back behind the car.

She drew her knife and cut the duct tape from Annie's hands and feet. The girl screamed when Shea ripped the tape off her mouth. "Mommy!"

Wendy wrapped her arms around Annie, both of them sobbing.

"I don't mean to cut short your reunion, but we gotta get outta here."

Wendy wiped her eyes and nodded. "I'm just so happy."

"Okay, when I say go, run for cover behind the building across the street. Got it?"

"Why don't we take the police car?"

"You smell that? Gasoline. Motherfucker musta hit the tank. Our best bet is to run for it. When I say go, you two run back the way we came while I provide cover. You ready?"

Wendy nodded, clinging to Annie.

"Go!" Shea stood up again, firing another four rounds into the house, then turned to follow them.

Motorcycles rumbled in the distance as they ran, while police cruisers came speeding down the street. They had nearly made it to the house across the street when another shot rang out. Wendy fell to the ground.

"Get up!" Shea pulled at her sister's limp body. "We're almost there."

Wendy didn't move. Annie grabbed at her. "Mommy! Please, Mommy, get up."

The ground around Wendy's head was wet with a dark liquid. Shea turned her over and half her face was missing. A blood-curdling scream erupted from Annie. "No! Mommy!"

Shea's throat filled with bile as grief, anger, and confusion overwhelmed her. *This can't be happening. Not after all of this.* Annie clung to her mother, both of them covered in blood. Shea gasped for air, wrestling with her emotions. *Got to save Annie.*

Shea lifted Annie up. "You gotta let her go!"

"No! Mommy!" She clung to Wendy's hand.

Shea shared Annie's reluctance to leave. She shouldn't abandon her sister's body on the street in that run-down neighborhood. No one should have to suffer that indignity. But the street was filling up with sheriff's deputies, and Willie had a warrant out for her arrest.

Shea wrapped her arm around Annie's middle and pulled her away screaming from her mother.

## 36

SHERIFF'S DEPUTIES emerged from a growing blockade of police cruisers. With weapons drawn, they chased after Shea and the girl. "Stop! Police!"

"C'mon or they'll catch us."

Annie stopped resisting and ran with her. Shea led them down a gravel-strewn alley between houses, past garbage cans and endless piles of junk. They emerged onto the next street and cut across several yards, keeping to the shadows. Shea pulled Annie behind a line of juniper shrubs that concealed their presence, yet offered a decent view of the street.

Three uniformed deputies emerged from the alley, scanning the area with guns and flashlights raised. Annie began to sob. Shea wrapped an arm around the girl. "Shhh. Can't let 'em hear us." Annie grew quiet, but trembled in Shea's embrace.

For fifteen tense minutes, the deputies searched the area, knocking on doors, looking behind bushes, and peering underneath cars. Deputy Aguilar sauntered into the yard where they were hiding. His flashlight swung back and forth, exploring the dark corners of the house's porch, then into the row of shrubs. With her heart thundering in her chest, Shea shrunk back further, sheltering her niece with her body. His boots crunched on the sandy soil a few feet away. Shea braced herself, ready to fight.

"Aguilar!" someone shouted from a few houses down. "Over here."

Aguilar turned away from them and hustled down the street toward his colleague.

When the deputies were out of sight, Shea guided Annie through another alley, avoiding the fenced yard, to where the borrowed Harley sat. Annie stared at the bike, shivering despite the warm, humid night. "What're ya gonna do to me?"

"Do to you? Oh, sweetie, I'm your Aunt Shea." She slipped the Windbreaker on Annie and zipped it up, the sleeves dangling several inches past her fingertips. The bandage over Annie's right ear smelled rank with infection. She needed medical attention.

"You're Aunt Shea?" Annie's half-lidded eyes met Shea's for the first time. The girl had Hunter's chestnut hair and her mother's eyes. My *mother's eyes,* thought Shea.

"Yes." Shea struggled for something more to say. Sorrow tightened her throat. "I'm ... I'm so sorry about your mom."

Annie hugged her, sobbing. "I want my Mommy."

"I know, kiddo. Me, too." Shea wanted to make it all okay, but she didn't know how. She wasn't a parent. She was barely an aunt.

A helicopter hovered nearby, scanning the ground with its searchlight. The *chup-chup-chup* of its rotor blades grew louder.

"We gotta get you out of here. You think you can ride on the back?"

Annie nodded. "I used to ride with my dad."

Shea put the helmet on Annie's head, careful not cinch the strap so tight it pushed on Annie's wounded ear. She threw a leg over the bike. "Put your left foot on the peg, then grab hold of my arm." Shea helped lift her onto the passenger seat.

Annie wrapped her arms around Shea's middle.

"Hold on."

Shea started the bike and cruised up the street slowly, puttering north. There was no sign of life anywhere. No cars, no pedestrians, no lights in the houses. Not even a stray dog or cat. At a T-intersection, she turned left toward the downtown area. A police car parked on the side of the road sprung to life, flashers and sirens going. *Was the deputy behind her working with the kidnappers?* She couldn't take the chance.

With the blue lights flashing in her mirrors, Shea pinned the throttle. Annie's arms tightened around her. Shea hoped the girl could hold on.

At the next intersection, Shea whipped right onto a main road, sending up a cascade of sparks as the footpegs scraped the pavement, then gunned the motor to put some distance between herself and the law.

They emerged from the desolate barrio back into the hustle and bustle of Prospector Avenue's downtown bar scene. The police cruiser on her tail had become three.

In a car, she'd be screwed, but on the bike, she could use the traffic to her advantage. She squeezed between two lines of cars, leaving the deputies stuck behind. A few inebriated college boys cheered her on from the sidewalk.

A block later, she turned off the main drag and parked the bike in a small honor pay lot. Sirens wailed in the distance, but there was no sign of flashing lights anywhere. Shea climbed off the bike, leaving Annie on the passenger seat. She put a hand to the girl's forehead. It was warm. "You're burning up. We gotta get you to a doctor."

"Mama always takes me to Dopey. He's nice," said Annie in a lifeless voice.

"I'm not sure Dopey's gonna be enough, sweetie."

Shea pulled out Oscar's phone and dialed.

"Hello?" Terrance sounded groggy. No surprise, considering it was well past midnight.

"Dude, I'm sorry to call you, but I'm in trouble."

"Again?"

"Wendy's dead. But I've got Annie with me. You still got her ear on ice?"

"Yeah."

"Meet me at Cortes General ER. And keep an eye out for cops."

"Cops? Why?"

"Willie's involved in the kidnapping. I don't know who to trust at this point."

"You've got to be kidding."

"Wish I were, T. This whole thing is fucked up."

"Where are you?"

"Downtown Ironwood. I should be at the hospital in about thirty minutes."

"All right. I'll meet you in the ER."

"Thanks, man. I'm turning off this phone in case the cops are tracking it. If I don't see you when I get to the ER, I'll give you a call."

As she hung up, an alert sounded on the phone. When she clicked the icon, an AMBER Alert appeared asking people to be on the lookout for Annie. "Great."

Shea turned off the phone. "Annie, you think you can hold on a little longer?"

"I'll try." Her face glistened with fever. She looked

barely conscious. A sharp turn on the bike could pitch her off.

Shea considered having the girl sit in front of her, but that would make driving nearly impossible. "I have an idea."

Shea climbed back onto the bike. "Okay, now wrap your arms around me."

Annie's arms only reached two-thirds of the way around. The overlong sleeves of the adult-sized windbreaker dangled and fluttered in the slight breeze. Shea tied the sleeves in a knot around her own waist. "Don't slip out of this jacket."

Shea started the engine and crept along side streets to avoid traffic until she got to Sycamore Highway leading south to the hospital. Then she opened up the throttle.

At ninety miles an hour, the wind made Shea's eyes water as she raced along the moonlit landscape. Her heart ached for her sister. *Why did I bring her along? Why couldn't I protect her? How could I leave her in middle of the fucking barrio?* Maybe it was karma, some sort of twisted divine punishment for killing Oscar. Or for defending Ralph so many years earlier. *What a fuckup I am!*

She screamed into the wind until her lungs ached and her body shook from sorrow. When she was cried out, she reached back and felt Annie's arm. She had to make this right, even if it meant going back to prison and losing everything she'd worked for.

∼

A HALF HOUR LATER, the bike squealed to a stop in front of the ER entrance. "Annie? You still with me?"

She didn't respond.

"Annie?" Shea reached back and shook her. "Annie, wake up."

The girl slumped to the side. Only the tied windbreaker sleeves kept her from falling to the pavement. Shea honked the bike's horn. Two Cortes County EMTs in navy blue T-shirts rushed through the automatic sliding doors. Terrance ran behind them carrying a small cooler.

"You need some help?" asked one of the EMTs, a young Hispanic man whose name, L. Cruz, was stitched on the shirt. Cruz grabbed Annie from the left, while his partner, a woman with V. Liu stitched on her shirt, held her up from the other side.

"Her ear's been cut off and she's running a fever." Shea untied the windbreaker's sleeves.

"I got her. Cruz, grab a gurney." Liu lifted her off the bike. Cruz rushed inside.

"I have the severed ear in here." Terrance held up the cooler.

Cruz returned a moment later with a gurney. They laid Annie on it, took the cooler from Terrance, and rushed her inside. Shea pulled the motorcycle into a nearby parking space and followed Terrance past the waiting area to a small examination room with a sliding glass door. A nurse in cornflower-blue scrubs attached EKG leads across Annie's chest, then swiped a thermometer across her forehead and took her blood pressure.

A nurse with coffee-colored skin and a seventies-style afro opened up a laptop near Shea. "Hi, I'm Emma, one of the RNs. Are you the mother?"

"I'm her aunt." Shea wiped the tears from her face.

"Where's her mother?"

Shea's chest tightened as she recalled the image of Wendy's shattered face.

"Out of town," said Terrance when Shea didn't respond.

"And her father?"

"Not sure. They recently separated," Shea said, struggling with her emotions

"Will you give consent to treat?" asked Emma.

"Yeah."

"The child's name?"

"Annie Stev—" Shea shook her head to ward off the fatigue. "Wittmann. Annie Wittmann."

"Age?"

"Eight."

Emma typed in the information into the laptop. "Birthdate November 14?"

"I guess so. How'd you know?"

"She's already in our system. Can you tell me what happened?"

"She was kidnapped a few days ago. We rescued her, but the kidnapper cut off her ear and sent it to us. We've kept it on ice."

Emma frowned and stopped typing. "Have you notified the police?"

"Yeah," said Shea. "They were there when we rescued her." Technically true, but she opted not to elaborate.

"Temp's 105.3 degrees," said the other nurse. "BP 80 over 50. Heart rate 130."

"Will you be able to save her ear?" Shea asked.

"We'll certainly try. We'll have to stabilize her first." Emma peeked under the bandage on Annie's ear. Her nose scrunched. "Her wound is infected. We need to get the doctor in here." She rushed out of the room while the tech set up an IV.

Emma returned a moment later with Dr. Sossaman. The doctor did a double take when she saw Shea. "You're in here again?"

"My niece, Annie."

Sossaman inspected the wound, lifted each of Annie's eyelids, and shined a penlight in them. "She's in shock."

An alarm on the vitals monitor began beeping. Dr. Sossaman turned to Shea and Terrance. "You two will need to step out of the room while we try to get her stabilized." The doctor made requests for medications from the nurses.

Terrance opened the room's sliding glass door for Shea. They stepped into the hallway, letting it close behind them.

"What the hell happened?" Terrance put an arm over Shea's shoulder as they sat down in a couple of chairs against the wall.

"Borrowed a bike from one of the Thunders' prospects. By the time we arrived, Hunter had sent one of their guys into the drop house in my place. Then Willie pulled up and went inside."

"Willie? What was *he* doing there?"

"He's in on it. Maybe the break-in at Iron Goddess, too. The guy who called with the ransom demand was sitting in Willie's police cruiser, probably keeping an eye on Annie."

"Unbelievable."

"Everything went to hell. Bullets were flying in all directions. Wendy and I found Annie in the trunk of Willie's cruiser, but when we tried to make a run for it, someone shot Wendy in the head." Shea pushed back against another wave of sorrow while her eyes watered.

"Shea, I'm so sorry."

"Suddenly the whole place was crawling with cops."

Movement out of the corner of her eye caught Shea's attention. Detectives Rios and Edelman approached the nurse's station at the other end of the hall. A tech pointed at Shea and Terrance. The detectives walked toward them.

"Shea Stevens, we need to talk to you," said Rios.

"Stall them." Shea said before bolting down the corridor.

## 37

SHEA DASHED toward the main part of the hospital, making random turns at hallway intersections to throw off her pursuers. In the quiet, early morning hours, the pounding of her boots echoed down the empty corridors. *Gotta get these things off!*

She ducked into a single-stall restroom, frantically kicked off her boots, and tucked them under her arms. A peek out the door revealed no one in sight, but distant voices suggested someone was coming. Leaving the vent fan and light on, she engaged the lock, shut the door from the outside, and took off in her stocking feet, hoping they'd think she was holed up inside.

The corridor emptied into the elevator bay, where all three elevators sat open for the night. Shea reached into one and slapped the sixth- and seventh-floor buttons, then ducked out before the doors closed. A sign led to a nearby stairwell, where she dashed up the stairs, gasping for air.

At the third floor, she glanced down the corridor. No sign of cops. No voices or the *clap-clap-clap* of leather soles on linoleum. She pulled out Oscar's phone and sent a text to Terrance: *I see you, Derek.* Would he figure out the code?

After another look down the length of the corridor, she slipped her boots back on and strolled casually to the ICU ward. Without looking up at any of the nurses, she slipped into Derek's dark room and drew the privacy curtain, taking a seat in a chair by the bed.

"God, I wish you'd wake up," she whispered.

Derek cleared his throat and opened one eye. "Huh?"

"You're awake?" For the first time in days, a ray of light split the gloom in her mind.

"Yeah." His voice was weak and raspy. Both eyes opened. "What're you doing here? What time is it?"

"Two or three in the morning. I'm happy to see you conscious for once. I thought we'd lost you."

"Sorry to disappoint." A halfhearted grin played across his face.

"Who did this to you?"

He rubbed his face with his hand, pulling against the pulse oximeter taped to his index finger. "Guy named Reyes."

"Oscar Reyes?"

"Yeah."

"Why would he shoot you?"

He frowned. "I fucked up."

"Whaddya mean? How'd you fuck up?"

The door opened. Shea whipped around, fearing the cops had found her. Terrance stood in the doorway. "Took me a minute to figure out your text. Hey! Look who's awake."

"Derek was just telling me why Oscar Reyes shot him."

A pained expression colored Derek's face. His eyes watered. "I got busted again. Meth. Cop gave me a choice— go back to prison or do him a favor."

"What favor?"

"You gotta understand. I can't go back to prison. My mama—she's on the dialysis. Without me around, she'll die."

Anger eroded her sympathy for him. "What'd you do, Derek?"

"Let them into Iron Goddess."

Shea clenched her fist and pounded the bed railing. "Who's *them*?"

"The cop. Foster's his name."

"Willie?" She shook her head. *Why would he do this to me?* "Who else?"

"Reyes and another big-ass Mexican named Tiburón. Oh, and this skinny kid—don't remember his name—had a teardrop inked by one eye. They're all Jaguars."

Terrance crossed his arms, glaring at Derek. "Why's Willie working with the Jaguars?"

"He ain't. It's a deal Foster and another cop got going. Jags don't know nothing about it." He coughed and winced in pain. "Somehow Foster recruited a few Jaguars."

"What deal?" Shea asked

"They're growing poppies here in Arizona to make heroin. Avoids the risk of smuggling it over the border. "

"That explains the poppy field Wendy and me stumbled onto," said Shea. "So why rob Iron Goddess?"

"Needed money for chemicals and equipment. Foster knew I worked for you, figured he could make an easy buck selling your bikes and gear. Told me to help him or he'd make sure I did serious time."

The feeling of betrayal overwhelmed Shea. She raised her fist to pummel him, but Terrance grabbed her arm before she could.

"Where are the bikes now?" Terrance asked. Shea paced the room like a caged animal.

"Don't know. Never told me."

Shea turned and pointed a finger at Derek. "Terrance and me gave you a second chance, you little piece of shit. You betrayed us."

"I didn't have no choice. I had to protect my mama."

"Maybe if you weren't using again, none of this would have happened," growled Terrance.

"If it's any consolation, I smashed the door to set off the alarm. Hoped the cops would get there in time to stop 'em." Derek's vitals monitor started beeping. A block on the screen flashed red, warning that his heart rate was too high. "That's why Reyes shot me."

"I heard the sheriff's deputies stopped by your room." Shea wondered if they would try to do the same to Annie. "How far up does this go in the Sheriff's Office?"

"Just Willie and another deputy, far as I know. Never got the other guy's name, but he was with Foster when they came in my room."

"What'd he look like?" Shea asked.

"White, I think. Maybe Mexican. And bald. It's all kinda fuzzy."

*Mexican and bald? Must be Aguilar—good ol' Deputy Commando.* "What'd they say?"

"Willie asked if I'd told anyone about what happened. Don't remember much after that. Doc says I went into a coma."

"Sounds like they tried to finish you off." Shea stared out the window at the nurses' station. Dr. Patel was talking to someone just out of view. "And now Annie's downstairs fighting for her life with a couple of Buzzkill's detectives running around looking for me."

"Who's Annie?"

"My niece. Your buddies kidnapped her and cut her damn ear off." Her chest tightened. "Oh shit."

At the nurses' station, Dr. Patel took a few steps back and Detective Rios came into view.

"Fuck! It's that female detective." Shea glanced around the room looking for a place to hide. In the bathroom? No, too obvious. Under the bed? No room. Cabinets? Again, too obvious. She would have to make a run for it.

"Hold this for me." Shea handed her Glock to Terrance, not wanting the weight and bulk of it to slow her down, much less get her in further trouble should they catch her.

Shea slipped open the door and duck-walked around the other side of the nurses' station. Her knees tightened with each step.

"Ms. Stevens, stop!" Rios doubled back to intercept her. Shea charged full-out down the corridor, knocking over wheelchairs, carts, and other equipment in her wake, anything to put more distance between her and the detective.

Shea made for the stairwell just past the elevator bay about fifty feet away. She pushed her battered body to its breaking point as she closed the distance. A tech rolled a patient on a bed out of an elevator in front of her. She veered left to avoid them, lost her footing, and slammed into the opposite wall, tumbling into a heap on the floor. Rios was on her instantly, cinching handcuffs around her wrists. Shea struggled to regain her footing, but Rios put a knee in her back, driving Shea's face down on the disinfectant-scented linoleum.

"Shea Stevens, you're under arrest for the kidnapping of Annie Wittmann."

"Fuck you! I'm the one who rescued her."

"You have the right to remain silent—"

Shea threw her weight to the side, rolling out from under Rios, then kicked the detective against the wall. Shea scrambled to her feet, but not before Rios drew her weapon. "Don't move!"

## 38

SHEA NARROWED her gaze at Rios a few feet away. "You fucking cops are all alike! You ask us to trust you. But y'all ain't nothing but thugs with badges." She took a step toward the detective.

"Shea, don't make me shoot you."

"You robbed my shop. You shot my employee." Rage consumed her as she advanced. "You kidnapped my niece! You cut off her ear! You goddamn people are fucking sick!"

Rios backed up until she reached the wall. "Shea, I don't know what you're talking about, but you need to stop where you are."

"You gonna kill me anyway. Can't leave any witnesses, right?" Shea pressed her chest against the gun barrel. "So fucking do it already. Pull the goddamned trigger."

Rios locked eyes with Shea. "Why would we kill you? What did you witness?"

Shea trembled with fury, her voice little more than a growl. "Willie showed up at the ransom drop with Annie in his goddamn trunk."

"Willie? You mean Sergeant Foster?"

"He's the one who kidnapped her. Now you're pinning it on me. Well, fuck you!"

"That's ridiculous. Why would Sergeant Foster kidnap a child?" There was a sincerity in Rios' eyes that broke through Shea's rage.

"He's making smack with help from a few Jaguars." Shea's head ached.

"Foster's working for the Jaguars?"

"He ain't working for them. This is a new scheme. They're growing poppies in the forest, two miles east of White Juniper Road."

"That's absurd. Foster's a highly decorated officer with nearly twenty years on the force."

"I saw Willie at the ransom drop. So did most of the Confederate Thunder. I'm the one who got Annie out of his trunk. I'm the one who brought her here."

Rios lowered her weapon. "Where's the girl's mother?"

Shea shook with anger, fighting back the tears, and glared at the detective. "Dead. Foster shot her."

Rios stood there, her gaze drifting, not saying a word.

*Would Rios believe her, or would she toe the blue line?*

"Let's assume for a moment you're telling the truth."

"I am."

"Fine. You're telling the truth. You got any proof?"

"Assuming Annie lives, yeah." Shea thought about it. "Who filed the arrest warrant?"

"Sergeant Foster." Rios frowned.

"Based on what evidence?" When Rios didn't respond, Shea smirked. "Who was first on the scene at the shootout in Ironwood earlier?"

"Foster called it in." Rios took a deep breath and let it out slowly. "But this is all circumstantial. Doesn't prove anything."

Shea thought about mentioning Oscar's phone showing

calls to Foster, but she had other plans for it and couldn't afford to lose it. "How much of your job I gotta do for you? Or maybe you're working with him?"

"You think *I'm* dirty?"

"Foster's working with Aguilar on this scheme. For all I know, you're involved, too. Why else would you be so determined to protect him?"

"I'm not protecting him. But if you want me to go to Internal Affairs, I need more than a wild accusation from an ex-con with a warrant out for her arrest."

"How about the fact that he's the one who broke into my motorcycle shop? Or that he tried to kill my employee Derek Williams—twice. But don't take my word for it. Go ask Derek. He's recovering down the hall in ICU."

"All right, let's talk to Mr. Williams." Rios grabbed Shea's arm and led her down the hall.

"Can you take these damn cuffs off? They fucking hurt."

"I want to hear what your friend has to say first."

A couple of men in blue scrubs came down the hallway, pushing a bed. Several IV bags hung from a hook like a cluster of red and white jellyfish. A child's choking cry drew her attention.

"Annie!" Shea pulled away from Rios and caught up with the bed.

Annie lay there, her face glowing with fever and streaked with tears. "Aunt Shea." Her pitiful cry ripped at Shea's heart.

"What's happening? Where are you taking her?" Shea asked.

"To the OR," replied one of the men pushing the bed, a startled expression on his face as he looked down at Shea's cuffed hands.

Rios pulled Shea backward, while the medical team

continued with Annie toward the operating room. "Let them do their thing."

Shea wanted to run after them, to hold Annie's hand and let her know everything would be okay. But nothing was okay. Wendy was dead. There was nothing Shea could do to help.

When they entered the ICU, all eyes were on Shea as Rios perp-walked her past the nurses' station. Shea stared at the floor, avoiding their gaze, until they came to Derek's room. Rios slid open the door.

Terrance stood up and stepped back when they entered. "What's going on?"

"It's all right, T. I told her about Willie's involvement in all this. She wants to confirm my story with Derek."

"Derek Williams?" Rios asked.

"Yes." Derek's voice wavered.

"Is Shea Stevens your employer?"

Derek looked at Terrance, then Shea, and back at Rios. "They both are. They own Iron Goddess."

"Who shot you?"

Derek glanced at Shea with a worried look. Shea nodded. "Tell her what happened."

"Sergeant Foster forced me to open up the shop, so he and some other guys could steal a bunch of bikes and stuff. I felt bad about betraying Shea and Terrance, so I smashed the front door to set off the alarm. That's when Oscar Reyes, one of Foster's guys, shot me." He winced as he adjusted his position in the bed. "The next day, Foster and some other deputy visited me here. I told 'em I'd keep my mouth shut. They tried to kill me anyway."

"Why would Sergeant Foster do this?"

"Got a heroin operation. Growing poppies. Needed money for equipment."

"Who else is working with him?"

"A few of the Jaguars—Reyes, the guy who shot me, and another guy they call Tiburón. I don't know any other names. He didn't want people to know too much about each other in case one of us got caught."

"What do you know about the kidnapping of Ms. Stevens' niece?"

Derek shrugged. "Nothing. Before the break-in, he talked about getting some of the money the Confederate Thunder was earning selling crystal. Didn't say how."

"Convinced?" asked Shea.

"I'll put in a call to Internal Affairs."

"What about me?" Shea raised her cuffed hands. "You letting me go or what?"

"I got a warrant for your arrest."

"It's bogus and you know it. Once you take me in, there's nothing to stop Willie from killing me. Not to mention Annie and Derek."

Rios' face twisted in frustration. "I can't pick and choose which arrest warrants I execute."

"Even if all the evidence points to the guy who issued the warrant in the first place? Just doing your job, right? Like all them Nazis." Shea stared at Rios, who wouldn't meet her gaze.

"Dammit." Rios pulled out her keys and released the cuffs.

Shea let out a sigh of relief, rubbing her wrists. "Thank you."

"Understand, I can't do anything about the warrant. Foster outranks me. So keep a low profile. But in the meantime, I will have IA look into these accusations. You got a number where I can reach you?"

"My cellphone got busted, but you can leave a message with Terrance if you need to reach me."

Terrance gave Rios the number, which she wrote down in a notepad. "I'll be in touch."

## 39

WITH RIOS GONE, decades of repressed hurt and anger tore at Shea's mind. The loss of her mother. Confused memories of Ralph's trial. The violation of the break-in. The betrayal by Derek and Willie. And now the loss of her sister, after seventeen years of blaming her for something she didn't do. Oscar's blood on her hands. She couldn't imagine ever being happy again. She didn't deserve to be happy. In so many ways, she had become what she despised in her father: a violent thug hungry for revenge. And it had cost her. The one glimmer of light in the ever-increasing darkness was Annie. She alone was innocent.

"I want to check on how Annie's doing."

"She's probably still in surgery," said Terrance.

Ignoring him, Shea walked back down the corridor to a nurses' station near the double-door entrance to the OR. A young blond nurse sat at a laptop, looking up as Shea approached.

"Uh . . . can I help you?" A cloud of concern crossed the nurse's face.

For the first time since she'd arrived at the hospital,

Shea noticed her borrowed shirt was covered with blood. Its metallic smell blended with the scents of floral laundry detergent, body odor, and dirty water. "I brought my niece, Annie Wittmann, into the ER a little bit ago. They took her into the OR. I was wondering how long she'll be in surgery."

"Let me see what I can find out." The nurse picked up the phone and punched in an extension. "Hey, it's Lucy. Can I get a status update on Annie Wittmann?" She nodded, thanked the person on the other end, and hung up. "They're reattaching her ear. Dr. Sossaman says another four hours at least. They'll be taking her to room 321 in the ICU after releasing her from recovery. You can wait for her there."

"Thanks."

Overwhelmed with grief and fatigue, Shea zombie-shuffled along the floor. Her boots dragged as if filled with concrete. The previous day's events played through her mind like a TV rerun she half paid attention to. She was beyond crying. Beyond anger. Beyond pain. The darkness had enveloped her, leaving her an empty shell.

"Shea?"

Someone was talking to her. Or was it a memory? Wendy cowering from the baseball bat. The SUV closing in on the Mustang. Flipping. Spinning. The biting cold of the river. Numbing her, pulling her down, beating her into submission with rocks and debris and forgotten memories.

∿

"Shea, you with us?"

She looked out on a sea of faces, strangers sitting on wooden benches, hungry for salacious bits of drama. In front, Ralph sat at a table. The man in the expensive suit stood nearby with a smile on his face that didn't reach his eyes.

"Mama picked up the frying pan," Shea said, trembling and trying not to remember Mama's blood-smeared face and the blood streaming between her fingers.

"The cast-iron pan?" asked the man in the suit.

"Yes, sir. The real heavy one." She glanced up at the judge wearing a robe the color of death. *Would he figure it out?*

"And what'd she do with the heavy pan?"

Shea looked at Ralph, then at the man in the suit. "Um . . ." Her chest tightened. The air felt thin. She gulped for a breath and held it as if she'd never get another one. *She was gonna get busted, she just knew it.*

"Shealene, what did your mama do with the heavy pan?"

She closed her eyes. Mama gasped, blood-filled mouth moving like a fish out of water. *Forgive me, Mama.* Shea clenched her jaw and opened her eyes. "She hit him with the pan. Hard. Several times."

Ralph grinned at her from the table. It was the grin that always meant trouble.

"You think she coulda killed him with that pan?"

"Objection, calls for speculation," said another man in a suit, sitting on the other side of the courtroom.

"Sustained."

"Shealene, what'd your daddy say when your mama hit him over and over with the pan?"

"He said, 'Don't hit me with that pan. You're going to kill me.'" Ralph would never talk that way, but the judge wouldn't know, would he?

"Shealene, help me." Mama's eyes pleaded with her. Blood everywhere. Half her head was missing. Because it was Wendy's head, not Mama's. Because Wendy stayed with the club. And married Hunter. And had a little girl. Annie. The girl without an ear. The bloody ear in the box. And it was all Shea's fault because she had believed the threats from the man in the expensive suit. She had lied. And then twisted it all up and blamed Wendy.

Shea lay down on the ground waiting for the people to shovel dirt on top of her. The way they did to Mama.

~

"Shea, you all right?" Terrance's skin glistened like liquid chocolate as he loomed over her.

She looked around. She was sitting in a chair in the intensive care unit. Vitals monitors in the ICU rooms played a disjointed melody of beeps and alarms. "What happened?"

"You wandered into the unit looking like something from *The Walking Dead*. Did something happen?"

"I'm just tired. And hungry."

Terrance held up a Snickers and a bag of beef jerky. "Got these from the vending machine down the hall. Take your pick."

Shea grabbed the candy bar. "Chocolate." She tore off the wrapper and bit into it. Her appetite woke like a wolf as she inhaled the candy.

"Any word on Annie?" he asked.

"Gonna be a few hours. They're supposed to bring her down here." She pulled her cracked phone from her pocket. "Wish I could check my voicemail. I'm expecting a call from Goblin."

Terrance took it from her hand. "You could always call your number from another phone and check it that way."

"Yeah, didn't think of that."

"Also, we could switch out the SIM card with a used phone I got at home. Should work."

"I don't want to leave Annie here alone."

"Or Derek."

"Fuck Derek. I saved his life and it turns out he helped them rob us. Willie can have him. All I care about now is getting the bikes back."

"Can't say as I blame you. You said Annie won't be out of surgery for a few hours?"

"Yeah."

"What do you say we go back to my place, get you cleaned up. You're covered in blood and you smell like ass."

Something about his words struck her funny. Shea laughed in spite of herself. Not a chuckle, but a full-on belly laugh that wouldn't stop, as if she were possessed. She gasped for breath between guffaws. Tears streamed down her face. "Smell like ass," she said between howls.

"Damn, I think that Snickers went straight to your head, girl." Terrance crossed his arms and shook his head, managing a smile himself.

"It's 'cause I smell like ass." She took a deep breath and blew it out. "Shit, I'm punch drunk."

Terrance lifted her up from the chair. "Yeah, and you smell like ass."

Shea convulsed into another laughing fit.

"She all right?" asked a nurse.

"I'm all right." Shea walked toward the corridor getting control of her body. "I just smell like ass."

The amber glow of streetlights cut through the deep dark of the parking lot. No hint of morning yet on the horizon.

By the time they reached Terrance's truck, Shea had laughed herself out. She was exhausted, but the unexpected hysterics left her feeling better. She still felt sad about losing Wendy and worried about Annie, but the darkness had retreated for the moment.

Inside the cab of the truck, Terrance pulled her Glock out of his waistband. "Next time use somebody else for a gun locker. They catch me with it, they'll shoot first and come up with excuses later."

"Sorry, didn't have nowhere else to put it." Shea tucked the gun in her waistband holster, while Terrance drove out of the parking lot toward home.

She leaned her head against the window and closed her eyes. The gentle bouncing of the truck rocked her to sleep. When she opened her eyes again, they were pulling into Terrance's driveway.

She had no energy left. Terrance opened her door and helped her down the sidewalk, which was lit by small electric lamps rooted in the ground. She must have drifted off a bit because before she knew it, they were in a bedroom. Terrance clicked on a small lamp. Jessica lay under the sheets of a double bed, rubbing her eyes. "Shea?"

Shea sat next to her on the bed. "Hey, baby."

"Sorry to wake you, Jess. Brought her back to get cleaned up and grab some shut-eye."

"Thanks, Terrance," said Jessica.

Terrance closed the door, leaving Shea alone with Jessica.

"I'm so tired." Shea lay on the bed.

Jessica leaned over to her and took a couple of sniffs. "Ugh, you smell—"

"Don't say it. I know. Please let me sleep."

"I'm sorry, but you are *not* lying next to me smelling all funky."

Shea felt herself pulled up again. "Jess, please."

"Not just no, but hell no. Come on, a shower'll do us both good."

Jessica led her down the hall to the guest bath and turned on the shower. Shea took a seat on the toilet. The sound of water reminded Shea of bacon sizzling.

Jess helped Shea off with her shirt. "Where'd all this blood come from?"

"Wendy." Sadness swept over her. "She's gone. Fucking cop shot her." She pulled off her boots, pants, and underwear. Her leg was raw and pink, but with no signs of infection.

"I'm so sorry." Jessica hugged her. Her skin smelled of lilac and lavender.

"What about your niece?"

"In surgery at Cortes General. They're trying to reattach her ear."

Jessica scrunched up her nose. "Ugh. I can't imagine what that poor girl's been through." She slid open the shower door. Clouds of steam billowed out. Jessica lifted Shea to her feet. "Up we go."

Shea wrapped her arms around her girlfriend, pulled her close, and kissed her. Jess kissed her back. It felt good to hold her, to kiss her. After a few moments, Shea pulled back, pressing her forehead against Jessica's, eyes closed. "I missed you so much."

"I missed you, too." Jessica said. "Now get in the damn shower, stinky girl."

"I smell like ass."

## 40

SHEA WOKE to morning light shining through the peach-colored curtains. She lay on her side, sorting out the crazy dreams she had. Motorcycle dreams. Running dreams. Dreams of her sister or maybe it was her mother; she wasn't sure which. Maybe both.

For the first time in days, she felt rested, though it didn't change her circumstances. The darkness and sadness haunted her. The bikes were still missing. If she failed to deliver, Iron Goddess would be ruined. But even if she found them in time, it wouldn't make up for the loss of her sister.

Shea's brain kept coming up with excuses for Wendy not to be dead, insisting it must have been a bad dream. It was dark after all. Maybe it only looked like a fatal wound. Maybe the cops called for an ambulance and she was somewhere in the hospital. But she didn't buy any of it. Wendy was gone.

Shea's thoughts turned to Annie. Was she alive? Was she out of surgery? What would happen to her when she woke up? Would she go back to living with Hunter and the twisted violent world of the MC? How long before she ended up dead like Wendy or Mama?

She sensed movement behind her and rolled over to see Jessica cuddled next to her. Shea wanted to lie in bed forever, hiding from the world, holding on to her girlfriend. But her bladder had other plans.

Shea slipped out of bed and walked out into the hallway to the bathroom. She was surprised to discover she was wearing a pink Tinker Bell nightshirt that came down to her mid-thighs. *Where'd this come from?* Jessica must have loaned it to her.

After taking care of business, she took a rare look at herself in the mirror. Bruises marked the left side of her face, as well as her arms and legs. She was tired of being the victim of other people's violence. It was time for a change in strategy.

Someone knocked on the door.

"Just a minute." She washed her hands and opened the door to see Terrance's sixteen-year-old son, Elon, standing there. He was about her height and skinny. "Morning, Elon. I swear every time I see you, you're a foot taller."

"Aunt Shea?" He asked, rubbing the sleep out of his eyes. "What're you doing here?"

"Your dad picked me up from the hospital last night. My niece is there."

He nodded. "You done?"

"Yeah." She smiled at the kid's singular focus and returned to the bedroom, where Jessica softly snored.

Shea thought about climbing back in bed with her, but she had things to take care of. She pulled on her jeans and boots. The smell of coffee led her down the hall to the kitchen.

Terrance sat at the table reading something on his

tablet. A coffeemaker with a half-filled pot sat next to a wooden stand of earthenware mugs.

She poured herself a cup and sat next to Terrance.

"Nice shirt, Tinker Bell," he said with a smirk. "You sleep all right?"

"As well as can be expected. Thanks again for everything."

"No worries. What are your plans?"

"I need to get back to the hospital and see how Annie's doing." The coffee gave Shea new energy.

"How soon before her father shows up?"

"That's what worries me. Wendy was trying to get Annie away from all that. If the MC wasn't dealing crystal meth all over the state, those guys never would have kidnapped Annie. Wendy'd still be alive."

"You looking for custody?"

Shea shook her head. "No, I'm just worried about her safety is all."

"You think she'd be better in foster care?"

"I dunno. Maybe."

"She belongs with family." Terrance gave her a knowing look.

"You think they'd award custody to her ex-con, lesbian aunt? Not likely."

"Why not you? Annie needs a loving, supportive environment. You've been through a lot of the same stuff."

"What do I know about raising a kid?"

"Who does? I didn't know shit when I gave birth to Elon. At least you care."

"I'll have to think about it." She sipped her coffee. "You said you had a phone I could use?"

"Yeah." He reached over to the counter and disconnected a black phone from a charger, plugged into the outlet shared with the coffeemaker. "You got your broken phone?"

She pulled it from her pocket and handed it to him. He popped off the back, pulled out the SIM card, and inserted it in the replacement phone.

"Cross your fingers," he said, handing her the new phone.

She pressed the on button and watched it cycle through the boot-up process. When the main screen came up, she saw she had two voicemail messages.

"Panterita, call me," said Goblin's recorded voice as she played the first message.

She dialed the number. "Goblin, gimme some good news."

"I was wondering if you was gonna call me back, *chica*. My acquaintance is supposed to meet with the guys selling your bikes this morning. Figured you'd wanna join the party."

"Hellz yeah! When and where?"

"Ten o'clock at a closed-up garage in Ironwood, Twelfth Street and Oakland. I'll be bringing a few of my guys to make sure things go smoothly."

"Thanks, my friend. I will see you at ten."

"*Órale*. Ride safe, amiga."

Shea hung up. "We may get the bikes back."

The second message was from Monster, asking Shea if she knew anything about where Wendy and Annie were. She would return that call later.

∾

AN HOUR LATER, Shea and Terrance arrived at Cortes General. Jessica had stayed at Terrance's to keep an eye on

Elon, despite his protests that at sixteen he didn't need a baby-sitter.

With no calls from Detective Rios, Shea assumed the arrest warrant was still in place. To avoid the gaze of deputies or hospital security who might be looking for her, Shea wore an Arizona Diamondbacks baseball cap and a checkered button-down shirt borrowed from Terrance.

When they walked into the intensive care unit, a uniformed deputy with narrow eyes and round cheeks stood at the entrance to room 312, where Annie was supposed to be recovering. Shea's pulse quickened. *Was he there to arrest her or to protect Annie?* Only one way to find out.

"I'm here to see my niece." Shea's voice was monotone and all business. Her body readied itself for another dash for freedom.

"Your name?"

"Shea Stevens."

The deputy looked her over, then glanced at Terrance. "You got ID?"

Shea let go of a breath she didn't realize she was holding. She pulled out her wallet and handed her driver's license to the man.

He studied it, glanced up at Shea again, then at Terrance. "Who's he?"

"Terrance Douglas, my business partner."

The deputy handed Shea back her driver's license. "Go on in."

Annie lay with eyes closed, bandages wrapped around her head. Her long hair was matted with blood. Several bags of fluids hung from an IV pole, feeding into a computer-controlled pump. Shea wondered if she should let her sleep. She walked around to the side of the bed farthest from the door and pulled up a chair. It squeaked when she sat down. Annie's eyes fluttered half open.

"Annie?"

"Mama?" she asked in a drowsy voice.

Shea tightened her jaw. "No, sweetie. It's Aunt Shea."

Annie's eyes opened wider and focused on Shea. "Aunt Shea?"

"Yeah, how ya doing?"

"Ear hurts."

"Yeah, I imagine it does." With all the bandages, she couldn't tell if the surgeon had reattached it or not. Shea gripped her small hand like they were the petals of a flower. "It'll get better soon."

"Who's that black man?"

Shea flushed with embarrassment and mouthed the word "sorry" to Terrance, who stood on the other side of the bed. "He's my friend Terrance."

Terrance nodded. "We're glad you're safe, Annie."

A phone rang. Shea pulled out her new phone, but it wasn't the one ringing. She reached into her other pocket and pulled out Oscar's phone. "Hello."

"¡Hola, mija!" Victor's icy voice tore apart her burgeoning hope.

## 41

SHEA'S BLOOD BOILED. "What the fuck do you want, Victor?" She stepped into the bathroom to keep from disturbing Annie.

"We have a debt to settle, you and I."

"You want your dope? Talk to Hunter Wittmann."

"I'm talking about Oscar Reyes."

"Oscar Reyes got what he deserved. He shouldn't have tortured my sister."

"Perhaps if you had not broken into my warehouse . . ." He cleared his throat. "But what's done is done. Oscar is dead. My product is missing. I hold you responsible."

"Fuck you, Victor. Tell it to someone who gives a shit."

"You can either pay your debt, or I will kill everyone you love. Your sister. Your niece. Your *marimacha* lover. I will make you watch as I gut each of them. Then I will hang you all from a bridge. Give a shit now?"

Shea considered mentioning that Wendy was already dead, but it wouldn't change anything. "I did you a favor killing Oscar."

"How dare you! Oscar was *familia*."

"Your *familia* sold you out, *Uncle* Victor. To the Sheriff's Office, no less. Oscar made a shitload of calls to Sergeant Willie Foster. You know all your heroin that got seized at the border recently? Ever wonder how the Border Patrol found it?"

"*¡Mentirosa!* Oscar would never betray me."

"I got the proof right here on Oscar's phone. The call history doesn't lie. And Oscar wasn't the only rat in your house. You heard from your buddy Tiburón?"

"What do you know, *mija*? *¿Dónde está* Tiburón?"

"In the morgue. He and Sergeant Foster kidnapped my niece. When Wendy and I went to rescue her, Tiburón got in our way. We put him down like a rabid dog. Like that dog of yours that chewed up my face."

"*¡Putas!*" Victor roared in frustration, causing Shea to smile.

*Time to twist the knife.* "Word on the street is yet another Jaguar is helping Foster grow opium poppies a few miles from your warehouse."

"Who are you talking about?"

"Not sure. Never got a name. Guess you'll have to figure that one out for yourself."

"Why should I believe any of this?"

"I don't give a shit whether you do or not. But let me make one thing clear, Victor. You hurt anyone I care about, I will hurt you back ten times over."

"Don't threaten me, *mija*. I am the president of the Los Jaguares. I am the king of this fucking jungle."

Shea hung up. She'd made her point.

"Was that Victor Ganado?" Terrance stared at her as she walked out the bathroom.

"You heard that, huh?"

"Should I be worried?"

"I don't think so. Victor has bigger problems than me to

worry about, specifically Willie and the Jaguars he recruited for this local heroin operation he's got going."

"Geez, Shea, you do love to stir up trouble."

"Me? I just wanna build motorcycles. But if Victor and Willie want to kill each other over the local heroin trade, I don't want to stand in their way."

"Speaking of motorcycles, it's time we meet up with your friend Goblin and get ours back."

She nodded, staring down Annie.

"Annie, honey" Shea whispered, putting a hand on her shoulder.

"Uh-huh."

"I gotta go out for a little bit."

"No, please don't leave me." She clung to Shea's hand.

Shea's chest tightened when their eyes locked. Annie's desperation and fear matched her own. She wanted nothing more than to curl up into the bed with Annie and hold her. "Just for a little bit."

Annie let go, eyes wet with tears. "Promise you'll be back soon?"

"I promise."

"How soon?"

"Maybe a couple hours."

"That ain't soon."

"Sorry, there's something I gotta do." Shea smiled and hugged her.

"I love you, Aunt Shea."

"Love you, too, Little Bug."

Shea stood up and followed Terrance down the corridor. "We'll need the cargo trailer at the shop."

They loaded into Terrance's pickup truck and drove south toward Sycamore Springs.

"How you holdin' up?" he asked.

"I'm having trouble believing Wendy's really gone. I

mean, I go seventeen years without seeing her. She pops
into my life with all the drama of a *Sons of Anarchy* episode.
Then right when I'm getting to know her again, she's dead."

"It's rough losing family."

"I keep playing everything over in my head. Why didn't
I insist she stay at the Church? Why couldn't I protect her?
Why didn't I get back in touch with her sooner?"

"Ain't your fault she's dead, sister. That guilt lies
squarely on the bastards who kidnapped Annie. Maybe the
Thunder, too, for dealing crystal and making Annie a
target."

"I keep thinking I coulda done something different. All
those years I spent mad at her, thinking she'd defended
Ralph on the stand, when it was me the whole time."

"Shoulda-woulda-coulda. It's all water under the bridge
now."

"Yeah, maybe." Shea stared out at the landscape.

"What's our plan for getting the bikes back? Who are
we meeting? Willie?"

"That's my guess." Shea pulled her Glock from the
glove box and tucked it in its holster.

"Maybe we oughta call Detective Rios."

Shea shook her head. "Hell no! Last thing we need is
bringing in more goddamn police. Chances are they'd
impound all the bikes for *evidence*." She used finger quotes
on the last word.

"What does Goblin want in return for his help?"

"We ain't talked specifics yet. Depending on what's
there, maybe a few of the production bikes. Insurance is
covering them anyway."

"Sounds suspiciously like insurance fraud."

"Naw, just the cost of doing business in a fucked-up
world. Besides, the cargo trailer only holds so many bikes at
a time. After we pick up what we can, what are the odds the

rest would still be here when we got back for a second trip?"

"Good point."

They picked up the cargo trailer from the back lot of Iron Goddess and raced back north to Ironwood. While Terrance drove, Shea kept a keen eye out for anyone following them. Luck must have been in their favor because they arrived at the meet-up spot without incident. Still, Shea remained uncertain how they were going to get the bikes back without getting killed in the process.

## 42

THE FORMER HOME to Kirkland Auto Repair had been abandoned for years. The painted letters on the sign were peeling from decades of heat and sunlight. Crabgrass grew from every crack in the blacktop. Rotting plywood had replaced the plate glass windows. The storage lot next to the building was overgrown with sow thistle and snakeweed—the only signs of life among the rusted hulks of cars.

A low rider, metal-flake purple Monte Carlo sat parked in the driveway. On the far side of the street, a full-size Dodge Ram truck sat idling. The words AA Ajo Auto Repair had been painted on the side of the truck—Goblin's shop.

Terrance parked along the street, positioning the back of the trailer next to the driveway. Shea and Terrance got out and walked over to Goblin's truck. He rolled down the window.

Goblin's face was a little rounder and his cholo-style mustache a little grayer since the last time they met. "Been awhile, Panterita."

"Yeah, it has. This here's my business partner, Terrance."

The two men nodded at each other.

"Looks like our contact's already inside," said Goblin. "How you wanna play it, *chica*?"

Shea looked at Terrance, then back to Goblin. "A couple of local deputies named Foster and Aguilar are behind all this. If they're in there, I want 'em dead. Anybody else, we'll see how it goes."

Terrance put a hand on her shoulder. "Shea, you can't go around executing cops, no matter what they done."

Shea drew her Glock and glared at him. "How many people gotta die before someone puts these dirty cops down, T?"

Terrance stared at Shea, but didn't say anything.

Shea turned to Goblin, "You with me on this?"

"We got your back, *chica*." Goblin and four burly men— two Latino, one black, and one white—climbed out of the truck, armed with an assortment of compact assault weapons and semiautomatic handguns. Goblin carried a shotgun.

"Let's go." Goblin waved them on.

The seven of them walked up the drive, with Shea in the lead, followed by Goblin and his men, Terrance bringing up the rear. Shea gave a gentle tug on front door. It was unlocked. The plywood prevented Shea from seeing who and what awaited them inside. Her chest tightened. "Here goes nothing."

Shea opened the door and raised her gun. Inside, a dimly lit service counter sat next to a small customer waiting area. Trash and dry leaves littered the floor. The place smelled of rat feces and motor oil. Shea took a quick glance behind the counter. No one there. She turned to her left and opened the door to the repair bay.

Sunlight coming through the garage door windows reflected off the pink metal flake paint of the Trinkets' bikes. Beside them sat the production bikes Willie and his cohorts had stolen. A large pile of jackets, helmets, and other motorcycle gear lay in a heap to the side. Relief at finding the bikes mixed with her apprehension.

"Getting worried you wouldn't show."

Shea whipped around to her right to see a tall, skinny kid in his mid-teens with cold, half-lidded eyes and a teardrop tattoo on the right side of his face. A gold cross dangled from one ear, below the yellow bandana wrapped around his head. He pointed a large-caliber, snub-nosed revolver sideways at her. *An amateur,* Shea thought.

"Where's Willie?" Shea put a second hand on the grip of the Glock and pointed it at his chest. The *clickety-clack* of the others cocking their guns boosted her confidence.

"Hey, lady! I'm the one making the deal." The kid patted his puffed-up chest, glancing from Shea to the others. "You in or out?"

"Put the fucking gun down, shithead, or we will end you."

The kid's eye twitched. His frown twisted. *"Puta."*

Shea caught a whiff of Axe body spray coming off the guy like a wave of desperation. She took a step toward him. "I already killed Oscar Reyes and Tiburón." A white lie, but necessary. "You wanna be next?"

The young Jaguar shifted from one foot to the other, staring at the half-dozen guns pointed at him. "Fuck it." He backed up, then pointed the barrel of the revolver upward in surrender and laid it on the floor. "Let's be cool, a'ight? You give me the money, I give you the goods. We all go home happy," he said with his hands raised.

Shea picked up his gun, a nickel-plated Taurus .45 caliber with a jaguar engraved near the grip. She holstered the Glock and pressed the revolver to the kid's chest. "What's your name?"

"Why?"

She ripped the cross out of his ear, splitting open his fleshy lobe.

"Jesus Christ!" he yelped, gripping his bloody ear in pain. "What the fuck'd you do that for?"

"What's your name, asshole?"

"Eduardo."

Shea narrowed her eyes and tilted her head. "Eduardo Ortega?"

"How the hell'd you know that?"

"You and your sister, Margaret, were supposed to help my sister Wendy." She smacked him in the face with his revolver.

"Shea, ease up," said Terrance.

"You're Wendy's sister?" He wiped blood from his nose and busted lip, smearing it across his face.

"Yeah. What the hell happened?"

Actual tears began to run over the inked ones on Eduardo's cheek. "Shit, it was my cousin Oscar. He got this all fucked up. He had this deal going with a fucking cop. Forced me into it. Then he shot my sister when she tried to stand in his way. Tell Wendy I'm sorry."

"Wendy's dead, asshole. Your buddy Willie Foster shot her."

"The cop? Goddamn. It wasn't supposed to go down like this."

"Well, thanks to you, it did. And these here are my bikes, Eduardo. Got it?"

"Yeah," he said, sounding defeated. "I got it."

"Great. Now where the fuck's Willie?"

"I don't know."

She pulled back the hammer on the revolver. "I'm getting tired of repeating myself, Eduardo."

"I don't know, and that's the truth. He told me to come down and collect the money or he'd throw my ass in jail for my sister's murder."

Another one of Willie's pawns. "You know you ain't leavin' here with no money right?"

"What? I can't do that. Foster'll have my ass."

"Or we can shoot you right here, leave you to the rats," said Goblin.

The kid sighed. "What the hell am I supposed to tell Foster?"

"Tell him he fucked with the wrong woman."

"Man, this is some fucked-up shit. He'll come after you. Ya know that, right?"

"You assholes robbed *my* shop and put *my* guy in the hospital. Y'all kidnapped *my* niece and murdered *my* sister. Give me one reason I shouldn't pull this trigger."

"Shea," said Terrance from behind the safety of Goblin's men.

She glanced back at Terrance, who shook his head. "Not worth it, sister girl."

She turned back to the kid and sighed. "Get the fuck outta here, Eduardo, before I kill you, anyway."

He raced out the back door like a frightened rabbit.

Shea looked to Terrance. "Happy?"

He frowned.

Goblin came up to Shea. "You said you'd make this worth our while, *chica*."

"We came for the Pink Trinkets' bikes. I can let you have a few of the production bikes. The gear, too, if you want it."

Goblin and his guys looked over the bikes and picked through the gear, trying on the women's jackets, but they didn't fit. After a brief discussion with them, Goblin said,

"Gimme those three flat black bikes on the end. You can keep the gear. Too damn small for my homies."

"You got a deal." Shea shook his hand.

Shea opened the garage bay door. After pulling the three bikes they'd chosen to the street, Goblin's guys helped them load the Trinkets' bikes and the remaining production bikes into the trailer. They piled the jackets and other gear in the bed of Terrance's pickup.

"Thanks for your help, man." Shea slapped Goblin on the back. "You saved our asses on this Trinkets deal."

"My pleasure, *chica*. You come down to Ajo sometime, we go for a ride."

"Sounds like a plan."

Goblin and his guys rode off.

When they climbed into the truck, Terrance said, "Well, that's one problem solved. What about the rest? Between the Jaguars and these dirty cops, I don't feel safe opening up the shop tomorrow."

"I'm hoping Detective Rios will have Internal Affairs deal with Willie and Aguilar. I don't know what else I can do about them." Shea picked out a jacket and helmet from the back of the truck. "As for Victor, I have a plan."

He looked at Shea. "Care to share?"

Shea frowned. "Better you don't know."

"Look, we're in this together. What's your idea?"

"Victor ain't gonna leave me alone till he gets his hex back, right?"

"Yeah."

"So I just have to convince Hunter to bring it to him."

"And how do you plan to do that?"

"Tell him Victor's holding me, Wendy, and Annie hostage until he brings it back."

"Wendy's dead. Annie's in the hospital."

"Yeah, but judging from Monster's voicemail message,

they don't know any of that. I reckon Hunter and the MC are keeping a low profile after what happened between them and Willie."

"Hunter will kill you once he finds out you lied to them."

"You got any better suggestions?"

"No." Terrance sighed. "Where do you plan to meet with Victor?"

"Dunno. Hopefully someplace neutral and public."

"I'm coming with you."

"No! I'm not risking anyone else's life."

"You can't do this alone. It's suicide."

"Then so be it. I already got Wendy killed for letting her come with me to rescue Annie. I can't risk losing you, too."

"Shea—"

"No, T! I won't do it. Elon needs you. And somebody needs to run Iron Goddess." The darkness crept up on her. She took a deep breath. "This is something I gotta do on my own."

## 43

WHILE TERRANCE DROVE them back to Iron Goddess, Shea pulled out Oscar's phone. "Victor!"

"*Mija,* unless you have my product, we have nothing to discuss."

"Listen, Victor. You still have a rat in your crew. I know who it is."

"More of your bullshit, *mija*?"

"No bullshit. Had a chat with this guy a little while ago. He's a helluva lot more scared of Sergeant Foster than he is of you. Wonder what he's telling the Sheriff's Department about the Jaguars."

"No more games, *mija*. Tell me who it is now."

"I tell you who it is, my debt to you is paid."

"Not hardly. You still owe me for the stolen product."

"As I said before, I ain't got it. But I might be able to convince Hunter to bring it back. But if I do, then we're square once and for all."

"The product, plus the name of the rat."

"Deal."

"Be at the warehouse in one hour with the product."

"Can't we meet somewhere a little more neutral?"

"*Mija,* you wanna talk. This is where I am. You come here, I know you on the up and up. If not, I know you full of shit."

"Fine. One hour."

Shea hung up. "I'll need you to drop me off at my place, so I can pick up one of my bikes."

"Take one of the ones in the truck."

Shea shook her head. "These are street bikes. I need something better suited for off-road."

"Cops are probably watching your house. Be better if I drive you in the truck."

"No. You've done enough. This is on me."

"Then how will you get your bike if the cops are at your place?"

"I'll figure something out."

A sly smile crept onto his face. "I think I can help you with that."

Shea looked at him. "How?"

"You'll see."

~

AFTER UNLOADING the bikes and merchandise at Iron Goddess, they unhooked the trailer. Terrance locked up his truck. While Shea grabbed a spare helmet and jacket from the workshop, Terrance pulled out an 1800 cc production sport bike.

"T, I told you, I need an off-road bike."

"And I told you I would help you do that." He pulled on a helmet "Now shut up and get on."

She climbed onto the passenger seat behind him and they maneuvered down Sycamore Mountain to Shea's neighborhood. Terrance stopped at the corner before turning onto her street. A dark blue sedan sat parked in front of her house.

"I wonder if that's your buddy Willie." Terrance said.

"Maybe, though he usually drives a marked cruiser. I don't have time to deal with him anyway. So what's your plan?"

"You sneak down behind the houses. I'll loop around from the next street over and draw them off."

"How do you know they'll follow you?"

"Trust me, I'm a black man. I know how to get a cop to follow me."

She held his gaze and put her hand on his arm. "Try not to get yourself shot. Or arrested. Don't need you going to men's prison."

"You're the one meeting with the head of a heroin-trafficking street gang. Don't get yourself killed. Annie needs you."

A low ridge ran behind the row of houses on her street, crested with boulders that rose like the ancient standing stones of Britain. Shea scurried along behind the boulders until she reached a small, overgrown path that meandered into her backyard. She sat for a moment, perched behind a boulder with a clear view of the blue sedan.

The rumble of Terrance's bike grew louder when he turned the corner onto Shea's street and pulled onto the gravel-covered shoulder ten feet in front of the sedan. For a few moments, nothing happened as dust from the disturbed gravel drifted down the street.

The sedan's passenger door opened and Detective Edelman stepped out. Shea suspected Rios was behind the wheel. Terrance's engine roared. The bike's back tire sent a rapid-fire barrage of gravel at the sedan. Edelman ducked back into the car. Rocks smacked the windshield, cracking it in several places. A moment later, Terrance took off in a cloud of dust, pursued by the sedan, siren wailing. No way would Rios and Edelman catch Terrance on the bike. Not on paved roads. But it would have been fun to watch.

Shea hustled down the path and let herself in the back door. The place had been ransacked. All of her chair cushions were slashed open. Papers from the desk in her bedroom covered the floor. The contents of her kitchen cabinets were everywhere. Ninja was eating something off the floor. She grabbed a spare garage door remote and tucked it into one of her jacket pockets.

In her garage, her tool chests had been dumped, but her bikes looked untouched. She decided to take Kali, a 600 cc adventure bike. It was lighter and better on gravel than a cruiser anyway. She opened the garage door, hopped on Kali, and took off, closing the door behind her with the remote.

Shea raced up Sycamore Mountain, burning through the corners, letting the adrenaline fill her system. Once past Olde Towne Sycamore Springs, she rode like a bullet toward Ironwood, then out into the Cortes National Forest, past the campgrounds, and up the maze of unpaved Forest Service roads.

A mile from the Jaguar warehouse, she passed a gauntlet of cars and trucks parked alongside the road. Large Latino men, armed with rifles and shotguns and wearing the distinctive yellow Jaguar bandanas, stood beside the vehicles. Maybe this would be a one-way trip after all.

As expected, Victor and two other Jaguars were waiting for her out front. She parked the bike at the edge of the driveway nearest the building's side door. Another black Pathfinder was parked on the side of the building. No bullet holes in the windshield. *Must be a different SUV from the one we had used to escape.*

The main garage door stood open. The two Jags she didn't know were holding AK-47s and both dressed in matching black flannel shirts with yellow bandanas encircling their heads. Both had the build of Mexican wrestlers.

Victor did not look happy to see her.

## 44

"WHERE IS MY PRODUCT, *MIJA*?"

"I told you I'd have Hunter bring it." She reached into her jacket for her phone. The AK twins raised their rifles in a flash.

Shea took a step back, raising her hands in surrender. "Easy! You want your dope? I gotta call someone in the MC to bring it."

"Rico, frisk her."

Rico, one of the AK twins, swung his rifle over his shoulder and patted her down, pulling out her Glock and Eduardo's revolver. He handed the guns to Victor, whose frown deepened. Rico returned to his original spot, AK-47 in hand. Shea breathed a sigh of relief, grateful she still had the knife tucked next to the now-empty holster.

"Happy now?" she asked.

Victor stashed the Glock in his belt, stepped forward with the revolver, his eyes cold and dark. He circled her, reached into her waistband, and pulled out her knife.

*Dammit,* she thought. *This is not going according to plan.*

"You missed this." He flicked open the knife and held it

up for Rico to see while glaring at her. "Planning to kill another one of my men?"

"A woman's gotta right to defend herself."

"Not in my house."

"Fine, you got my weapons. Now if you want your fucking dope, I'll have to make a phone call."

"If you try something, I will shoot you myself." He closed and pocketed the knife, keeping the revolver trained on her. "I want Hunter to bring my product. No one else."

"Fine." She pulled out Monster's business card, along with her cellphone. It rang three times. Her hand tightened on the phone. If he didn't pick up, things would go downhill quickly.

"Yello."

"Monster, you told me to call if I needed anything."

"Sure, but now's not the best time. The MC's laying low at the moment. Is Wendy with you? I can't get ahold of her."

Shea let a wave of hurt and anger pass before she answered. "Yeah, she is. Annie, too."

"Oh, thank God. I's afraid something mighta happened."

"Something did happen. The Jaguars got us and are holding us at their warehouse."

"What? You gotta be kidding me."

"If Hunter don't bring back the hex he stole, they'll gut all three of us, starting with Annie."

"Goddamn fucking Mexicans!" He didn't say anything for a minute.

"Monster, you still there?"

"Yeah, I'm here. Hunter knows where this place is?"

"Yes. And he's gotta come alone."

"Can you put Wendy on?"

"I want to, but the guy with the gun won't let me."

"Let me talk to this guy."

Shea looked at Victor. The corners of his crocodile grin curled as he reached for the phone. "Bring me my product or these *putas* die." He handed it back to Shea.

"Hello?" she asked.

"You hang tight, girlie. Help is on the way."

"Thanks, Monster."

She hung up, heart pounding. *What would happen when Hunter discovered the deception? Am I swapping one enemy for another? Do I have a choice?*

"Who is this Monster?"

"He took care of Wendy after Ralph went to prison."

"Will he convince Hunter to bring me what I want?"

"If anyone can, it would be Monster."

"Very well. We wait inside and you will tell me the name of the rat." He gestured toward the open garage door with her Glock.

Memories of her previous experiences in the warehouse came crashing down on her like fifty-foot waves. She took a step backward. "I'm fine out here."

"I was not asking," he said through gritted teeth.

Rico and his buddy raised their rifles, gazing down the gun sights at her. "Move," said Rico.

Her boots dragged along the ground as she followed Victor inside, the AK twins at her back. Victor gestured toward a couple of chairs along the wall—the same ones they'd tied her and Wendy to last time. Someone had tried to clean up Oscar's blood, but the concrete still bore the brick-red stains, including smudge prints from Shea's boots.

Victor sat next to her, facing her, left arm hanging over the back of the chair. So casual, as if two men armed with Russian automatic rifles weren't standing a few feet away from them.

"So, *mija,* who is the rat in my house?"

"A kid named Eduardo Ortega. Got a tear-shaped tat by his eye. Him along with his cousin Oscar and Tiburón were all working with Sergeant Foster of the Cortes County Sheriff's Office."

"Angel, tell Eduardo to come up here."

Angel, the other AK twin, pulled out his phone and spoke with someone in Spanish.

The wrinkles on Victor's face deepened. "Why should I believe you?"

"I will show you." Shea cautiously pulled out Oscar's phone, pulled up the call history showing the calls made to Willie, and handed it to Victor. "Oscar made these calls before I took his phone."

Victor dialed the number and put it on speaker.

"Reyes, where the hell you been?" asked a familiar voice.

Victor's eyes met Shea's, but conveyed no emotion. "Oscar is not here. Who is this?"

"Sergeant Foster of the Cortes County Sheriff's Office. Who the hell's this?"

"Wrong number." Victor cut the connection. "What does this prove?"

"It proves I wasn't lying about Oscar working for Foster. As for Tiburón, I killed him last night."

"You want?"

"He and Foster kidnapped my niece and cut off her ear. When I tried to rescue her, he attacked me. He got what he deserved."

"Hmmph. And how does Eduardo figure into this?"

"A couple hours ago, Eduardo tried to sell me back the motorcycles they stole from me." Shea decided to leave out the part about his plan to help Wendy. "That revolver's his. Nice engraving work, by the way. Remind me when he gets here to ask him where he got it done."

Victor examined the engraving, then popped open the cylinder. Five pinkie-sized bullets slid out and pinged off the concrete. He kicked them under the table and flicked the gun closed.

Eduardo pulled up in his purple Monte Carlo. When his eyes met Shea's, his jaw dropped. "What's she doing here?"

Shea and Victor stood while the skinny teenager approached.

"This nice lady was kind enough to return something you lost." Victor handed Eduardo the revolver.

Suspicion crept into the kid's eyes as he accepted the gun. "Uh, thanks."

"She also says you are working with the police."

Eduardo raised the revolver and pointed it at Shea. "She lying, *jefe*."

Victor, cool as ice, approached the kid. "Why you sweating, *mijo*? Is there something I should know?"

"*Jefe,* you know me!" His voice squeaked with fear. "I wouldn't ever betray you."

"Oh *mijo*! I believe you." Victor put a reassuring hand on the boy's shoulder.

Shea's stomach knotted. Her plan was backfiring. Perhaps she underestimated Victor's loyalty to his crew. "Ask him how I got his gun."

"Eduardo?"

The young man grew increasingly restless. "It's not what you think."

"I grabbed it from him after he tried to sell us back the motorcycles he and Foster stole from my shop."

Eduardo glared at Shea, eyes hooded, then at Victor. "It's not true."

"Tell me the truth, *mijo*." The consoling parent was gone. The sociopathic gangster was back.

Eduardo pointed the gun at Victor. "No."

Victor growled and drew the Glock. "Put the gun down."

The revolver clicked several times. Eduardo's face crumpled with realization. "No, *jefe!*" Eduardo screamed. "You . . ."

Victor fired. Eduardo fell, a gaping hole where his right eye used to be. Blood pooled around his head and dripped down the side of his face, obscuring the inked tear on his cheek.

"*Mija,* when you shoot a rat, you make sure he's dead." Victor slapped his chest and set the Glock down on the table. "Never know when someone's wearing a vest."

Shea's ears were ringing from the gunshot; the darkness swirled inside her. The color drained from Eduardo's face, stripping away the thug and leaving the broken body of a child. She felt the urge to kneel down and cradle him. The roar of an approaching vehicle tore her away from the dead teenager.

## 45

"LET'S hope Hunter followed your instructions." Victor walked toward the open garage door as the thunder of the engine grew louder. While everyone focused on the approaching vehicle, Shea eased slowly back toward the table, grabbed her Glock and held it behind her back.

Hunter's Bronco rounded the curve at the bottom of the hill and raced up the driveway, skidding to a halt on the gravel between Eduardo's Monte Carlo and Shea's bike.

Rico and Angel pointed their rifles at Hunter when he climbed out of the truck.

"Where's my wife and kid?" shouted Hunter, pointing a SIG Sauer at Victor.

Hunter crossed the threshold of the garage and spotted Eduardo's body laying in a puddle of blood. "What the hell's going on? Who is that?"

"Someone who thought he could steal from me," said Victor. "I showed him he could not."

"Where's Wendy and Annie?" Hunter asked, looking at Shea.

*How would Victor play this?* Shea's grip on the Glock

tightened. The jig was up. The situation was about to go bad fast.

"I will give you what you want, *ese*. First, show me you brought what you stole."

Hunter looked at Victor, then at the AK twins and stepped to the rear of the Bronco. He pulled out the plastic bins he'd taken, set them down on the concrete slab, and kicked them toward Victor. The Jaguar leader popped the latches on the first bin and lifted the lid.

"What the hell is this?" Victor scowled at Hunter, his face darkening. He lifted a package from the bin wrapped in duct tape and wires.

Hunter held up what looked like a garage door opener with a telescoping antenna. His thumb rested on the device's red button. "It's a little thank-you gift." His voice was cold and monotone.

A strange calm came over Shea as she realized they were all going to die. "What'd you do, Hunter?"

"A little insurance—a bag of screws taped around three pounds of C-4 and wired to a remote receiver." Hunter extended the antenna on the detonator. "I'll ask again. Where the hell are my wife and daughter?"

"Wendy's dead," Shea said.

Hunter glared at her, his nostrils flaring. "The fuck you say?"

"Last night when we were rescuing Annie."

"Who the hell shot her?" His voice grew ragged while his face reddened.

"Sergeant Foster," said Shea, "the deputy who showed up at the drop house."

"Fuck!" He pressed his hands to his face, pacing around like a caged animal.

"I'm sorry, Hunter. I really am." Perspiration dotted Shea's forehead as her eye stayed glued to the detonator.

Hunter twisted and bobbed back and forth, unable to contain his anguish. He turned to her, eyes blazing, and pointed the SIG at her. "What about Annie? She dead, too?"

"No, she's safe." Shea brought the Glock to her side. "She's recovering at Cortes General."

"You fucking lied, bitch." The SIG shook in his hand.

Shea pointed the Glock at him. "I didn't have a choice. They'da killed me if I didn't get you to return the hex you stole. You wouldn'ta come if you knew they only had me."

"Damn straight, I wouldn't. Why would I save your perverted, rug-munching ass?"

"Hate me all you want, but this is your fault."

"My fault? How in the *hell* is this my fault?"

"You're the one who stole the Jaguars' dope."

"You stupid bitch. You stupid, stupid bitch." The pain reflected in his eyes was burning through his sanity like a wildfire. His face was bright red and shiny with sweat. His finger trembled on the detonator's trigger.

Shea resisted the urge to shoot him, fearing he could still set off the bomb. "Put down the detonator, Hunter, and go home. Everybody lives."

"That's bullshit. Wendy's dead." He closed his eyes and took long, slow breaths. When he opened them he pointed the SIG at Victor. "And your boys down the road are just itchin' to kill me. Call them off. Tell 'em to go home. Then I'll leave." His voice resonated with a sudden confidence that set Shea on edge.

"Put down the detonator, and I will do as you ask." Victor took a step toward Hunter.

Hunter shook his head. "No way. I'm done listening to your lies. All of y'all. Now call off your boys, or I will blow us all to kingdom come. Ya got me?"

"Okay, *ese*." Victor inched toward Hunter—a jaguar

stalking its prey. He pulled out his cellphone, held it up for Hunter to see, then dialed a number. "Emilio, *prepárate para venir aquí, por favor.*"

Shea didn't understand much Spanish, but something in Victor's eyes told her he wasn't calling off his fellow Jaguars.

"In English, motherfucker!" insisted Hunter, his voice hoarse but commanding.

"Emilio, go back to the house. *¡Andale!*" Victor enunciated each word, then hung up. "Satisfied? Now you are free to leave."

Hunter pointed the SIG at the AK twins. "You two, put down your guns."

They looked at Victor, who shook his head. Victor's voice turned icy. "It is time for you to go, hombre."

"I ain't leaving here empty-handed, you fucking beaner." Hunter whistled a call. Red laser dots appeared on Victor and each of the AK twins. Hunter laughed. "You screw me; I screw you. How 'bout that? Guess neither of us can be trusted."

Victor's frown twisted into a bitter mask of hatred. "You were told to come alone, *pendejo.*"

"Deal with it. Tell your spic buddies to drop their weapons."

"This is my house. I give the orders here, not some *pinche gringo.*"

From the woods, a gunshot shattered the relative quiet. Angel cried out and fell. Bullets shot from his rifle in random directions as he went down. Hunter disappeared on the far side of the Bronco.

Shea took cover behind a shelving unit filled with fifty-pound bags of cornstarch. She stayed low, keeping an eye on what was going on. Ten feet away, Rico fired several rounds into the woods, ripping through leaves and trees.

Another volley of bullets came from the woods, hitting Rico in the chest. He stumbled and fell next to Angel's body.

Victor picked up one of the AK-47s and ducked behind the parked forklift. "I gave you a chance, Hunter. All you had to do was return our product." He fired several rounds on full-auto at the Bronco, putting holes in the windshield and hood. Hunter returned fire.

From the woods, Mackey, One-Shot, Monster, and several other Thundermen emerged, all armed with assault rifles. They took up positions by the edge of the garage door and joined Hunter in shooting at Victor.

"Goddammit." Shea's plan, like so many of her previous plans, had gone to shit.

## 46

A GROWING rumble in the distance confirmed the rest of the Jaguars were on their way. This was turning into an all-out gang war. *I gotta get outta here.*

Going out the front wasn't an option. The back door was her only escape route. Shea crept behind the shelves. The door was locked. She had left her lock pick set at home.

She glanced back at the melee. Victor fired a few more shots and stopped. He pounded his rifle several times. *Out of ammo,* she thought.

Hunter appeared from behind the Bronco, joined by the Thundermen. Hunter passed the detonator to Monster and pointed his SIG at Victor.

*"Por favor, amigo."* Victor stood with his hands held up in surrender. "Let us stop this madness."

Hunter pulled the trigger, showering the forklift with Victor's brains.

"Where the fuck are you, bitch?" Hunter peered around the room. "I got a bullet with your name on it."

Shea fired her Glock at him, but it pinged off the metal

shelf support a few inches from his head. He shot back. What felt like a sledgehammer to her left shoulder knocked her to the ground. Shea gritted her teeth while examining the hole in her jacket. No blood. The bullet must have gone through the jacket's shoulder guard, missing her skin by a fraction of an inch.

"Leave her be, Hunter," said Monster. "We got bigger fish to fry."

As the sound of the approaching Jaguars grew louder, the Thundermen took up defensive positions inside the warehouse, hiding behind overturned tables, sacks of cornstarch, plastic bins, and wooden crates. Shea pulled herself to her feet and stumbled to the back door.

Several cars and a couple of trucks charged up the driveway in rows of two. People shouted in English and Spanish, followed by a random drum solo of gunfire.

Shea again pressed on the release bar of the back door, but it didn't budge. Without a key or her picks, there was only one way through. She pointed the Glock at the lock. Before she could pull the trigger, a bullet whizzed past making a quarter-sized hole in the warehouse's aluminum wall. Three more holes appeared next to the first, each one closer to her.

Shea whipped around. A Jaguar wearing a yellow bandana across his face stood behind the open driver's door of the Bronco, firing an AR-15 at her. Shea shot back a couple of rounds, but he was a small target at this range. She hit the Bronco's fender twice, but missed her attacker.

He fired again at Shea. Bullets hit a bag of cornstarch next to her, sending up a cloud of white powder. She ducked, turned back to the door, and put two bullets through the lock. The door opened a crack. Keeping her head down, she bolted out the door and emerged into sunlight. The land sloped away into the trees. The juniper and pines were densely packed with waist-high undergrowth.

Even if she could reach her motorcycle undiscovered, she'd never start it without getting shot by either the Jaguars or the Thunder. Her best option was to hide out in the woods until the situation in the warehouse resolved itself one way or another. She looked for a good spot to wait out the fight.

"Where the fuck you going, lesbo?" someone shouted over the intermittent bursts of gunfire coming from the other side of the warehouse.

Shea whirled around. Hunter stood by the backdoor twenty feet away from her, pointing an AK-47 at her. A few bullets burst through the warehouse walls from inside. He didn't flinch, keeping his focus on her instead.

Shea pointed the Glock at his chest. "You and the Mexicans wanna play king of the mountain? Be my guest. This ain't my battle."

"On the contrary, you're the one who invited me, remember?"

"Didn't tell you to bring the whole goddamn club."

"Think I'm stupid enough to come here alone? You're dumber than you look."

Shea ducked behind an old twisted pine tree as he fired three rounds. The smell of fresh sap filled her nose from two bullets hitting the tree trunk. The third zipped past, deep into the forest.

Shea popped out and fired two rounds at his chest. He stumbled back but didn't fall. No blood oozed from the two holes she'd put in his T-shirt.

He straightened up and pounded his chest with his left hand. "Body armor, bitch! Military grade." He raised the rifle again, but there was no shot. He pulled on the bolt handle, but it was locked back.

Shea smiled. "Out of ammo, bitch!"

He charged her. Shea fired at his head, but only nicked his ear. Before she could fire again, he swung the empty rifle, knocking the pistol out of her hand. When he swung it again, she grabbed the rifle's stock and the top of the receiver.

She grappled with him, using all her strength and weight to try and wrest the rifle from him. But he had the strength advantage. Her grip was slipping. She kneed him in the groin, but hit something hard instead—he was wearing a cup.

He headbutted her. She stumbled backward and collided with a tree before she regained her footing. He came at her again with the rifle, swinging at her head. She dodged left, extended her leg, and used his momentum to send him tumbling to the ground.

"I'm sorry I lied about Wendy and Annie." She glanced around looking for the Glock, but didn't see it. She grabbed a large tree branch instead.

He came at her again. "Not as sorry as you will be." He swung the rifle. Shea ducked and brought the tree branch down on his hands with a sharp crack. He dropped the AK with a yelp.

Before she could swing the stick again, he tackled her to the ground. She twisted, struggled, and rolled on her side, but before she knew it, he was partially underneath her with his arm around her throat.

As she faced heavenward, she pulled, but his arm was like a vice. She elbowed, but hit the body armor. She tried to scratch at his eyes, but couldn't reach his face. His grip tightened and she struggled for breath. Her vision grayed.

With her remaining strength, she curled her body and launched her knees into his head. He let go.

As she rolled away, she retrieved the Glock and blew a hole in Hunter's forehead. He collapsed.

She sat on the ground, dizzy and sick to her stomach. While she struggled to clear her head, two Jaguars with yellow bandanas over their face came running around the outside of the warehouse, both armed with Uzis. As they raised their weapons, she fired two shots at each of them. They dropped with blood pouring from their chests.

A moment later an explosion rocked the mountainside. Shea's ears rang from the blast. She struggled to her feet as smoke rose from the other side of the warehouse.

Engines roared and tires squealed. The occasional gunshot punctuated the agonized screams for help.

Disoriented from the blast, she stumbled to building, pistol ready, leaning against the wall for support. She shuffled past Victor's Pathfinder. Acrid smoke billowed from where the Jaguars' cars had been parked. Pieces of metal and bits of rubber rained down from above. She cautiously approached the front of the warehouse.

All the Bronco's windows were blown out. To her surprise, her bike still stood next to it with no signs of damage. The Bronco must have shielded the bike from the blast.

The bomb had ripped apart two of the Jaguars' cars and blown them to opposite sides of the road. They were barely recognizable as cars. Just twisted scraps of smoldering, black metal. Pieces had embedded themselves in tree trunks. A pickup truck and a car that had been parked behind the first two were each missing their front ends. The engine block from the truck was now embedded in the front seat. The entire top of the car next to it was gone as well. All the other cars had driven away, leaving deep ruts in the gravel from their rapid retreat.

Her eyes were drawn to the human carnage. Body parts

littered the gravel, blood soaking into the sand. Shea counted a half dozen Jaguar bodies, most missing limbs or a head.

She stood there dazed, mouth gaping like a grouper. How many times had she seen news video following bombings and other mass killings? It didn't prepare her for the heartrending cries of dying men or the bitter perfume of burned flesh and melted plastic, mixed with the reek of death. In that moment, she wanted to be at home holding Jessica.

"Helluva blast, wasn't it?"

She spun around with her gun raised. Monster stood a few yards away, surveying the carnage with a proud smile. He held an AR-15 under one arm, muzzle pointed at the ground.

"Tossed that bomb right in the middle of them Jaguars. You shoulda seen 'em scatter. Like Mexican cockroaches."

His amusement at the bloodshed and chaos made her want to puke.

## 47

"You all right?" Monster asked Shea.

She nodded, eyeing him warily. "I think I'm in one piece."

"You ain't seen where Hunter went, did ya?"

For half a second, Shea thought about telling him the truth. *Yeah, asshole, I shot your precious president.* But it would only get her killed.

"A couple of Jaguars came around the back of the building. I killed them, but not before they shot Hunter in the head."

Bitterness replaced Monster's amused expression. "One-Shot! Mackey! Follow me!" He ran toward the back of the building, with the other two following.

Shea walked to her motorcycle and swept broken glass from the Bronco off the seat. Tires looked okay. No damage to the block. Hoses and cables all secured. Seemed in better shape than she was.

The guys returned moments later carrying Hunter's body and laid him on the ground next to the Bronco, blocking her escape route. The rest of the Thundermen gathered around, kneeling in front of the body, silent.

One-Shot walked up to her with a stern look on his face. "The Jaguars shot Hunter?"

"Yeah." She rested a hand on the grip of her Glock, unsure where this was headed.

"Hey One-Shot, ease up on the girl," said Monster.

"Shut up, Monster. I'm in charge now." One-Shot kept his eyes on her. "How I know you didn't kill him yourself?"

Shea stared into his eyes, heart pounding in her chest. "Guess you'll have to take my word for it."

"Better be telling the truth." One-Shot held her gaze for a moment then turned away. "Mackey, you and Monster put Hunter's body in the Pathfinder and park it somewhere. His death lands on the Jaguars."

"What're ya gonna do?" Shea asked. "Hang him from a bridge?"

Mackey stood up, face red and eyes puffy. "Jesus, One-Shot, tell me you ain't gonna disrespect Hunter like that."

"Do as I say. Rest of you grab as much dope as you can. Might as well get something out of this deal."

Shea needed to leave these idiots while she could. She pulled on her helmet and gloves. Directly above, the sky was bright and cobalt blue, but another afternoon monsoon was fast approaching from the south.

Shea started the bike and eased her way through the smoldering scraps of the four Jaguar vehicles that remained. She hoped it would be the last she'd see of the Jaguars, but she doubted it. Cortes wasn't a big county.

She'd gone maybe half a mile when she realized she wasn't sure where she was headed. Should she return to the hospital or Terrance's? She pulled over to the side of the road and called him. It rang until she got his voicemail. She hung up without leaving a message. She'd drive back to the hospital and take her chances. While she put away her phone, the Pathfinder rumbled past her, followed by the Bronco and the Thundermen on their motorcycles. She waited until the roar of their engines died down and the forest was once again quiet.

Raindrops pelted her windshield as she pulled her helmet back on. She wasn't a big fan of driving in the rain, especially on a gravel road. However, Kali's suspension and knobby tires were built for this kind of terrain. Besides, the rain-cooled air was always a nice treat during monsoon season. She started up the bike again and rode back toward civilization.

She was halfway to the highway when a white sedan appeared coming from the other direction. Maybe it was someone staying at one of the campgrounds or a university student looking to spend a little time in nature. Or it could be one of the Jaguars returning.

As it got closer, she noticed the push bumper covering the grill and the spotlight by the side mirror. It was a cop.

*Just play it cool,* she told herself.

The gravel road was narrow with deep gullies on either side. She pulled as close to the right as she dared without risking ending up in the ditch. She expected the car to pull the other way, in order to get by, but it didn't. It kept coming right at her, taking up the whole damned road.

What the hell's wrong with this guy? Doesn't Buzzkill train these jokers how to drive?

She laid on the motorcycle's tinny horn. The unmarked cruiser continued hogging the road.

*Fucking cop!*

In a desperate move, she pulled over to the left while the car closed in on her. The cruiser did the same. This idiot wasn't letting her past.

At the last second, she swerved right again, hit a large

rock, and flipped over the handle bars. She landed on her right side next to the cruiser.

The impact knocked the wind out of her. Her body trembled as if it had been rung like a bell. Everything hurt, especially her right arm and shoulder. A car door opened. She lifted the visor on her helmet.

Willie stood over her, pointing his service weapon at her. "Geez, Shea. That must have hurt."

"Fucking murderer." She considered reaching for her Glock, but he'd shoot her dead before she could get it out of the holster.

"Quit yer bitchin'. Where's Oscar?"

"He's dead, asshole. I killed him."

"Guess that makes both of us murderers, don't it?"

"You're a real piece of shit, you know that? Kidnapping and mutilating little girls."

He patted the brass shield attached to his belt. "Yeah, but a piece of shit with a badge, a gun, and a warrant for your arrest."

A blue sedan with a cracked windshield came barreling down the road, siren wailing, and screeched to a stop behind Willie's car.

Rios climbed out. "Sergeant Foster, put the gun down."

Edelman emerged from the blue sedan's passenger's side and unholstered his weapon.

"Detective Rios, you need leave. I have the situation under control."

Shea hoped he would turn and face Rios, so she could shoot him. He kept his gun trained on Shea instead.

"Sergeant," said Rios, "you need to come with me."

"Detective, as your superior, I am ordering you to leave the scene, or I will have you charged with insubordination."

Rios drew her weapon and pointed it at Willie. "I have

orders from IA to bring you in for questioning. Please drop your weapon. I really don't want to shoot you."

"Detective Edelman, please relieve your partner of her weapon."

"Put the gun down, Toni, or I will shoot you." Edelman aimed his pistol at Rios.

A chill ran up Shea's spine. *Edelman was the one working with Willie? Not Aguilar? He so didn't fit the type.*

"Micah? What the hell's going on?"

Willie turned toward the two detectives. "Edelman, if Detective Rios does not lower her weapon, I'm ordering you to shoot her."

With her right arm out of commission, Shea pulled the Glock with her left hand and shot Willie in the throat. Edelman turned his gun toward Shea.

She tried to roll for cover until a white-hot jolt of pain erupted in her lower back. She wanted to run but her legs weren't working. Another two gunshots shattered the air as everything went dark.

## 48

Detective Rios told her to hold on, but Shea had trouble focusing her mind. She felt like she was lying with a rock sticking into her back, even though she was on her stomach. Pain and darkness filled her consciousness.

A man in a dark blue shirt rolled her over, intensifying the pain in her back.

"Can you tell me your name?"

Brown eyes. Thick lashes. Was he wearing eyeliner? Why all the questions? Do I know what happened to me? What happened?

Something was put over her mouth. A cup of some kind. Everything started bouncing. *What's that loud chup-chup-chup sound? Helicopter.* The pain lessened, but she still couldn't focus. Everything was happening too fast.

When she came to again, she was lying in a hospital bed. Her body hurt all over, especially her back and right shoulder. A brace and sling held her right arm firmly across her chest. A vitals monitor beeped nonstop, giving her a headache. "Can someone turn off that goddamned beeping?"

"Shea?" Jessica walked into view, her eyes red and swollen. Dark streaks of mascara lined her cheeks.

"Hey, Jess." She struggled to keep her eyes open. "Where am I?"

"You're in the hospital. Someone shot you."

She tried to remember. "Willie. I shot Willie." She took a deep breath and winced. "Someone shot me. The geeky detective. What's his name? Edelweiss. No. Edelman."

"I'm glad just you're alive." Jessica's soft hand felt warm on Shea's cheek. "Doctor said the bullet hit one of your ribs, but stopped short of your kidney." Her eyes filled with tears again. "You also have a fractured collarbone."

"It'll be all right, honey." Shea wanted to kiss away her tears. "Can you make the beeping stop?"

"I pressed the button. Nurse should be here in a minute."

A young gal wearing oversized eyeglasses and teal scrubs walked in the room. Brown-black hair framed her heart-shaped face. Her name tag read Svetlana. She pressed a few buttons on the vitals monitor. The beeping stopped. "Can I get you anything, darling?" she asked with a slight accent.

"Water." Her mouth felt full of cotton.

"I'll go fill up a pitcher for you." She walked out as Terrance came in.

He hugged Jessica and pulled up a chair next to the bed. "Good morning."

"Is it morning already? Damn."

"I found something that might cheer you up." Terrance smiled and pulled something out of his pocket.

"What?"

"The lighter Lenny gave you." He handed it to her. "I felt bad about throwing it out, so I went back and looked on the side of the road and found it. Even had Lakota polish out the scratches."

Shea wrapped her fingers around it, the metal still warm from being in Terrance's pocket. "Thanks, dude. That means a lot."

"Want to tell me what happened?" he asked.

"Hunter and the MC showed up at the Jaguars' warehouse. Everybody started shooting."

"Do I want to know any more?"

"Probably best you don't."

"No, but *I* do." Rios walked in the room with a stack of folders under one arm. "I need to question Ms. Stevens."

Terrance looked at her. "Jessica, maybe you and I should go for a walk."

"No," Shea mumbled. "Don't leave."

He stood up. "I'll be back shortly, girl."

Rios closed the door to the room and sat down in the chair Terrance had just vacated.

"What do you want?" Shea asked.

"Gee, where do I begin?" She held up a couple of files and set it down on the bedside table. "You, an ex-con, were found at the scene of a murder four days ago in possession of a gun that's tied to no less than eleven other unsolved murders. Then there's the multiple casualties at the warehouse found just up the road from where you crashed your motorcycle."

She set down another file on the first. "Two days ago, we found a Ford Mustang registered to your sister wrecked and abandoned at the bottom of a hill off I-17 along with numerous shell casings from a 40-caliber semiautomatic that matches the Glock we found on you."

"Seriously?"

"That same evening your sister, four members of the Confederate Thunder, and one member of the Jaguars were found dead in a south Ironwood neighborhood. According to the report, a woman was spotted leaving the scene on a motorcycle with a young girl on the back. I'm guessing that was you and your niece."

She pulled out two more files and laid them on the stack. "And finally, there's the incident that landed you in here, where you shot and killed a Cortes County Sheriff's deputy."

"I want my lawyer."

"Someone called for me?" Justin knocked and opened the door.

Shea wondered if the pain meds were messing with her sense of time. "How'd you get here so fast?"

"Your friend Mr. Douglas rang me up a little bit ago, said the Sheriff's Office was camped outside your room. So I camped out in the waiting room until Mr. Douglas said I was needed." He nodded at Detective Rios. "Nice to see you again, Detective."

"Mr. Bryce, your client appears to be involved with multiple criminal incidents. I have a lot of questions that need answering."

"Detective, would you mind if I consult with my client? Then perhaps we can answer those questions."

"I'll be outside." She left.

Justin looked at Shea and sighed. "Want to give me a rundown?"

For the next forty minutes, Shea recounted the events of the past few days. Justin listened and made notes. Svetlana interrupted briefly with a much-needed pitcher of water.

When Shea finished, Justin said, "Well, I must say, you have had an exciting week. Sorry to hear about your sister."

"Thanks. Do they got a case against me?"

"Maybe. We can argue self-defense on your shooting Sergeant Foster. However, running from the cops on the

motorcycle, possession of the Beretta, and your involvement at the Jaguars' warehouse are a bit more problematic
from a defense point of view."

Not what she wanted to hear. "You're saying I'm
screwed?"

"Not necessarily. Tell her what you know about the
Thunder, the Jaguars, and Sergeant Foster's pet project. If
we play this right, I might be able to get the charges
waived."

He stood up and ushered Detective Rios back in.

"So?" she asked.

Justin smiled. Shea liked it when he smiled. "My client
would be happy to provide information related to your
investigations into these matters, provided she is given full
immunity from all charges."

"What kind of information could your client provide?"

"She witnessed multiple felonies, including murders
and drug trafficking, committed by members of the
Confederate Thunder Motorcycle Club, the Jaguars street
gang, and your very own Sergeant Foster and Detective
Edelman."

"Let me hear what she has to say. If it's of value, I can
talk with the DA about a possible deal."

Once again, Shea ran down the events of the past few
days starting with the break-in through to her rescuing
Annie at the shootout in Ironwood's barrio. She didn't like
ratting anyone else out. But after all she'd been through
with Willie, the Jags, and the MC, she was happy to name
names.

Rios asked a lot of probing questions that put Shea on
the defensive. Justin ran interference, making sure Shea
didn't stick her foot in her mouth and blow her chances at
immunity.

After two hours of questioning, the pain in her back

was getting to her. "I've told you all I know. Now someone get the nurse in here. My back is killing me."

"I think that should be enough to earn my client immunity. Yes?"

Rios looked at Shea as she processed the idea. "I think the DA can be persuaded on one condition—Ms. Stevens agrees to be a confidential informant for the Sheriff's Office on future interactions with the Confederate Thunder, the Jaguars, or any other organization we deem criminal in nature."

"I don't deal with any criminal organizations. Not normally, anyway. I build motorcycles. That's it."

"And I want to stop organized crime in this county. Word on the street is an all-female motorcycle club called the Athena Sisterhood is establishing a charter somewhere here in central Arizona. That could lead to conflicts with the Thunder. I may need you to be my eyes and ears."

Justin whispered into her ear. "Take the offer. No one's saying you have to get involved with anyone. But if you happen to hear about something going on, let the detective know. No big deal."

"I don't like snitching, Justin. I just wanna build motorcycles."

"This deal will keep you doing that. I suggest you take it."

Shea looked up at Detective Rios. "Fine. I'll be your snitch."

"Glad to hear it." Rios reached over and shook Shea's hand. "I look forward to working with you."

"What about Annie?"

"Once she's released from the hospital, she'll be put in a temporary foster home until the court can decide—"

"I want her." The words came out of her mouth before she realized she was saying it.

"You?" Rios raised an eyebrow. "You want custody?"

"Why not? She's my niece. I'm all the family she's got left, right?"

"You sure about this, kiddo?" asked Justin. "An eight-year-old is a big responsibility. Trust me, I raised four kids and now have three grandkids."

"I'll figure it out. Now that all this nonsense is over, I should be able to provide her a loving, stable home."

Rios sighed. "All right, I'll get with the Department of Child Safety and see about transferring custody once you're released from here."

An unexpected wave of calm filled Shea, more than when she finished the Pink Trinkets' bikes. "Thanks. Now can a girl get some pain meds up in here?"

"I'll get a nurse," said Justin as he ducked out of the room.

"I'll let you know when I hear back from DCS. In the meantime, get some rest." Rios put a gentle hand on Shea's arm. "And off the record, I'm glad you shot Sergeant Foster."

"For the record," said Shea with a smirk, "I wish you had shot your asshole partner sooner."

∾

THE NEXT MORNING, Shea woke to find Jessica reading in a chair next to the bed.

"Hey." Shea's throat felt dry and raw, but much of the pain from the day before was gone.

"Morning, sunshine." Jessica's smile made the room feel brighter. "How ya feeling?"

"Like I lost a fight with a Mack truck. How's Annie?"

"They moved her to a regular room just down the hall. Don't know much else."

"I gotta see her." Shea pressed the button on the bed's control panel to lower her legs and raise her head.

Jessica lowered the railing on one side. "You sure you're up for walking?"

Shea harrumphed. "Damn nurse forced me to get outta bed last night and I felt like shit. Can't be any worse today."

With help from Jess, she maneuvered her legs to the edge of the bed, feeling twinges of pain in her back from the bullet and along her calf from the road rash. She tightened her jaw and pushed through it. Jessica grabbed Shea's left arm and pulled her up into a sitting position. Shea waited a minute to catch her breath, then lowered her feet to the floor.

An exhausting ten-minute walk later, Shea and Jessica arrived at Annie's room. There was no guard posted, which Shea took as a positive sign.

Jess opened the door. Shea shuffled in and saw Dr. Patel standing over the bed. "Oh, hello. Are you Annie's family?"

"I'm her aunt,"

Annie's head popped out from behind the doctor. "Aunt Shea?"

"Hey, kiddo."

Dr. Patel tilted his head, as if trying to remember something. "Have I seen you here before?"

"You're treating my employee Derek Williams down in ICU. Gunshot victim."

"Well, I hope you can control yourself better than last time." His nostrils flared as his Indian accent grew thicker. "I will not put up with any shenanigans this time."

"Seriously? Does it look like I'm up to shenanigans? I can barely walk." She held his gaze for a moment. "What's going on with Annie?"

"We were able to reattach the ear, though we had to remove some necrotic tissue. We are using leeches to help maintain blood flow until her body can repair the veins that return the blood to the body."

"Did you say leeches?" Shea plopped into a chair as a wave of nausea hit her. "Is this some third-world, holistic bullshit from India?"

Dr. Patel shook his head. "Not at all. The leeches drain blood from the injury site to prevent clotting. They do a far better job restoring blood flow than the best vascular surgeons. Trust me, it's state-of-the-art medical practice."

The idea made Shea's stomach churn. "Is it painful?"

"Not at all. She'll hardly know it's there."

"How about her infection?"

"We have given her antibiotics to treat the sepsis. Her temperature is returning to normal and her blood pressure is improving."

"How soon before she's released?" asked Jessica.

"Let me take a look real quick." The doctor stepped toward the head of the bed. Shea moved back to allow him to check Annie's ear.

Annie whimpered and scrunched her face when he lifted the bandage and examined it using a penlight. "Yes, it looks good. The redness around the wound site is much improved." He put the bandage back in place and stepped away. "It should take about five days to restore the circulation in the ear. Assuming there are no more signs of infection, we will release her then."

Shea thought about Terrance's suggestion of her getting custody. *Would Annie want to live with her? And what would Jessica think?*

"Thanks for your help."

"You are most welcome. Goodbye, Annie." He waved as he walked out.

"Bye." Annie looked up at Shea. "What happened to you?"

Shea grunted as she stood up and shuffled toward the bed. "Had a little motorcycle accident. I'll live." She frowned. "I don't know if now's the right time, but there's something I gotta tell ya. I don't even know how to say it."

"What's wrong, Aunt Shea?"

"It's about your dad."

"He's dead, isn't he?"

Shea's mouth tightened into a thin line. "I'm afraid so. How did you know?"

"If he were alive, he woulda been here." There was sadness in her voice, but not as much as Shea had expected. *Maybe that's a good thing,* she thought.

"I'm sorry, sweetie." The memory of shooting Hunter grew vivid in her mind. She didn't regret it, but was sorry Annie was now an orphan.

"What's gonna happen to me?"

Shea looked at Jessica and their eyes met. Jess nodded. Shea forced a smile.

"I'm gonna see if you can come live with Jess and me. Would that be all right with you?"

Annie studied Jessica's face. "Are you Aunt Shea's girlfriend?"

Jessica cleared her throat. "Um, yeah, actually I am."

An awkward moment dragged on that felt to Shea like time had come to a halt. She tried to think of something to say.

"Okay," said Annie. "I'll come to live with you."

## 49

A WEEK LATER, Shea lay on the loveseat watching cartoons, bored out of her skull and more than a little grumpy. The hospital had released her after twenty-four hours. Her right arm and shoulder were immobilized with a sling, forcing her to eat left-handed.

"How's the pain?" Jessica handed Shea a plate with eggs over easy, bacon, and toast.

"It hurts." She cut a piece of egg, but dropped it onto her shirt as she tried to eat it. She adjusted her grip on the fork. It slipped from her hand onto the floor. "Goddammit."

"When was the last time you took your pain meds?"

"I don't know. I don't want 'em. Makes me feel like I'm thinking through a fog."

Outside, a car pulled up in the driveway. Jessica glanced out the window. "I think that's them."

"Shit, I got egg all over my shirt." *I'm such a klutz,* she thought. "Great first impression I'm gonna make with the social worker."

"Everything'll be fine."

Jessica opened the door the second they knocked.

Detective Rios walked in carrying two full-size suitcases, followed by Annie and a woman with dark
mocha skin, high cheekbones, and a head full of shoulder-length braids. She wore a tan suit that matched her
shoes and nails. Bandages still covered Annie's reattached ear.

"Shea Stevens," said Detective Rios, "this is Evelyn
Langdon with the Department of Child Safety. And you
know Annie."

"Hi, Ms. Langdon." Shea tried to stand, but had trouble
getting her feet under her.

"Oh, don't get up. I heard about your accident. And
please, call me Evelyn." Her eyes scanned the room.

"Hi, I'm Jessica, Shea's . . . friend." She shook hands with
Rios and Evelyn, then kneeled down to Annie. "Hi, Annie.
Nice to see you again."

"Hi," said Annie in a timid voice.

Evelyn looked at Jess. "You live here, too?"

Jess smiled nervously. "I'm helping take care of her until
she can move her arm again."

They were dancing around the lesbian issue. Shea
wasn't in the mood for games. "She's my girlfriend. Is that a
problem?"

Evelyn shook her head. "No, not a problem with DCS,
as long it isn't an issue with Annie."

Shea handed her plate to Jessica, got to her feet, and
walked over to Annie. "Hey, Little Bug."

"Hey, Aunt Shea." Annie hugged her tight. A little too
tight.

"Easy there, kiddo. I'm still a little tender."

She let go. "Sorry."

Evelyn scanned the living room. "I'd like to see where
Annie will be sleeping."

"Jess, can you give them the tour?"

"Sure. This way, ladies." She led them to the spare bedroom.

Shea turned back to Annie. "Wanna watch cartoons?"

A smile crept up on her face. "Yes, please."

She sat beside Shea on the couch and Shea turned the TV back on. Not nearly as boring with Annie there.

~

A COUPLE OF DAYS LATER, Shea showed up at Iron Goddess with Annie, who'd volunteered to be her personal assistant until she recovered from her broken collarbone. The place looked much as it had before the break-in, complete with four Pink Trinkets' bikes front and center on the showroom floor.

"Looks a little different, huh?" Monica stepped out from behind the sales counter.

Shea couldn't help but grin, despite the persistent pain in her back and shoulder. "God, I missed this place."

Monica crouched down to Annie's height. "And who is this cutie?"

"This is my niece, Annie."

Annie took a step back and grabbed Shea's hand, a worried expression on her face.

Shea chuckled. "Don't worry, kiddo. Monica's my friend. She won't hurt ya."

Annie looked up at her. "Hi," she said in a small, timid voice.

"Hi, Annie. I'm glad to meet you."

"Glad to meet you, too."

"So when's Derek coming back?" asked Monica.

Shea's smile faded. "He's not."

"Why not?"

"He started using again. I can't have that in my shop."

Shea had decided not to mention his involvement in the robbery.

"Can't blame you there."

The bells on the front door jingled. Shea turned to see the Pink Trinkets walk in. Wicked, Vicious, and Nasty, as they were known, sported their signature pink leather jackets, skintight chaps, and pink-tinted shades.

"I hear we got us some motorcycles in here." Wicked sashayed through the showroom, flipping back her kinky long blond hair.

Annie's eyes went wide, and her jaw dropped open. "Is that the Pink Trinkets?"

"Yeah, they're my clients. You like the Trinks?"

Annie nodded vigorously.

"Welcome back to Iron Goddess, ladies," Shea said.

"Damn, girl, what the hell happened to you?" Wicked looked Shea up and down while Vicious and Nasty strolled over to the bikes.

"Long story. Wicked, meet my niece, Annie. She's a fan of your music."

Wicked glanced at Annie. "My goodness! What'd you do to your head?"

"Someone cut my ear off." Annie's face darkened with sadness.

"Oh my gawd! You poor thing." Wicked gave her a hug. As she pulled away, she reached into her jacket and pulled out a CD in a jewel case. "Maybe this'll make you feel better. It's our new album. No one else has it yet. Would you like it?" Wicked glanced at Shea with a nervous grin. "Most of the lyrics are PG."

"Yes, please," said Annie, eyes bursting with excitement.

Wicked laughed. "Well, aren't you precious." She pulled out a black marker and signed the CD in the case. "Here you go, doll. Autographed just for you. Now let's go see what your auntie made for us."

Shea followed Wicked over to the new motorcycles. Each gas tank bore the name of a band member. The fourth simply had the band's name.

Vicious, running her hand through her signature half-hawk haircut, sat astride her café racer–style bike. Nasty glanced over her heart-shaped shades to inspect the long and low cruiser with ape hanger handlebars.

"These are amazing, Shea," said Wicked. "But I contracted for three bikes, not four."

"The fourth one was sort of a backup. It's on us."

"Yeah, I heard you had a little trouble."

Shea looked over at Terrance, who was walking over. "We did," she said, giving Terrance the stink eye. "But we got it sorted out. Like I *knew* we would."

Terrance patted the seat of the fourth bike. "We were thinking about auctioning off this one to raise money for the charity of your choice."

Wicked threw a leg over the bike with her name on the tank. "I like it. There's a rock music camp for girls we support. I think they'd be the perfect choice."

"Well then, ladies." Terrance walked toward the office. "Shall we settle up?" Ever the businessman wanting to get paid.

"I don't think so," Wicked said. "Not until after a test ride."

The office phone rang. Monica ran. "I'll get it."

Wicked gave Shea a seductive grin. "So whaddya say, Leftie? Wanna ride bitch?"

Before Shea could answer, Monica hollered from the office. "Hey, boss, phone for you."

"Take a message."

"I think you'll want to take this."

Shea rolled her eyes, fearing Detective Rios was calling with new demands on her freedom. She walked into the office.

Monica handed Shea the receiver with a sour expression on her face. "It's your ex, Debbie."

"Hello?" Shea said into the phone.

"Hey, darling! Guess who's the president of the new Ironwood charter of the Athena Sisterhood? This girl! I was thinking you could meet us for drinks, considering you're a hotshot bike builder now. Whaddya say?"

"Oh fuck."

### Ready for Another Adventure?

*Download a free copy of "Kissing Asphalt", a Jinx Ballou short story, by subscribing to Dharma's newsletter, The Gritty Gritty at dharmakelleher.com.*

*This semi-monthly newsletter features interviews with up-and-coming crime fiction authors, book reviews, release announcements, giveaways, and more.*

# BOOKS BY DHARMA KELLEHER

## Jinx Ballou Bounty Hunter series

Chaser

Extreme Prejudice

A Broken Woman (Dec. 2019)

## Shea Stevens Outlaw Biker series

Iron Goddess

Snitch

# ABOUT THE AUTHOR

Dharma Kelleher writes gritty crime fiction with a feminist kick and is one of the only openly transgender voices in the genre.

She is the author of the Jinx Ballou Bounty Hunter series and the Shea Stevens Outlaw Biker. Her work has also appeared in anthologies and on Shotgun Honey.

She is a former journalist and a member of Sisters in Crime, the International Thriller Writers, and the Alliance of Independent Authors. She lives in Arizona with her wife and three feline overlords.

Learn more about Dharma and her work at https://dharmakelleher.com.

CPSIA information can be obtained
at www.ICGtesting.com
Printed in the USA
LVHW031527211021
701109LV00001B/94